DODGING AND BURNING

DODGING AND BURNING

A MYSTERY

JOHN COPENHAVER

PEGASUS CRIME
NEW YORK LONDON

Dodging and Burning

Pegasus Books Ltd.
148 West 37th Street, 13th Floor
New York, NY 10018

First Pegasus Books hardcover edition March 2018

Interior design by Sabrina Plomitallo-González, Pegasus Books

ISBN: 978-1-68177-659-0

10 9 8 7 6 5 4 3 2 1

Printed in the United States of America
Distributed by W. W. Norton & Company, Inc.

To Mom, because without you, there would be no Ceola, no Bunny.

Why print this picture anyway of three American boys, dead on an alien shore? The reason is that words are never enough. The eye sees. The mind knows. The heart feels. But the words do not exist to make us see, or know, or feel what it is like, what actually happens . . .

—Life magazine, September 20, 1943

PART I

February 6, 2000

Washington, DC

Dear Ceola,

I thought I might begin this letter by reminding you who I was, but that would be pure pretense, and I know you wouldn't stand for it. I would like to say I'm writing to reminisce, to recall those "halcyon days" of our childhood in Royal Oak, but knowing you as I once did, I suspect you would prefer I just get to the point.

It's been fifty-five years, but I still recall your last words to me and the terrible look on your face. Your eyes were bright and wet, and you had blood on your lips—no longer the face of a girl, but something fiercer and finer—and you said to me, "Bunny, you're a murderer." To this day, I believe it. I really do.

Someone, it seems, wants me to remember that time in our lives. Two days ago I received one of Jay Greenwood's photos of Lily. It arrived in the mail with no return address, no clue to its origin. I need to know—did you send it to me? If you didn't, do you know who did?

I must admit, as horrible as it is to say, I still see beauty in the photo—or perhaps allure. That's really the word for it. I'm looking through his eyes when I'm looking at her. It's what he saw in her poor broken body that makes it extraordinary.

If you are willing, please write to me or phone me as soon as you can. I've enclosed my home address and number. I would be so grateful to you.

With sincerest regards,

Bunny Prescott

1
CEOLA

There we are, Robbie, at the train station seeing you off. It's July 1943, and you're headed to Bainbridge, Maryland, for basic training. Mama, in that dim way of hers, suggested Papa shoot it. She's clutching you tight to her, her arm around you, her fingers squeezing you through your striped shirt, digging into the cotton and pulling the fabric tight across your body. You're staring at the camera with a blank, hot look on your face, your anger boring back through the lens and piercing the surface of the photo. And I'm standing away from you a little, my small hand around two of your lanky fingers, like I'm trying not to let go.

I'm sure I was sad at the time, but all I remember is your anger at Papa, at Mama, and—although I hope it wasn't true—at me. Two days before, you came to me with that same look: eyes bright, cheeks flushed, turbulence roiling underneath. You asked me if I wanted to go to Hersh's, because the new *Dime Detective* might be in. I said yes, punching as much good cheer into my reply as I could muster. We made our way to town, mostly in silence. You were withdrawn, your hands buried deep in your pockets and your shoulders high and tight. Like a barometer before a storm, I could feel the pressure of your emotion. I wanted to touch you, but I didn't dare. Even at that age, barely ten, I could tell how distraught you were.

Our narrow wooded road gave way to open stretches of rolling farmland and then the paved streets of Royal Oak. The town, just a cluster of well-appointed brick buildings, fanned out from the county courthouse with its impressive columns and wide steps. The First Presbyterian Church, the tallest building in town, sat across from it, both its counterpart and its challenger: God's law versus man's. As we passed by, the American flag over the courthouse lawn swished against its pole and fluttered a weak salute.

We went to Hersh's Pharmacy and found only old issues in the magazine stand. You cursed at it several times. The buxom models, grim politicians, and handsome soldiers on the covers of *Life*, *Harper's Bazaar*, and *Photoplay* all seemed a little startled and flustered to me, like they didn't understand why you were angry at them. It wasn't like you to be so short tempered.

We turned to the counter for a consolation prize, two vanilla malts. With our drinks in hand, we sat on the bench outside, sucked on our straws, and nursed our disappointment, watching an afternoon thunderstorm edge its way over the mountain ridge. You'd cooled off, but you remained distant, fidgety. I began to believe your mood wasn't so much about the war as about me.

"Cee," you said, after tossing your empty cup in the trash and sitting beside me again, "I want to tell you that I . . ." You looked out across Main Street, studying something, maybe our blurry reflections in Brickles' wide windows, or the chipped plaster mannequins staring back through the plate glass. "There's something I need to . . ."

You looked at me, your face strained, your left knee bouncing up and down. "Jesus Christ," you said, shaking your head and standing again.

"What?" I said, feeling the swell of the rich ice cream in my stomach.

You rubbed your forehead, smoothed your hair back, and gave me a long hard stare, like I was the Sphinx and had just told you some impossible riddle. "It doesn't matter. Forget it," you said, and began to pace the sidewalk.

"What is it?" My stomach gurgled.

"Just forget it."

"Come on!"

You stopped and gave me a hot look—part agitation, part humiliation, and part fear. Suddenly your eyes lost their intensity and your expression caved in. Something was very wrong, but I had no way to nudge it out of you. At least that's what I recall now, as I hold this photo of you, Mama, and me.

"Let's go," you said, turning to the street. "This was a waste of time."

As we made our way home, I remained silent. You walked loosely and quickly, leaving me a few paces behind you, struggling to catch up. I felt like an afterthought, like I was being punished, making me wonder if I'd somehow been to blame for your fickle mood. The air grew heavier, closer, and by the time we reached our driveway, my head was throbbing and my stomach was doing somersaults. I took a step or two toward the house and heaved, and out came my malt: a frothy white streak across the dirt, soon to be washed away by the storm. You guided me down the drive, and as we walked together, your arm loose around me, I felt like we were moving in different directions, that by the time we reached the porch, you'd be gone.

Two days later, the train swept you away for real, and all I had was this photo. It has hung above my desk for years, shaping how I remember you; that look on your face is what I think of when I remember the days leading up to you leaving. Photos have that power. Photographers have that power, whether they realize it or not. Papa didn't understand that, of course. He was just commemorating you at the threshold of manhood—a proud occasion, in his view of things.

Unlike Papa, Jay Greenwood did know what he was doing when, two years later, after you went to war, after you died in the Pacific, he showed us the photos of that murdered woman. Like any good photographer, he saw everyone and everything as open to interpretation, as *in need of* interpretation. Even his own demons, God love him.

It all began on another summer day not so different from the day you boarded the train. The weather was swampy and thick, and I was stretched across that slab of cool limestone near the Greenwoods' pond—you know the spot, near the weeping willows, a little down the hill from the Greenwood house—swatting mosquitos with my bare feet, reading "A Date with Death" for the umpteenth time.

I'd just come across the lines, *She heard the door open behind her and felt someone approach. A man.*, when a shadow flitted over me. I sat up like a spooked rabbit.

Jay loomed above me, his long bangs swept forward, shading his eyes, his strong chin tilted down, and the collar of his loose linen shirt twisted out of shape, catching the sunlight behind him. He seemed vague and uneasy, like he couldn't quite maintain his balance and needed his cane. He was only twenty, but he seemed so much older.

The war had done that to him, knocked him off-center, but I didn't fully understand that at the time. That spring, he'd returned to Royal Oak, honorably discharged from the army because of his wounded leg and physically changed, a bony and blue-veined ghost of himself. His civilian clothes were loose around him, his hands always shoved deep in his pockets and his posture bent, like he was avoiding looking directly at anyone. With a little rest, some decent food, and sunshine, he'd begun to resemble the young man who'd been your best friend, if skewed.

He had started coming around earlier in the summer, when I was outside escaping Mama and Papa's den of despair. He'd talk about you and tell me about the fun things you did, like exploring the old quarry, or fishing in the lake, or sneaking into the Sunday matinee at the Lincoln to see creature features or detective dramas. He'd tell me what you were like—how you were funnier than most people realized, or how you could quote movies after seeing them only once, or how you could make up ghost stories on demand. Of course, I already knew most of those things, but I liked hearing him tell them. It brought you back, if only for a moment or two. We had even taken to reading your pulp magazines together. We pored over Bradbury and Wellman tales and whatever was in *Dime Detective* and *Weird Stories* that month—and of course, there was "A Date with Death." He liked it more than I did.

"I just saw something, Cee," he said, ending the awkward, wavering moment. "I've witnessed something, something terrible." He stepped into the sun and offered me his hand. His blue eyes lit up, glossy and intense. He looked shaken.

"What was it?" I said, as I took his hand. He faltered a little—in pain from his injured leg—then pulled me to my feet.

I softened my voice, a little guilty that I'd been the cause of his pain. "What'd you see? Are you going to tell me?"

"I'll tell you when we get there," he replied, standing straight again, seeming to ignore his leg. "Let's go."

We crossed his family's overgrown pasture, as forgotten and unkempt as their huge farmhouse, tore through a haze of pesky gnats, and hoofed it to the oak-lined drive that curved up the hill to his home. When Jay and I were only several yards from the drive, he stopped short and tilted his ear up. I heard it, too: the faint grind of a motor. A sedan rounded the bend and barreled down the road, kicking up streamers of dust, its windshield glinting in the sun. He grabbed my arm and we rushed toward a large oak, knobby and twisted. Before we could duck behind it, a gloved hand popped out the driver's side and waved us down.

Jay dropped his shoulders and, through his teeth, hissed, "Jesus Christ."

The dark green, chrome-trimmed Oldsmobile rolled to a stop a few yards away. The engine idled and died, and Bunny Prescott, in all her glory, leaned out the window.

"Hello, you two!" she called, removing tortoiseshell sunglasses with pitch-black lenses and squinting at us. I knew what she was thinking— *Ceola Bliss is such a tomboy. Look at those dirty cheeks. That grass-stained sailor's middy. That sloppy ponytail.* I wasn't a bit interested being girly, but all the same, she made me feel dumpy.

"I apologize for all the dust," she said, "but Mother has sent me on a very important errand. I'm to deliver not one but *two* pies to you, Jay. A cherry-vanilla thing she made this morning. Really, it's quite good. And the lemon pie—your favorite."

I could smell the warm crusts wrapped in cheesecloth on the seat beside her.

"Leave them with Grandma," Jay said, a rough edge to his voice.

"Oh, do I have to? She hates me. She *really* does. Can't I just leave them with you? Besides, they're for you, not her."

"We're in a hurry," I said. "We're on our way to see something." I wanted her to go away. *Vanish.*

"Oh, all right." She frowned, then leaned toward us, parting her waxy lined lips. "What sort of something?"

"Got to go," he said, taking my arm and spinning me around. My feet sent a little cloud of dust across the road. Over his shoulder, he tossed out, "Tell your mother thank you for the pies."

"Hold on!" The heavy door of the Olds swung wide, its hinges squeaking and popping with the weight of the steel. Bunny's footsteps crunched on the gravel behind us, moving toward us with a determined gait.

Despite Jay's bum leg, we kept up our pace, but it didn't matter. When I felt Bunny's grip on my elbow, I whirled around like I'd been stung by a wasp.

"What are you up to?" she demanded to know.

"Damn it, Bunny," he said, his face flushed. "Just leave us alone."

"Why are you being so cagey? Both of you?"

"You really don't want to know."

"Of course I do."

"You don't."

"*Jay.*"

They regarded each other for a moment. Tinged with sweat, her silky makeup glowed in the midday sun, and even as a rush of humid air swept across the drive and rattled the branches above us, her chestnut curls didn't budge. With that practiced posture of hers, not to mention the professional tailoring of her strawberry-red halter dress, she could've passed for one of those mannequins in the windows at Brickles'. I wanted to topple her over to see if she'd look as polished and manicured on the ground. If I'd known then how much you hated her, Robbie, I would've done it.

All summer long, she had been our shadow, wagging her finger at Jay and me and chirping criticisms. She would find us sitting out in front of the courthouse having ice cream, or perched on the library steps reading, or getting malts at Hersh's. "You two," she'd say, "do nothing but lay around, soak in sunshine, and use up oxygen." She thought she was being funny, I guess.

She even gave us a hard time for liking pulp stories. She'd creep up behind us while we were reading and say something like, "That looks positively grisly. Your father and mother wouldn't approve of that sort of thing, Ceola." Jay fended her off by explaining that I knew the difference between fiction and real life. He always blocked her attacks, which I was grateful for, but I wasn't sure how he really felt about her. I knew they'd met up several times that summer and hadn't included me.

Jay broke eye contact with her and glanced around, concerned, it seemed, that the trees and the meadow grass might be listening in. He said, "You really want to know?"

"That's why I'm asking," she said.

His eyes shone. An impulse was emerging, pushing itself out. I'd seen film stars have the same dazed look moments before they blurted out declarations of love or admitted guilty secrets. I thought of Mary

Astor's pale cheeks and pleading eyes as Bogart pressed a confession out of her in *The Maltese Falcon*.

Jay took a deep breath and said, "I'm a witness to a murder." In a whisper, he added, "At least, I think I am."

I took a step back, mouth open, speechless.

"What?" Bunny said, startled into a laugh. "You're joking, right?"

"I found her body in the woods, badly beaten." He straightened his back and frowned at her.

She cocked her head to the side. "Are you serious?"

His still eyes and straight lips told us he was. "I'm not a witness to the act itself," he explained, cupping his elbows in his hands, as if a chill had run through him, "but I was going to meet her to take her photo. Her name's Lily—Lily Williams, I think—and she lives just over the mountain in Jitters Gap. I don't know her, not really."

"Where were you meeting her?" Bunny asked.

"You know the spot, where we picnicked a few months ago." Again, he made a show of studying the field and the edge of the forest behind us.

"You should report it to the police," she said, narrowing her gaze at him. "That's what's done in situations like this."

He shook his head. "It's too risky."

"How's that?"

"The police treat witnesses like they're suspects. I don't want them to come calling at the house. I know what they think of Grandma."

"When she waves her gun at the neighbors on a regular basis, what can you expect?"

"That's my point. They'll say, 'That grandson of crazy, drunk Letitia Greenwood—he must be even crazier and drunker than she is.'"

"I don't think they'll say—"

"That's not all," he interrupted, glancing to the ground.

She crossed her arms. "What else?"

"I dropped my camera, not far from the clearing. I heard something in the woods, maybe just a deer or something, but it startled me and I ran. I snagged the strap on a branch, and it yanked it off."

"Is that why you've been looking around?" I said. "You're worried it wasn't a deer."

He nodded. "We need to go back." He glanced at Bunny, who gave him a stony, challenging stare. "I'm sure whoever killed Lily was long gone by the time I found her. I'm just being careful, that's all."

"Okay," Bunny said. "You've *completely* baffled me. Why—even for a second—would you consider taking Ceola with you?"

"She understands these sorts of things." He flashed a smile at me, and I smiled back. "We've been reading about them all summer. In Robbie's magazines." He cleared his throat and added, "I didn't want to go back alone, Bunny. Would you?"

She mulled it over, blushing slightly. "I see," she said with surprising tenderness.

I was relieved at first, glad that she seemed to understand, but her dark eyes lingered on him too long. Desire surfaced through layers of makeup. My stomach did a nervous flip-flop, and I blurted out, "Are we going to investigate the scene of the crime or not?" I emphasized "the scene of the crime." I wanted Jay to know I really knew the lingo, that I was taking him seriously.

"I certainly hope not," Bunny said without much force.

Jay brightened. He appreciated my enthusiasm. He raised his eyebrows at Bunny.

She planted a hand on her waist and glared at me. "I guess you're all in, aren't you, Nancy Drew?"

I nodded my head yes and gave an impatient hop.

She rolled her eyes. "Fine, I'll go, but as soon as you find your camera, and we see this—this crime scene, we'll go directly to the police. Promise me that. Both of you. Directly to the police."

"Agreed," Jay said. "Let's drive to your house, Bunny, and walk in from there, the back way up the creek. If the murderer was still there, I bet he went out another way, either toward the train station or up to the road. They're more direct routes."

"Okay," she said, still reticent. "I suppose the pies will keep."

📷

Royal Oak was such a different place then, Robbie. From an outsider's standpoint, it wouldn't seem that way, I suppose; small towns change so slow, like the creeping of continental plates. But if you were here now, you'd know what I mean. The energy and pride have seeped out of the place. The downtown is a strip of empty storefronts with grimy plate-glass windows, God-awful vinyl siding slapped on in the '60s and '70s to give the town a "facelift," and rusty signs, letters burned out, neon drained. It's been sucked dry by the monster stores that sit like fat spiders by the interstate, breeding other little spiders—and no one wants to raise a hand to change things. No one cares. We don't even talk to one another like we used to. When I walk down Main Street, I look my fellow townspeople in the eye—and usually jowly faces from drinking Big Gulps and eating bottomless bags of Doritos stare back—and I wonder, who *are* all these strangers?

If only you'd been here the summer before the end of the war. Royal Oak buzzed with chitchat and goodwill. Peace was on the horizon. We'd lost eleven young men, including you, and many more were still serving, but the war had pulled us together, from the dairy farmers in the valley to the shop owners on Main Street, from blue-collar men like Papa to those wealthy folks behind their hedgerows and columns. Main Street, all pleasant brick storefronts and cleanly swept sidewalks then, was a place people went to get what they needed, and to see one another and to be seen, whether it was at Kessler's Hardware for feed; or Brickles' wide linoleum aisles for a new hat; or Hersh's polished chrome counter for a grilled cheese; or Elroy's Cafeteria for a Sunday dinner of fried chicken, corn pudding, and roasted potatoes; or the Hoot Owl for a bourbon and Dixie Cola. Oh, I don't mean to say we all loved one another. That's far from the truth. But we understood ourselves as belonging to one another. I even belonged to Bunny Prescott, although, at the time, I would never have admitted as much.

During the car ride through town, Bunny pressed Jay for more details about Lily. "Start at the beginning," she said. "I want to know *everything*."

He looked back at me, eyes restless, as if tracing a fly around the inside of the cab. "I met her, Lily, on the train coming back from Washington three days ago, and we struck up a conversation, just friendly chitchat." He gave me a brief nod, like he wanted me to know he was talking about it for my sake, not Bunny's. "She saw my camera and asked me if I was a photographer. I told her I was, of a sort, and she told me she was trying for a modeling job in the city. She wanted to model dresses, hats, shoes, nylons—that type of thing. She wanted to be on the floor in a big department store like Woodies." He shifted in his seat and bit his lip. "Could you drive a little faster, Bunny?"

"Yes, okay," she said. Her gloved hands tightened around the steering wheel, the motor surged, and a cluster of colorful, freshly painted bungalows whooshed by. We were on King Street, headed to the better part of town, Bunny's part. "Well, go on," she said.

"I told Lily I'd meet her there, at the clearing in the woods, to take some shots for her modeling application."

"Really? Why there?" I said.

"The light is good at that spot midmorning and the mountains make a great backdrop, and, of course, I didn't have a studio to offer her." His arm was stretched across the back of the seat, shirtsleeve rolled to the elbow, veins twitching as he fiddled with the raised seam of the leather upholstery. I had the urge to put my hand on his to calm his fidgeting.

"I didn't want her coming to the house and having to explain her to Grandma," he continued. "So when she rang up yesterday and told me she'd be passing through, I explained how to get to the clearing from the train station. It seemed easiest to meet her there since it's fairly close to the station. After all, I was doing her a favor." He fell silent and pulled his arm back.

"And?" Bunny prompted, taking a moment to change gears. "What happened when you went to the clearing?"

"Just wait. You'll see for yourself."

"I'm not sure I want to." She scrunched her nose.

"Then why are you here?"

Creases appeared in her clean, white forehead. "I just need to be prepared. I haven't seen something like this firsthand."

"You can't prepare for this sort of thing. Trust me."

She caught my eyes in the rearview mirror. "Ceola, we should take you home. You *really* are too young to go with us."

"No!" I said, grabbing the back of the seat and thrusting my head between them. "I should go! I wanna go!"

"She'll be okay," Jay said, shooting me a half-smile. "She may be more prepared than you, Bunny." I knew he was talking about you, Robbie, about me losing you. He knew that loss was a kind of violence; the war was closer to me at that point than to her. A dead body was nothing compared to my nightmares about what had happened to you.

We turned onto North Street, heading west. The Prescotts' two-story colonial was wedged between the old Bixby place and the Matthews' home at the end of the cul-de-sac. With its white bricks and black shutters, its canvas-draped pergola, and its oversize second-story gallery shaded by a navy-and-white-striped awning, it looked like a ridiculous cruise ship; its flat lawn, a stagnant green sea.

We used to wander through that neighborhood, Robbie, with its tall oaks and elms, whitewashed fences, boxwood bushes, and fancy rose gardens, and dream about what it'd be like to live in one of those ritzy places. You'd say, "Someday, little sis, we're going to live in a house with columns all down the front and a paved driveway in the back. We're going to play baseball in our Sunday best and not care, not one bit. We'll even have a butler in a tuxedo and some maids and eat off silver trays."

Well, I never lived on North Street or ate off a silver tray, but I have a paved drive, for what it's worth.

Bunny parked the car. We flung ourselves across the lawn, shielding our eyes from the afternoon sun, and clamored into the cool shade of the forest. After scrambling down the bank, we followed the creek upstream, the locust trees, maples, and birches bending over us, casting a tangle of shadows on the shallow water. We did our best to maintain our footing on the slippery limestone slabs and smooth river stones. Bunny sounded off frequently, a namby-pamby Little Red Riding Hood, clutching her dress close to her, shooing away mosquitos and water bugs. Jay struggled with the uneven surface, but he'd trained himself to work through physical adversity, and to my surprise, about a quarter mile in, he leaped to a stone at the center of the creek and balanced on his good leg like a circus performer in a high-wire act.

"Aren't you worried about hurting yourself?" I said.

"Nah," he said, grinding his teeth together. "I'm fine."

"You should be more careful," Bunny said. "Wounds like that take a long time to heal."

"Yes, Mother Dear," he said. "Now, jump. Come on."

"Why don't we cross over on the bridge?" she said, putting a hand to her chest to calm her breathing. "It's just upstream a little."

"We shouldn't risk it."

"I can't believe this Lily person would've dragged herself all the way out here for a silly photograph. I mean—"

"It's not that far. Come on."

"If I fall, Jay, you'll have to fish me out of the creek and carry me home."

"*Come on.*"

"All right. Okay."

After taking off her muddy pumps, she skipped to the rock in a bustle of red, like some enormous cardinal trying to take flight. Once she found her balance, she curtsied, pleased as punch, her cheeks pink, a film of moisture coating the ridge of her nose. She held her hand out to me, smiling like she wanted to eat me, but I waved her off. No thank you. As soon as she moved, I jumped.

"That's the way to do it, Cee!" Jay called out.

I smiled at him.

"Let's go," he said. "We need to move faster."

I sensed eagerness just under his impatience. What he'd witnessed, it seemed, had cranked something up in him, a brashness as well as an unease. I couldn't tell if we were running toward something or away from it. I wondered if he had been thinking of you, too, of how you, with your love of detective stories, would've reacted to seeing a real murder victim.

You'd been beside me the entire journey, my hand in yours, pulling me along, whispering in my ear, transforming the woods into the set of a matinee thriller. I was no longer a twelve-year-old girl but a PI, a Philip Marlowe or Sam Spade sort, ducking limbs and skirting dead trees, headed to the scene of a crime and the clues that would lead us to the black-hearted killer. There was an evil out there that we would wrestle to the ground, handcuff, and bring to justice.

"That's it," Jay said, nodding to a bend in the trail just ahead. "That's where I dropped it." I took a step forward, and he held out a hand to stop me. "Let me."

Jay scanned the trees and undergrowth—so he *did* think the murderer could still be nearby!—and staggered to the spot: the rim of an old sinkhole stuffed with debris, mostly branches and rotten leaves. "I almost fell in when I was running away," he said. He smacked the side of a spindly, leafless locust. "Here's the tree that caused the problem."

Using it to brace himself, he kneeled and began rummaging through the leaves and twigs just over the edge. The muscle underneath the soft fabric of his pants trembled, and he recoiled in pain.

"Cee, could you get it?" he said. A foot or so beyond his reach, I spotted the ripped leatherette casing of his Speed Graphic. Without much trouble, I scooted down the incline, grabbed the shoulder strap, and dragged the clunky camera up. He took it and slung it over his shoulder. "Thanks, Cee."

Down the trail a few hundred feet, we passed through a row of feathery pines and, still being watchful of movement in the woods, approached a small clearing about thirty yards wide, a wasteland of rocks and dry grass. A narrow path passed east to west through it. In the center was a large, igloo-shaped boulder, like the skull of a half-buried giant.

"That's where she is," he said, stopping abruptly. "Over there. Behind the boulder." He looked at me, his eyes urging me on. "When I first saw her, I didn't know what I was looking at. For a split second, I thought she might be asleep, like she'd been waiting for me and dozed off. That was stupid, of course. Blood was all over her and the ground. I stood there for the longest time. Then instinct kicked in, like I was back on the front, and I started shooting photos."

"You took pictures of the body?" Bunny said with a little gasp.

"I feel safer behind the camera, you know, looking through a view-finder."

Bunny's stunned glare dissolved into a sympathetic frown. But he didn't like her pity, not at all, because that's when I first saw *it*, or at least became aware of it—the actual shifting of his mood, like a cloud passing over the sun. His eyes darkened, his features fell quiet, and his adventurous spirit retreated, pulled back through a thick curtain of anxiety. The bone structure of his face seemed to change. His skin grew pale, his eyes flickered, his muscles contracted, pulling and pinching the flesh in his cheeks, at his temples, and across his forehead. I didn't really understand what it meant. Was it the murder? The war? Bunny? Some blurred combination of the three?

"Go and tell me what you see," he said.

Bunny gave me a quick glance and swallowed. Was she waiting for me to make the first move? Or was she going to object to my age again and hold me back as soon as I took a step forward? She opened her mouth but said nothing. Maybe she thought the killer was still lurking in the woods, or maybe she thought Jay was playing an elaborate joke, or maybe she was just as caught up in the moment as I was and was frightened by her own curiosity.

"Go ahead," he said softly. "Please."

In front of me, the boulder's smooth, sun-warmed surface promised so much—a corpse, a mystery, a chance for me to put my detective skills to use. On the other side was something, I just knew, that would change my life, but I was confused. Jay had been protective of me, of us, and now he wanted us to go ahead of him and expose ourselves to whatever was waiting. My heart was running laps around my lungs.

"We've come this far," he said in a whisper. "I need you to tell me what you see. I'll watch out for you. I promise."

I edged forward with Bunny inches behind me, her shadow falling over mine, gobbling it up. Was I ready for the shock, the strange thrill of the dead woman on display? Unlike losing you to the ocean, there would be a body—something real, someone to bury. Worried that Bunny would grab me, I shot ahead and clambered up the giant's skull.

But there was nothing. No woman. No blood. Not a damn thing.

At first, I thought I hadn't looked in the right spot. I dashed to a clump of grass at the far end like a frantic squirrel searching for nuts. I saw something white—maybe a hand?—but it was only quartz in a piece of sandstone. I swore at it.

By this time, Bunny had seen the big nothing too. "This isn't funny," she said.

"What is it?" Jay said, rounding the side of the boulder.

"I'm going home. It's just a game, Ceola. A lark, to make fun of us."

He stopped cold and furrowed his eyebrows. "She was right here. Lily's body was right here." He pointed to a rough mess of weeds, twigs, and rocks a few paces in front of him. His tone was flat, drained of energy. "I know what I saw. She was beaten and bloody. I'll develop the photos and you can see for yourself."

"Someone must've moved her," I said. "Someone *was* in the woods."

"The ground is damp where her body was," he said, bending down and pressing a finger into a large, oval-shaped patch of mud. He showed us the evidence on his fingertip. "The murderer could've cleaned up, washed away all the blood."

"Do you think he saw you?" I said. "If he watched you take the photos, you could be in danger."

"I'd like to see these photos, Jay," Bunny said. She searched his face, like she was looking for a tell, but he didn't move, not even a twitch or a blink. I wanted to kick her in the shins and give her a shove. *Leave Jay alone.* But she gave up soon enough, wobbled on her heels over to the boulder, and leaned against it with a huff. She smoothed out her dress and began picking milkweed pods out of its folds, flicking them away.

I leaped to action, combing the area for clues, hoping I would find an incriminating matchbook or torn piece of cloth from a coat or dress. The matchbook would have a phone number scrawled on the inside flap, or the scrap of fabric would smell like cheap drugstore perfume that, using my bloodhound nose, I'd identify with just a whiff.

In a patch of Queen Anne's lace near the edge of the woods, I spotted a dark, triangular shape wedged between the long stalks. As I reached down, a group of butterflies sprang to life and spiraled into the trees. When I glanced back to the shape, I saw that it was a woman's shoe. I hooked it with my forefinger and brought it to eye level. I held it away from me, the open toe pointing toward the ground, its ripped bow hanging by a thread, its black velvet dirty. It was a classic clue. All we needed now was a smashed watch and a broken strand of pearls, and we were on our way to pulp magazine paradise.

"I found something," I said.

Jay was sitting on top of the giant's skull, his eyes far off, his arms crossed tight over his chest. Bunny was leaning back and holding her face to the sun like some ridiculous postcard—"Come to Royal Oak and Stay A-While!" Neither of them made a move.

I called to them again, this time louder. They popped out of their daydreams and came quick.

"See, Bunny, there's blood on it," Jay said, jabbing his finger at a rust-colored stain that covered up the size and make on the insole of the shoe. "I'm not inventing this."

Bunny wrinkled her nose as if it was the woman's foot itself and took a step back.

"Was there another shoe?" Jay asked me.

"I don't know."

"Where did you find this one?"

I pointed to the spot. He rooted around until he found the shoe's mate. He gave it a quick once-over and set it on the ground by his feet. He pulled his camera strap over his head and stripped off his linen shirt, leaving him in a T-shirt with sweat stains at the armpits. He spread his shirt on the ground and wrapped his new discovery in one side of it.

"We need to keep these safe," he said. I offered him the other shoe, still dangling from my forefinger, and he took it and folded the shirt over it.

"So you can take them to the police?" Bunny said.

"I can't go to the police," he said. "The body's gone. The blood's washed away."

"But the shoes," Bunny said. "You can show them the shoes. And the photos. What about the photos?"

"The photos make me look guilty. They won't understand why I took them. I'll just be crazy Letitia's grandson, back from the war, murdering helpless women and taking their pictures. And the shoes. We've tampered with them. Cee's fingerprints are all over one of them."

She hesitated, sizing him up, her lips separated but motionless. "You are too frustrating," she finally said. "You really are. The truth is, I'm not sure I believe you."

"I believe you!" I chimed in. "I do."

She frowned at me, her mouth a bright red boomerang.

"Thank you, Cee," he said. "It's nice to know someone does."

Bunny glared at him. "You need to develop those photos, I think."

2

BUNNY

began falling in love with Jay Greenwood at my eighteenth birthday party—oh, and what a fall it was! It was the summer of '43, two years before Ceola and I were privy to his lurid photos of Lily.

My party fanned out from a large gazebo on the Point, a peninsula that jutted into the center of Culler's Lake, and my mother, in her usual grand fashion, had hired a five-piece band from Roanoke to play dance music (the trumpeter was an old beau of hers). The caterers, also imports, rearranged and clustered picnic tables, draping them with linen tablecloths and topping them with gardenia centerpieces flanked with hurricane lamps. From the roof of the gazebo to surrounding trees, she had them stretch shimmering white streamers and a large, breeze-whipped Happy Birthday banner. Mother had such fine taste and she liked to show it off, but, as usual, she extended herself too far and invited half the town, including all of Father's employees and their families.

Dixie Dew employees often welcomed my mother's generosity, but on occasion, they resented the show of wealth, particularly during wartime. Father encouraged both my mother and me to wear simple, muted colors and avoid glitzy jewelry—no bangles or pearl-drop earrings. It was gauche to overdo it in those days; bright colors were thought unpatriotic because of the ration on fabric dyes. "Be women of grace, not status and place," he intoned. Mother often challenged him on this. She loved color. My party was a strike of independence on her part, and though Father didn't approve of all the folderol, he conceded for the occasion, for me.

Counted among the truly resentful Dixie Dewers were Bob and Margery Bliss. (On reflection, I can see why Ceola despised them.) Of course, they arrived early so as not to be avoided.

Margery thrust her thin hand out at me. "Happy, happy birthday," she muttered, as I shook it lightly. She had a thin, angular nose and a wilting smile. Although her eyes drooped at the edges, they lurked nervously under the hood of her brow. She wore her hair long and close to her cheeks in an attempt to hide a red birthmark that crept from her left eye and down her jaw to her neck. I could tell she hated me, but I could also tell she was frightened of me—or at least the prospect of having to make conversation.

Bob Bliss—short, potbellied, and mostly bald, save the thin web of a comb-over—stood like a tree trunk beside her. His cheeks were firm and fat like full water balloons, and the ruddy skin of his face constantly fluctuated in intensity. He shook my hand and said, "You look very pretty tonight, Bunny." He said it loudly so that my father, who was just a few feet away, could hear. His blue eyes remained sharp and fixed, pinpoints of concealed anger.

I smiled at him and told him to enjoy the party.

Behind them, a pace or two back, was their only son, Robbie, looking ill at ease. Underneath a wave of thick brown hair, his warm brown eyes moved restlessly, a little mischievous, a little cautious.

"Hello," I said to him, pushing brightness into my voice and holding out my hand.

"I hope you're having a good birthday," he said. He was preoccupied by something over my shoulder.

"It's wonderful. I just—"

Laughter exploded behind me. He blinked, almost flinched.

"Are you all right?"

"It's not important." He was still searching past me.

"Are you looking for someone?"

But he didn't answer me. He shook my hand and walked away. As he vanished into the party, his head was lowered, and his thin arms and legs were loose in their sockets, giving his gait a gawky femininity, a wounded deer searching for shelter.

After greeting the guests, my mother excused me, and I began mingling with the crowd. I moved from circle to circle of my parents' acquaintances, making small talk and flashing smiles, telling them how I wanted to be an actress after the war ended. One guest—I have no idea who—suggested I should begin my career immediately: "The troops need pleasant, pretty distractions."

I was flattered, but Father needed my help at the plant, sorting large-size food cans, which would be recycled into crowns for the Dixie Dew bottles. Rationing was in full swing, making it difficult to find enough sugar for the soft drinks and enough tinplate for bottle caps. He insisted I work at the plant until the war ended. So I had to put my dream on hold, which turned out to be a blessing. Believe me, I had no business acting.

Eventually I found myself in front of my birthday cake. It was a large pink slab of buttercream icing, with "18" written across the top in bright pink. It was girlish and silly, but I hid my resentment from Mother and Father. Accompanied by the band, the crowd sang "Happy Birthday," then I made a wish and blew out the candles. The cake was cut, and I served several pieces until my mother took over.

"Go on, Bonita," she said, calling me by my proper name. "Have some fun."

When I was young, instead of saying Bonnie, I said Bunny, and unfortunately, the nickname stuck. When I decided I wanted to be a writer later on, I made my pen name B. B. Prescott—the name "Bunny" wouldn't sell many novels, especially mysteries.

I danced several songs with different partners, spinning through old standbys like "Begin the Beguine" and "Georgia on My Mind." Then I saw Jay. He stood beside a tree, half-submerged in the shadow of the overhanging branches, and he was staring at me. For the first time, in just a blink, I saw the man in him. His facial contours were sharpening, losing their adolescent thickness; his shoulders were rounding out and his chest widening. Even his legs had filled out his trousers, shortening the hem. But I could tell by his eyes, with all their guarded passion, that he hadn't lost the boyishness I found so appealing. The dance steps forced me to turn away, and when I glanced in his direction again, he was gone.

I excused myself and began searching for him. I found him in a small group of six adults: two women in their forties; Mr. Hersh, the pharmacist; his wife, Bernice; and on Jay's arm, Letitia Greenwood, his grandmother. I kept my distance. Marion Hersh was pontificating on the war, and the women listened attentively, all impressed by his proclamations and prognostications, which he claimed were the result of "inside knowledge" he had elicited from a friend, a colonel in the 2nd Armored Division. Jay was shackled to the spot by his grand-mother's grip. Even in all her frailty, the woman had absolutely myth-ological strength.

Letitia wore an elaborately ruched, dusty green evening dress that was much too fancy for the occasion, flower petal earrings set with dia-monds (most likely real), and thickly applied makeup that had cracked and collected in the wrinkles at the edges of her mouth. All around her, like a cloud of despair, hung the heavy scent of an old, acrid perfume, tinged with an underlying odor of whiskey. Father felt duty-bound to invite her to all the parties. "You must have sympathy for her," he always reminded me. Our family, although unintentionally, had bene-fited from the Greenwoods' misfortunes. Jay's parents had been killed in a car accident when he was a young boy, plunging George Greenwood, his grandfather, into grief. He began drinking heavily and allowed Dixie Dew Bottling, which he had founded, to slip into the red. He sold the company to my father for a bargain price in 1933 and, two years later, died of cirrhosis of the liver. My father revived Dixie Dew with an infu-sion of Prescott money, strong work ethic, and good business sense.

As I approached the group, Letitia saw me and tightened her harpy grip. Jay's clunky camera hung close to his side. Using my birthday-girl authority, I said, "Excuse me, everyone. May I borrow Jay? I want him to take a photograph of me before it gets too dark."

"My dear," Letitia said with a frown, "it's already dark. It'll never turn out."

"You look beautiful this evening, Bonita," Mr. Hersh said, nodding his head and swirling the ice cubes in his drink.

Letitia hissed, "There's no point. It's a waste of film. It's nonsense."

Bernice Hersh frowned at Letitia and touched her husband on the arm in commiseration with me. "Let him go, Letty," Hersh said jovially. "After all, Bunny *is* the birthday girl."

Letitia watched us leave, fuming, her hands locked together like a tight dovetail joint. I felt the warm flush of victory.

Peeking through the ridge that surrounded the lake, the light from the setting sun only hit the Point in triangular patches. We scouted out one of these patches, away from the party. With his back to the sun, Jay paced, paused, and studied his viewfinder, and then paced again, paused again, and studied again.

"The sun *will* go down," I said.

He was gently adjusting knobs on the side of the camera. "Step to the left," he said. "Just half a step." I moved, and the sun was in my eyes. "Look at the top of the mountain and place your hands on your hips." He pointed, and I looked. I didn't like being posed.

"Drop your right arm and make it loose, then be still."

"Maybe your grandmother had a point."

I was aware of the warmth on my skin, the intense scarlet of the sun, and like that, he took the photograph. When he lowered the camera, the intensity of his eyes unsettled me. I glanced at the glittering black water of the lake and said, "Why were you staring at me when I was dancing?"

"I wasn't."

"Yes, you were."

"You may have thought that, but I wasn't."

"Then *who* were you staring at? Jenny Sprinkle, or one of the other pretty girls?"

"I wasn't staring at all."

"It's rude to stare," I said.

He smiled and said, "You're beautiful. You shouldn't need validation from me or from the camera."

"Pretty girls need the most validation," I said. "They've been told they're pretty so often, it has lost its meaning."

From the party behind me, the band began an orchestral version of "Haunted Town." I knew Lena Horne's version from my mother's record collection. The lovelorn lyrics stirred at the back of my mind. I wanted to be back under the lights and throwing myself into the tipsy clamor of partygoers. But even as the sun crept below the edge of the mountain, Jay wanted to continue. He produced a flash. I begrudgingly agreed to about a dozen more shots.

When we finished, he said, "I'll develop these for you soon."

"Good." I stepped back, nearly blind. My eyes swam with ghostly spots. "I really should go."

The warm, dark music guided me back to the party. As my vision cleared, I saw couples dancing close together, my parents among them, my mother's fingers laced together behind my father's head. She was a little drunk and happy. My father's hands rested quietly, patiently, at her waist, never touching her hips, always respectable. A shift in the music—or was it the dying light?—and Mother leaned in, the elegant shape of her sculpted and set hair disappearing in a shadow. *She is kissing him*, I thought. *I want to kiss someone.*

Again I drifted from group to group, engaging in small talk about the war and making cheerful promises to have lunch or dinner.

Bernice Hersh caught me by the arm and said, "I'm sorry Letitia behaved that way. She's really such a monster, you know. Your father is too kind to invite her."

I nodded, smiled, and drifted on, needing a break from the chatter.

I wandered down to the edge of the water, near where Jay had taken the photographs. To my surprise, Robbie Bliss was sitting quietly on a thin band of man-made beach. I stopped a few feet away, not wanting to disturb him. He tossed a rock in the water and listened to it plop. He raised his head a little and studied the ripples as they came toward him. A pang of sympathy shot through me. He seemed so lonely.

Being careful of my white dress, I sat beside him on the gritty terrain. I remained silent for a few moments, observing him as he, again, lobbed a stone into the black water. He seemed unwilling to acknowledge my presence, so I said, "Have you had fun this evening? I didn't see you dancing."

"It's a good party," he said with little enthusiasm.

"Well, my mother insists on inviting the entire town. She calls it 'good public relations.' I suppose she's right, but it always seems horribly political to me." I paused, then said, "Don't you think the lake is beautiful? I like the reflection of the night sky on it."

"I'm sorry," he said. "I want to be alone."

"You're not having fun, are you?"

"My birthday is next week. I'll be eighteen too."

"And you're enlisting?"

"That's right."

"Are you frightened?"

He let my question hang in the air. "No," he said at last. "I mean, I'm not scared of going to combat, if that's what you're getting at. It's just that all this . . ." He looked out at the lake. "It feels out of my control, like I have no say-so in it, like I never will."

Pushing brightness in my voice, I said, "You could be drafted anyway. At least this way, you have some control over where you'll end up. It's the smart thing to do."

"Jesus, you sound like my father."

A shadow flickered over me; someone was behind us. I turned and saw Jay's silhouette framed by the light from the gazebo.

"What are you two talking about?" he said.

"Birthdays," I said.

"Robbie's going to be a warrior for Uncle Sam," he said, and walked past us to the shoreline. He paused, then looked back: "Want to skinny-dip?" He pulled out a pack of cigarettes, selected one, fished a lighter out of his breast pocket, and lit it. Neither Robbie nor I responded, but Robbie released the stiffness in his shoulders and leaned back, uncrossing his legs. Jay asked again, and Robbie nodded and smiled.

"Mother would throw a fit if we skinny-dipped," I said. "I simply can't."

"Public relations?" Robbie said.

"That's right," Jay said.

Robbie chuckled.

I didn't like being made fun of. "I don't know why I invited you," I said to Jay.

He leaned toward me, offering me his cigarette, and said, "Keep this safe for me."

I took it between my fingers and held it away from me. He quickly writhed out of his shirt, and Robbie jumped to his feet and began undoing his belt, but guided by a greater modesty than Jay, he stopped and retreated to the shadow of a nearby birch tree. Jay continued to strip. His pants came down, his shoes and socks came off. He was naked except for his shorts. He retrieved his cigarette from me and took a drag. The hair on his legs caught the light from the party, deep shadows delineated the muscles of his torso, and a corona of smoke floated over his head. He was mysterious in a seductive, even dangerous, way—like one of William Blake's angels, all fiery watercolor and moody ink. I was hooked.

Since the bottom of the lake sloped gradually, Jay was able to walk out far enough to be obscured by darkness. I heard him swishing and stirring for a moment or two, the faint glow of his cigarette bobbing in the night. Then, like a ghostly bird, his underwear flew out of the void and landed beside me with a plop. From under the tree, Robbie— no longer reserved and shy—streaked into the lake, splashing and laughing, his thin, naked body vanishing as quickly as it appeared.

I glanced back at the party to see if anyone noticed. No one had.

Under the same tree, driven by some insane impulse, I unstrapped my sandals, kicking them off, and unzipped and removed my dress, carefully hooking it on a low branch. In my slip, I approached the water, which was now gently lapping against the beach, and dipped a toe in. It was tepid. I checked the party again. It seemed distant and intensely concerned with itself, as if it had nothing to do with me anymore. "Wait for me!" I called to the boys, and began inching into the lake, feeling sticks and slime on the bottom. I rubbed against something slick and ropy, and sure I was trudging through a family of water snakes, jerked away, slinging curse words at the water, realizing a breath later, it must be algae.

Once I was up to my waist, I heard the boys' laughter yards away, somewhere in the low mist creeping in from across the lake. I cried again, "Wait for me!" but heard nothing in response. I gave in, flopped into the warm water, and began swimming. *Wait for me.* I swam steadily for a few minutes, frustrated by the slip's thin fabric cleaving to my legs. I stopped and listened. I heard no voices, no splashing. *Wait for me.*

Lights from Royal Oak, situated a valley over, outlined the mountains, and the Milky Way stretched across the sky in a bright swath. I could no longer feel the bottom of the lake; the liquid universe below seemed as vast and endless and unknown as the night sky above. I imagined a pale, decaying hand, fingers hairy with algae, like something from a horror matinee, reaching up through the murk and grabbing my ankle. I yelled, "Jay! Robbie!" Nothing. I repeated the call. Nothing.

I might drown, I thought. *I might deserve to drown.* That horrible feeling, a mixture of desertion and embarrassment, was wrapping its tentacles around my heart. I listened again, more deeply. I heard music echoing in the valley. It seemed far away and I was afraid, but it gave me a sense of the distance to shore, like a bat's sonar. I started swimming furiously toward it, toward the partygoers, toward my mother and father dancing together. Soon I hit the sludgy bottom, and the black magic of the lake receded. Then I was climbing out of the water, pushing my feet through the mud and running across grit and stones and grass to my soft, white dress, suspended in the shadows.

I sat underneath the tree. I was soiled with black mud, and my hair and my makeup were ruined. *Why, why did I do this to myself?* My pristine white dress hung on the branch above me, stirring in a breeze like a mobile. I knew what I had to do.

I slipped the dress over my head and zipped it up, cringing at the grime bleeding through the starched cotton bodice. I strapped on my sandals and, walking in a semicircle to avoid the party, made my way to a boating dock on the other side of the peninsula. Taking care no one spotted me, I slinked to the end of it, about thirty feet out. The lake's glassy surface reflected the moon, and I could see the North Star, the Big Dipper, perhaps even vain Cassiopeia herself.

So when I jumped, I was jumping up, into the heavens.

As I surfaced, I screamed for help and thrashed around, doing my best impression of a damsel in distress. Eventually partygoers came to my aid. When I was on land again, surrounded by pale adult faces, I explained how I had wandered away from the party to stargaze. I told them I had been so distracted by the constellations, looking up, not ahead, that I had misjudged the end of the dock. Father propped me up, put his coat around me, and drove me home.

In the morning, Mother offered to scrub the dress for me, but I told her not to bother, I would never wear it again.

3

CEOLA

Bunny and I waited while Jay processed the photos in his make-shift darkroom, a bathroom just off the glassed-in porch—what was once a showpiece of the Greenwood home (so I've been told)—that Jay had transformed into his private space after the war by draping sheets and bolts of cloth over the inside of its roof and walls.

Bunny lingered over a *Royal Oak Times* she'd plucked from a stack of well-worn periodicals scattered beside the cot in the corner, and I nosed around the room. The sun glistened on the panes Jay had failed to cover, its rays penetrating the damp glass and playing this way and that across the clutter. I flipped through several of the books piled high on the picnic table in the center of the room, holding them up to the light to read a sentence or two. Most of them were detective fiction and pulp rags, some military manuals and cartography books. At the far end of the room beside Bunny, who had positioned herself on his sagging, hospital-cornered mattress, sat a phonograph on a small table, its horn twisted outward like a big brass flower in bloom. Jay had propped records against it, including Billie Holiday, Artie Shaw, and my favorite, Anita O'Day, who I'd sneak from Mama and Papa's collection and listen to when I was on my own. At the end of the cot was a U.S. Army–issue trunk, topped with half-empty bottles, many bearing the same labels I'd seen in Papa's liquor cabinet. Pinned to the blanket over the head of the bed were photos of soldiers—maybe even a picture of you, Robbie—and above the photos, his Purple Heart and Bronze Star, dangling like icicles.

Even though I'd never tagged along with you when you went to Jay's—kid sisters are rarely welcome around teenage boys, doing boy things—I imagined you in this space: Your strong, rangy frame. Your dark flop of hair, tamed with a little tonic. The handsome sharpness of your nose, your chin. The softness of your mouth, a whisperer's mouth. You would've been attracted to Jay's stacks of books. I could see you circling the table, picking up novels and flipping through them, sizing them up. I could see you and Jay sitting across from each other on the cot, playing pinochle, silently studying your cards and deciding your bids. I wondered what you two talked about. In the months leading up to your birthday, I'm sure you discussed the war and how much you hated it, or how much you hated Papa and Mama for forcing you to sign up—or maybe you just told stupid jokes ("How does Hitler tie his shoes? . . . In little knotzies!"), or made up scary stories, or talked about movies.

Jay eventually emerged from his darkroom, holding an eight-by-ten photo with a pair of rubber-tipped tongs. "The other prints are still drying," he said, "but you can have a look at this one."

I scooped up an armload of books from the picnic table to make space for the photo. Bunny flung down her newspaper and crossed the room, determined to be the first to have a look. I dumped the books and returned, but she shot out an arm, holding me back.

"Let her see," Jay said.

"It's not—she's too young," she said.

"I want both of you to see. *Move.*"

Bunny shifted to the side, flapping her hands in exasperation.

Still as a statue, trying not to give away the pounding of my heart, I looked at it. I could tell Jay had been close to her when he took it, about five paces from where she was lying with her head bent back over a rock, her curly blond hair all tangled like a web of spun sugar. Just above her breasts, blood was seeping into the edge of her light-colored, button-front suit, and her skirt was crooked over her hips. Her whole body seemed to be broken in two and twisted like some bad-mannered child's baby-doll. Her arms were thrown wide, her dirty palms open to the sky. I imagined a horrible demonic force had hold of her, pinning her wrists to the ground. She was missing a shoe on her left foot but still wore a scuffed-up pump on her right, and her legs were crossed over each other, a swimmer frozen mid–scissors kick. All around her it was rocky and dusty, littered with twigs and dead weeds. Thin streams of blood, black as oil, fanned out from her head, running downhill and flowing around the edges of her stone pillow.

Once we had gawked long enough, Jay trapped the photo with his tongs and carried it back to the darkroom. He brought out more photos, each similar to the first but shot at different angles, different distances, some a little blurry, others a little overexposed.

I didn't know how to react. Hell, I'd never seen a real dead body. How was I supposed to feel? Afraid? Spooked? Excited? Sad? The emotions floated by like a line of theater masks, each carved expression shifting, bending, becoming something else, none reflecting exactly what was inside my head.

I thought of you, Robbie, of what you might have made of the photos. I hoped that, in thinking of you, I'd know what to do with what I saw, as if you, now somewhere between the living and the dead, the purgatory of all those missing in action, had some secret understanding of the dead—or at least how they'd want us to feel when looking at their corpses.

A few weeks after word about you came, I swiped the letter from Papa's desk. After studying step-by-step instructions in one of your magazines, I picked the desk drawer's lock with a bobby pin. Hiding underneath the desk, I read the report one word at a time, sounding it out, like it was written in a foreign language. It said you and more than ninety other soldiers were missing in action after the Japs sunk the USS *Johnston* during a battle off Samar in the Philippines. It proclaimed your bravery and patriotism, it declared your sacrifice as the greatest sacrifice a man could make for his country, but it seemed distant, like the writer didn't know you, like he was talking about some other Robbie. I wasn't convinced. Although Papa was fit to be tied and Mama was harboring doubtful fantasies of your return, I knew, I just knew, that you would come home. There was no body, no dog tags to hold, no proof. So every day, I watched as the mail truck lurched to a stop at the mailbox, dust from the road curling around it, shimmering in the sun. I imagined when the cloud settled, you would be standing there in your fatigues, that somehow it had all been a terrible mistake. After all, a letter brought news of your death; why shouldn't it bring you back to me?

Jay gathered up the photos and returned them to the darkroom. Bunny started circling the table like a caged tiger. When he appeared again, she said, "We need to—no, *you* need to go to the police. There's no question about it."

"Look, Bunny—"

"There's no question," she said, delivering it like an order.

"There's still no body." He flared with anger. "And the photos only incriminate me more. I wish you'd knock it off about the police."

She stopped and stared at him, her nose, chin, and lips like sharp points on a shield. I almost expected her to snatch her lipstick from her purse and unsheathe it like a sword. Part of me looked up to her, the part that admired her willfulness and her beauty, but another part, the bigger part, the *meaner* part, wished she'd go the hell away.

"There's no question," she repeated, but faintly, then took a step forward, a move that seemed to throw her off-balance. "Oh," she muttered, steadying herself, "it couldn't be . . . ?"

"What is it?" he said.

She held up a hand, her eyes bright. "What was the dead woman's full name?"

"Lily Williams, I think. She mentioned her last name once. I wasn't really listening."

"Could her name be Vellum? Lily Vellum?" She swung herself across the room and grabbed the newspaper from Jay's cot. "I read the headline, but I didn't make it to the article." She fussed with the pages, found what she was looking for, and scanned a paragraph or two. "Look," she said, thrusting the paper at Jay.

He read the story out loud, which went something like this: *Jitters Gap—July 16. Lily Vellum, the daughter of Frank Vellum, a*

prominent attorney in Jitters Gap, went missing from her home on
Friday evening between 9:00 p.m. and 12:00 a.m. Because the Haden
County police found signs of a struggle, and only a few personal items
were taken and no note was left, they suspect foul play. The article
also noted that the window to her bedroom had been forced open
from the outside. I remember that in particular. Frank Vellum made a
plea to anyone who knew about her disappearance to come forward.
The police were searching for her boyfriend, William R. Witherspoon,
for questioning. He went by Billy.

There was a yearbook photo of Lily. She was thin and pretty and
had short, curly blond hair, like the girl did in Jay's photos. Her facial
features were muted by the newsprint—except her smile, which was
more of a tight-lipped grimace, a failed performance. She wore a
double strand of pearls and a black V-neck. She couldn't have been
much older than Bunny.

"That's her," Jay said. "That's the girl I met on the train."

"Are you sure?" Bunny said.

"Yes, that's her."

We fell silent and moved away from one another. I plopped down
on the cot, pulled my dirty knees to my chest, and stared at motes
of dust filtering through the light. Bunny perched on the edge of a
rickety chair with ripped caning like she was practicing her posture for
finishing school. Her eyes had a shine to them. Jay paced the room,
swiping his hand through his thick hair, molding it into a different
shape with each gesture.

"If Robbie was here," I said, wanting to conjure you up, to feel you
there with me, egging me on, "he'd say we should do something. Solve
the mystery. Something. He'd know how too."

Jay looked at me, his eyes warm but sad, a blur of pain stirring quietly behind them. "You know, Cee's right," he said with a sudden punch of energy. "We should go to Jitters Gap and spy on Frank Vellum."

"Yes!" I said, jumping to my feet. "We have to." I'm still shocked I didn't say something gritty, like, *We have to act now. We're hot on the trail of a cold-blooded killer.*

He grinned at me.

"Jay," Bunny said, not acknowledging my enthusiasm. "You met Lily when you were coming back from Washington, right?"

"That's right."

"That was three days ago, on the seventeenth."

"Yes."

"Well, Lily was missing by the sixteenth. What was she doing here, having her picture taken, today?"

He looked puzzled, his energy waning.

"If she were kidnapped," Bunny went on, "she wouldn't be walking around Royal Oak. If she wanted to skip town, she would've taken the first train out of here."

"Good point," he said dully.

"And the shoes."

"What about them?"

"I don't know. She has on one in the photo, but you found both. That seems odd."

"Maybe the other came off when the murderer was moving the body," I said, pleased with myself.

"Okay," she said. "But why take time to move the body, then leave both shoes behind?"

"You're right," Jay said, shaking his head. "You're absolutely right."

She offered him a vague smile but retreated again into a frown. "I really do think you should go to the police," she said. "If you don't, I will."

"What will you tell them?" he said.

"You can't decide to hold your own investigation, Jay. It just isn't done. This isn't one of Ceola's trashy detective magazines."

"Hey!" I said.

"But I'm the only witness," he said, beginning to simmer.

"That you know of," she countered.

"If you tell the police, I'll look suspicious. They'll suspect *me*. Don't you get that?" His temples throbbed; his jaw muscles flexed. He was shifting again.

Bunny bit her lip and studied his face. She was trying to put him together, it seemed—the curve of his mouth, the angle of his nose, the loose drift of his eyes—trying to figure out if the sum of his parts equaled a whole. But Jay couldn't be assembled so easily, and Bunny's expression, a stew of colliding emotions, melted, and she looked away. She had her principles, sure, but she didn't want Jay to be falsely accused and dragged through hell any more than I did.

"How do we get to Jitters Gap?" I said. "It's over the mountain."

"My grandmother won't let me take her station wagon," Jay said, the heat in his cheeks and forehead cooling. "She keeps the keys hidden—from herself mainly, I think, so she won't get in it if she's had a few." He raised an eyebrow at Bunny.

"No. Don't ask." She crossed her arms.

"Pleeease," he said, curling out his bottom lip. I liked seeing him joke around.

"Absolutely not. I can't believe you would even—"

Jay began whimpering like a puppy.

"You're ridiculous," she said.

"Please," he said, dropping the act.

She uncrossed her arms and shook her head.

"Would your mother let you go out this evening?" Jay asked.

"She'll let me take it out if I gave her a good reason—but I'm not going to."

"What's on at the Lincoln?"

"*Murder, My Sweet*," I answered immediately. I'd been waiting for Papa to take me to see it.

"Tell her we're going to a movie."

"I don't like lying to my mother."

Jay smiled. "You've lied to her before—and your father. Remember your birthday party?"

Bunny shot him a look. "Don't push it."

"But you *are* going to do it?" he said.

She blinked.

📷

We all agreed to meet back at the Prescotts' around eight that evening. Bunny took off in her mother's car, and Jay walked me across the pasture to the border of the Greenwood farm. When we passed by the spot where he'd found me reading earlier, I saw the pages of your magazine waving at us through the grass.

"So you were reading 'A Date with Death' again?" He stooped to pick up your *Weird Stories*, July 1943. The Grim Reaper on the cover leered at his victim, a silly blonde in a form-fitting green dress. It was the third time that week I'd read it. He handed it to me, and I rolled it up and slid it into the front pocket of my middy.

"Yep," I said.

"I thought you didn't like it."

"I want to. I really do."

"But you just don't."

"That's right."

"Why?"

"The ending, I guess. There should've been a way out of it. That's always the best part of a story—the way out, the escape. But Robbie didn't see it like that. He said a scary ending stayed with you longer."

"Fate runs the show," he said wearily.

"I guess."

"So why do you read it over and over again?"

"I don't know. It's just . . ." I faltered. I couldn't explain it to him.

"You miss him, don't you?"

I didn't answer.

"Stupid question," he said. "I miss him too."

We set out for the fallen oak that bridged the gully, which ran the length of the property. We were quiet, taking in the sky, feeling the evening coming on. A breeze rushed across the pond and stirred the thin branches of the weeping willows. The next day would be stormy.

I could see from the strained look on Jay's face that his leg was bothering him. I wanted to offer to help, but something stopped me, a dark and shapeless thing tugging at my heart. At first, I thought it was sadness, that I was missing you, but that wasn't it, not quite. It was something more troubling. Maybe I was sensing the seriousness of what we were up to. After all, someone had been killed, and that meant that someone in town was a killer. But it was more than that; it was akin to fear, but fear as a premonition—a holy dread, Mama called it.

"Your brother used to make up stories," Jay said, as we approached the oak. "Like the ones in his magazines. He'd tell them to me."

"He told me stories, too," I said, and climbed on the log. Underneath, cold spring water trickled through tufts of wiry grass and black mud. I held my arms out, fingertips forming little circles in the air, and began a balancing act to the other side.

"That's something I miss the most," he said. "He could tell the best stories."

"He wrote some of them down," I said.

"He did? Do you have any?"

I stopped and let my arms fall to my sides. I was a little possessive of you, Robbie. I wasn't sure I wanted to share you with him. "I don't know where they are."

"Oh, okay," he said in a thin voice, then leaped on the tree, jostling it and making me reel. "Whoa!" He caught my shoulders and added, "Sorry about that."

I pulled away and edged forward, arms out, focused on my feet. The cool, damp smell of the stream drifted up, and a dragonfly, a glimmer of iridescent blue and green, zoomed past me. Foot over foot, I made it to the roots, navigated their gnarled twists and bumps, and dropped to the mushy ground. Jay was moving slow, being careful with his leg, his face pulled tight in concentration. Again, I felt you there beside me, watching your friend cross the log for me.

"The stories," I blurted out, "they might be in his journal." I immediately regretted mentioning it. I could feel you draw back from me and grow dim.

"That's right, he kept a journal. I forgot." He glanced up and smiled at me. "Do you know where it is?"

"No, he didn't want me nosing around in it. Besides, he probably took it with him when he left."

"Are you sure?" Jay asked, hovering above me, a shadow against the high white cloud passing behind him. A few stray hairs on his head flipped up in the breeze and glowed in the hazy sun like lightbulb filaments. "We wrote letters a lot, but he never mentioned taking his journal with him when he enlisted. I guess that's why I forgot about it. It'd be swell to have something of his."

"He told me if I ever read it," I said, "he'd box my ears."

Jay laughed. "That sounds like him." He sat on the edge of the tree and slid to the ground.

"Besides, Mama doesn't like me messing with his things. She'd be so mad if she caught me in his room."

"But you swiped his magazines, didn't you?"

"Some of them—but I wasn't supposed to."

He looked at me for a minute or two, turning something over in his mind, his eyes flashing as the clouds parted and the sun fell directly on his face. "Cee, look, it'd be bad if your mama or papa found his journal. There could be more in it than just stories, you know."

"Yes," I said, but I didn't know. I'd seen you writing in it, but I'd never dared look. None of my business; you made that clear.

"Trust me." He reached out and touched the side of my arm. "Can you do that?"

"He wouldn't want us reading it."

The corner of his mouth trembled, and his expression narrowed. "Please. Do some detective work and find it. I'd feel better if I knew it was safe."

"Okay. I'll look." But I wasn't sure I would.

"I didn't know you was married," the mail boy said, his dopey eyes drooping at the edges like a sad puppy. "*Mrs.* Addison." He grinned, showing his crooked front teeth, and handed her an envelope. It was addressed to Waverly Insurance Co., Attn. Mrs. Kenneth Addison, 402 West 92nd Street, New York, NY.

Addison. The name put a bad taste in her mouth, like stale bread. Soon Sheila would no longer be Mrs. Kenneth Addison. She frowned at the boy, making her lips an upside-down horse-shoe. He knew to leave her alone.

The envelope was of heavy paper, very official. It was from the law firm of Morgan and Ayres. Perhaps Kenneth's lawyers? She opened it quickly, stabbing her finger at it. The paper slit her fingertip, and she let out a little cry. She sucked her finger to stop the bleeding. The other girls in the room glanced up like chickens at feeding time. The clacking of typewriter keys stopped.

They were foolish, these girls, typing up insurance claims by day, dressing up and hunting for beaus by night. "Chickens" was right. *Be careful what you wish for, gals,* she thought. *Once you snag your prince, he might turn into a frog.* She shot a smile at them and reassured them she was fine, just fine. Then, she read the contents of the envelope:

Dear Mrs. Addison,

I regret to inform you that your aunt Majestica Fury of 300 Meadowlark Lane, Berlin, New Hampshire, passed from this world on November 13th. You are the sole beneficiary of her estate, including her home, Brimblevine House . . .

Sheila read on. Her face flushed with excitement, and she could feel herself sit up straighter, chills flowing through her in waves. Her great-aunt had left her a treasure, a hoard, a pot of gold! She had landed at the end of the rainbow, and right when she was feeling so blue. Golly!

She knew nothing about her aunt other than she had called herself "Madame Majestic" and was lousy with cash after conning the New York elite into believing she could tell their fortunes. She had fled the city and retreated into the White Mountains of New Hampshire to avoid scandal—and the clink.

Sheila's father, who had owned a dirty little potato farm outside of Parsippany, New Jersey, considered her aunt a dark stain on her God-fearing family's honor. He'd once shown Sheila a newspaper clipping of the notorious woman.

In it, Madame Majestic wore an elaborate silk turban iced with an expensive brooch, heavy diamond earrings, and a triple-strand pearl choker. Her raccoon eyes peered out from a smooth white face and sparkled with an uncanny light.

"She's a jezebel," Sheila's father had told her. "She had a different man on her arm every time I saw her. We don't speak to her anymore. A shameful woman." Sheila had thought she was beautiful and exotic. She had wished she could meet her. If she could only be as glamorous at her aunt, she could wash off the farm once and for all!

"What are you smiling about, Sheila?" Betty Blakely said. "You look like the cat that ate the canary." Betty was her prim, bespectacled desk-mate, and Sheila disliked her and her tight sausage curls. What a busybody!

"Some good news."

"What's that?"

"I'm rich. I just received word—"

"No?"

"I'm an heiress."

"Girls! Did you hear that? Sheila's a woman of means."

The girls began chattering and asking Sheila questions. She enjoyed their attention, their jealousy. She was about to burst her cocoon and turn into a butterfly and fly away from them all.

In the midst of the commotion, she thought of her soon-to-be ex-husband, Kenneth. She was divorcing the no-good, two-timing scoundrel, because he had broken her heart to be with a cheap floozy who performed in sequins at the Pink Elephant. He would never touch her aunt's money. Never.

During lunch, she would visit Morgan and Ayres. Until then, she daydreamed . . . What was her aunt's house like? Was it romantic? Was it at the end of a long driveway? Did it have marble bathrooms? What would she do with all that loot? Would she sell it and travel the world? Would she have an affair with a handsome Englishman, a blueblood, like she read about in the pulp romances? Possibilities floated out in front of her. She wanted to reach out and take each one, make them all hers. She wanted to leave memories of her shabby Parsippany upbringing behind; she wanted to walk out of Waverly Insurance and never look back; and most of all, she wanted to forget she had ever been Mrs. Kenneth Addison.

4

BUNNY

several weeks after my eighteenth birthday, Jay invited me over to peruse the photos he'd taken at the party. I wore a thin, gray dress, cinched at the waist with a strip of red patent leather, and applied a thick layer of lipstick to match the belt. I held an umbrella over my curled hair to protect the entire ensemble from the damp summer weather. I wanted Jay to see me as mature and womanly, and to forget the horrible business at Culler's Lake.

In the years after George Greenwood died but before Jay went to war, the Greenwood home hadn't yet taken on its gothic cast. The large Victorian still retained its white paint and glossy green trim. The windows were clean and the front walk swept. The lawn was freshly mown and lush in the rain. Several potted geraniums burst forth, bright red, on the front porch. Letitia Greenwood had managed to maintain the house with what she'd made in the sale of Dixie Dew, but it would be only a few years before that resource ran dry.

I wanted to avoid Letitia, so it was an absolute relief when Jay answered the door. He looked particularly handsome that day, not in the casual way I had come to expect. His hair was greased and combed, and his white shirt, its sleeves rolled to his elbows and smooth across his chest, was tucked into his linen pants. His brown suspenders matched his polished brown loafers. Before he welcomed me in, I felt a rush of emotion—a very definite and identifiable attraction to him, but less mysterious, less dangerous than what I felt at the party. Or so I thought. All the feelings of embarrassment over being stranded alone in the middle of the lake and my subsequent plunge back into the water lifted. Jay had cleaned up and dressed up for *me*.

I offered my hand to him, and he took it and held it firmly. A muscle in his forearm twitched, and a thought entered my mind, something particularly carnal and lovely. It felt good to feel that way, to have identified what I wanted.

He showed me through the house to the conservatory that would become his shrouded lair when he returned from the war. The walls then were foggy glass panes fused together with lead and wood supports. Above, reinforced with steel rods, was a domed roof made of the same damp glass, glowing from the cloud-muted sunshine and echoing the soft patter of rain. The moist air smelled clean and rich with oxygen. Potted plants of various sizes—ferns, violets, cacti, evergreens, even a lemon tree—thrived in the corners and along the edges of the room. It was the Greenwoods' private jungle.

Jay gestured toward a wrought iron patio chair. I positioned myself on it and he sat casually on a matching settee, catty-corner from me. As we fumbled through a few remarks about the weather, he rubbed his knees, unintentionally drawing attention to the way his tight pants pulled against his crotch. I was a little embarrassed for him, or perhaps

I was embarrassed by my own desire to touch him. Not knowing what to do, I blurted out a question: "So when did you take up photography as a hobby?"

His eyes brightened, and he leaned forward. "A while ago, Grandma ordered me to clean out my father's closet in his study. I found a dusty leather case behind some old boxes, and inside was his old camera. After lots of trial and error, I figured out how to use it. Eventually it broke, but I bought a new one with my allowance, the Miniature Graflex I still have now."

"Was it expensive?"

"Yeah—but it was worth it. I'd fallen in love at that point."

"In love?" Disappointment slipped into my voice.

"A love triangle, really."

"Sorry, I don't understand."

"It's like this: I walk around outside, or wherever, usually when the weather or the light is doing something interesting, and I search for the right moment, where everything is balanced. Like bright leaves against a stormy sky, that sort of thing. And then I stop it, just like that. That moment is my first love."

"And your second?"

"When I develop it. The black-and-white image adds something new to the original moment, a layer. Once the process is over, I usually can't decide what I love more, the experience of taking the photo or the photo I took of it. The two are inseparable, beyond comparison."

I lingered in silence.

"I should've asked," he said, standing up and startling me a little. "Do you want something to drink?"

"A glass of water?"

He left the room, and when he returned, he had an envelope, pre-sumably the photographs, tucked under his arm.

"Some of these turned out nicely," he said.

"Good," I said, taking the glass of water and the envelope.

"I didn't expect them to."

"Too dark?"

"I just didn't expect them to. My concentration was off that night."

"You were distracted, a bit self-involved—" I caught myself. "I don't mean that as a criticism. It's just—"

"I had a lot on my mind."

"Of course you did."

"Would you like to look at them?"

I sipped my water, which he then gingerly lifted from my hands and placed on the tile floor beside his seat. I slipped my finger under the flap of the envelope and, being careful not to bend the photographs, slid them out. The first few were panoramic shots of the party before dusk. They were well composed but not especially remarkable. We noted some of the bad dresses and laughed at the unfortunate facial expressions on several of the guests—eyes half shut, double chins, that sort of thing. There was a photograph of my mother and father dancing; my father's eyes were a bit dim and my mother's arms were loose around his neck. Her chestnut hair was pulled back carelessly, and her silver half-moon earrings reflected light onto her face, warming the hollow under her high cheeks and softening her jawline. They appeared tipsy, and their posture was a little inappropriate.

"I don't like this one," I said.

Jay removed the photo and flipped it facedown beside him. He didn't seem offended.

The photographs of me were at the bottom of the stack.

This is what I expected to see: A lovely young woman with rich, dark hair in a clean white cotton dress, posing playfully in front of the camera. There would be equal amounts of carelessness and caution to the image. The right arm stretched out, the left hand planted firmly on a hip, leaning forward a little, inviting the viewer, but gently, with grace—the same poise I had always admired in my mother. This young lady would be bright about the eyes, might even be thought flirtatious, but not indiscreet. She would approximate the perky Carole King dress models in *Ladies' Home Journal*, or an elegant fashion model juxtaposed with a handsome military man in *Life* magazine.

Oh, what vanity.

A few years ago, I stumbled upon a retrospective of Weegee's work. His photographs of the underbelly of New York City during the 1940s—the winos, the prostitutes, the exotic dancers, the transvestites, the crooks, the dead bodies, his obsessive love for sensational grit—reminded me of these photographs.

These images were phantasmagoric, a sort of nightmare of myself. The background of each was inky darkness, and in the foreground, I glowed so white that the folds of my dress had disappeared and my skin shone pale gray, almost two-dimensional. My face, however, was distinct in each photograph. In one, the expression was exceedingly desperate, almost angry. In another, slack-jawed and empty-eyed, arms straight at my sides—graceless, even absurd. The last image had me bending forward, my cleavage luridly, if carelessly, accentuated. I looked to be folding in on myself, white enveloping white, a phantom preparing to vanish in a ripple of cold vapor.

I touched the surface of that final photo, leaving my fingerprint over my face. Jay caught my hand, gently moved it away, and said, "I dodged it in the darkroom to make that effect."

I liked that he was touching me. "What does that mean?" I asked.

"I covered you with a piece of cardboard for a few seconds during exposure to create more contrast between you and the night sky. I wanted you to float in the darkness, like a white bird."

I thought he was telling me my photos were beautiful, that the real me, the absurd, frightened, desperate me, was something extraordinary and desirable. If I had stripped down in front of him, I thought, it wouldn't have been more intimate than those photographs.

Of course, that wasn't the case. But I didn't know it at the time, so I kissed him.

He returned the kiss forcefully, earnestly, surprising me a little. He pushed us together into a wider, deeper connection. His arms went around me, and he hoisted me onto his lap, opening my thighs with his knees. His hand slid up the back of my leg, under my dress. He fumbled with my garter belt. He seemed urgent, impatient, even schoolboyish. He was releasing something in me—a rougher, less mannered passion, part of me I didn't understand yet.

But the way he was handling me, and the way his kisses met mine, was awkward and faltering. At last, he stopped, and we deflated like punctured balloons, the air seeping slowly out. I panicked, aware how delicate young men's egos were, but, to be honest, more deeply afraid of being rejected myself. I quickly covered our failure with a more acceptable anxiety—Letitia. I wanted her to walk in right then. I wanted to shock her and lay claim to Jay, to see her curse and carry on, her bile uniting us against a common enemy.

I said, "Your grandmother might—"

"Yeah, you're right," he said, and helped me off him.

His starched shirt was wrinkled, and his suspenders were loose at his shoulders. His face was smeared with lipstick. He looked dopey and sweet.

"I love you," I said stupidly. His face went blank. "I'm sorry. That's not what I meant to say."

"It's okay."

"Those pictures you took of me are . . . I'm not sure I can . . ."

"When I turn eighteen, I'm enlisting. Like Robbie."

"I know."

"I'm not sure what to tell you."

We stared at each other for a moment, a long moment. Finding it unbearable, I directed my eyes out at the rows of vegetation and the foggy glass panels. "In all those pictures, there's not a single picture of you," I said.

"It's the burden of being the photographer. Always behind the lens."

"May I have a picture of you?"

He didn't answer. He just gestured toward his lips and said, "Your lipstick."

"You need to clean up too."

"There's a bathroom just inside the door."

"What about you?"

"I'll use my handkerchief."

The windowless bathroom, which reeked of developer and fixer, was Jay's makeshift darkroom. There, two years later, with the greatest care, he would develop the photos of poor, murdered Lily. Back then, it was strung with drying photos and cluttered with trays, bottles, and stacks of photographic paper. The enlarger sat on a table over the toilet. I found the sink, washed my face, and straightened my dress. I decided we needed to approach our mutual attraction in a more conservative, more appropriate fashion. I would be frank with him. He needed to know I was falling for him but also that untamed passion could run amok and cause problems. He also needed to know that I would wait for him to return from the war. I was loyal.

When I returned to the conservatory, he was gone. He had left the envelope containing the photos propped up on the settee. On the side of the envelope was scrawled:

> DEAR BUNNY,
>   HAD TO GO. PLEASE TAKE THE PHOTOS AND LET YOURSELF OUT.
>   YOURS, J

The door to the porch was open, and the gray sky still hung low over the mountains. I angrily snatched up the photos and my umbrella and stepped out into the dripping afternoon. I opened my black canopy against the sky.

It was only after Jay left for boot camp that I looked at those photos again. That's when I discovered he had included one of himself, the only photo I still have of him.

He is leaning against the side of a building, the clapboard sloughing off paint in wide strips as thin and curled as birch bark. His shirt is unbuttoned, and the collar is pulled back from his neck, revealing the smooth hollow of his collarbone. He is smiling a particularly wry smile, his eyes squinting a little.

It was a photo taken by a lover, but all I saw was a handsome boy, offering a gorgeous smile to the camera, to me.

Mother and Father insisted I go to Robbie's funeral. I hadn't wanted to attend, but there I was, carefully made up and dressed in a black wool suit and pearls. It was a chilly March day, 1945.

Three pews in front of me, Bob Bliss stood as stiff and blank as a slab of limestone, his eyes fixed on an invisible point at the front of the church and his jaw set against tears. Every time his wife reached for him, he shrank from her, as if her touch might send him to the floor in sobs. Her eyes moved from the empty pine coffin draped with the American flag to her open hymnal then to her husband. She wanted to know why her son had died and why she had been denied his body. She seemed to demand it from the service, from the congregation, even from God Almighty Himself.

Ceola stood apart from her parents. She wore a dark blue dress with a twisted white collar. (I wanted to reach across the pews and straighten it.) She sang loud and off-key, her long brunette pigtails swinging like twin pendulums as she aimed at the high notes. During the sermon, she bowed her head and clutched the ends of her pigtails together over her breastbone. When she released them, I realized she was reading the prayer book, gently flipping its pages as if she were reading a magazine in a doctor's office. After a while, Margery made her close it and sit up straight.

As I exited the church with my parents, bracing myself against the cold wind, I saw Jay with his grandmother on his arm. I had heard he had been wounded and he was coming home, but I didn't know when. I was genuinely happy to see him.

When he looked my way, I waved and smiled. He nodded and

excused himself from Letitia, who, buried in a shambling sable coat, was preoccupied with the minister, registering some officious complaint, I imagined. As Jay limped toward me, he smiled. He looked older and thinner. His dark blazer no longer fit him; it was roomy at the shoulders and chest. His skin was pale, and his eyes were brighter but less focused.

"Hello, Jay. How are you? I didn't see you come in." I offered my hand to him, and he gave it a weak shake.

"I didn't want the Blisses to see me. They don't want me here."

"I'm so sorry about Robbie."

"Are you?"

"Of course."

"You should be sorry for his kid sister. She's a good kid."

We were silent for a second, watching our breath escape in the cold air.

"How are you, Jay? I mean, are you okay?"

"I'm here, aren't I?"

"I've missed you."

He didn't respond at first, but he smiled a little.

"Have you . . ." He paused. "Met anyone?"

"No, I've been too busy working in the plant. My mind has been on the war, not on boys. Are you home for good?"

"I'm taking the train back to Washington this afternoon, but I'm moving home again in April or May. My grandmother needs me to help her around the house, and I need a little time to think." He looked directly at me, the silver fog in his eyes lifting. "The things I've seen, Bunny," he said softly, and I withdrew, a little afraid of him.

"Jay Greenwood!" I heard Mother call out. She immediately took him in her arms and hugged him. Standing back from him and giving him an admiring once-over, she said, "Are you back with us? Please, tell me you are. Tell me you've had enough of this war, and this war has had enough of you."

"I have, and it has," he said.

"That's wonderful. We should celebrate. I hear you're quite the hero."

"No, I'm not," he said firmly.

"You've been so brave, and that should be celebrated."

"It's not necessary."

"Jason!" his grandmother brayed. "It's time." She hooked her arm in his and tugged on him like a child, loose sable fur drifting away from her, caught by the icy breeze. She glared at my mother and me.

Mother frowned and said to him, "When you move back, come and see us."

"Yes," I added. "Please do."

Once Jay returned to Royal Oak, we began cobbling our friendship back together. We made a habit of rendezvousing for picnics down by the creek and going on photo expeditions around the countryside. We usually met in a small, secluded clearing in the middle of a wooded area on the edge of his family's property.

I remember one picnic in particular, not long before he showed us the photos of Lily. After we had finished eating (he had just gobbled up a piece of Mother's rich chocolate cake), he leaned back on the blanket and put his hands behind his head and closed his eyes. His chest spread wide, revealing the thickness of muscle underneath. He had gained weight and was looking much healthier.

"What are you thinking about?" I said.

"Nothing."

"Are you napping?"

"No."

"Well, that's not very polite, if you are."

"I'm trying not to think. I want it to be blank."

"*Tabula rasa.*"

"Yes."

"Is it working?"

"Not if you're talking to me."

I tried to lie down and nap, but I was restless. So I watched him sleep and listened to the whine of the cicadas and the breeze shifting through the trees. From his milky skin to his soft blond hair to his red lips, he had an almost feminine beauty I found deeply moving. He seemed like a ghostly vision, a Keatsian evocation:

> *Fair youth, beneath the trees, thou canst not leave*
> *Thy song, nor ever can those trees be bare;*
> *Bold lover, never, never canst thou kiss,*
> *Though winning near the goal . . .*

I touched his shoulder and, punching positive energy into my voice, said, "Take my picture. You haven't taken my picture since before you went away."

He rose slowly, went to his case, retrieved his camera, and assembled it. He circled me with his head bowed over the viewfinder, stepping sideways and crouching, as if I were the game and he the hunter. Being a target made me nervous. He noticed and dropped the camera from his face.

"Don't be so stiff," he said.

"Just take my picture and stop creeping around."

"I'm trying to find the best light. You want it to be flattering, don't you?"

"Flattering or perverse?" I said.

"Perverse . . . You'd like that wouldn't you?"

I laughed. I arched my back and thrust my breasts out a little, exaggerating my posture, hamming it up. He snapped a photograph and then several more, changing the film between each shot with an exuberant frenzy. Feeling particularly private in the woods, I gave in to the moment and flaunted myself a bit. When I was younger, I was shy about my body, but by this time, I had begun wearing tighter dresses and higher heels. I had received compliments on my good figure and my dark, curly hair—a Gene Tierney look-alike, or so I was told.

Jay stopped, lowered his camera, closed the viewfinder, and tossed it on the blanket like an alcoholic shoving away a drink.

"Did I do something?" I asked.

"No. It's not you."

His eyes clouded over like the translucent film of cataracts, and he dropped his head forward. I wanted to comfort him—but something in his body language told me not to. He was still in shock from the war, and I was ill-equipped to help him.

He lay down again, with his right arm over his eyes. I watched his chest rise and fall and his feathery hair flare in the breeze. I studied the shifting shadows from the trees on the blanket and on his shirtsleeve.

"Look," I said. "I wish you would talk to me. I don't bite."

He sat up, searched my eyes, then flopped back down and said, "I've been reading this book. *An American Tragedy*. Have you heard of it?"

"Dreiser, right? Didn't he base it on a true crime?"

"Yeah, but the story is more about the chip on his shoulder. He's really writing about himself growing up poor."

"I started to read *Sister Carrie* once but put it down. It was dreadful."

"Writing about someone else's tragedy was his way of saying something about himself. Writers do that all the time."

"I suppose. So, why are you telling me this?"

"Just trying to make conversation, as requested." He shrugged and smiled, but his smile was ever so slightly smug.

"What are you *really* thinking about?" He turned away from me. "The war?"

He didn't respond.

"Can't you tell me? Can't you try? I haven't forgotten about what happened between us, before you went away—"

"Bunny," he said, his tone a little sharp. "That was a long time ago. At least it feels that way." His voice softened. "We're different people now."

"I know. Of course. I just—I care about you. That hasn't changed. I can't change that."

"I know you can't." He stood up, brushing off his pants, and strapped his camera over his shoulder. "I should go, or Grandma will wonder where I am."

"Ooooh, not yet," I said, standing. "Please don't run off."

I reached to grab his arm, and in a surge of violence, he caught my wrist and twisted it. "Bunny! Just leave it alone." His fingers were digging into the flesh on the inside of my wrist.

"Let go!" I demanded, wresting my arm away from him.

He glared at me, his cheeks flushed; then he lowered his chin and whispered, "Sorry. You're really pushing my buttons."

Before I could respond, he disappeared into the woods. The underbrush swallowed him whole.

I stood there for a few moments, listening to my own breathing and the gentle flap of the leaves high in the trees. Then, like an automaton, I began to clean up the picnic. After I scraped the uneaten food into the woods, neatly stacked the plates and cups, wrapped the utensils in the dirty napkins, and packed it all up, I stared at my work, that stupidly quaint wicker basket painted with primroses and lined with pink and white gingham Mother had bought for us, and I rushed to it, snatched it up by its handles, and with a little scream, like a tennis player hitting a serve, flung it at the nearest tree.

Sheila had first met Kenneth on the elevator. They both worked in the same building; he on the twelfth floor, she on the eighth. He cut a figure with his wide shoulders, close-cropped hair, and coppery brown eyes. He also knew how to dress—he wore a sharp blue Brooks Brothers suit, powder blue tie and matching pocket square, buffed Italian leather shoes, and a gold college ring set with a garnet. Glad rags, indeed. He had gloss, real polish, like those Wall Street sorts, nothing like the rough, muddy looks of the only other man she was close to, her father the farmer.

So one day, she smiled at him. She had a good smile. She practiced it in her mirror often, tilting her head at different angles in search of the most flattering position. Her mother's advice. From a certain viewpoint, she looked a bit like Jean Harlow; from another, like Barbara Stanwyck.

He nodded in return, but no smile. She tried again the next day, but still, no smile. Just his handsome mug. This went on for a week, until finally, she said, "Are you going to flirt with me or not, mister?"

"I will if you want me to," he said.

"I *do* want you to, I do."

"Well, then. Let's see . . ." He looked her up and down. "You look swell in that skirt. And those shoes do your gams justice." He whistled lightly.

She was wearing a green wool suit she'd made from a Woolworths pattern. She raised the hem by an inch; a little more leg didn't hurt. And her green pumps she'd bought on sale at L & T. What a find!

"Oh, so you *are* good at flirting. I thought you might be."

"I didn't know I was being tested."

"I've been testing you for the past two weeks."

"Have I passed?"

"Not yet."

"What did I do wrong?"

"You haven't asked me for a cup of coffee."

He smiled again and asked her to dinner. She liked his smile, his teeth so bright and even.

She said yes.

Today, however, she was dreaming of dollar signs and her new life, not Kenneth Addison, so when the elevator door opened, she was surprised to see him standing there.

He wore a gray suit and a vermillion tie. His face was grim, even tarnished, but still handsome. Sheila glared at him and, holding her blond head high, entered the elevator. The doors closed. She glanced over at him. His black shoes shone like mirrors, and his trousers were pressed. Was the cheap sequined canary taking care of him? A woman like that didn't know how to look after a man.

She cleared her throat and said, "I received a bit of good news today." He didn't respond. "I received a letter. I've inherited my great-aunt's estate."

"Why are you telling me?"

She didn't answer. Then, she said, "Are you still with that harlot?"

"She's not a harlot."

"Oh, really?"

"You need to move on, Sheila."

"I have. I am."

"We were a mistake—"

"I'm a woman of means now."

"Well, good for you."

"I don't need you. At all."

"You don't have me. At all."

The elevator door opened and

several birds got on, squawking and cooing over one another. The car went a few floors, and the women got off. Kenneth gave Sheila a hard look, his irises cool as steel, and followed them out.

Before the elevator door slid closed, he turned and said, "And another thing: Stop ringing me in the middle of the night. I know it's you."

5

CEOLA

I couldn't be late for our trip to Jitters Gap, so I cooked up a plan to sneak out. I decided I'd do my best impression of a sad little girl with a tummy ache and tell Mama and Papa I had to go to bed. Once they thought I was dead to the world, I would stuff the bed with a spare quilt and slip out one of the windows in your room, Robbie.

I hoped and prayed Papa wouldn't decide to go out in the yard after dinner. A month or two after word came about you, he threw himself into planting trees along the driveway as a kind of tribute. Maples, evergreens—it's a goddamned forest now. He said he wanted to plant a tree for every day you were a part of this godforsaken world. I'm not sure what he was really hoping to accomplish. Just down the road in Bedford, they'd lost more boys during D-Day than any other town in America, and you didn't see them running around tearing up their yards like crazy people. It was some sort of self-imposed punishment, digging holes like he was a member of an invisible chain gang.

Anyway, it wouldn't be dark by the time I needed to leave. I'd be visible when I climbed down the trellis by the edge of the porch, so I needed Papa to stay inside. Luckily, he poured himself a whiskey and settled in to listen to Bob Hope on the radio. I heard the comedian's familiar voice from the living room—"What rugged guys these marines are! Today, one of them pulled off his shirt and handed me a tattoo needle and said, 'Okay, make with the autograph, boy.'"

By the time I came to the edge of the woods behind the Prescott house, the sun had dipped below a bank of clouds and the air felt cooler. I was a little nervous. It wasn't that I was afraid of the danger. In fact, I thought it was exciting, and it was keeping me from being blue about you. But I was worried about your journal. Jay didn't want Mama and Papa to discover it, which believe you me, I understood. But even if I found it first, I wasn't sure I wanted to give it to Jay. He'd made me feel uneasy by asking for it. For the time being, though, I chose to ignore my gut for the sake of our adventure. When I arrived at Mrs. Prescott's dusty Olds parked beside the house, I gave Jay a timid wave.

"Hey, sleuth," he said. "These are for you." He handed me binoculars. "Get in the passenger's side, but keep your head down. Mrs. Prescott wouldn't approve of you going to the movie with us, much less doing what we're actually going to do."

I slid over the slick leather seat and tilted my head to the side. Bunny was in the driver's seat, dressed from neck to knees in midnight blue. She kept her head still, her glossy lips pressed together like they had been painted shut. Jay dropped into the back seat, propping up his damaged leg. It was irritating him. Bunny adjusted the rearview mirror, gave her reflection a self-satisfied glance, and started the car.

Once out of the neighborhood, I sat up. But Jay gestured for me to stay down and said, "This town is full of gossips. We don't want them to see you. Just wait until we get out of the city limits."

I slid to the floor quick, catching a whiff of Bunny's perfume. It smelled heavy, like gaudy gold jewelry. She'd probably worn it for Jay. I got comfortable and watched the shadows move across the ceiling of the Olds, my imagination wandering, as it tended to do in those days. I made up a B detective movie called *A Drive into Darkness* to entertain myself, casting Bunny as the desperate vamp—she'd get it in the end. I cast yours truly as the sly private eye, C. C. Steele. Just as I was working out the plot, something about a car trunk full of stolen money, Jay said, "Okay. You can sit up. We're out of town."

📷

Jitters Gap was—and still is—a gloomy place. The Basin Coal Company opened Kildare and Gaylord Mines and established the town in the 1890s. The company kept the town running until the mid-1980s, closing its doors due to the Clean Air Act's requirement for low-sulfur coal, which, of course, Basin couldn't supply.

It's now a ghost town, Robbie, but in '45 it wasn't much better. Along its streets were rows of whitewashed clapboard company homes made grimy and rotten by the damp winters and, because the steep Appalachians clipped the day short at both ends, a lack of sunlight. The downtown, just a block or two long, wasn't much to see. Besides a general store, a butcher, a gas station, a doctor's office, and the company bank (the best-looking building in town), its storefronts were empty shells, selling nothing but dust and vermin.

At night, though, in the vicinity of Glade's Dine-In, there was life. As the three of us passed the diner in the Prescotts' car, I could see people inside huddled around the bar, laughing and carrying on. I even caught a whiff of buttery roasted chicken. I must've been hungry, because it smelled delicious. As we turned the corner, the diner's door swung open and a man and woman spilled out onto the street, her hand in his, both tipsy from beer or moonshine, both giggling and falling into each other. Call it girlish stupidity, but I wondered if Jay might ever hold my hand like that, pulling me out into the night.

We drove deeper into town, circling a more residential neighborhood. We eventually parked in the shadow of an old oak, far away from a streetlight, and set out on foot, searching the maze of streets.

Jay knew where to find the house, generally speaking. He had chatted up his grandmother and asked if she knew Lily Vellum, keeping it casual, he told us, so as not to raise her suspicions. She didn't know Lily, but she knew of the Vellum clan. Both families had been bigwigs in Haden County society years ago. The Vellums had been the politicians and the Greenwoods, the business folk. Letitia had explained to Jay where the Vellum home was, although she wasn't sure the Vellums still lived there. The Depression had been as rough on that family as it had the Greenwoods.

"Up there," Jay said, and pointed.

The house sat high on the hill at the end of Jitters Rock Drive, lording its four chimneys, its fancy Victorian curlicues, and its wrought iron weather vanes over the smaller, one-story homes on either side of the street. Its bay window glowed orange, peering down at us like the open eye of a drowsy watchdog. I didn't like it, not one bit. It reminded me of the haunted houses from storybooks.

Jay nodded toward the car parked at the front gate. Somebody was home. Moving from tree to tree like some silly Warner Bros. cartoon, we crept past the house and up a side street, hoping to sneak up on it from the rear.

"We shouldn't trespass," Bunny said, stopping in her tracks. "Wouldn't he be in his rights to shoot us?"

"We came all this way," Jay said.

"I don't want to be shot, thank you very much."

"Nobody's getting shot."

"We should just go home."

"Stop pretending you're above being curious."

"I'm not *above* anything. I just—"

He looked at her and she, him. His long eyelashes threw thin, spider-leg shadows across his cheeks. I felt cut off from them.

"What?" she said, with a puff of exasperation.

He placed his hand on her forearm, squeezing it a little, and said, "I'll watch out for you."

She seemed flustered at first, even embarrassed, but his touch calmed her. She twisted sluggishly away from him.

"Okay," she said. "Let's pray the man doesn't have a gun."

We trudged up a dirt road that dead-ended at a wall of blasted limestone, the Basin Coal Company's deep scar on the side of the mountain. To the right was a long gravel driveway, which snaked along the limestone and behind the houses. A screen of humidity blurred the moon, weakening the light and making it difficult to see. Every few feet, the trees seemed to grow thicker and the buzz of insects louder. We followed Jay through tall grass and into a bramble of blackberry bushes that tore up my arms and my thin cotton blouse. It felt like the beginning of a fairy tale—*Beware what lurks in the woods!*

Bunny caught her hair on a briar and let out a cry. "I don't want to be here!"

"You'll be just fine," Jay said, his voice cool and soft. He fumbled around in the darkness and freed her hair. There was something both familiar and distant about how those two were behaving toward each other, like everything they said was in a secret code.

Once we found the Vellum place, we leaned on the fence that ran the perimeter of the property. Jay spotted the silhouette of a man in the kitchen window and called our attention to it. He asked for the binoculars, and I handed them to him. He whispered, "That's him," then passed the binoculars to Bunny, and in turn, she handed them to me.

I found it difficult to focus the lens. Blobs formed into shapes of things then slipped back into clouds of light. Eventually, I saw Frank Vellum. He was a tall, proper-looking man with gray hair, a slick mustache, and ferrety black eyes. If he'd had a top hat and black cape, he could've been Professor Moriarty. He was sitting, chatting with someone who was out of sight.

"I'm going in for a closer look," Jay said.

"No," Bunny whispered.

Jay grabbed the top of the fence, about four feet high, and pulled his body up like it was nothing. He teetered on the edge of the wooden slats and dropped into the backyard, grunting as his right foot hit the ground. He crept up to the window and peeked in. Bunny situated herself close to me—practically on top of me—and watched over my shoulder as I watched Frank Vellum, who seemed to be explaining something, his hands moving up and down and back and forth like he

was directing a band. Although his voice began as a murmur, the more
he gestured, the louder he became. I was able to make out a word or
two, names and pronouns—Lily. Billy. They. To me. He said "to me"
twice. He seemed angry.

I guessed that he meant *How could they do this to me?* But was he
talking about Billy and Lily? What had they done?

Then a woman stepped into sight. I couldn't place her at first, but
then it dawned on me. "I know that lady!" I said a little too loud. "I've
seen her at the store. It's Mr. Hersh's wife."

Bunny gasped and said, "Bernice Hersh? Really?"

Bernice positioned herself behind Frank while he was ranting and
raving. She was wearing one of those tight, high-necked suits so popular in the 1940s, and her red hair was tidied up into a swirl. She
began rubbing Frank's shoulders, easing his temper, her fingernails
brushing against his neck. I'd once overheard Mama say that Bernice
had something of a reputation. When Bernice ran her index finger up
Frank's neck and around his ear, he fidgeted and stood up. She was
flustered for a second, pressing her lips together and massaging her
lipstick, like she wanted to make sure it wasn't going anywhere. Then
she collected herself and said something. He walked away from her
and she followed him, both of them moving out of sight.

Jay motioned to us. He was going to try another window around
the corner of the house.

Bunny shook her head and whispered a shrill "No!"

I gave her an angry, shut-your-mouth-now look, and when I glanced
back at the spot where Jay had been crouching, he was gone. I searched
the shadows for him but saw nothing. I searched all the windows of
the house. Nothing.

"Where did he go?" Bunny said. "Where is he?"

I didn't answer her.

She snatched the binoculars away from me, jerking the strap over my head. "Do you see him?" Her head darted back and forth like a chicken.

What would a private dick do? What would C. C. Steele do? I thought. *I can handle it. Keep cool—nothing fazes me, nothing. Cool as they come.* I stared down the darkness at the side of the house and readied myself for the next move, a regular Sam Spade in saddle shoes.

And then Jay flew out of the shadows, flashing through the night, his feet pounding the earth as hard as they could, and, despite his bad leg, he flung himself over the fence like a crazed deer. "He saw me!" he yelled. "Run!"

And that is exactly what we did. We ran through the grass and the blackberry bushes, Bunny hissing at the thorns like a rabid cat. We ran between the trees and down the road, kicking and crunching the gravel. We ran, forgetting to breathe, our bodies screaming at us. We ran until we hit the car. Literally. Hands, arms, and legs bounced off the metal. Jay jumped in the back seat, I hopped into the front passenger seat, and Bunny, her forearms scratched and bleeding from the briars, fell into the driver's seat. She fumbled with the keys and started the Olds, the motor flaring to life. She put the car in gear and pulled out, headlights swiping their claws at the bug-infested night. We screeched down Jitters Rock Drive and bolted past Glade's Dine-In, the smell of roasted chicken still high in the air, the car not slowing until we hit the town limits.

Jay's bad leg had to be shooting bullets. His breathing was labored, he was coated head to toe with sweat, and his face was red and tortured.

We were quiet.

Bunny rolled down her window, and the cool mountain air soothed us. She locked on Jay in the rearview mirror and said, "What *were* you thinking? You can't just run away from us without an explanation! That's not fair."

"What happened?" I asked. "Did he really get a good look at you?"

"Take me back to the farm . . . and I'll tell you all about it," he said, massaging his leg. "If we're going to . . . do this right . . . we need to establish a base of operations." His eyes were tearing from the pain.

"Base of operations!" Bunny echoed. "Oh no. This fool's errand is over. *Over.*"

"I don't believe you," he said, gritting his teeth and sucking in his breath. "You want to know what happened to Lily as much as Cee or me . . . You're hooked. I know you."

"I don't want you to get hurt. Look at you. I mean, my God."

Maybe it was those black animal eyes of hers, or her teeth biting into her lower lip like a frightened little kid, or the wrinkle of concern just above her nose. I don't know. But whatever it was, Bunny's expression at that moment struck me as real, like there was a heart under all that primp and polish. It's strange to say now, but right then and there, I liked her.

"I'll be fine," Jay said, touching her shoulder over the car seat.

📷

"We need to make a plan," Jay said. "Decide on some rules."

The converted sun porch's glass peeked through the draped fabric, reflecting the candles we'd just lit. The room felt brighter and more welcoming at night than it had during the day.

Jay poured himself a drink and offered Bunny a sip, but she waved it away. I wanted him to offer me some, but he didn't. Instead, he cocked his eyebrow, gave me a sly look, and said, "First of all, we need some secret way to communicate with one another."

I thought about how you had taught me to use lemon juice as invisible ink and how we nearly burned down the house trying to decode the message with a match. "What are we going to do?" I said.

"What about use a telephone, like most civilized people?" Bunny said.

"No, we don't want anyone figuring out what we're up to," Jay said.

She was about to respond, but he held up his finger, shushing her. He kneeled in front of his bed, easing through the pain of his sore leg, and began rummaging under it. He pulled out a small book and dusted it off.

"Have you heard of a cipher?" he asked, and flipped to a page of the book with lines of numbers and letters and unfamiliar symbols. "The military encrypts messages so the Nazis and Japs can't read them. We could do the same."

He handed me the book, and I stared at the sea of code and pretended I understood what he was talking about.

"Look," he said, "we can do something simple. Say, B equals A, C equals D, and on like that for the entire alphabet."

Then he wrote—

XF XJMM LFFQ B TFDSFU

"Translate it," he said.

Both Bunny and I worked on it, but Bunny was quicker and, wouldn't you know it, blurted out the answer—"WE WILL KEEP A SECRET." She seemed so pleased with herself. "It's just simple substitution," she said. "You gave us the pattern."

"Okay," Jay said. "Here's another cipher clue and encryption."

He wrote—

$$A - 4$$

and then—

FYRRC ERH GISPE

Bunny and I stared at it, breathing loud, thinking hard. We both scrawled some ideas on paper, my twelve-year-old mind moving lightning fast but not making much progress. After a few frustrating seconds, I glanced back at the original cipher and had a thought. All the letters of the message were four letters further down the alphabet than the original letter. So, A - 4 = W. I quickly began to decipher it, set on proving myself to Jay. FYRRC became BUNNY, and ERH became AND, and GISPE was my name. I held up the paper, and Jay congratulated me.

"Why are we doing this?" Bunny grumbled.

"We'll leave an encrypted note with its cipher clue at a designated hiding place in the woods. I know an old tree with a hollow trunk near the pond that will do the trick. Each day, we'll leave notes as a way of communicating and calling meetings. We'll use my room as a base of operations."

"This is just too much," she said.

"I like it," I said, giving her an angry squint.

Jay grinned. "But our group needs a name, a club name. What do you think, Cee?"

My stomach fluttered with nervousness. I'd been given a very important task. I scanned the books scattered across the picnic table; titles like *The Thin Man* and *Death on the Nile* and *Poison in Jest* jumped out at me, but nothing inspired me. I didn't know what to say. I looked at the cot, Jay's collection of bottles, the photos of the soldiers tacked above his pillow, and his Purple Heart glimmering in the weak light of the room. "What about the Purple Hearts?" I said, before I'd really thought about it.

"Is that appropriate?" Bunny said.

"What's your favorite color?" he asked me.

"These days, blue, I guess."

"Well, what about the Blue Hearts?" Jay said. "Purple is an ugly color."

I nodded, a little embarrassed.

"The Blue Hearts Club it is," he said.

Bunny made a show of looking at her dainty gold wristwatch and said, "Mother will be worried."

"Don't you want to know what happened at the Vellums'?"

"Okay, what happened?" she said, cocking her hip. "Tell us."

"Well," he replied, enjoying himself, "after I left you, I snuck around the corner of the house. I heard voices and tracked them to a window, which was a foot or so above my head. I listened for a few minutes. Bernice Hersh and Frank Vellum are definitely having an affair. I can confirm that. I decided to have a closer look, so I wedged my toes between loose boards and pulled myself up by the windowsill. Inside was dark, but I could see their silhouettes moving in the room and, most importantly, I could hear them. Bernice was trying to calm Vellum down by complimenting him and loving him up, but he wasn't in the mood to screw—"

"Jay!" Bunny said. "Not in front of Ceola."

Bunny was so prudish. I knew about sex at that age—the biological facts, anyway. What goes in where, that sort of thing. I thought it was some awkward medical procedure. It was what a married couple *had* to do to make babies. It certainly had nothing to do with finding a boy handsome and wanting to kiss him.

Jay ignored her and went on with his story. "Frank kept muttering, 'Damn Billy. Damn him to hell.' He said it several times before the piece of rotten clapboard I was standing on broke, and I went down. I didn't wait around, but I know he heard me and saw me. He didn't know who I was, though. He yelled, 'Come back here, Billy! You're not going to get away with this!'"

"Billy's the boyfriend," Bunny said.

"Yes," Jay said. "That's significant. We need to focus on him next."

"Where does he live?" I asked.

"I don't know. We'll figure it out."

Fidgeting with her watch again, Bunny said, "I've got to go. My mother will have a fit. I'll take you home, Ceola."

Jay had been hobbling around the room as he spoke and at this point, he was behind Bunny. He shook his head no, signaling to me what I should do. At first, I was confused, but the lightbulb went on, and I shook my head. "No thanks. I'll walk."

Bunny stepped forward, about to argue with me, but apparently

decided against it. She shrugged and said, "Fine, have it your way."
She turned to Jay. "Good night. And rest your leg." She gave us both
a suspicious once-over and then left without another word.

Once Bunny was out of earshot, Jay gestured for me to have a
seat on his bed. "I've got something to show you before you go."
He opened the bottom drawer of his dresser and laid a black leather
photo album in my lap. I thought of you. It reminded me of the creepy
photo album Sheila finds in "A Date with Death." "Look at it," he
said. I liked the attention he was giving me. I liked that this was just
between the two of us.

On the first page was a photo of you in a swimsuit, your legs dangling off the edge of a dock, probably at Culler's Lake. You were
smiling and squinting, having a good ol' time. You were healthy and
tan, like it was the end of a summer. The photo was natural, easy, and
something about it, some little detail I couldn't put my finger on—the
life in it, I guess—made me sad, but I stayed stock-still. I wasn't going
to let on I was emotional, no way, not in the presence of a fellow hard-
boiled detective.

Jay turned the page, and there was another picture of you, and then
another and another, some near the lake, others up by Hardy's quarry.
I picked up the album and started flipping through it, coming across
more photos of you shuffled in with shots of Main Street, the mountains, the creek, the railroad crossing at Culler's Mountain, and even
strange shots of Bunny in a white dress.

I stopped at an eight-by-ten of you reclining in the prow of a rowboat, hands tucked behind your head, your lanky arms flexed, your
chest spread wide, emphasizing those sinewy muscles of yours. The
photo bothered me. Your face was sly and impish, not a familiar

expression. Your thin swimming trunks were wet and plastered to your skin, the waist tie all undone and the top button unbuttoned. I closed the album with a snap and handed it back to Jay, a little queasy. He took it and sat beside me on the cot, the mattress bowing with his weight, our arms touching.

"I loved him very much," he said, and flipped to the back of the album. "Here's a photograph he took of me."

It was a picture of Jay in the buck. Can you imagine? His body was stretched out, catlike, on the very cot we were sitting on! His skin glowed like it had been dusted with phosphorescent powder, and his face was blurry like he was reclining behind a plate of frosted glass. All of this contrasted with the sharp focus on his midsection and his manhood, which lay a little stiff on one of his thighs. I felt dizzy and sick at my stomach. What shocked me the most when I saw him wasn't that he was showing it to me but that it stirred feelings in me I didn't understand, *couldn't* understand. All I could think about was his body and how I liked looking at it—at him. I'm sure you don't want to hear about this, Robbie, but I need to say it to someone. They say the dead are the most forgiving. I hope it's true in your case.

I stood up and let out a nervous half-laugh, half-hiccup, and when I did, I knocked the album with my knee. Photos that had been hidden in the back flap spilled out.

At odd angles, spread across the floor, were pictures of corpses—soldiers planted in snow like frostbitten flowers, faces black with gangrene and eyes filmy and white; boys' bodies thrown across a field, tangled in one another, some appearing to have three arms, others none, like some sort of confused monster. Other photos were stranger.

In one, a woman was spread wide across a pile of bricks like she'd been tossed there by a giant. I thought of King Kong and Fay Wray. Her floral print dress was open from the shoulder to the waist, exposing her left breast and long strip of dry blood from her navel to her shoulder. In another, a young child, a rumple of lace and curls, abstract in black-and-white, lay on her side, grasping a little stuffed giraffe. I remember wishing I had a toy like that—and then looking away.

Jay jumped to his feet and snatched up the photos, shoving them back in the album, like he was cleaning up a crime scene.

When he finished, we sat beside each other again. He turned to me, wearing a feverish blank stare like a mask. For the longest time, he just looked at me, almost like he'd been struck dumb. Slow, like the changing of light on a summer afternoon, softness crept into his eyes. It was odd, even spooky, but appealing somehow, very appealing, like he wanted to ask me to comfort him or he wanted to comfort me, but couldn't manage either. I was drawn to him like Sheila in "A Date with Death" is drawn to Brimblevine House—and that horrible man. I remember thinking that right then. Part of me wanted to fall on him and kiss him like I'd seen willowy damsels do to their knights in shining armor—B-movie-pantomimed lovemaking. But I hiccupped again, and another part of me, the smarter part, the part that couldn't shake the photos I'd just seen, said, *Take a step back, Cee*, and I did.

"You understand now. Don't you?" he said.

I nodded yes, but I didn't.

"Okay," he said, grabbing my hand. I gasped a little, ending the hiccups. He held my palm firm, applying too much pressure, and said, "That's why I need Robbie's journal. It's sure to have more than the stories he made up in it. I never want your parents to find it. They'll destroy it. It's what I have left of him—other than you. Please understand. I need it." Dark swirls of emotion filled his eyes.

"Okay," I said.

He released my hand and said, "Thank you, Cee."

Mr. Morgan was an old curmudgeon, slumped behind his desk, glowering over stacks of papers and dusty law books. His owlish partner, Edwin Ayres, was more pleasant—and younger. He showed Sheila her seat and offered to get her coffee. She refused politely.

Mr. Morgan coughed and sputtered out a welcome. "Mrs. Addison, are you well?"

"Please," she said. "The name is Sheila. Sheila Fury."

"I see," he said.

"Thank you for seeing me on such short notice. As soon as I received the letter, I simply had to know the details."

"Indeed. Well, it's quite simple. You, being your aunt's only living heir, inherit the entirety of her fortune."

"Miss Fury," Mr. Ayres said, "you are a wealthy woman now."

"Indeed she is," Mr. Morgan snorted.

"What happens next?"

"We have some papers for you to sign, and you'll want to sell your aunt's home, unless, of course, you plan to live in it. But I can't imagine a young woman such as yourself would want to live in a big old house in the wilds of New Hampshire."

"No—but I should see it, shouldn't I?"

"Of course."

"I imagine it's a beautiful place."

Mr. Morgan grimaced. He had intended it to be a smile. It unsettled Sheila. "Your aunt added a codicil to the will when she became ill. She gave me special instructions to have you read it in my presence."

Mr. Ayres walked around the desk and took the envelope from Mr. Morgan and then handed it to Sheila. She broke the seal and unfolded the note inside.

Scrawled in a jagged script, the handwriting of a dying woman, were the following words:

Dearest Niece,

Whatever you do, do not tamper with ACTUS DEI. Fate is cruelest to those who don't respect her power.

Dearly Yours,
Aunt Madge

Sheila handed the note to Mr. Ayres. He removed his glasses, read it, and handed it to Mr. Morgan, who glanced at it and chuckled. "Your aunt certainly loved mystery," he said.

"What does it mean?" she said.

"I have no idea."

"She wasn't very lucid at the end," Mr. Ayres said. "It may mean nothing."

"What is 'ACTUS DEI'?" Sheila asked.

"It's Latin. It means 'act of God,'" Mr. Ayres said.

"Oh." She smiled. "That really doesn't make sense. Poor woman."

Mr. Morgan lurched forward: "There's nothing 'poor' about your aunt, Miss Fury." His eyes were severe. "Telling the future made her a millionaire. If she warns you about fate, I would heed it. She saw much and understood more. She was a very insightful woman."

Sheila detected sadness in his tone and around his eyes. What sort of woman was her aunt? Had her father been right to cut off ties? Was she a grifter—or was she the real thing? What did she really know about the future? After all, fate wasn't cruel to everyone.

"I just don't understand what she means," she said.

"Perhaps you will. Just remember her advice."

Sheila signed several documents and then was on her way. That evening, she celebrated with the girls from work. She bought drinks and dinner for all of them. The next morning, she gave notice at work and made plans to travel to Berlin, New Hampshire.

6

BUNNY

I leaned over the banister at the top of the stairs, being careful not to make a sound, and watched the reflection of my mother and Letitia Greenwood in the large mirror in the foyer.

"I'm not here to socialize, Carla," she said in a prickly tone. Letitia wore an ill-fitted gray dress and a mauve turban, decades past its prime. Her lipstick was bright orange, thick, and haphazardly applied. She was clutching a paper bag in her hands, her fingers nervously crinkling it as she spoke.

"May I ask *why* you're here?" my mother said gently.

"Because of your daughter."

"Yes?"

"She was at my house last night."

"Was she?"

"Without announcing herself. That is—*surreptitiously*."

"If it's true, then I'm sure there's a good reason for it."

"It *is* true, my dear. I saw her slinking away in the darkness, like a stray cat."

"I'm not sure I understand."

"Your daughter was in my grandson's room."

Although I could see only the back of Mother's head, I could tell by the pause in the conversation and the slight slump in her posture she was no longer coming to my defense.

"Your daughter, my dear, is a little seductress." The bag crinkled. "And I won't have her around Jason. He has enough to contend with. The war wasn't kind to him. This town hasn't been kind to him, either. I won't have your daughter toying with him. The Prescotts have taken enough from the Greenwoods."

"We wanted to have a celebration for him. We should always celebrate our survivors, but town politics got in the way. We're as broken up about it as—"

"All of you are scavengers! You, your husband, *and* your daughter—picking over the dead and dying."

"That is hardly fair, Letitia."

"Scavengers!"

"Perhaps you should—"

"*These* are your daughter's!" Letitia foisted the bag out in front of her. "She left them in my son's room."

Mother opened the bag and pulled out a pair of women's pumps. I recognized them immediately; they were Lily's shoes. Mother knew my wardrobe well and knew they weren't mine. She relaxed her posture a little. "I'll get my daughter to verify they're hers." She called out, "Bonita. Bo-neee-tah!"

I backed away from the stairs. My first instinct was to retreat to my room, but I thought better of it. Being falsely accused by Letitia— *especially* Letitia—burned me. I wanted to prove her wrong. I was not her Cinderella.

"Yes, Mother!" I called, as cheerfully as possible. Mother and I locked eyes as I approached the top step. Since she was headed to the Ladies Auxiliary that afternoon, her hair was swept up from the sides of her face and tucked into a bun; she had on full makeup, eyebrows carefully sculpted; and she wore her favorite mother-of-pearl earrings—all of which made her seem professional and formidable.

"Would you come down here? We have a visitor who wishes to ask you a question."

I obeyed but didn't hurry.

"Mrs. Greenwood claims you were in her grandson's room last night," Mother explained, "and you left these shoes."

She handed the dirty, black velvet shoes to me as I reached the bottom of the stairs. Once in my hands, I saw immediately they were too big to be mine. I wore a woman's eight, and these were at least a ten. I hadn't been close enough when we discovered them in the clearing to get a sense of their size. "I couldn't possibly keep these on my feet," I said. "They're several sizes larger than I wear." I reached down and plucked the sandal off my foot and held it to the other shoe for comparison.

Letitia was annoyed. "Still," she said, "I saw you last night. You *were* at my house."

"I dropped Jay off after the movie, if that's what you mean." I replaced my shoe.

"I saw you. You were slinking away."

"No, you're mistaken," I said, keeping my voice bright and cheerful.

"You're lying."

"Now, Letitia," my mother said, "are you sure you saw my daughter?"

"I know a Prescott when I see one."

"Be kind," my mother said firmly.

While I was holding the shoes, it occurred to me Lily must have been quite tall, even striking. From her photos in the grainy newsprint, it was difficult to decide what sort of woman she was—tall, graceful, self-possessed? I looked again at the bloodstain on the instep of the right shoe; it struck me as odd that dry blood was such an unpleasant rust color. I then noticed, on the instep of the other shoe, the name of the designer was partially visible:

Ferrag . . .

Ferragamos! That shocked me. Not only were they expensive, but they were made in Italy—not at all what you would expect to find on an American woman from Jitters Gap, Virginia. They also couldn't be more than a season or two old, because materials like velvet, cork, and raffia had been used during the war due to the shortages of the nicer leather and steel. Also curious was that on the inside of one heel, "FL L" was written and on the other, "FL R." The L and the R stood for left and right obviously, which was something I'd seen actresses do. During quick costume changes, they couldn't waste time sorting out which shoe belonged to which foot. I assumed, then, that F and L were someone's initials. Perhaps the L stood for Lily—but the F? I didn't know.

I held out the shoes. Letitia snatched them from me and shoved them back into the bag.

"Are you sure I can't offer you some iced tea or lemonade?" Mother said.

"No," she growled. "I need to get back to the house."

Once she was safely down the walk, Mother turned to me and smiled.

"I wasn't there," I said.

"I believe you," she said. "I think Jay needs you. I'm glad you're spending time with him." She shook her head. "Poor Letitia. She really believes we forced her to sell Dixie Dew. She would've lost everything—her house, *everything*—if your father hadn't made such a generous offer."

Father had deeply admired Jay's grandfather. He had told me that if the shoe had been on the other foot, he might have crumbled just as George Sr. did after he lost his son and daughter-in-law in that horrible accident. "George Greenwood was a true entrepreneur," he told me once. "He knew our region needed more industry, and he knew soft drinks were going to be big. He had vision. I'm sure he'd hoped to pass that vision along to his son."

He didn't think much of Georgie, Jay's father, though. When I'd ask him, he'd just shake his head and say, "Well, he was handsome. I'll give him that." But most surprising to me was Father's opinion of Letitia: "She was a beautiful woman in her day. Brilliant too. She set the tone for local society. She had real elegance." That was hard to believe.

So I *was* in Jay's room, of course. Letitia may have been eccentric and an alcoholic, but she wasn't crazy.

Jay hadn't been particularly subtle in dismissing me after we returned from spying on Frank Vellum. I wanted to know what he and Ceola were up to, why they were having their own secret club of two, so I pretended to leave and crept around the corner of the summer porch to listen. I could hear them moving around, but they weren't talking. After some rustling of pages and a period of stillness, I heard Jay say, "You understand now. Don't you?" Then he asked for Robbie's journal, which I knew nothing about at that point. He said, "I never want your parents to find it, because that's all I have left of him," or something to that effect. She promised to give it to him.

Why hadn't Jay said anything about the journal to me? Again, I felt like I had in the middle of Culler's Lake: my feet swiping the darkness below me, my arms beating the black water, my body out of accord with my better sense. *Wait for me! Wait for me!* What was I doing lurking in the bushes outside of the Greenwoods' house, or for that matter, Lily Vellum's home? Why was I always running after Jay?

As I stepped away from the porch, the night was silent and expectant. The fireflies drifted noiselessly across the overgrown lawn, and heat lightning flashed in the distance. Using the dim light from the house as a guide, I crossed the backyard and found my way around several obstacles—an overturned wheelbarrow, a slack clothesline, an attempt at a stone-lined decorative pond. I could see the house faintly, only suggestive of how it appeared in the light of day, the white paint peeling off in dirty ribbons, the roof over the porch sagging under the weight of a fallen tree limb, water pooling around the edge of the house, forming a fetid moat, out of which algae and feathery mosses spread over the brick foundations. Miss Havisham's lair—only this Miss Havisham had long traded her wedding dress for muck boots and yellow rubber gloves.

"Bonita Prescott, that you? That you?"

I flinched when I heard my name.

"What are you doing slinking around my home?"

I ducked into a shadow by the edge of the woods. Letitia was standing at the back door of the house, framed by light.

"Fucking Prescotts," she grumbled, and I could tell she was drunk. She switched on another light, and I saw that she held a bottle in one hand and a shotgun in the other, grasping it by the barrel. In a soiled housedress and a toppling updo, she was a far more pitiful creature than I had first imagined. She tossed the bottle off the porch, wedged the shotgun's stock in her armpit, and waved the barrel around, stumbling forward a little. I was frightened.

"Bo-NEEE-tahhh!" she cried, steadying herself against a porch support. That was my cue to move. I dashed back through the forest and made my way to the car. I heard her calling my name again in the distance.

📷

A day or two after Letitia's visit, I found Jay at our kitchen table finishing off a piece of lemon pie. Mother, her dark Spanish features particularly radiant, sat across from him, making small talk, genuinely pleased he was there. When I saw them together, I hesitated at the door. Jay seemed so content, so handsome. Then he glanced up at me and said, "This pie is amazing."

"You can have a slice any time," Mother said, getting up from the table. "I've got chores to do. Bunny, do you want a piece?"

"No, thank you."

"I'll leave you two. Remember what I said." She winked at Jay.

"I promise," he said.

After she left the room, I said, "*Where* have you been, and *what* were you promising my mother?"

"I've been keeping off my leg. It feels better today."

"And the promise?"

"To drop by more often."

"She feels responsible."

Jay took his last bite of pie.

"We need to talk," I said.

"I've got to show you something."

"Your grandmother came by the other day, and she had Lily's shoes. She claimed they were mine. She saw me leaving your room. She thinks we're . . . that I'm your girl."

"I want to show you something. Come with me." He pushed away his plate and got up.

"Aren't you going to respond?"

"Pssh. Don't worry about her."

I followed him to a grove of trees near the pond on his grandmother's property, my attempts at conversation batted away like badminton birdies. In the center of the grove was a dead tree, an old oak, which a few years before had been struck by lightning. Jay had used it as the subject for several of his photographs. It was out of place next to the thick foliage of the other trees. It had been hollowed out by termites and had shed most of its bark, which revealed the brittle, bone-white wood underneath. Jay cleared some cobwebs from a small opening at its base.

"This is the spot," he said. "If we can't communicate any other way, leave a message here. It's going to be an important place for everyone. Especially Cee. Her parents don't want me anywhere near their house. It was very difficult to get news to her to meet today."

"They don't like you, do they?"

"Check the tree at least once a day. In the morning."

"Why don't they like you?"

"Will you check the tree?"

"And why do you want Robbie's journal?"

He looked at me with a flicker of surprise.

"You asked Ceola for it," I said. "You thought I had left the other night, but I wanted to know what you two were up to. I wanted to know if this was all an elaborate practical joke at my expense."

"It's not a joke."

"What's in the journal? Why do you care?"

"I told her to meet us here, so I could explain the tree to her too."

"Answer me," I said firmly.

"His stories. Robbie used to tell us stories, like the ones in Cee's rags. Turns out he wrote his stories down. Some of them might be in his journal. I just wanted something of his. That's all."

"Why didn't you tell me this before?"

"I didn't know until Cee mentioned it the day I found Lily. Let's talk about it later. She'll be here soon." He was looking over my shoulder, avoiding eye contact.

"So that's what I had to pry out of you? Robbie's silly stories?"

"Here she comes." He waved to her.

I was determined to get more from him. "And what about those shoes? They're expensive. Italian. Why would a girl from Jitters Gap have such expensive shoes?"

"Employee discount. Department stores give those, right?"

"I thought you said she was applying for a job to be a store model. She was already working as one?"

He grabbed my shoulders. His blue eyes blazed; a curtain had been swept back and something indescribable and unpredictable lurked behind them. It was the same danger I'd felt when he'd twisted my wrist during our picnic. "She was *murdered*," he said. "She was murdered, and we need to understand it. *I* need to understand it."

I pulled away from him sharply, and he wilted again into the wounded, war-struck boy.

"Okay," I said. "But you have to explain all this to me."

"I will," he said, looking down. "When we understand each other better."

I shrugged and leaned against the dead tree. "When will that be?"

He leveled his gaze at me. "When you open your eyes."

Royal Oak, VA
2/12/2000

Bunny,

I was damn sure that if I ever heard from you, I'd ignore you, or send a nasty reply. Jesus, the things I had lined up to say to you. But it seems old age has done something truly terrible to me—it's made me soft. The spit and fire of that girl you remember has dulled to just a flicker.

It's not been easy for me, not that I'm complaining. I married a good man, Sam Richardson. Did you know his family? He managed the Piggly Wiggly downtown for eight years. He gave me three handsome and headstrong sons, Rob, Eddie, and Ray. But in '75, right around the holidays, he fell from the roof cleaning leaves out of the gutters, hit his head, and died, leaving me on my own to raise those boys.

Needing to support my children, I began working at Twin Oaks as a secretary to the superintendent. My boys turned out better than I could've hoped, and, just recently, after twenty-three years, I retired from the hospital. Thank Heaven! These days, I spend my time drinking coffee at Hardee's or writing in my journal or reading mystery books. I've read all your novels. Not bad. I mean that. I guess you learned a thing or two that summer too.

Well, I don't know what to tell you about the photo that was mailed to you. Other than to say I didn't send it. The last time I ever talked to Jay, I asked him about the photos of that woman, but he said he didn't have them. He said they were safe. Of course, he didn't burn them—or at least not the negatives—so he must've sent them to someone. But who? I haven't the slightest.

I'm not sure what else to tell you. It's good to know you kept the summer of '45 so close.

-C

7

CEOLA

ama's grief ruled the house with an iron fist after your death,
Robbie. Her first almighty decree was: *All who live in this
house must live in silence.*

Papa ordered me not to play records or listen to the radio or make
too much noise of any kind. I was even told to take off my shoes before
entering the house. The quiet was hell. I curled up on my bed for hours
at a time, yearning to hear the Andrews Sisters or Anita O'Day or *The
Shadow* or anything for relief. Despite his dutiful enforcement of the
rules, Papa was as much a prisoner of them as I was.

One night, he was taking in the news on the radio in the living
room, like he did, and I was sitting at the top of the staircase, straining
to hear, real happy for the distraction. Mama stormed into the room,
and the radio clicked off. I heard her say, "I have a headache, Bob. I've
already asked you to turn it down once."

I heard Papa's heavy footsteps, and then the radio came back on but louder—"World News Today. Brought to you by the Admiral Corporation makers of Admiral Radio, America's Smart Set—"

She snapped, *"Turn it off!* I've had enough bad news for one lifetime."

The radio went dead. Seconds later, I heard Papa trudge out of the house. He didn't come back that night. Soon after that, he began spending evenings and weekends digging holes, planting trees, surrounding the house with a forest of saplings. Although it was intended as a memorial, it surely felt more like he was trying to wall us in.

Mama's second decree was: *When Robbie is spoken of, he must be spoken of in if-then statements.*

Mama would carry your photo with her around the house, setting it in the kitchen while she cooked or propping it against a book in the living room while she knitted. If I entered the room, she would begin her usual litany of conditionals. "If Robbie had survived the war," she'd say, "he would've lived in Royal Oak, to be close to his family. If he had survived, he would've married a nice girl—that Donna Smith or Rachel Richfield or the King girl—or no, not the King girl, she's too easy with the boys." She was certain whoever you would've married, the two of you would've had beautiful children. She even chose names for the ghost grandchildren—Robert Jr. and Mary Jane. Little Mary Jane had blond curls just like she did as a young girl.

"If he had returned from the Pacific," the chant went, "he would've studied law, or maybe medicine. He certainly would have gone to UVA or Virginia Tech. He would've loved his community and, particularly, his church, where he would have become a lay reader. He would've joined the Kiwanis Club like his father. He would've set a good example. He would've taken care of us, as we got older. He would've held my hand when God calls to me in my last hour."

Her third and final decree was: *No one, under any circumstances, can enter Robbie's bedroom or touch his belongings.*

Mama made it into her own personal shrine to you. Her grief was greedy, claiming your stamp collection, your saved Dixie Dew bottles, your favorite red sweater with the hole in the sleeve, your Roy Rogers cowboy hat with gold trim, the bone-handled pocketknife Papa gave you when you were twelve, your baseball mitt, the pocket watch you inherited from Grandpa that was inscribed with Great-Grandpa's name (*Terrence Henbone Bliss, 1854*), and the broken-in deck of cards you used to teach me pinochle. All of them became holy relics.

For months, I thought that if I went into your bedroom, sirens would blast and police would rush in, seize me, and haul me off to jail, hands cuffed and hunched over in disgrace. Papa made me promise I would never, *ever* disturb your room. "If Mama finds out," he said, "we'll both be in terrible trouble."

But the limbo of mourning became too much for me, and, in the worst sort of way, I wanted to claim something of my own from Mama's police state.

About midsummer, I said to hell with the rules and started poking around. That's when I found the stack of magazines under your nightstand and started sneaking off to read them. But of course, I hadn't come across your journal.

Right after Jay had shown Bunny and me the hiding place in the tree and Bunny had marched off in a tizzy, he said, "Cee, I have to know Robbie's journal is safe. Please. Before anyone else finds it. It's killing me."

His blue eyes were on fire. He loomed over me, so agitated and afraid.

I still wasn't sure if I wanted to give him your journal, but I sure wanted to find it. I wanted to keep it safe. I suppose what I really wanted was to keep it for myself, because deep down, I wanted to know you better. So when I got home, I crept upstairs and down the hall to your room. Mama was running errands, and Papa wasn't home from work yet.

The door to your room was cracked—you remember, it was warped and never came to—so I nudged it open. The afternoon sun was peeking through the limbs of that old locust tree outside your window and throwing flecks of light across the floor. I hesitated, worried Mama might come home and catch me but also worried I was doing something sacrilegious, like spitting in a baptismal font or walking across a grave. I moved forward on tiptoes. With each step, the floor groaned like demons calling out to me—*What are you doin', Ceola? You'll get in big trouble. Mama and Papa will never forgive you. You're desecrating the memory of your brother.*

The slanted ceilings and dormer windows and sideways light gave your room a sadness I still feel when I'm by myself in the church sanctuary, fixing flowers or replacing candles for Sunday services. But those red cowboys galloping across the walls, lassos whipping through the air, herding and roping cattle, reminded me that it was your space, your sanctuary, not Mama's. Between the windows, I saw your small, beat-up dresser with both of our initials carved into the side of it, displaying bits and pieces of your life, from school awards to postcards from Virginia Beach. Along the bottom of the mirror, you had wedged several school photos of friends, maybe there was even a picture of Jay—no, surely Mama would've seen it and thrown it in the wood stove.

I rummaged under your bed and riffled through your closet—nothing but sports equipment, schoolbooks, and dusty clothes. Underneath the neatly folded T-shirts and boxer shorts in your dresser, I found even more magazines—*Dime Detective, Astonishing Tales, Weird Stories,* and a stack of comics. I'd struck gold. Right there, on the floor, I fanned out this new treasure trove so I could see all of it, forgetting about how angry Mama and Papa would be if they caught me.

I picked up the comics and let the pages fall through my fingers, reading bits of dialogue and glancing at the pictures. The handsome fedora-ed detectives, holding their pistols close to their hips, spat phrases like, "It's time to meet your Maker. I hope you're wearing your best dress." Or, "Baby-doll, you'll make a beautiful corpse." And the femme fatales, wrapped like maypoles in red-and-black satin gowns, every curl on their head as tight as a spring and eyes aimed like twin Colt .38s.

I can still hear you, clear as a bell, reading in a low voice so you wouldn't draw Mama and Papa's attention: *It was a hot, damp, mean August day, and the city streets were crying black tears. Detective Rod Magnum leaned back in his chair, unbuttoned his collar, and drifted into an uneasy slumber. When he heard the* click-clack *of her heels and smelled her perfume through the open door, he sat up and straightened his tie. Sweet trouble was coming his way . . .*

When you read to me, you always held out at the cliffhanger—a dame with a knife dangling over her head or the hero slipping from a crumbling ledge, some melodramatic climax or other—and made me beg for the ending. You loved to make me beg. I remembered you reading "A Date with Death" to me but stopping just before the final page. Oh, I really wanted you to finish it! But it was just as well you didn't. When you were finally done reading, we'd talk the stories over, going on about the parts we liked and picking at the parts we didn't, our talks all out of joint if we thought the story was a cheat.

As I flipped, I caught a glimpse of something wedged between the fluttering pages of an issue of *Dime Detective*. I thought it was a paper doll, but then it was something I hadn't expected—a male underwear model. You must've cut him out of a Sears catalog, trimming his outline, not sacrificing a finger or a flip of hair or a fold of fabric to the scissors. In other magazines, I found more cutouts of men, from smiling boys with their hands on their hips to cool customers trailing ribbons of cigarette smoke to muscle men, Charles Atlas sorts, flexing their greased biceps and sporting sculpted pompadours. I didn't understand what they meant. How could I at that age? I just imagined you bent over magazines and catalog pages, tongue caught between your teeth, concentrating as you traced the outlines of these men with Mama's sewing scissors. I knew they were secret, and I knew I wanted to keep them safe—and far from Mama's and Papa's eyes.

I grabbed everything you had hidden under your T-shirts, and that's when I saw it at the back of the drawer—your journal, bound in dark brown leather and tied with a black shoelace, almost invisible against the cedar lining. I took it and unknotted the lace. On the first page, you had written, *DO NOT OPEN!!! TOP SECRET!!! That means you, Cee!*

I closed it with a slap. I wasn't going to read it—and neither was Jay. Not now. I added it to the pile of magazines and hid everything behind a blanket on the top shelf of my closet.

That night I had a dream.

It was dusk, and you emerged from the dark woods at the edge of the yard wearing jeans and a white T-shirt. Everything was quiet, like one of those silent movies from the '20s that Grandpa used to like. You saw me and smiled and waved. Your face, shoes, and the knees of your dark jeans were muddy—or was it blood? You were smiling and waving, and I wanted to go to you, but I didn't. I just watched, and the more I watched, the more confused I became and the more the mud seemed like blood. In the next instant, you were beside me, whispering in my ear, but as hard as I listened, all I could hear was the blood rushing through my ears, like the roar of the ocean in a seashell. Then—*pow!*—there was an explosion, as if a thousand firecrackers had gone off all at once, and I woke up.

That's when I remembered it.

It was early summer, not long before you enlisted, and I was in a good mood. The end of my fifth-grade year was a week away. I had just come home from school and dropped my books on the hall table when I heard raised voices in the kitchen. I crept to the edge of the kitchen door and listened.

"That family just isn't right," Mama said. "They're cursed. I mean, first Georgie and Elizabeth, then George Sr. God doesn't smile on them—or the grandson."

"The guys down at the plant talk about him," Papa said. "They say—"

"He's my friend," you said.

"It doesn't matter," Papa replied. "Because in a couple of weeks, you're going to enlist. It'll be your birthday, and you're going to serve your country. I won't have you hanging around here, waiting for the draft. You need to be with real men, learning how to be a real man."

"You can't force me to enlist. I won't do it."

"I'll throw you out of my house if you don't."

"You won't do that."

"You *will* go and fight for your country. It's what proud young men do."

"You really hate me, don't you?"

"You'll do what's right, son."

"I see through you," you said, your voice sharp-edged. "*Right* through you."

I heard the sound of shoes on linoleum and a crack. I stepped into view, and Mama stood up, setting a colander of snapped beans on the table.

"Go to your room, Cee," she said, nodding toward the staircase behind me. You were holding your cheek. Papa stood back from you, leaning against the kitchen counter, panting and rubbing his right hand.

I could tell you were crying. But then, channeling some hidden fire in you, you straightened your posture, cocked your chin back, and, in high-riding hauteur, said, "He has dark hair and thick eyebrows. He talks in a loud blustery way. He gives the impression of being—a violent man." You were quoting Mary Astor's lines from *The Maltese Falcon*. We knew that movie inside and out. After all, we'd spent our allowance on it three weeks in a row.

Papa scowled at you, then dropped and shook his head, a vicious show of disappointment.

You sprang forward and flipped Mama's colander off the table, sending beans scattering across the floor.

"Robbie!" she gasped, but you were already out the door.

I dashed after you as you crossed the yard and moved toward the forest. When I caught up, you were in the high grass at the edge of the woods. I grabbed you by the shirtsleeve and you twisted around, shoving me back. I fell on the ground. You stammered something, spit flying. I'd never seen you like that, so out of control, so full of anger. We stared at each other awhile, stunned but not crying, unable to speak. I studied the red mark on your cheek and wondered if it would bruise. I wanted you to tell me that what Papa said wasn't true, that you didn't have to enlist, but I couldn't ask. I thought that if I did, it would make it true.

"Cee," you said, your eyes wide and intense like spotlights shining directly at me. "If they send me away, I'm never coming home. Ever! I never want to see them or this goddamn place again. I'm going to go live my life and do what I want to do, be who I want to be."

Then, like that, you spun around and disappeared into the trees, a leafy branch snapping back into place after you, the forest swallowing you up with one gulp.

A sob burst from me and tears followed. After a few minutes, I found my feet, wiped my eyes dry, and inspected my dress. I brushed off the grass and went home, banging up the stairs and into my room. I didn't hear you come in that night. When I asked Mama about it in the morning, she said, "Your brother is doing a very brave thing by enlisting. That's all that's important."

Sheila made the final leg of her trip into the wilds of New Hampshire by car. The tangled, curvy road took her through deep, misty valleys, only widening briefly for the small community of Berlin, then narrowed again as it followed a rocky stream into an overgrown meadow at the end of which stood Brimblevine House.

As she got out of her car and walked the stone path to the front door, Sheila took in its gothic architecture—its four impressive three-story stone turrets, its ornate ironwork along the faux battlements, its line of shadowy arches across its northern façade, not to mention the pine-covered inclines surrounding it like waves of black water on the verge of cresting. All it needed was a strike of lightning slicing the sky in two and a banshee wailing in the distance, and it would be the perfect setting for a haunted house matinee.

After fiddling with the keys, she entered the house and switched on the lights. The mammoth wood-paneled interior seemed to burst into existence. She dropped her suitcase and coat and began wandering the house. She found herself mesmerized in each new room by expensive bric-a-brac: bronze statues, bone china, silver platters, and on and on. Dark oil paintings of gloomy landscapes in gold-leaf frames hung from walls papered in dark velveteen patterns. Most of the furniture was hand-carved hardwood, decorated with laughing cherubs and stern angels. Polished black granite framed every fireplace, thick Turkish carpets spread across the floors, and heavy silk window treatments covered the panes.

This was hers. It was all hers.

At the end of her tour, she found her aunt's bedroom. Over

the fireplace hung an oil portrait of Majestica. A rose-tinted silk turban framed her opalescent face, which shimmered like a Chinese mask in the dark room, and her flowing, sea-green dress matched the green gleam in her eyes. Her expression—a sort of half-smile, half-smirk—was a little off-putting. In the center of the room was a canopy bed draped in purple, and under a large three-quarters bay window sat a crystal ball displayed on a decorative brass stand. It glowed in the late-afternoon sunlight. Sheila touched it with her finger, and the filtered light flickered out like a candle. A cloud had passed over the sun.

She remembered her aunt's note: "Do not tamper with ACTUS DEI. Fate is cruelest to those who don't respect her power." But she respected its power and understood that her destiny, with all its promise and potential, lay in this house. She was a new gal already, and she deeply appreciated Majestica's gift. She would honor her legacy by living richly and fully, by grabbing life by the heels and not letting go.

Sheila went to her aunt's bedside. The bed looked inviting. She felt suddenly chilled and tired from her long journey. She sat on the edge of the bed and, after a moment of awkwardness—she wondered if her aunt had died in this bed—she was compelled to lie down and shut her eyes, the soft pillow molding itself around her head, the down cover cupping her body.

She woke up gasping for air, her heart pounding, tears streaming down her cheeks. She threw her legs over the side of the bed and steadied herself. The room came into focus. Her throat hurt, stinging when she touched it. She'd had a horrible nightmare. She still felt the fear, the grip of adrenaline, but she couldn't remember what she had dreamed.

She made her way to the bathroom and inspected her neck. It was raw and chafed; a hot scarlet blotch ran across her throat, as if someone had been trying to choke her with something large and rough. Was it an allergic reaction to something on the bed? Or had she done it herself?

Loneliness fell over her. She sat on the edge of the marble tub and began to cry. She remembered how safe Kenneth had made her feel, his hand on her shoulder, pulling her toward him, kissing her. But then she also remembered coming home midday—she hadn't been feeling well—and catching him in bed with that tramp, their bodies tangled in the sheets that Sheila had smoothed and folded into place that morning. She had loved him so much. She still loved him—no, it had turned to hate! Bitter hatred.

She collected herself, stood in front of the mirror, and gave herself a pep talk. She told herself she really was a doll, admiring the fullness of her blond curls and her thin, perfectly straight nose and her full, pink lips—lips some girls would die for! She would be fine, she told herself. No, she would be *wonderful*! She had so much to look forward to. She fantasized about her future happiness—expensive clothes, exotic vacation spots, foreign lovers. She thought about the man she might marry one day. Dashing, muscular, perched on the bow of a yacht with the warm breeze glancing off his twice-bronzed skin. A living magazine ad. It was all there for her now. All possible.

She made her way to her aunt's study. Mr. Morgan and Mr. Ayres had told her that several of her aunt's most valuable possessions, including the deed to the property, were in a safe in that room. They had given her a sealed envelope containing the combination.

She opened the safe as instructed. The air inside smelled stale and metallic. She scanned old stock certificates and popped open jewelry boxes full of necklaces and earrings dripping with precious and semiprecious stones. Were they paste or the real deal? She found gold coins and an envelope stuffed with cash. At the bottom of the safe was an object wrapped in a black cloth. It was some sort of book. It was too heavy to hold comfortably in her arms, so she set it on her aunt's large mahogany desk. She carefully removed the cloth, revealing a large, flat, leather-bound photo album. On the cover, stamped in dim gold, it said simply: "Photographs."

"Oh," she said aloud. She was excited by the prospect of getting to know her aunt better, if only after her death. She cracked its cover, and in her aunt's handwriting on the first page was:

ACTUS DEI
SEEK NOT THE FUTURE
TO ESCAPE THE PAST

Sheila slapped the album closed, wrapped it in the cloth, and placed it back in the safe. She would heed her aunt's warning: "Fate is cruelest to those who don't respect her power."

8

BUNNY

J ay left this bit of intrigue in the tree:

17.9.9.24 5.24 24.22.9.9 5.24 23.9.26.9.18 20.17
24.19.17.19.22.22.19.1
A=5

I saw no point in having elaborate codes. We weren't spies. No one was going to discover the rendezvous spot. No one was stumbling around in the woods but us. In truth, I didn't appreciate being subjected to Jay's fancies, because he had been so cagey the last time I saw him. But in a few minutes, I had the translation:

MEET AT TREE AT SEVEN PM

TOMORROW

And so I was there the next day by the dead tree. While I waited, I peeled some of the dry bark from the trunk with my fingernails and flicked it across the clearing. The tree itself was rather large, its dead branches stretching irregularly toward the sky. It was an appropriately melodramatic hiding place for encoded notes.

I considered everything we knew. The body. Lily. Her father, who was carrying on with Bernice Hersh. And Lily's bloody shoes. But why was Jay being so evasive about Robbie's journal? What was he hiding?

I thought about defying Jay and going to the police, but two things stopped me. First, Jay was so enthusiastic about solving the mystery that it was keeping his mind off the war, a welcome distraction that felt cruel to me to remove. Second, Lily Vellum *was* missing. That was a fact.

The day was clear and dry for the first week of August, making it easy to see Ceola trudging through the tall grass. She was scowling when she approached me. Her legs were covered with a pink calamine crust.

"Poison ivy?" I said.

She nodded.

"Somehow I avoided it. Not a bump."

"It's going away."

We were quiet for a few minutes, not knowing what to say to each other, both of us resting on the same log and studying the fading tinctures of the afternoon sky.

I speculated, as I studied her profile, if she would grow into a beautiful woman. The oval of her face was elongating, her cheeks sharpening, her lips reddening and fleshing out, and even her nose, if a bit hooked, seemed to be softening as her features filled in. Her sloppy ponytail, dirty fingernails, and legs caked with calamine were signs of her childish lack of self-consciousness, but I could detect the woman growing underneath, breasts shadowing under her blue sailor middy and hips pressing out at the fabric of her skirt. With time, she would transform into a striking woman—but about those nails, I had to bite my tongue.

"You may not have known this," I said, fumbling for something to break the silence, "but I thought your brother was a nice fellow."

I was lying. I had formed only a vague opinion of Robbie, and it wasn't good. He seemed to me to be a touch churlish and certainly disrespectful. He had been rude to me the night of my party.

"Yeah?" she responded, but wasn't hooked.

"I had a conversation with him before he went away."

She didn't respond. Her eyes were focused on a pale butterfly that had landed on a rock in front of her.

"He didn't want to leave home," I continued. "He seemed sad about it."

"Is that what he said?" She scratched at the raw sores on her leg.

"He was especially sad about leaving you." He had never said that to me, but I needed a way in.

"Why would he tell you that? You hardly even knew him."

"He came to my birthday party, right? You know that."

"Sure."

"That's where we had our conversation."

"My parents hate your parents. Your dad only gave my papa a week off work after we heard about Robbie."

"I had no idea." Again I wasn't telling the truth.

"Sure you didn't."

"Look," I said. "The other day, Jay's grandmother came by. She saw me leaving the house the night we spied on Mr. Vellum. She warned me never to come around the house or visit Jay again. Believe me, she hates my family more than your parents do. Much more. She brought Lily's shoes thinking they were mine, that I had left them, and when she showed them to me, I held them in my hands, and I noticed how big they were and that they were Italian."

"So?"

"They're very expensive shoes."

"So what?"

"Italian shoes on a woman from Jitters Gap. Doesn't that seem odd?"

"I guess."

"May I confess something else to you?

She flaked dry calamine off her right shin with a fingernail, making it clear I was boring her.

"When I was leaving Jay's the other night, I overheard him talking to you," I said. "He said something about Robbie's journal."

Her face turned bright red, and her hands curled into little fists. "Why were you spying on us?"

"I felt left out. I knew you were keeping things from me."

"Jay doesn't want you around. That's why."

"He does."

"He doesn't like you."

Her jealousy was too innocent and desperate to anger me, but I was tiring of her childishness. I wanted to put her in her place.

"You don't understand what he went through in Europe," I said. "What he saw, what seeing something like that does to you—just seeing it. You're too young to understand something like that."

"He doesn't love you," she said. The conviction in her voice pricked me.

"I want to see Robbie's journal."

"No way."

"Why?"

"It's none of your business."

"Jay's not telling us something, Ceola."

Her grimace tightened, and then she was distracted by something behind me. I spun and saw Jay approaching quickly, using a walking stick to support his bad leg. His face was flushed and his hair feathery gold. His hectic, careless manner made him even more striking.

"I've got news," he said, out of breath. "I've found another clue."

"What is it?" Ceola said, standing back from him a little, her hands by her sides.

"I found the keys to my grandmother's car, just by luck. She wanted me to help her bake zucchini bread. We have a surplus of zucchinis this year, so she decided she'd make bread and take it to all the neighbors—the neighbors she doesn't hate. So when I was preparing the batter, I scooped a cup of sugar from the canister, and lo and behold, there was the key. The old bat had hidden it in the sugar. Well, that's what gave me the idea to go hunting for some clues on my own. I was worried I was involving both of you in too many dangerous things."

He was in a good mood, but it wasn't rubbing off on Ceola. She seemed aloof, disenchanted. Something was going on between them.

"I was flipping through a copy of *Detective World*," he said, "and I came across an article about police procedures. When they can't get a warrant for someone's house, they'll check the garbage. Since it's on the street, it's free game. That got me thinking—maybe I should check out Frank Vellum's garbage. So last night, I went to Jitters Gap. His garbage can was on its side and empty, but when I inspected it more closely, I found a plastic bag stuck to the inside of the container. In the bag, there were a few pieces of trash, and this . . ."

He produced a wrinkled piece of paper from his pocket. The paper had a blue tint and the feel and shape of stationery. "It's the last page of a letter. That's all there was, but it's very interesting."

Ceola and I sat down to read it.

> I didn't love him and I wanted nothing to do with him. Now I hate him so much it's hard to write his name.
>
> Honestly, until I met George, I was so lost. If it ~~weren't~~ hadn't been for my stay with Aunt Kathy, I don't think I would've ever figured things out. Of course, I couldn't tell Kathy about my current state. I'm sorry to be so blunt, but I can't have ~~his~~ this baby. Please help me find a way out. I've written to George—but I need to know I can count on you too.
>
> Take good care of yourself and write soon.
>
>   Love, Lily

"She was pregnant," I said.

Ceola nodded her head slowly.

"And?" Jay prompted.

"*And* her boyfriend Billy Witherspoon got her pregnant," Ceola said, her moodiness melting a little. "He's the crossed out 'his.' Don't you think? *And* she wants to give the baby away."

"That's what I think," he said, looking at me.

So it seemed Jay was going to allow Ceola to interpret *But I can't have ~~his~~ this baby* as Lily's desire to put her unborn child up for adoption. I felt that if that had been the truth, then it should've read, *But I can't raise ~~his~~ this baby.* Jay obviously wanted to protect Ceola, and it frustrated me. How dare he shove photos of a murdered woman under our noses and then shy away from the truth about Lily? It was a blatant contradiction. But Jay understood all too well which sins could be spoken of and which couldn't. Murder, rape, blackmail, thievery—the black-and-white sins—were fine, but abortion was off-limits as a topic for twelve-year-old girls.

"Who is the letter addressed to?" Jay said.

"And who are Aunt Kathy and George?" Ceola said.

"I've been checking *The Times* for news about Lily's disappearance. The police haven't come up with much—at least nothing that's been published," Jay replied. "But I did come across news of a plea from a Katherine Vellum of Washington, DC—Frank's sister. She asked for anyone with any knowledge of Lily's whereabouts to come forward. It was also in *The Washington Post*, which means that the police are looking for Lily in DC as well. If they're focusing on her, maybe we should focus on Billy, the boyfriend."

"How do we find him?" Ceola said.

"I don't know. We have to assume he'll communicate with Frank at some point. We're going to have to follow Frank and wait to see what happens."

"When?" Ceola said.

"Tomorrow," Jay said. "But we need to use your mother's car, Bunny. My grandmother's going to be home all day, so we can't take hers."

"You want me to lie to her *again*," I said.

"Tell her we're going on a picnic."

"I won't do that, Jay."

"You want to know what happened to Lily as much as we do."

He had me; I did want to know. But more than that, I wanted to know what Jay was up to.

Jay and Ceola materialized at my house early the next morning. After grabbing the new picnic basket Mother had packed for us (I told her I'd dropped the old one on some rocks, not flung it against a tree), a pair of sunglasses, and my wide-brimmed straw hat, I joined the others in the car, and we made our journey across the mountain to Jitters Gap.

It was midmorning when we parked down the street from the Vellum house and settled in. The day was sunny and humid, and the car was hot. The coal-mining town seemed grubbier in the daylight, all the flaking paint, dirty windows, and missing shingles exposed. I wasn't as frightened as I had been when we snooped the first time. Perhaps it was the time of day, or perhaps I'd just grown bolder. I don't know.

For a long time, we waited in silence. I stared out at the empty street, bored and listless, and was thrilled when I saw movement of any sort—though it was usually only a haggard housewife on her way to do laundry or shop at the market, or the milk-and-egg truck making its rounds. Eventually, we ate our picnic lunch of soggy sandwiches and warm lemonade, then waited some more.

I thought about Jay and Ceola, and about Robbie. He was their bond, their connection, but he was stifling me. I tried to remember him more clearly, but all I could conjure was the stilted conversation we had at my birthday party two years earlier. There he was—floppy brown hair and delicate features, his hands spinning in little circles while he was speaking. The boys in school called him a sissy, but that's not what I saw. He was mild and a bit rarified—not at all prepared for war and certainly not enthusiastic about enlisting. Perhaps he knew instinctually, cosmically, he wouldn't be returning. That would explain his hell-may-care sprint into the lake.

"Bunny," Jay said. "Look!"

Frank Vellum emerged from his house dressed in a light brown suit and a chocolate fedora. He was groomed and professional, as if he were on his way to a business deal, but his face was sharp like a hawk's, all directive. He walked to his truck and started the engine, and we followed him into downtown Jitters Gap. He parked in front of Glade's Dine-In, its dingy, stain-streaked chrome siding catching the morning sun, the reflected light harsh and dull. I parked across the street, and we watched him enter Glade's, disappear for a moment, then reappear through the diner's wide plate-glass windows. I could see the heads of other customers, bobbing and dipping as they chatted and ate; it was clearly a popular place. A few moments passed, and then we saw Frank, hat in hand, cross the diner and, with an air of determination and undue speed, head to a young man with blond hair. The man stood up, the two exchanged words but didn't shake, and then they both sat again, vanishing behind the glare of the sunlight.

"You two need to go in and eavesdrop," Jay said. "I can't. Frank might have seen me the other night. Just sit near him and have a milkshake."

"I don't think it's a good idea," I said. "Too dangerous."

In the rearview mirror, I saw Ceola roll her eyes, and before I could stop her, she hopped out.

"Go," Jay said. "*Now.*" I went after her.

Glade's was a hodgepodge—the sleekness of its chrome-fixtured, art deco design was cluttered, if not a little concealed, by gingham tablecloths, rustic trinkets, and local knickknacks. Between the windows hung dusty paintings of local landscapes—mountains, valleys, sunsets—and behind the register, nailed haphazardly, were framed clichés like, "As ye sow, so shall ye reap," and, "Many hands make light work." From the ceiling, a billowy, faded quilt had been draped like a canopy in an attempt, I imagine, to produce a cozy feel. The thick smell of bacon grease permeated the air.

Before Ceola could rush to the open booth beside Frank Vellum and the other man, I grabbed her hand and gave it a squeeze. The softness of her small palm made me aware again of her age. She didn't move to pull away from me, which I'd expected, and I felt a brief flush of tenderness for her.

Although it was difficult to look at the two men without being conspicuous, I did note the mystery man wore grimy blue overalls, and, although he was young, perhaps mid-twenties, his face was creased and his eyes were dark, a mask of hard living, covering up something, some wound, some story.

We calmly moved to a booth and slid across the cracked leather cushions. I had my back to the men; my eyes were on Ceola and hers on me, and we eavesdropped:

"I haven't come to talk," Frank said. He was seething.

"Why are we here?" the blond man said.

"The police have asked you, and now I'm going to ask you—"

"I don't know where your daughter is. Sir."

"You do, Billy. Don't lie to me."

The waitress arrived at their table, placing a coffee in front of Frank. Billy, who I assumed was Billy Witherspoon, had his coffee already. She attended to us, muttering something about the sausage and cheddar pie of the day.

"Just a vanilla milkshake for her," I said, "and coffee with cream for me."

"How about some breakfast, or maybe lunch?" she said. She was a large, frumpy woman, her curly hair fizzy and damp at its ends.

"I'm watching my figure."

"Pancakes for the young lady?"

"Just the milkshake and coffee. Thank you."

She frowned at us and left the table. Ceola and I stared at each other, acknowledging a bond of commiseration.

Behind me, Billy said, "She wanted to get away from you, didn't she? You were smothering her, locking her up."

"She came back here on her own," Frank said. "You shamed her, and she needed me." His voice was thin, even shaky. Ceola's eyes grew wide, almost gleeful.

"I don't know what you're talking about, old man."

"And now you've kidnapped her. *Haven't you?*"

"Of course not. Why would I?" Billy's voice squeaked.

"I can see it in your eyes. I can see what you've done."

"You're goddamn nuts. You're trying to throw the blame my way, make me into the thug that did her in. *You* know more than I do."

"You've taken her, haven't you?" Frank's voice was shrill, desperate; heads around the restaurant stopped bobbing, forks went down. "Tell me, you son of a bitch!"

There was commotion behind me—a rustle of fabric followed by the smashing of crockery, the clatter of silverware, and the sensation of hot liquid across my feet—and a scream. My scream? I'm not even sure now. Later I discovered that the coffee had scalded me through my nylons.

From the corners of my eyes, I saw Billy fly across the restaurant and heard the bell over the front door jingle violently.

From above me, a hand offered a napkin—it was Frank. I took it and, stammering a little, said thank you. He grimaced and said nothing in return. For an older man, he was handsome, weathered like the sheriff in a Western matinee, but his eyes were still watery with rage and his chin turned down in embarrassment. He seemed to be hiding behind his finely coifed gray mustache.

"We got to go," Ceola said. "Right now."

I glared at her incredulously, but her earnestness suddenly made me frightened, as if she knew something bad would soon happen if we didn't leave immediately. I quickly dabbed my ankles and feet and threw some money on the table. We left in a flourish, not looking back at Frank, who was still standing, stunned, it seemed, by his own behavior.

Jay was waiting in the driver's seat when we arrived at the car. He asked what happened, but Ceola, bright-eyed with excitement and out of breath, just gasped, "We got to follow him!" She hadn't been afraid in Glade's; she just didn't want to miss the action. She was still playing pretend.

"What?" I said. "We're not going to—"

"Who?" Jay said. "Billy?"

"Did you see which way he went?" she said.

"A blond guy went that way." Jay nodded to the west.

"That's him," Ceola confirmed.

Jay turned the key in the ignition, and we set out. We drove a block before Ceola spotted Billy. He was moving vigorously away from the center of town, and he was clearly still boiling with anger. To avoid giving ourselves away, we parked and hopped out and began shadowing him on foot. Billy crossed the cracked pavement under a lattice-work arch that spanned Main Street and announced in soot-streaked letters, JITTERS GAP, VA, PRIDE OF THE MOUNTAINS. Billy then took a sharp left down a steep incline. We followed him to the bottom of the street and watched as he approached a filling station.

The hollowed-out body of a Chevy truck sat out front, propped up on cinder blocks and tangled in Virginia creeper; beside it, another junked car was unrecognizable under the layers of rust. The door to the garage was open, and yet another car—a glossy black two-door Ford—was up on the platform, mid-repair. Across the wide window to the front office, the owners had stenciled WITHERSPOON FILL AND FIX in bold red letters. Billy entered the office.

"That's where he works," Jay said. We stepped into the doorway of a derelict storefront to regroup.

"That explains the overalls," I said.

"What happened back there at Glade's?" Jay asked.

"Mr. Vellum swung at Billy across the booth and tipped a waitress's tray over," Ceola said. "Bunny got splashed with hot coffee."

Jay looked at me with concern.

"I'm okay," I said. "But the two of them. They were really steamed at each other. Frank wanted to kill Billy."

"Really?"

"Billy's hiding something," Ceola said. "You can tell."

"But there was something about Frank . . . ," I said. "I don't think he's telling the truth, either."

"We need to know more." A slim smile crept onto Jay's face.

"What?" I said. "I don't like that look."

"Follow me."

He led us back to the car. When I asked him again what he was up to, he didn't respond. He just popped the trunk, located my father's toolbox, rummaged for something—a wrench, I would come to find out—and stooped beside the front left tire. I heard the hiss of escaping air and gasped.

"What are you doing?" I said. I was ready to push him down and take the car keys from him. "How will we get home—especially over that mountain?" I could hear the high, unpleasant anxiety in my voice.

"We'll be fine. There's a filling station around the corner, didn't you know?" Jay just smiled.

"Oh no," I said. "It's dangerous. We can't. We *mustn't*."

"You two don't even need to get out of the car."

"You're taking this too far."

"Billy *was* really mad," Ceola said, a tremor in her voice. "If he's the murderer, he could've seen you in the woods when you found the body."

"That's right," I said. "He could be looking for you. You can't show yourself."

"We're going to have to do something," he said, raising his eyebrows at me. "The tire's flat now."

"This is absurd," I said.

We piled into the car, but before Jay started the engine, I insisted we come up with a plan. First, Ceola and I had to conceal our identities. We didn't want Billy recognizing us from the restaurant. I put on my straw hat and sunglasses—the picnic apparel that had served as part of the cover story for our trip—and I made Ceola use one of the gingham napkins, which Mother had packed, as a kerchief for her head. Of course, she looked ridiculous, but I didn't know what else to do. I made Ceola promise to stay in the car with me while Jay sorted things out with Billy. Since he had put us in this position, he should be the one to take the risk, I thought, and after all, he was the most able to defend himself. I made him promise to keep his interactions with Billy all business.

We drove slowly down Main Street and made a left, the car tipping forward at an awkward angle as we rolled down the steep grade to the bottom of the hill. We swung into the station, the bell chiming to alert an attendant.

For what felt like hours, we saw no one, heard no one. Several cars passed by on the street, but none of them stopped for gas like I'd hoped they would. The potential witness would help keep everyone safe. I imagined Billy lurking in the undergrowth, watching Jay stumble on Lily's corpse, his dark, carnivorous eyes roiling with venom. I felt certain we were being watched now. I looked over at Jay but said nothing.

"Let me see what's going on," he said, and swung the car door open. I almost made to grab him and pull him back, but I knew I couldn't stop him. "Hello," he called. Still nothing.

Just as he was about to return, Billy appeared at the edge of the garage door. He'd rolled the top of his overalls to his waist, exposing a clean white T-shirt underneath. He was more muscular than I'd imagined, biceps thick and leaden in his sleeves, and a neck like a telephone pole, but this bulk, besides being intimidating, made him seem squat and dwarfish, a caricature.

"What you need?" he said. "Fill 'er up?"

"The left tire. It's lost some air."

"It'll be a buck to use the compressor—that includes labor." That was price gouging. He must have sized up the Olds and figured we had money.

"Fine."

Billy disappeared into the garage, switched on the compressor, and then reappeared with a thin red hose. As he approached the front of the car, he noticed Ceola and me, squinting a little and giving us a polite nod. I don't think he could quite make out either of us. Perhaps it was the glare on the windshield.

"Nice weather, isn't it?" Jay said, making small talk. He was leaning against the fender, feigning nonchalance.

"Yep, suppose so," Billy said, seemingly uninterested.

Jay smiled faintly at him.

I heard a click and the smooth whistle of air entering the tire. Immediately, I felt better. This would all be over soon, and we'd be on our way.

"Witherspoon," Jay said loudly. "That name seems familiar to me."

My heart leapt. What was he doing?!

"Does it?" Billy said.

"The newspaper—that's right. It was about that missing girl. Lily Vellum."

"That's none of your business, sir," Billy said.

"Wasn't someone named Billy Witherspoon suspected of doing it? Of taking her?"

"What's it to you?" he said, standing up. I could still hear the air seeping in. *Faster*, I thought. *Faster.* He glanced our direction again and stepped closer, craning his neck to get a better look at me. I tilted my head forward, the wide brim of my hat shielding against his gaze. Why was he looking at me? I thought of those predatory eyes, leering at Jay from the woods.

"We're just passing through, pal. Visiting family," Jay said.

Billy sneered at him but didn't make a move. Something clicked, and Billy returned to the hose. The tire was finally full. Thank God.

Jay fished a dollar out of his shirt pocket and walked around the front of the Olds. When Billy stood again, Jay held it out to him. "You're the one they suspect," he said. "Did you do it? Did you kill her?"

Billy dropped the hose and grabbed Jay by the collar, shoving him hard against the side of the car. The dollar fluttered to the ground. "Who the fuck are you?" he said. "Did Frank send you?"

Jay didn't respond. He seemed oddly serene, considering the damage a man like Billy could do.

"That man better watch himself," Billy said.

"Why?" Jay said.

Billy jerked him up by the shirt and flopped him against the hood of the car. I could tell it hurt Jay, especially his leg.

"You tell him I don't know a damn thing, and if he comes asking again, I'll—" And he bounced Jay again, making it clear what he would do. Jay's back landed hard against the green metal, and his face flushed with pain. I didn't know what to do, so I slammed my hand on the horn. The blast confused Billy, and Jay slid down the hood and slithered out of reach. He swung around the front of the car and pulled the driver's door shut just as Billy—face glazed with sweat and teeth bared like a rabid fox—collided with the outside of the door. He beat his fists against the window, leaving star-shaped grease marks and even a smear of blood on the glass. Jay started the engine, and before Billy could crack the window and break in, we were off, screeching across the street, nearly ramming a hay truck.

On the drive back over the mountain, after Jay had recovered a little, Jay and Ceola launched into a mania of questions and hypotheses: *What if Billy really doesn't know what happened to Lily? But he has the best motive, doesn't he? She was pregnant after all. Why does Billy think Frank knows more than he does? Does he have a motive? And what about the other people in the letter—George and Aunt Kathy? What, if anything, does Bernice Hersh, the pharmacist's wife, have to do with this?*

I said nothing. I didn't understand how they could go on spinning circles in the air with their wild suspicions. Jay had been reckless. He had blithely thrown himself in harm's way, first by jumping fences at the Vellum house and now by getting assaulted by that horrible thug. Even if he didn't care about himself, he should have cared that he was placing us in danger. Wasn't it real for him? Or was it just a game? More than ever, I wanted to read Robbie's journal. It was my right to know why Jay wanted it. I'd earned that privilege by undergoing this ordeal.

What a goddamn fool I was.

The first morning at her aunt's house, Sheila walked the estate. Her mood lightened as she followed the trails that wound in and out of the woods and switchbacked down the side of the mountain. When she and Kenneth had been in love, they'd taken weekends in the country. One day in particular came back to her.

It was fall, and they were visiting the Adirondacks. They had slept in, and after a big breakfast, they decided on a hike. The sky was blue and the leaves were in full color, and Kenneth held her hand in his. As they crossed a wide field, he looked back at her from time to time, a warm smile on his face. Suddenly he let go and started running, his scarf unwinding from his neck. "Weeeee!" he screamed. He headed for a large mound of leaves that a tidy farmer had gathered. Like a schoolboy chump,

he flopped into the center of it, expecting a fluffy cushion. He came out cursing and stomping, covered in muck and dead leaves. It was compost.

When their eyes met, she began laughing. "You're a queer one, aren't you?" she said.

He wanted to be mad, it seemed, but he began laughing too. Then he started chasing her, his arms outstretched. "Give me a kiss, sweetheart. A big kiss!"

Eventually, she got a muddy smooch. She had wanted that moment to last forever.

As black rain clouds thickened in the west, Sheila became lonely again and headed back to the house. After lunch, she took a nap in her aunt's dayroom. She awoke to the patter of rain on the windowpanes. Slowly she became aware that the sleeves of her blouse were wet, and her shoes were soaked.

She gasped and shook the dampness from her arms and her feet. She searched for a leak in the ceiling but found none. She felt the sofa and the carpet, but they were bone dry. Like the evening before, it didn't make sense. She touched her neck. It was still sore. What was going on?

She made a cup of coffee and spiked it with whiskey to steady her nerves. As she sipped the bitter black liquid, she watched it rain. She couldn't wait to get back to the city, to her little apartment, cheerful despite its dinginess. She had no desire to live in this house. She would visit a real estate agent tomorrow. She began to cry softly.

She dabbed away the tears and snatched up the telephone receiver and immediately slammed it back in place. After a sip or two more of her concoction, she plucked the receiver from the cradle and dialed. The operator connected her, and it rang several times before Kenneth answered, "Hello." She didn't respond immediately. "Is anyone there?" he asked.

"It's me."

"So you're calling me at work now."

"Please, don't."

"What do you want?"

"I needed to hear your voice. I miss you."

"We're finished. You made that clear when you ordered up the divorce papers."

"If you ask me to forgive you, I will. We could start over."

"I don't want you to forgive me. Why should I? I'm not sorry."

"I'll be rich soon. Lousy rich. We could build a new life together."

"I don't care about your money, She."

"Is that tramp really going to make you happy?"

"We plan to marry."

"Already?"

"Good-bye, She."

The line went dead, and she just sat there, numb, for a time. Did she mean nothing to Kenneth? How could he be so cold? She thought back on that happy weekend in the Adirondacks—but she caught herself, peevish tears forming, then stood up and stamped her foot—once, twice, beating away the emotion like a child. She wiped her eyes with the back of her hand. She wanted to think about something else. She wanted something to look forward to. The future was out there. Kenneth was the past. Damn him to hell.

9

CEOLA

Mama had been waiting for me. Her hands were folded over the wool blanket she had been making, her needles stabbed into its scratchy pink web—she was always knitting something, *always*.

Papa stepped around the corner, bracing himself against the living room wall, drunk as a skunk. His cheeks were red, and his whiskey-glazed eyes were loose in their sockets. He steadied himself and, for the longest time, stared at me. Slow, like demons out of a pit, his thoughts climbed out of his soupy mind, and with a hiccup, he started.

"I met some of the men for refreshments after work, and we got to talkin'." He was slurring his speech. "Sam Sprinkle tells me he was out making deliveries in Jitters Gap today. He said he saw the damnedest thing. The damnedest thing. He said he saw Jay Greenwood and Bunny Prescott and you in a slick green Oldsmobile. Yes, ma'am, that's what he said. And I thought to myself, how could it be that my daughter was with a Prescott *and* a Greenwood? It didn't make one bit of sense.

"So I asked Sam if he had made a mistake. I told him my daughter knows how I feel about both of those families, she wouldn't be driving around with them. He said he was making a delivery to Glade's Dine-In, and he saw you and Bunny walk out of the place and get into the car with the Greenwood boy. There was no mistakin' it, he said." Papa dropped his heavy hand on my shoulder and bent toward me, his 100-proof breath made my eyes sting. "Out with it! Why were you with them?"

Mama's lips twitched and tightened as if she was about to speak, the birthmark on the side of her face blazing bright red like the scorch on a freshly branded cow.

"Why were you driving around in that fancy car with that queer boy and Princess Prescott? It was embarrassing for me. Goddamn humiliating."

"Bob," my mother said with caution.

"I wasn't there," I said. Papa's grip on my shoulder tightened. His face was close to mine, his eyes like licks of blue flame. I thought about Billy's vicious mug as he beat the side of Bunny's car. I was more afraid of Papa.

"Tell the truth," he demanded.

"They're my friends."

"Your friends?" He let go. "Your friends!"

"We're a club."

"How could you be friends? Why would you want to be friends with either of those two?"

"I missed Robbie, and Jay was Robbie's friend. They were best friends. He loved Robbie. Robbie loved him too."

That's when Papa hauled off and hit me.

His hand clipped the side of my face, and his garnet-studded Royal Oak High ring bit into my cheek just under my eye. I can still remember the twinkle of gold before the pain, like light flashing through that prism Mama had hanging in the kitchen window. He had done it to me only a few times before and never before you died, Robbie, so I didn't expect it. To this day, I don't like it when light catches my eyes.

I stumbled, slapping the wall with my back. The shock of it brought tears, and I cried into my hands, easing my body to the floor. I heard the front door swing open, then the flop of the screen against the door-frame and Papa's feet pounding the wood slats of the porch. Soon he would be breaking ground and tossing dirt, planting trees like a man possessed, building a forest to hide us in.

Mama stood up, her blanket spilling from her lap. She didn't say a word. Her eyes were as blank as polished stone, like a zombie from one of your scary comics. Did she want to help me? Did she care? Hell if I knew. I couldn't take my sticky, snotty hands away from my cheeks. I retreated like a turtle into its shell, and my thoughts—like many times before and after—turned to you.

You were sitting on your bed and it was the afternoon—one of those chilly fall afternoons where the world is dark at its edges. I had just been playing outside, racing my bike down the hill, jumping in the leaves, tunneling through the tall grass, all the things a young girl isn't supposed to do. I wasn't ready to settle down to finish my arithmetic or my book report on *The Red Badge of Courage* or whatever school-work I had to do.

On your lap, in a jumble, were sheets of notebook paper, curled at the edges and scrawled with your messy handwriting like some loony's graf-fiti. For a minute or two, I leaned against the doorframe and watched you read, your long fingers fidgeting with your pants pocket and your lips pressed together as if giving the air in front of you a little kiss.

I cleared my throat, and without looking up, you said, "What do you want?"

I came into the room and sat on the opposite end of the bed from you. "What you working on?"

"Nothing."

"Is it good?"

"I guess. I don't know."

"What's it about?"

"Don't be so nosy."

I leaned toward you, being as nosy as possible. "Why don't you read it to me?"

"It's not finished."

"What kind of story is it?"

"It's scary, but it's not ready. Go away."

"Come on. Read it to me."

"No—you're bugging me."

"Read it to me, pleeease."

"No."

"I'll tell Mama about it!"

You rolled your eyes. "Okay, okay—but you have to sit there and be quiet. Not a peep."

You cleared your throat and breathed in and out like you were about to sing high opera. When you read scary stories to me, it was like being on the deck of a ship in a storm. I could hang over the edge and stare at the dark, bubbly waters below, imagining what it might feel like to let go and take the plunge and be sucked under, but all the time knowing you had your hands around my waist and would never let me go.

Annoyed with your main character, I blurted out, "Why is she doing that? Going there alone? Shouldn't she know better?"

"You want me to stop? I'll stop right now. I swear."

"Sorry, sorry. I'll be quiet."

As you read on, I forgot *you* had written this story. It was professional, official, like something in one of your magazines. It was so much better than the last one you wrote, "The Case of the Creepy Cradle." Do you remember that one? It was about a policeman who falls for a woman who ends up being the mama of a vampire-monster with bat wings, red eyes, tusks, and fangs. The mother gets angry with the cop and feeds him to her baby. Now, mind you, my tastes weren't terribly sophisticated at that age, but I knew a good story when I read one, and "Creepy Cradle" was not good. You had become a much better writer since then.

"Stories need to hold together," you told me, like you had read that somewhere. "Everything should click into place at the end. The endings are so important."

Your new story had me hooked. It was damn good. Being the excitable girl I was, I interrupted you again, and again you threatened to stop reading. I begged and apologized, and you gave in. As the story reached its climax, I was on the edge of your bed, my knees pinned to my chest by my crossed arms. Would you reach the end before Mama called us for dinner? Oh please oh please oh please! I could hardly stand it. Then you stopped, and I let out a scream—more of a squeal, really. I leaped toward you and hugged you, the pages falling to the floor. "It's too much!" I said. "I want to know how it turns out!"

"It's just a story, Cee!" you said, laughing.

"I have to know now!"

"Mr. Spade," you said, assuming an aristocratic posture, your voice low and feminine. I released you, and we assumed our carefully studied roles. "I've a terrible, terrible confession to make. That—that story I told you yesterday was all—a story."

"Oh, that—" I said, doing my best tough guy, putting my hands on my hips. "We didn't exactly believe your story, Miss—Miss—is your name Wonderly or Leblanc?"

"It's really O'Shaughnessy, Brigid O'Shaughnessy."

"We didn't exactly believe your story, Miss O'Shaughnessy. We believed your two hundred dollars— Wait a second," I said, breaking character. "You're not fooling me. I still want to hear the end!"

You smiled and shrugged. I knew the answer was no.

I loved acting out those scenes from *The Maltese Falcon*. You did all the voices so good. Spade, Gutman, O'Shaughnessy. Cairo was the funniest, in that squeaky, high-pitched voice of his, like an evil chipmunk—*You . . . you imbecile. You bloated idiot. You stupid fat-head, you.*

I wish you were here to remember those old times with me. We'd have so many stories to tell each other. We could sit in my kitchen where the light is good in the winter, sip coffee, smoke, talk about our favorite mystery novels, and quote our favorite movies. You were my best friend, have *always* been my best friend. I even named my first son after you. Hell, it was your namesake who helped me track down a copy of *Weird Stories*, July 1943, on eBay, the issue with "A Date with Death" in it. I wish you had seen it published, even if it had to be under a pseudonym. If you'd lived to be a writer, I wonder what sort of stories you would've written. Can you imagine what Mama and Papa would've thought? You, a real short story writer!

📷

But I've gone off course.

I was telling you I was there, bunched up on the floor, hiding in my hands. Once my crying mellowed, I took my hands away from my face. I noticed a pattern of blood in the grooves of my left palm. Papa had got me good. I wiped it on my skirt and stood up.

I wanted Mama to come and put her arms around me. I wanted her to bandage the scratch or rub my shoulders or just say a few kind words. I needed her to do something. But she had already left the room. So I went upstairs, cleaned my face, treated the cut, and barricaded myself in my bedroom by wedging a book under the bottom of the door. I took your journal out from its hiding place and curled up on my bed.

Before I began reading, I hesitated for a second, a little afraid I might be breaking a sacred oath that would conjure up your ghost. But that was the point—I needed you. I wanted your ghost. On the inside of the cover, you had written:

DO NOT OPEN!!! TOP SECRET!!!
That means you, Cee!
Property of: Robert H. Bliss III
Date: June 20, 1941 to _____

The pages inside were cluttered with notes, sketches, crossword puzzles, lines of dialogue from movies, and even several of your favorite quotations: "I dare not tell it in words, not even in these songs—Here I shade and hide my thoughts, I myself do not expose them, and yet they expose me more than all my other poems." Walt Whitman.

Although there were fragments of several stories, most of it was your personal diary. Some entries I've returned to again and again throughout the years, hoping to get closer to you with each read, like the way I go to pictures of you and just look and look. I suppose there's only so much you can get from a few words, but still I hunt for you in them, harder than I ever searched for Lily Vellum.

1941

September 29th

Today Mr. Martin was lecturing about the sex organs of flowers, droning on about stamens and anthers, when my lab partner Jay opened to the glossary of my Bio book. He took his pencil, circled HOMOSEXUAL, and put a question mark beside it. I looked at him, and he gave me the Charlie Chaplin eyebrow wiggle and wagged an invisible cigar in my face. Then he ~~scram~~ scribbled something else in the margin of the book. Mr. Martin snapped at us, and Jay slapped the book closed. We didn't look at each other for the rest of class. When I got home, I opened it. In the margin it read, MARTIN HAS A BIG STAMEN.

September 30th

Jay wrote another note today. It said, "Don't be scared. Want to be friends?" I quickly wrote back, "No." He wrote back, "Please." I wrote "No" again and then again. He replied with "Please" and "Why not?" Finally I wrote, "Yes, but I'm no fairy." I was scared Mr. Martin would catch us.

October 18th

Jay and I explored Hardy's quarry today, walking along the cliffs, squeezing ourselves into the mouths of caves, pretending to be spelunkers searching for hidden treasure, but we'd always chicken out after a few feet in. It was as black as tar in there—and there were bats. We also played this great game. We'd each find the biggest rock we could carry, haul it to the edge of the quarry, yell, "Bombs away," and toss it over, counting how long it would take for each stone to hit the water. The fastest one won.

I told Jay I liked detective stories and ghost stories and would he like to hear one, so I made one up about a haunted cave with an evil witch in it and the two boys who defeat her. It made Jay laugh. That's all that mattered. Maybe if I get good at stories, I can do it for a job someday.

He told me he liked taking pictures with his father's camera. I told him he'd have to show it to me one day. He said he would, he'd like that.

Nov 2nd

I asked Papa if Jay could come for dinner and listen to _The Shadow_ on the radio with us, and he told me Jay wasn't welcome at our house. He said he was still mad at Mr. Greenwood for selling the company to Mr. Prescott years ago. I got hot with him, but he just steamed and told me I can't be Jay's friend and he didn't approve of him or his grandma. The end. He told me I should look for other friends, boys who liked to play sports and go hunting and not the sort who toy around with telling stories, playing pinochle, and doing crossword puzzles.

Dec 15th

In the newspaper today, I read a story about a man who was beaten to death at a bar in Roanoke. A group of five men took turns hitting him with a tire iron fifty-six times. He was only twenty-one. Although there was nothing in the article about why they did it, when I mentioned it to Papa, he said it was because the man was an invert, hanging out at a fairy bar, and probably deserved it. He said I had to read between the lines. The _Times_ was being tasteful and just implying the truth. They didn't want to burden young minds like mine. He told me if one of those queers was to ever get his hands on me, I should just sock him as hard as I can. Any decent person would understand that.

The thought of doing something like that made me sick to my stomach, but I lied to Papa and told him I would do just that, right in the fella's kisser.

May 14th

I want to tell Jay about what happened at Hersh's Pharmacy, but I don't know how. I don't have the nerve, but I got to—I just got to tell somebody.

It was about closing time, and I was there flipping through magazines. Mr. H came up to me and asked me if I wanted a soda before he went home. "A Snap Cola float with vanilla ice cream," I told him. He said it was on the house, but he wanted to talk to me. I thought, okay.

After he handed me the float, he led me into his back room and told me to sit on a stool in front of his desk. He took off his lab coat and leaned against the wall, trying to be suave like James Cagney or something. He smiled at me, rubbing the stubble on his chin. He's a handsome guy, but he had a few teeth missing at the left side of his mouth, making his smile a little lopsided. I sipped my float and watched the ice cream foam and melt.

Then he started asking me about what I was studying in school, and he told me he had noticed that I liked reading magazines. I told him I liked <u>Dime Detective</u> and <u>Weird Stories</u>, because I liked writing those kinds of stories, and I wanted to be a writer someday. He smiled like that was all okay by him. Then he said, "Any other sorts of magazines you like?"

I said, "I don't know."

And he said, "I keep a good eye on my store, son. You've lifted a particular magazine from the rack twice. Be honest with me."

I shrugged, trying to hide my nerves.

"It's called ~~Phsy~~ Physique," he said. "I'm sure you remember."

So I fessed up and told him I'd pay for what I took.

He said, "You don't look like much of a body builder. If you were only interested in bodybuilding, I don't think you would've stolen those magazines at all. No sir. You certainly paid for all that detective pulp, didn't you? I'm thinking you like looking at those men. That's what I'm thinking."

I was shaking. He reached over and took the soda glass from my hand and placed it on the desk. He knelt on one knee in front of me, putting one hand on my thigh and another on my shoulder.

He said, "I'm no muscle man, but may I kiss you?"

I was afraid, but I nodded my head. As he leaned toward me, his hand slid up my leg. His big, cigarette-smelling mouth pressed hard against mine. I kissed him back. It was deeper and messier than I'd seen done in the movies. It felt so good and awful at the same time—that's the only way to describe it. Good and awful.

I said, "I've got to go," and pulled away.

He said, "You're a good kisser. A real natural."

I stood up, knocking the stool over like an ass.

"Don't tell anyone," he said. "This needs to be between us, hear? Only us. And if you ever want to drop by after I close up, there'll always be a free float for you."

May 18th

I've been feeling rotten, worried to pieces about what happened with Mr. H. It was a horrible thing we did, sinful, but I can't get it out of my head. I'd be lying if I said I didn't like it, if I hadn't thought about going back, but as soon as I begin entertaining those notions, I want to throw myself in front of a train or into Hardy's quarry. I got excited thinking about it the other day and did myself in the bathroom—but I felt like dying after it was over. What's wrong with me? Mama and Papa would beat me to a pulp if they knew what I did. I should hate Mr. H, but I don't. I wonder if Jay would understand. I wonder what he'd think. I don't know. Oh God, I hate this.

May 22nd

I told Jay about what happened with Mr. H, and for the longest time, he just looked at me and smiled like he knew something I didn't. I wondered if Mr. H had done the same thing to him. He put his hand on mine, leaned in, and kissed me. When we were touching, that rotten feeling boring a hole in my gut disappeared, but once we separated, I could still feel the rumble of it in my stomach. I told him I wanted to leave Royal Oak, I wanted to live in a city or some foreign country, I wanted to be a famous writer and write under a pen name. He smiled and said what would your pen name be? It needs to sound impressive and recognizable, don't you think? What about Raymond Christie? Or Dashiell Carr? Doing Bette Davis, I said, "Jay, darling, my name is Aaagatha Chandler, so pleeeased to make your acquaintance."

May 27th

It's a rainy day, and the eaves of the house are spilling over like waterfalls. I wish I could see Jay today. All I can think about is the kiss we had and how it calmed everything inside me. I feel so rotten and worried when we're not together. Even Cee, who played cards with me for a while, makes me feel low, like if she really knew how I felt, she'd hate me. I'm trapped until the rain stops. I've got to get out of this place.

June 9th

Yesterday we took a dinghy out on Culler's Lake. Jay packed lunch and toted his camera. I brought a fishing pole and some binoculars. The day was clear, not a cloud in the sky from start to finish. We fished for several hours. I caught five or six bluegill and threw them back. They're worthless to eat. We rowed into an inlet and went for a swim. After that, we stretched out in the bottom of the boat, ate lunch, and took a nap.

I woke up to Jay taking pictures of me. I felt a little uneasy about it at first, but Jay seemed to enjoy himself, and I liked watching him move around. He posed me, even undoing the top of my trunks a little. "To accentuate your best feature," he said, smiling like a devil. He taught me how to change the film and adjust the camera, and I took photos of him too.

We put the camera away and rowed the boat deep into an alcove and hid it behind a fallen tree. In the shade on the bank, hidden from everything and everyone, we took off our trunks and saw each other naked for the first time. I thought I would feel guilty if I touched him or if he touched me, but when he kissed me and I felt him against me, none of that mattered, and when he kneeled in front of me, I touched the top of his head. His wet hair was nice and cool against my palm. I wanted to bend down and kiss him, but he took me in his mouth and the rest was shooting stars.

June 13th

When I got to Bunny's birthday party last night, Jay avoided me. Bunny, as pushy as ever, started shining her blinding light on him. I watched from a distance as she made him take her picture. How he spoke to her, like he was flirting with her, really burned me. Later, he jumped me and pulled me behind a tree and kissed me—but no thank you! How could he flirt with Bunny and then grab me behind a tree? I was so mad I was out of my head. I wanted to kick him, but instead I kicked the tree really hard and, like a chump, hurt my toe. I landed on the ground. He looked at me like I was crazy. "What's wrong with you?" he said, and I blurted it out I would be eighteen in a week. He just walked away.

I didn't want to be around anyone. I was feeling pretty hopeless, like going to war meant the end for Jay and me, maybe the end of everything. So I hid down by the shoreline until, of all people, Bunny found me and started grilling me about what I thought of her party and lecturing me about the benefits of enlisting versus being drafted. I really, truly wanted to stick it to her.

Then Jay arrived, ripped off all his clothes, and ran into the lake! It was his way of asking forgiveness. So I followed him, streaking right in front of Bunny. Fuck you, Bunny! We swam across the lake, over a hundred yards to the opposite bank.

In the moonlight, Jay pulled me close to him, and we did it—all the way. It hurt so much at first I thought I couldn't do it, but then it was like nothing else, and the pain didn't matter. When it was over and we were lying there holding each other, ignoring the dirt and rocks and the poison oak, I began to cry, keeping my head on his chest so he couldn't see my eyes. I didn't want him to know I was going to pieces.

June 18th

I'm eighteen on the 18th. Happy Goddamn Birthday. I've never felt so blue. Mama, Papa, and Cee escorted me to the recruiting station on Main Street, and I joined the Navy. They told me to go home and wait for my orders. I tried to see myself standing on the bow of one of those big blue-gray monsters with the wind whipping my clothes and the sun on my face. If I had enough moments like that, I thought, I might just survive the war. But as soon as I felt hopeful, the blues came rushing back. I knew it wasn't going to be at all like I imagined. I could sense it—how hard the war would make it to dream about the future.

June 20th

This morning I walked down to the creek with Cee. We messed around for a while, skipping stones, trying to catch dragonflies, and reading an old issue of <u>Dime Detective</u>. On our way back, she asked me if I knew why Papa hated the Greenwoods. I told her Papa was angry because they sold the Dixie Dew plant, but that's not the truth. I know he senses Jay is queer and I am too. I wanted to tell her that's why he was sending me away. She deserves to know, doesn't she? Instead, I started to do a dramatic reading of "The Nervous Doorbell," one of stories in <u>Dime</u>, in my best Orson Welles. She grabbed me around the waist and hugged me. It surprised me, and I almost pushed her away. But instead I hugged her back, crinkling the magazine. She said, "Don't go!" But I told her I had to. I said it was my duty to my country. She just repeated over and over, "Don't go."

July 1st

I've been doing some final edits to "A Date with Death." I've decided on a ~~psue~~ pseudonym to publish it under in <u>Weird Stories</u>—Robert Wonderly. Cee's idea. I don't know if the story's any good, but I'm glad <u>Weird Stories</u> likes it. Maybe during downtime at boot camp or overseas, I'll have time to write. I can send Jay my stories. Cee too. What if I really do become a writer when I return from service? That'd be just swell. I could live the high life in one of those big cities. New York, here I come, and all that. But I shouldn't take a shine to the idea. Right now my only ticket out of this town is the war. It's not how I wanted to make my grand exit. It feels more like an ending than a beginning. I'd be lying if I didn't say I was frightened. Actus Dei, right? My fate is in another's hands, but is it God's? More like Uncle Sam's.

July 4th

Jay and I met up at Culler's Lake at nightfall. We watched the fireworks crash over the lake from a secluded place on the east shore—but I was in a mood. Jay, always the optimist, kissed me and told me not to worry, to think about him, and only him, while I'm gone. Then he began to undress. He said he wanted us to look at each other, to really look, it would be better than any stupid photo. This is what I saw—

   his thick blond hair

   his straight (perfect) nose

   his square chin—a Superman chin

   his blue-aquamarine eyes like shallow swimming holes

   his wide, bird shoulders

   his slim waist

   his cock at attention, leaning a little to the right

   his muscular runner's legs

   his long calves

   his slender-boney feet

   the mole on his forearm shaped like West Virginia

That's him. That's Jay. I'm not sure what he saw in me, but I know I'm not as beautiful, or as manly—but he says he loves my hair and my eyes and my arms and even the deep grooves of my rib cage—and I believe him.

July 10th

I'm going to report for duty on the 16th. My stomach is doing flips. I'm already getting seasick! I tried to escape and find Jay but wasn't successful. Mama caught me and called me back to the house. She's never been happier. She was wearing a yellow dress, which looked odd on her, like something Bunny might wear. As I was walking back, she said to me, "You'll look so handsome in your uniform. The girls will be lining up to meet you. A well-pressed uniform always makes a positive impression!"

I slammed the door as I passed her on the porch. I imagined catching her fingers between the door and frame. Wham! I hate her. I've decided I won't speak to her or Papa from now on. How can they pretend to love me?

Cee hugged me when I told her the news. I'll miss her so much. I'll miss reading to her and telling her stories and playing pinochle. I wish I could tell her about Jay, but she won't understand. She's only ten.

July 13th

I tried to tell Cee today. I found her hanging laundry out back and asked her if she wanted to go to town to see if Hersh's had the new <u>Dime Detective</u>. Of course, it hadn't come in yet, so we had malts and, after a while, I made an attempt to tell her. But looking at her, seeing those wide brown eyes, that stupid goofy look on her face, I couldn't. I just couldn't. She won't understand. How can she? I must've made her a nervous wreck with all my stammering, though. She threw up her malt on the way home. All over the road. Jesus Christ. This is goddamned awful.

July 15th

I'm in bed now, and I'm looking out of my window at the edge of the woods. The moon is so bright, and the mountains, fields, and trees look like they were all carved from blue stone. Not far from the trees, I see a figure standing at the edge of the woods. It could be a scarecrow, but I don't remember it being there. I hope it's Jay. I want him to climb the side of the house and knock on the window and kiss me. If he comes, I will give him this journal and tell him to read it and think of me. He'll come. I know it. We haven't said good-bye.

When I had finished reading it, I tied the shoelace around it, triple-knotted the bow, and shoved it under my pillow. I stuffed my face into the mound of feathers. The journal felt hard as stone underneath. Cold too. It was just a sorry piece of you, a one-way conversation, a lousy epitaph. I had so many things to say to you, angry things, things I needed a response to. I didn't understand what Mr. Hersh had done to you, or why you'd kiss him back like you said, or why you would tell Jay about it. It was beyond the boundaries of what I knew about boys and men. It was the punch line of a dirty joke I was too young to understand.

But your voice coming off those pages was saying something I *did* understand—that you and Jay loved each other, a love that I'd never in my life seen an example of and, as far as I could tell, wasn't supposed to happen in the world I knew. And that, above all else, infuriated me. I felt foolish and blind. I wanted you right there in front of me, so I could grab hold of you and give you a shake and say, "Robbie, why didn't you tell me? Why didn't you let me in on your secret? Why didn't you trust me?"

Of course, I couldn't do that. You weren't there, you couldn't hear me, and your journal couldn't answer—so I screamed into the down fluff, the muffled howl parting the feathers and stretching the fabric, a whisper by the time it reached you underneath.

That night, I dreamed of you again. I heard your voice deep in my ear, a sharp, low babbling. I didn't understand what you were saying, but it sounded urgent, like you were repeating the same words over and over, so I got out of bed, crossed the room, and went to my window. I'd left it open and a breeze was stirring the draperies. I felt compelled to peer out, certain it was what you wanted me to do. Drenched in cool, uncanny moonlight, I saw you standing on the lawn in your navy blues, long shadows stretching in front of you, and your Dixie cup cap tipped forward on your forehead, casting a deep shadow over your face. You weren't looking at me; you were looking at something at the edge of the woods, a movement in the underbrush. My heart began racing. I was sure something bad was waiting under the canopy of the trees.

I called out to you and you looked up at me. "Robbie," I said, "get inside! Quick!" But when you tried to move, you couldn't. Your feet were buried up to the ankles in the yard, the soil packed tight around your pants legs, planted there like one of Papa's trees! I called again. The look on your face was so blank, so empty. I'll never forget it. That's when I woke up and let out a little scream.

The next morning, I dropped a note at the tree.

> TO: JAY.
> MEET ME HERE AT 2:00 PM.
> FROM: C.

I wrote it in big, messy block letters, holding the crayon like a dagger.

He was there before I was, leaning against the dead tree, smiling, holding his cane. His leg must've been acting up.

I trotted up to him, pulled out your journal, and shoved it at him. I gave him my damn-you-to-hell stare. He held out his hand, slow and easy like it was no big deal, and I forced the book into it.

"Are you okay?" he asked, clamping his fingers around the leather binding.

I did an about-face, stirring dirt at my feet, and started my journey back up the hill. He called after me until he caught up. He rapped the side of my leg with his cane, and I stopped.

"What's the matter?" he said. His face was sweaty and as white as a sheet.

"Leave me alone," I said.

"Why?"

"Mama and Papa told me to never talk to you again. Ever. Period."

"What happened to your cheek?"

I had tried to comb my hair close to my face, so he wouldn't see the cut and bruise.

"Papa."

"He did that!"

"I can't talk to you."

"What about Lily? We're getting close to a breakthrough."

"It's not important."

"What do you mean 'it's not important'?"

He had you, and now he had your journal. What else did he want? "It's not important. *You're* not important," I said.

He was leaning forward in pain, putting pressure on his cane, the tip sinking in the soft ground. He looked defeated and weak, and I hated him for it. I saw his body slamming hard against the side of Bunny's Olds. I wanted to do that to him, break him in two. I wanted to channel Billy's rage. Instead, I stepped forward and gave him my best playground shove. He stumbled back a few feet, wobbled, and hit the hillside with a thud, bracing himself so he wouldn't roll into the valley. His cane clattered against a few stones.

"Why did you do that?" he yelped, his face pinched and horrible. "You pushed me. Why would you do that?"

"I don't care about Lily or your stupid clues or any of it!"

"You don't mean that." Tears were welling in his eyes. He made like he was going to stand, reaching out his hand. "Please," he croaked. "Help me up."

"Stay away from me!" I said. "Just stay away."

"You don't really mean it?" he said. His face was red and feverish.

I said nothing. We just stared at each other. When he reached for me again, I jumped back and started to run. He called after me, but I didn't turn around. I didn't stop until I was home.

Sheila found herself back in the study with the photo album. She felt braver now. Kenneth wasn't going to hold her back anymore. She wasn't going to be just another lonely sucker waiting for a man, like those silly birds at the office. The future was out there, hers for the taking. She wanted to know what was inside the photo album. She wanted to take the dare, her aunt's warning be damned.

She paused, exhaled, and opened the leather-bound cover, skipping the first page. The photos on the second page were weathered black-and-whites of the house. The first photo was of the house at a distance, deep in the valley and encircled by fog. How imposing it looked! In the next photo, the house was closer and the image crisper. All the architectural details stood out, but the house's windows were black as pitch.

Shelia flipped the page. These photos were faded color shots of the interior of the house: the front parlor, with its hues of deep purple and dusty scarlet; the hall, with its mahogany wainscoting; the three-quarters staircase, on the landing of which stood sentinel an imposing grandfather clock. It was odd, she thought, that she hadn't seen a single photo of a person.

The next page was stiff and difficult to turn, the spine of the album cracking as she flattened it out. The first photo on this page was strange. It was the back of a woman sitting in the study, much as she was right then. The next photo made her gasp. She stopped, collected herself, and tried to reason it out, but there was no logic, no clear explanation for what she was seeing. Pictured in bright Technicolor was a photo of her leaning over the album!

Suddenly, the room burst with light, followed by the pop and crackle of a flashbulb—or was it lightning? She heard no thunder. She looked at the photos again. In the next one, her face was in full view. Her eyes were wide and her mouth open. A mask of fear. She glanced around the room, sure she was being watched by some boogeyman with a camera. No one was there. She began furiously flipping pages of the album.

There was a photo of her in her car, rain beating the windshield. In another photo, she was running with an umbrella over her head, her feet in a puddle. In another, she was sitting at a bar having a drink. She turned the pages faster. Then she was with a man in a dark blue suit—an Errol Flynn look-alike with eyes of black onyx and a full, glowing set of teeth. She was talking to him. He was smiling at her. Then they were in the house, in the bedroom. In the next photo, his arms were around her, holding her.

She closed the book, wrapped it in the cloth, shoved it in the safe, and spun the dial. Her breath was shallow, and she was light-headed. She needed to leave the house. Now.

10

BUNNY

I didn't touch anything at first.

Quilts and sheets Jay had hung as curtains glowed in the afternoon sun like the sooty stained glass of a medieval church. In the middle of the room, his rickety picnic table was piled high with books and papers. One book called *The Science of Codes* lay open, dog-eared and yellowed with age. Another book jumped out at me: *An American Tragedy*, an equally weathered, two-volume set. His cot was unmade, the sheets twisted into a tight ball. His Purple Heart and an assortment of photographs of soldiers were pinned to the fabric above his bed, all askew. On his dresser, among old cologne bottles and empty film cartons, was a worn photo of Robbie. He sat at the end of the rowboat, shirtless, fishing pole in hand. I picked it up. On the back, it was dated June 8, 1943.

In his dresser, I found clothes shoved in haphazardly, mismatched socks rolled together and undershirts in wads, and in the bottom drawer, a jumble of camera equipment, but no journal. I searched under his bed and came across the shoes from the crime scene wrapped in a paper bag. Letitia must have returned them to him, or he took them away from her when she was distracted.

I cleared the bottles of liquor and a pair of muddy shoes off the top of his military trunk at the foot of his bed. I pulled on the top a few times before I realized it wasn't stuck but locked. A thin gap opened between the trunk's lid—which had been warped with use—and the base. I struggled with it until I heard voices coming around the edge of the conservatory. I swiftly crossed the room and plunged deeper into the house.

I considered hiding in the bathroom-cum-darkroom, but I didn't want to get trapped, so I found myself in a dusty, unused dining room. A thin ribbon of light peeked between the heavy brocade curtains, hitting the crystal chandelier and casting brilliant fragments on the opposite wall. I wedged myself between wainscoting and a large china cabinet.

I listened for the squeak of the porch's door, but I heard nothing, not even the murmur of voices. I held my breath and concentrated. Silence—not even the whine of cicadas. I stepped out of the shadow, and then the doorbell—presumably to the front door—chimed. It was loud and metallic. I leapt back into the shadow.

Slow and steady footsteps emerged from some distant corner of the house, muffled by carpet, then loud again, moving closer and closer. I debated whether to dash through the dining room and out Jay's porch or to stay put. When I heard Letitia's clunky shoes knocking at the floorboards in the next room, I flattened myself against the wall.

She cursed at the doorbell, mumbled something about door-to-door salesmen, and opened the door with a vicious tug. Light poured in, illuminating the rich reds and browns of the carved three-quarters stairway. I heard the voices of two other people, a man and a woman.

"Mrs. Greenwood," the man said.

"Yes."

"We need to speak to you. May we come in?" the woman said.

"I'm in the middle of something."

"This is very important," the man said.

"Say what you've come to say right here. I'm not letting a soul past this door. The house isn't prepared to receive company."

"It's about your grandson," the woman said.

"What about him?"

"His behavior."

"Say what you've come to say, or I'm closing this door."

"Your grandson is a deviant, an invert," the man said. "You know that."

Silence.

"I don't want him anywhere near my daughter," he continued.

"He isn't bothering anyone."

"He corrupted my son, and now he's after Ceola."

"That's nonsense. He's a good boy."

"Our Robbie *was* a good boy!" Margery cried. So it was Ceola's parents at the door. The door hinges squeaked and then stopped. It seemed Letitia was trying to close the door on them. "Our son was a good, brave boy, who gave his life—"

"Jay's a good boy too. You don't know what he's suffered. How he's still suffering."

I recalled Letitia's frail body in those floppy yellow gloves and big muck boots. She was a force to be reckoned with. She didn't give a damn what people thought of her. Although the struggle with the Blisses was primarily a verbal one, I imagined her pushing the door closed on them, digging her heels into the wood, dropping her thin shoulders for more leverage. Like B-movie werewolves, the Blisses clawed at the front door, their nails tearing at the paint, teeth gnashing.

For a moment, I thought I might help Letitia. "Go away!" I would yell. "Leave her alone." But I remained silent, listening as she shut the door.

I heard Margery say, "Some of us have suffered more than others," before the lock clicked into place.

Letitia didn't move for some time. Then she said, "Fools," and left the hall, her shoes slapping the wood as she retreated to the other side of the house.

I wanted to run to her and tell her I loved Jay, that although I didn't fully understand him, I knew he wasn't a deviant. But that would've been unwise, to say the least. I would have to explain to her why I was in the house, that when I discovered Ceola's note in the tree calling a meeting with Jay, I had felt marginalized again. I would have to tell her I decided to snoop while he and Ceola were rendezvousing. But I knew I wouldn't have time to explain any of that; if she saw me, she would head straight for her shotgun.

I counted to ten, stepped out of the shadows, and made my way back to Jay's lair. I took a few minutes to put things back in order. I didn't want Jay to know I'd been there. As I was doing so, the corner of a piece of paper, sticking out from under the lid of Jay's locked trunk, caught my eye. I recognized its powder-blue color. I must have dislodged it while tugging on the lid. With little effort, it slid out. Its size and feel were immediately familiar to me. It was the first page of Lily's letter Jay told us he had found in Frank Vellum's garbage:

May 22, 1945

Jay,

You know what it's like to be from the mountains and to be so trapped. The city is the only place I could be really, truly happy. I imagine you feel the same way. And yet here we are. You in Royal Oak, me in Jitters Gap. Can you picture us, the three of us, living fancy-free in DC at the Howard and having nights out on the town? Oh, I want to feel that free!

I'm tickled you and I stumbled on each other. Those backstreet places aren't the dark, seedy dives everyone makes them out to be. I can do without the pushy girls at the Showboat or the boys in uniform at Carroll's (but I'm sure you don't mind a look!). Croc's is a good place, but that Teddie B.—where does she get those get-ups? What a mess! Oh, but I wish I was there now.

So I should get to the point. I really need your help. I'm pregnant. That no-good bastard Billy forced himself on me this winter even after I told him many times . . .

She was his friend. He knew her well, from the beginning.

I felt like I had been struck in the stomach by something heavy; I sat on the edge of his cot to catch my breath. To have lied so boldly to Ceola and me was simply astonishing.

My mind bounced from question to question like a ball in a pinball machine. What were these "backstreet places" she mentioned?

The Showboat, Carroll's, Croc's? Were they bars? Dance clubs? What about the Howard? Was it a boardinghouse? A hotel? Who was Teddie B.? And what did Lily mean when she wrote Jay wouldn't "mind a look" at the boys in uniform?

The old questions returned too. Where was Lily's body? Who was George? What about Aunt Kathy? Was Billy or was Frank responsible for Lily's disappearance and murder, or was it someone else, perhaps Bernice Hersh, the pharmacist's wife, or—and I didn't want to admit it—Jay himself? It seemed impossible that he could be responsible for her murder, so I pushed the thought from my mind. But what was his relationship to her? Had she been his girlfriend? I now knew undeniably that he had misled us, so everything he had shown us or said to us was in question.

I wanted another look at the photos he'd taken of her. So I searched his room again, checking under the bed and in his dresser a second time. I didn't know how to pick the lock on the trunk, but I did give his darkroom a thorough going over. I couldn't find a single print, which was odd. I decided the photos must be in the trunk, but I couldn't break it open without giving away that I'd been snooping. Since I couldn't see the photos, I decided I'd do the next best thing and return to the scene of the crime.

A quarter of an hour later, I found myself again perched on top of the boulder, staring down at the rocky terrain where Jay had discovered Lily's body. The sky above was darkening with afternoon storm clouds, and the shadows shifted and deepened. I heard the breeze sweeping through the trees, coming toward me. Jay had never indicated exactly where he found Lily's body. He'd just allowed us to interpret the location, to make our best guess. Then Ceola had discovered her shoes.

I closed my eyes and tried to summon Lily to me, but all I saw was her head twisted to one side, hair white against the dark soil, her blank white body against darkness, suspended there as if by a string, dangling just out of reach. That, of course, was the point. Focus on *her*. On her hair. On her dress. On her gloves. On her shoes. On the blood. But not the backdrop. Not the shape of the stones behind her. Not the contours of the earth underneath her. Although I had no proof, I felt certain Lily hadn't been killed where Jay told us she'd been. But why?

I felt a force—that Prescott determination—rising up through me. I was going to confront Jay and demand an explanation. He would have to explain, and his response would tell me something.

Royal Oak, VA
2/15/2000

Bunny,

Wouldn't you know it, but a "mysterious" envelope showed up on my doorstep too! It came just after I mailed my first letter to you. Someone wants us to pay attention to old times.

When I pulled the photo out of the envelope and saw her again, chills came over me, toes to fingertips. That made me start thinking about it, everything that happened that summer—what Jay was trying show us and the horrible things that happened because of it.

I also thought about everything that happened afterward. Things I don't think you know about, or if you do, it's second- or third-hand.

Papa was charged with assault for what he did. But did you know that even though he was acquitted, he still lost his job at Dixie Dew? Maybe you did. It was hard on us, even though he deserved it. He spent years working at Hills' dairy farm and died with a bottle in his hand, literally.

Mama had to go to work too. She scrubbed floors and bathrooms in the big homes on North Street, like the one you grew up in. She doubled over mopping Milly Evans's kitchen floor. Struck dead at age 70. But I'll be the first to say it, her bitterness kept her alive too long. Oh, now I'm just rambling on . . .

So what do we do? Whoever sent the photos wants us to talk. Should we?

-C

11

CEOLA

When I was in my thirties, I ran into Sylvester Hughes, of all places, outside of Hersh's Pharmacy. Remember him, Robbie? Would you have known him? He was that nice black man who worked for Letitia Greenwood for a time, before the money from the sale of Dixie Dew ran dry. He was sitting outside the pharmacy on a bench, sipping a milk shake. His long torso was bent with age, and his face was baggy and scored with wrinkles. We exchanged howdy-dos and talked about Dixie Dew for a while. I asked him how many years he worked for the Greenwoods, and he pouted his lips and shook his head.

"Five or so," he said, his voice deep and rough, but easy to understand. "Mrs. Greenwood was demanding. I tell you, she could keep you busy from sunup to sundown. That woman had endless energy, and she always expected me to move at the same rate she was moving. Good Lord, I remember the day she hit me with a broom because I wasn't sweeping the back porch fast enough. She just snatched it from my hands and swatted me in the bottom with it. 'Mr. Hughes, you're a ne'er-do-well!' she said, her face beet red, about to spit fire. I just smiled at her. She gave me a mean look and said, 'An imperturbable ne'er-do-well at that.' She left me alone for the rest of the day. Imperturbable—what a word to come out of that lady! I guess you could say we understood each other. But I can't say I liked it."

"How about Jay?"

He guided the straw to his mouth, his fingers like tentacles, moving slow and gentle, not fumbling or fidgeting, and took a sip of his shake. "He didn't talk to me much. Mrs. Greenwood wouldn't allow it. He'd come home from school and she'd send him directly to the study. After a bit, she'd join him and help him with his homework. I could hear them when I was working in the kitchen. Her voice was different. Gentler. The only times I heard her laugh—or the young man, to think of it—was through the walls of that room."

"So she was good to him?"

He caught me with those dark eyes of his. He knew my story. He knew what I wanted to know.

"In one way of thinking, she treated him like a prince. She loved him and wanted to keep him safe. In another way of thinking, he was her prisoner." He rubbed his knee. "What's all the attention and knowledge in this world, if you don't have your freedom?"

"I see what you mean."

Papa used to say that if you know a man's family, you know him. I don't think you can know everything about a person from his family, but you can get a pretty good idea. Not long after I ran into Sylvester at the drugstore, I began asking everyone, anyone, about Jay and his family. Mama and Papa wouldn't talk to me about the Greenwoods, but other people, particularly the First Presbyterian Church ladies in their bouffants, pastel knit suits, and pearl chokers, would. Letitia, from time to time, still attended church, so even when I was an adult, gossip about her was still alive and well. Sam and I, just newlyweds then, joined the church, and I began nosing around, always the detective, I guess. Missy West, Barbara King, and Amy Matthews, whose husband I worked for at Twin Oaks after Sam's death, were all, at one point in time, close friends of Letitia's, and all of them wanted to spill the beans on the Greenwoods.

Over time, I pieced together their stories.

The part that has to do with Jay, the only part worth mentioning, began the night Georgie Greenwood knelt in the middle of the Harvest Ball and asked Betty Blackwell for her hand in marriage. Missy West told me the whole story while we were arranging flowers on the altar one Saturday. Supposedly, when Betty said yes, friends and family applauded and popped up from their seats, napkins falling from their laps and glasses overturning on the tables. Georgie kissed her, bending her back in his arms.

"Georgie and Betty seemed to promise a bright future for our little town," Missy said. "You don't remember this, but the walls of that ballroom were at one time painted with murals of cattle farmers, salt miners, and local tradesmen, all depicted hard at work, milking cows or hauling salt or stitching quilts or what have you, and behind them, completing the scene, were our blue mountains and valleys of pink rhododendron. Georgie and Betty fit right in, like they had been painted there too."

Over coffee at the Pie Shop, Barbara King told me George Greenwood Sr. took the engagement as a sign his son was settling down and

would soon take over the family business. She explained that George
Sr. had toyed with the formula for Sid's Snappy Soda and had reintro-
duced it as Snap Cola, which was well on its way to becoming a hit. So
he needed his son to take on greater responsibility at Dixie Dew and
behave like a proper heir apparent.

"Betty, the dear," Barbara said, after another sip of coffee, "tempered Georgie's wild streak—well, for a time."

Soon Jason George Greenwood was born. His grandmother was
particularly fond of him, always cooing over him, calling him her
"beautiful boy." But after Jay's birth, the marriage began to crack.

"Rumor had it Georgie was stepping out with some horrible girl in
Washington," Barbara said, dropping her voice and leaning in, "but no
one had proof. About the time whispers of his infidelity became parlor
gossip—which of course is their first stop before becoming stone-cold
fact—news of the terrible car accident came, and the scandal quickly
became a downright tragedy. Just awful."

The entire town went into mourning. George Sr. proceeded to drink
himself into a stupor and lose control of Dixie Dew, selling it to Wayne
Prescott in 1933 and dying soon after.

After saying my good-byes to Barbara, I went to the library and
looked up the article about the accident. The *Royal Oak Times*
reported that the couple had been driving back from a late-night
party in DC. Georgie had gunned his car to beat the 12:20 freight
train to the Culler's Mountain crossing. The Duesenberg won the race
initially but bounded over the tracks at an awkward angle, couldn't
manage a sharp right turn, and collided with the cliff on the other
side, rolling back under the passing train. Betty was thrown from the
car, her neck broken on impact. Georgie was still in the car when it

toppled, side-over-side, underneath the moving train. Under the headline TWO DEAD AT CULLER'S CROSSING, a photograph of the mangled black Duesenberg peered out, its silver fender bent out of shape like a crooked smile.

"Can you imagine?" Amy Matthews said over dessert at a church picnic, her white-gloved hands darting back and forth. "Letitia went through all of it. The confusion, the grieving, the loneliness. As a young lady, she wasn't a beauty, but she had a sparkle, a real intelligence, I remember. That must've been what intrigued George Greenwood."

George and Letitia fell in love, married, and made a happy home together, but she nearly died giving birth to Georgie and, because of it, couldn't have a second child. She had wanted a large family. To make peace with her situation, she poured all her love into raising the one son, spoiling him, by all accounts. When Georgie entered school, she became involved in Junior League and dedicated herself to the community, toiling away at the church bazaar and set-designing the Harvest Ball. Royal Oak society followed her lead. Dixie Dew Bottling Company thrived, and for years she was queen of the town.

"A real belle," Amy said. "But after her son's accident and husband's decline, the queen became a hermit. Fodder for ghost stories." She shook her head and touched her gloved hands to her heart. She wanted me to understand that it was a real tragedy.

It was this Letitia you and I knew, Robbie. The witch in the ramshackle farmhouse, the town kook. It was this Letitia that poor Sylvester Hughes went to work for, God rest his soul.

He told me something else that day outside Hersh's.

One blistering summer afternoon, only a few weeks before Letitia would fire him, he was standing outside watering the azaleas, letting the mist from the hose cool him off, when he overheard raised voices from the porch. He listened at a window, which he had cracked for ventilation earlier that day.

"I love him, Grandma," Jay said several times, each time louder, more forceful. "I *love* him."

Letitia wailed with desperation, "No, oh no, oh no!" as if someone had her arm twisted behind her back and was wrenching it hard. "How could you, Jay?" she groaned. "Stupid fool. You break my heart—a heart that's already been broken so many times. Shattered in pieces so many times. *Shattered*."

Sylvester wondered if he should get help. But instead, he backed away from the porch and finished the watering on the other side of the house.

"Better to mind my own business," he told me.

But during the summer of '45, I was far from piecing Jay's life together.

Days after I had given him your journal and pushed him down, I could still hear him reeling in pain on the side of the hill: "Why did you do that?" It was a mean thing to do, and I knew it, but I didn't want to admit it.

So I kept to my room, passing the days reading adventure stories and flipping through detective magazines, avoiding Mama and Papa—particularly Papa, who obliged me by avoiding me, too, his conscience apparently still raw from his outburst. Along with Jay's, his voice rang in my ears: "Why were you driving around in that fancy car with that queer boy and Princess Prescott?"

The cut under my eye was puffy and pink. I wanted it to get infected and scar, so whenever he would look at me, he'd remember what he'd done. But it healed smooth.

Jay guessed I'd come out from under my shell and get curious again. After all, I wasn't angry with him, not really, just frustrated at the things I didn't understand about you and him. One morning, about a week later, I went to the tree, hoping for a cryptogram or a clue, some attempt to communicate. As if he could read my thoughts, he had left a note on the back of a flyer for a traveling carnival called Zelkos.

On the front of the flyer, a magician beamed with sparkles in his eyes and an exaggerated top hat on his head. Behind him was a carnival scene complete with a Ferris wheel, a carousel, and grinning cartoon circus animals. Over the top, it read, THE AMAZING ZELKOS CARNIVAL. THE BEST TRAVELING ATTRACTION ON THE EAST COAST!!! And at the bottom, AUGUST 12TH-18TH AT THE FAIRGROUND CROSSINGS, and it listed the attractions:

HERCULEAN 50-FOOT BIG WHEEL

MARVELOUS MERRY-GO-ROUND

HAUNTED CASTLE FUNHOUSE

MADAME ZEPHYR FORTUNE-TELLER

ZELKOS PETTING ZOO

MASSIVE MIDWAY

AND MUCH, MUCH MORE!!!

On the back, Jay had scrawled, "Cee—Do you want to go?" I slid the flyer into my dress pocket and set out for the Greenwood farm.

When I arrived, Jay was lounging under a tree. His back was against the gnarled bark, his head tilted forward over a book and his cane propped beside him. A breeze stirred his blond hair, a moment right out of a Norman Rockwell painting, and he looked up. I wasn't sure what to expect. He might have lured me there for an argument or, at the very least, to demand I apologize for pushing him down. I didn't want him to try to squeeze an apology from me. When I saw his face, all smile and goodwill, I knew he wasn't going to try. I also knew something had changed in him.

He snapped his book closed, a well-worn Agatha Christie novel, and said, "Well, it took you long enough."

"I was busy."

"I see."

"Papa and Mama needed me at home."

The light in his eyes dimmed. "Did they?"

"Yes."

"Well, all right." He grabbed his cane and hoisted himself up. "Do you want to go to the carnival? It's only here for another day."

I considered it for a moment. "How will we get there?"

"Grandma's car. She won't know we're gone until we're halfway there."

"Okay."

The station wagon's wood paneling was gray with wear and rot, and its black paint was scored with gravel marks. The front passenger's-side window had been shattered and removed. Jay put the car in neutral, and we pushed it a few yards to the downward slope of the driveway.

"It hasn't run in a while," he said, "so it needs a little help."

It began rolling slowly, its wheels crunching the gravel, and we hopped in. Jay jiggled the key in the ignition and, after several tries, the engine roared to life. A thrill passed through me. I was with Jay, and the adventure was back on. I wondered if Letitia would hear us and tear out of the house waving a gun like a maniac. But she didn't. Jay shifted gears, which squealed and popped into place, and we were on our way, letting the dust spin little tornadoes behind us.

As we reached the ridge above the Fairground Crossings, we saw rows and rows of parked cars to the east, bumpers and headlights winking at us in the morning sun. The midway stretched out past the parking lot in that large field situated smack-dab between the north and south forks of the river. Bunches of bright helium balloons yanked at the corners of the booths, as if any minute, the midway might detach from the ground and float away. Two billowy yellow-and-white tents were pitched at the back of the field, one housing the petting zoo and the other the funhouse and hall of mirrors. At the center, just behind the blur of a spinning merry-go-round, the Ferris wheel rotated slowly, offering its passengers to the sky and then, with an unwilling lurch, bringing them to the ground again.

We walked down into the crowd and weaved our way to the ticket booth. On the wooden fence beside the entrance, the carnies had pasted war posters—"Buy War Bonds!" "Rub Out the Axis!" "Let 'em Have It!" "Give 'em Both Barrels!" "YOU Back the Attack," and "Food is a Weapon, Don't Waste It!" I thought of you, Robbie. But one poster in particular stopped me. It was of a dead American airborne soldier strapped into a parachute, his body limp, arms at his sides, head forward, floating toward the ground through a night sky full of yellow parachutes, and lit up by bursts of artillery fire. His rifle was pointed toward the ground, emphasizing the pointlessness of the mission. Across the top of the poster, in a banner of bold black letters, it said, "CARELESS TALK . . . got there first."

I wanted Jay's arm around me, my head close to his chest. I wanted to pretend he was you. I wanted him to tell me that being with him and disobeying Papa's wishes wasn't wrong. He gently put his hand on my shoulder and guided me to the window of the ticket booth, where a leathery old woman with white hair on her chin sold us tickets. She smiled and asked if I was his kid sister. Jay said I was.

The midway was a river of excited boys and girls and their bothered parents, who were steering the kids to and from a confusion of smells—popcorn, hay, fried bread, grease, manure. The crowd parted for a second, and the shine of chrome from a cotton candy machine caught my eye. Inside it, a perfect cone of pink sugar spun like a ballerina in a music box. My mouth fell open.

"I had you pegged for more of a caramel apple kid," Jay said.

I smiled and shook my head.

He bought me a small spindle of "Strawberry Heaven," and as soon as he handed it to me, I tore off a piece and gobbled it up. The flavoring reminded me of the Jell-O salad Mama made every Christmas. Do you remember you told me Jell-O was made from jellyfish that were raised and bred in big vats of strawberry juice? You were so full of it, Robbie. I was never that gullible. Of course, when you told me it was actually made of cow and pig bones, I didn't believe you, either.

"Let's go to the funhouse," Jay said.

"Is it scary?"

"Nah, not really."

A large, sickle-shaped mouth with two jewel-green cat's eyes leered at us from over the entrance to the funhouse. The entrance was manned by an old guy with droopy, watery eyes and a nose purple with a web of burst blood vessels. As we presented our pass, he grinned, flashing us his rotten teeth, and said, "Have fun, you two."

I gasped a little but pretended it was a burp. Jay didn't seem to notice. We stepped through the cat's mouth, and it was nearly dark inside. In front of us, framed by the dim glow of low-wattage bulbs, was a sign that read **THE HAUNTED CASTLE, 13 METERS A HEAD** in bloody letters. We heard a scream and then nervous laughter echoing back through the tunnel. I grabbed Jay's arm.

"Is this okay?" he said.

"Sure," I said.

And we entered.

My best defense was—and still is—to explain horror away, to break it into its parts, to drag it out into the open. So I thought about how the Amazing Zelkos Carnival created the illusion. For instance, the mist that snaked across our path, I just knew, was evaporating from a trough of dry ice backstage, blown our way by a system of fans. I'd read about dry ice in a *Weird Stories* article called "How to Make Your Own Haunted House: Ten Terrifying Effects." The howls, screams, and moans sounded hollow, tinny, and if you listened closely, you could tell they were on a prerecorded loop. The flying bats were rubber, and the dancing skeletons were papier-mâché. Both bounced on thin elastic cords suspended from the ceiling.

When Dracula popped up from his coffin and the Mummy sprung out of his sarcophagus, I'll tell you, I jumped sky-high, but I wasn't fooled. I knew they were carnies. I caught a whiff of their ripe, sweaty clothes. When Lizzie Borden, all rosy-cheeked and crazy-eyed, swung her cardboard ax at us, and when the giant hooded executioner dangled a noose in front of us and groaned, "You're next!" I wanted to yell back at them, "I know you're not real. I know who you are. I can smell you." All the same, I held Jay tightly, digging my fingers into his arm, just in case I was wrong.

We made our way into the hall of mirrors. A fat, egg-headed Jay and a tall, skinny Cee stared back at us, plumping up and thinning out as we stepped side to side. I giggled. Jay's eyes stretched back across his forehead like Mickey Mouse's, and his chin disappeared into his neck. I turned to him to make sure the real Jay hadn't lost his proportions, and behind him, just leaving the room, I saw a greasy blond head and wide shoulders that were familiar to me. For a heartbeat, I couldn't place who it was. Then I bit my lip—I knew it! It was Billy Witherspoon.

Was he really here? Or was I just seeing things, my real fears mingling with my pretend fears? I stepped forward, and Jay caught my arm, leading me to the exit and into the bright sun.

"That was pretty scary," he said. I didn't believe him. "What scared you the most?"

I wanted to say something about Billy, but now, in the light of day, I'd begun doubting what I saw.

"When the Mummy popped out, my heart stopped," I said. It *had* frightened the bejesus out of me. "How about you?"

He thought about it. "The flashing lights."

"Huh . . . why?"

"I don't know."

We stopped at the carousel for a minute and watched it go. The other kids were lost in the movement of the ride—up and down, around and around, their screams cut loose from the blurs of colorful clothing. I'd started to reason that if I had actually seen Billy, he wouldn't have left us alone. There would've been a tussle—or at least words. I looked up at Jay. His cheeks were as pale as shaved ice, and his lips were clamped tight. I wanted him to tease me about being jumpy, about being a scaredy-cat, the way you used to, Robbie. But he was somewhere else.

"I guess you weren't very scared," I said.

"No. I'm sorry."

"You've seen scarier."

"It was swell—I just—"

"The war was a lot scarier, I bet."

"That's it. That's it, exactly."

I took his hand and, as best I could, held it in mine, a little embarrassed about being so forward. He didn't look at me, but he squeezed my hand and held it tight. My heart started thumping. I was blushing.

At last, he let go and said, "I've got something to tell you. I'll tell you at the top of the Ferris wheel."

So we made our way to the wheel and stood in line, not saying a word to each other. I felt uncomfortable and curious. Was it something about Lily? We hadn't talked about her at all that day. Or was it about your journal, about him loving you? That was something I already knew. Whatever it was, it seemed like it would flow out of his darkening mood.

The line started moving and we were ushered to a carriage by a fat, dark-haired woman with a thick Russian accent. "Keep hands and arms inside," she growled, as we slid into the cool metal seat.

After a minute or two, the wheel jerked to life, and our chair swung back and forth. I grabbed the edge of the seat, a little nervous. The machinery of the wheel smelled of fresh oil, but the cogs clicked and gnashed like grinding teeth. As we began to lift, the midday sun warmed my face, and I released my grip on the seat. I noticed people crisscrossing the midway, arms filled with stuffed animals and multicolored balloons. One of the latter escaped a little girl's hand and drifted above the trees, a dot of red against the sky. I heard braying and a squawk or two from a rare bird at the petting zoo. I smelled the fresh hay and the slightly comforting, slightly repugnant odor of animals. I watched as teenage girls and boys entered the Haunted Castle, each couple stalling before the entrance, and then, after the usual pleading and joking, the boys urged the girls on, feeding themselves to the cat at its entrance, gobbled up by its smile.

As we reached the top, the shape of the hills past the carnival, past the river, drew me in. They felt nearer to me, like I could just reach out and touch them, as if from this viewpoint I could understand them better. Maybe that's why I didn't react when Jay reached across me and placed his hand over my heart, pressing the light fabric of my dress against my skin. He leaned into me and kissed me. It was a long, motionless kiss, lips against lips, warm but not rude, not forceful. When he released me, he looked pained, his complexion flat and bloodless.

"You smell like him," he said.

For a long while, there was nothing, just the sky and the mountains. Then the wheel broke forward, and we began our journey back to earth.

"What were you going to tell me?" I said, scooting away from him, the chair tilting to one side.

"It's something I need to show you. I need to pull back the—"

He didn't finish his sentence.

Something on the ground caught his eye and he leaned forward. His hands, wrapped around the security bar, tensed, his knuckles white as bleached bone. His forehead wrinkled with concern—or was it fear? What—or who—did he see? Was it Billy? Had I really seen him? I searched the crowd, but all I could see were dots of color moving this way and that.

I bit my lip and felt a terrible shiver—"a presentiment of doom," Mama had once called it. She said it was when you see the future but you can't understand it. As I stared at the swirling crowd, was I seeing the future, all mixed up and out of order, like a spilled jigsaw puzzle?

Once we were on the ground, Jay took my hand without saying a word and we made a beeline for the back exit of the carnival.

The rain was whipping hard against the windshield, making it difficult for Sheila to see the sign: WHITE MOUNTAIN LOUNGE, 1 MILE ON THE RIGHT. She needed to be with people. She almost missed the birds at the office. The more distance she put between herself and her aunt's house, the better she felt. She thought of Kenneth and again found herself yearning for his hands, his touch. She shook the thought from her head and focused on the road.

She was pleased to see so many cars parked at the lounge, a one-story log cabin–style building with an eight-foot carved bear on its hind legs guarding the front door and a welcoming red glow at its windows.

As she opened her car door and popped her umbrella open, a strong gust of wind rushed at her and tugged her forward. "Oh, golly," she said, and, after a brief struggle, she steadied herself and aimed the point of the umbrella into the wind. Her feet and arms were completely soaked, but it was only after she dashed across the parking lot and into the bar that she remembered that her feet and arms had been wet earlier that day. The thought chilled her, and it was staved off only by the promise of a drink.

The jukebox murmured the soft, sultry squeak of Duke Ellington's saxophonist. Couples danced together in the far corner, silhouettes against the rose-tinted light cast by dim sconces along the back wall. Sheila approached the wood-paneled bar, and a broad-shouldered bartender the size of a lumberjack glowered at her. He had a bit of food caught in his beard.

She smiled and said, "A gimlet with a twist of lime, please."

"Coming up, girlie," he said.

She turned and looked around the room. In the corner, nestled in a booth, was a woman who reminded her of herself. She looked her age. She was laughing and flirting with a man who Sheila couldn't see. Her hair was pushed back with a headband, and loose blond curls spilled out the back; her lips were red and full and expressive. Smoke was trailing from her cigarette, curling around the edge of the overhanging light fixture. She was enjoying herself. It was Saturday night, after all. That's what Sheila would have been doing, if she'd been back in the city. That's what she *would* be doing all over the world, once she sold Brimblevine and cashed in her inheritance.

The gimlet warmed her stomach, and the shock of the experience had begun to subside. She had heard of this sort of thing before—extended hallucinations after an emotional event. She found a seat at the bar and leaned over her drink, swirling it with a swizzle stick. Maybe she had eaten something bad, she thought. Or perhaps it was mold? She had read somewhere about hallucinogenic mold. But then what about her aunt's warning? "Seek not the future to escape the past"—what did it even mean? If she was being honest with herself, she didn't believe in warnings and curses and that sort of voodoo. She was a common-sense girl at heart.

She heard the door open behind her and felt someone approach. A man. She smelled his cologne, a deep musky scent. She glanced up and saw his profile. It was a good profile. He had a large, shapely nose, a stern jaw, and a thin, well-maintained mustache. His complexion was smooth, almost polished. What was such a refined fellow doing in rural New Hampshire? Then he looked at her and smiled. A chill of recognition ran through her. Was he the man from the photograph? It couldn't be, could it? Certainly not.

"Hello," he said, extending his hand and flashing his straight, perfectly white teeth. "I'm Thomas."

12

BUNNY

For several days, questions spun through my head as I built up the nerve to confront Jay with the first page of Lily's letter that I'd found in his room. I considered the places she had mentioned—DC, the Howard, Carroll's, the Showboat, Croc's—and the people she had mentioned—Teddie B. and Billy, and in the second page of the letter, George and Aunt Kathy. I wanted to know, *I had to know*, what these places really meant and who these people really were. So finally I set off for the Greenwood farm to find Jay.

Like a diligent Blue Hearts Club member, I checked for an encoded message as I passed by the dead tree. The hollow was empty. I took the shortcut over a ridge, the way Ceola often took, but one I usually avoided because of the scraggly underbrush and the steepness of the grade.

On the climb up the ridge, I grabbed tree limbs above me to hoist myself over the outcroppings of limestone bedrock. Toward the top of the climb, I noticed a bright yellow piece of paper caught in a mesh of blackberry bushes. I would've dismissed it as trash if it had been in a more frequently trafficked area, but here it was out of place.

I plucked it from the bramble. It was a flyer for the Amazing Zelkos Carnival. On the back, Jay had written: "Cee—Do you want to go?" I stuffed the flyer into the pocket of my dress and quickened my pace.

When I arrived at the house, I threw open the door to Jay's lair in an impulsive, almost cavalier gesture. Again, I had been left out. I wanted Jay to pay attention. But to my surprise (and I *was* quite startled), Letitia was there on his cot, a faint outline in the semidarkness of the room. She didn't bother to look up.

"Mrs. Greenwood?" I said rather loudly, fear registering in my voice. She didn't respond. I repeated myself, but more softly this time.

"He's gone," she said.

"Where? To the carnival?" I held up the flyer.

She raised her head, and a thin bar of light fell across her face. Her watery blue eye blinked. For an instant, I felt certain she knew everything. I stepped forward.

"Stop!" she said, and I stopped.

"I don't understand."

"These shoes aren't your shoes?" In her lap were the ribbon-bowed Ferragamos.

"They don't fit. I already showed you."

"You did. Yes, you did."

"They belong to a dead woman."

She looked away.

"Mrs. Greenwood, do you know anything about Lily Vellum?"

"I couldn't say."

"Jay knew her."

"And you believe the shoes belong to her?"

"Yes."

"You're wrong about that."

"Why?"

"Get out of here. Leave me alone."

"Who do they belong to? Who is FL?"

"Ask my grandson. Now, get out of here!"

"Please."

She reached behind her and pulled her shotgun across her lap. The end of its polished black barrel caught the light from the door. One of the shoes fell from her knees and clattered on the tiles, the *FL R* showing on its sole. She didn't move to pick it up.

I backed out of the room, keeping my eyes on her and clutching the side of the doorframe as a guide. Even out in the sunlight again, I could still see Letitia's pale form through the open door, a slumped crescent on the bed. I was unsure what to do, so I just backed away, eventually turning and springing forward, wanting to break into a run but afraid to admit I was that frightened.

If I lose someone at a concert or a flea market or a public event of any sort, they have to find me, not the other way around. I simply can't spot individuals in a crowd. Often, however, I do find what I'm *not* looking for. That, it seems, is my talent.

This time it was Bob Bliss. I saw him because, like me, he was going against the current, both of us looking at the carnival-goers, not at the attractions.

His face was flushed and puffed out at the jowls, and his hands were balled into tight fists. I ducked behind a kiosk plastered with clown faces and anthropomorphized circus animals, all glowering back at me, grinning, jeering. As Bob blazed through the crowd, I followed him, searching for Jay and Ceola as I went and hoping to locate them before he did.

My father knew something of Bob Bliss's temperament. When news of Robbie's death had come, Bob had asked for two weeks off of work, and Father, who was sympathetic, told Bob he could take a few days off, but not weeks. He had told him, "A man needs to keep working, especially during these dark times, or he'll lose his way in grief." Bob had sneered at him, called him a tyrant, and stormed out of his office. Within a week, Bob had spread word of his grievance. He went as far as to have several of the other men sign a petition on his behalf.

"In ordinary circumstances," Father had told us over the dinner table, "I would fire an employee for such behavior, but the man has lost his son." He looked at me. "I can't imagine what it would be like to lose a child." Bob simmered down eventually and the angry petition evaporated, but my father remained wary of him.

On the fairway, Bob looked up and stopped, as if he had suddenly grown roots. The carnival-goers flowed around him, giving him a wide berth, as if they too sensed his volatility. His eyes were bright, and his hands came together, fingers interlocking—a disingenuous supplicant, rage nearly splitting his false prayer in two. The top of the Ferris wheel was in his line of sight.

There they were, legs dangling against the sky. Time seemed to slow and expand, and details flashed before me: first, Jay's blond hair, a feathery, flame-tipped corona in the sun. Then, his arm bent loosely, almost languidly. His shirt, denim blue and thin over his shoulders, held in place by a pair of brown suspenders. His body—a man's body—moving toward Ceola, covering her. Her white sailor dress, billowing with the breeze, its navy middy collar turned back against her neck. Her small hands by her sides, an elbow and forearm still exposed to the light. The bucket seat gently swaying.

Although concealed in a shadow, what I saw was clearly a kiss.

Bob's knuckles reddened. Veins stood out on the tops of his hands and down his forearms. His jaw muscles rippled.

I could only stand there and take it in, my jealousy of Ceola and my love for Jay locked in a furious stalemate. I was angry with Jay, but I was confused too. What did it mean, his kissing her? I felt certain he did have something to do with Lily's disappearance and death, but as the cliché goes, it didn't add up.

As the Ferris wheel began to rotate again, I saw Bob move toward the base. I went after him and called out: "Mr. Bliss! Mr. Bliss!" He didn't respond. I caught up to him and grabbed his arm.

"What!" he growled, and whirled around. He glared at me, his whiskey breath hot on my face, and shook my grip, knocking me backward. My heels caught in the dirt, and I stumbled into a mother and her daughter, the girl's cotton candy sticking to my blouse. The mother caught me by the elbows and propped me up.

"That awful man!" she said. "Are you okay, sweetie?" I saw the little girl's face; she must've been just five or six. Her eyes were round as quarters.

"I'm fine," I said, finding my footing. Then to the little girl, "I'll be just fine."

By this time, the wheel had deposited Jay and Ceola at the bottom. I began searching for them but couldn't find them. Bob had vanished too.

13

CEOLA

s we drove—houses passing by, pastures passing by, trees passing by—my poor brain was still numb from the episode on the Ferris wheel. It was like Jay had dangled a pocket watch in front of me and hypnotized me, like I was at his command, but instead of sticking a new thought in my head, he had only left it blank.

When we started up the mountain, the station wagon took the sharp switchbacks hard, slinging me across the cracked leather seat, chafing the backs of my legs. I slammed against the door on a steep curve and, waking from my stupor, said, "You're driving too . . . fast." Were we running from something? It sure felt like running. Had I really seen Billy in the funhouse? Had Jay spotted him from the Ferris wheel? I sat up, feeling a little queasy, and let out a groan.

Jay smiled. "Do you know how to drive?"

"When would have I learned to do that?"

"I thought Robbie might've taught you."

I shook my head, wishing you had.

My stomach was doing somersaults, and I needed a break something bad. So when we made it to the top of the ridge, Jay pulled the wagon off the road at an overlook. We got out to take in the mountain air, which was lighter and cooler than the humidity that had settled in the valley. We walked to the edge of the overlook, leaned against a crumbling stone barrier, and peered down at the soupy haze clinging to the sides of the mountains. A hawk drifted into view, circled far above the valley, and then glided toward Jitters Gap, down and down until it vanished.

Jay suddenly hopped on the barrier and stepped to the edge, pieces of mortar flying into the valley and striking the rocks and bushes below. He peered down into the haze. He even seemed to lean into it, like he was giving into the pull of gravity, like he wanted to go headlong into the valley.

"Jay," I said, frightened for him. But he didn't reply. "Don't get so close to the edge."

I reached out and grabbed the back of his leg. He flinched when I touched him and lost his balance, his arms twirling like a cartoon, and then he fell—not forward, but back on me. I threw out my hands and deflected his clumsy collapse to the ground. He emerged out of a cloud of dust, grinning and gripping his bad leg.

"That was a close one," he said.

I glared at him, stomped back to the car, and slammed the rickety door with a metallic screech.

He followed me, leaning on the door and poking his head in the window. "It's time you learned to drive. Besides, my leg is no good for the next little bit."

"Where are we going?" I demanded, refusing to look at him.

"Just wait and see."

"I'm not going to drive, and I want to know where we're going, *and* I want to know who we're running from."

I looked up at him. He was smiling at me, handsome and bright-eyed and all charm. I seemed to be entertaining him.

"What sort of detective can't tail a suspect because she doesn't know how to drive?" he said. "Besides, if you're driving, you're a lot less likely to get sick."

I wasn't convinced. Besides, it wasn't his driving that was making me sick.

"At the end of this," he said, a pall of seriousness falling over him, "you'll know all I can tell you. I promise."

"Even what happened to Lily?"

"I'll tell you everything I can." He smacked his hands together. "Okay, it's driving lesson time."

I thought he was crazy. I was tall for my age, but how could I press down the clutch *and* the gas? Jay had a solution. He took off his beat-up black boots and his thick socks, and stuffed the socks in the toes of the boots, and then told me to put them on. I felt like a drunk horse clopping around in them, but they were what I needed to push the pedals to the floor. He also rummaged in the back seat and pulled out an old blanket, which he folded into a square and wedged between the seat and my back.

He checked with me to see if I was comfortable. I told him I was, even though I wasn't, not one bit. I was scared. But I didn't want to disappoint him.

He adjusted the rearview and side mirrors so I could see out the back and the sides. I followed his instructions as he described the process for starting the car—hold clutch down, put car in neutral, turn key, release clutch, let engine warm up, press clutch again, and put car in gear. He walked me through downshifting, since we were heading downhill.

"Just ease off the clutch," he directed.

I popped the clutch several times and the wagon lurched forward, coming dangerously close to the stone barrier. I felt like a fool, the awkwardness of the boots making me even more self-conscious.

"It's all about balance," he said, "finding the sweet spot between the clutch and the gas. You have to think about both."

I've always had good coordination, so I caught on quick, even if at times awful grinding and clicking noises, barely muffled by the hood, reverberated through that old car. It sounded like the gears were going to shatter, but I was doing it.

The road hugged the rocky mountainside, twisting in and out of the ridge, dipping into and out of shadows cast by the sinking sun. The turns were terrifying at first. The edge of the cliff was only a foot or two from the asphalt, and the byway was trimmed with only a flimsy wooden guardrail. If I'd lost control of the station wagon, we would've plunged into the valley, tumbling side over side to the Jitters Gap city limits, a twisted mess of metal and glass, like Jay's parents' train-trampled Duesenberg.

Jay held the steering wheel with his left hand and called out instructions, calm as ice. The wagon galloped down straight stretches, and in the turns, it leaned, top-heavy, toward the valley on the left, and then back into the looming, water-slick limestone mountainside. My adrenaline was high. I was aware of Jay's hand on the steering wheel, of him beside me, of his voice.

Suddenly, a truck—an old rust bucket—was coming around the bend smack in the middle of the road! I swerved, and the right fender of the wagon caught the side of the mountain, spraying the hood with dirt and ripping a leafy sapling out from between limestone slabs, which released the moist smell of earthworms into the car.

I screamed; Jay was laughing.

I remember being worried about the brakes. As you well know, those detective stories loved to bump off characters by a severed brake line. The car—usually a shiny new sports car—would speed down a lonely highway, its driver soon discovering that the brakes didn't work. There would be a few frantic, heart-pounding moments, and then the victim would drive off the cliff and fall to the black ocean below, the expensive car—and it was *always* an expensive car—exploding on the rocks. Fantasy and reality had overlapped so much that day; anything was possible.

Luckily, the brakes worked, but for a split second at every turn, I wondered what it would feel like to shoot out over the valley and fall into it like the hawk I had watched minutes before. Down, down, down.

When we reached the bottom and came to a stop at a railroad crossing, I was sweating something awful, my white dress damp and stained at the armpits and collar. Jay ordered me to pull over, so he could drive. I screeched to a halt on the side of the road, dust billowing around the station wagon and drifting into the twilight.

Jay took the wheel again, and we drove into town. "We almost hit that truck," he said. "You did a hundred-dollar job of avoiding disaster."

"Your grandma's going to be *so* mad at me."

"She's not going to notice."

"She won't?"

"She lost count of all the scratches years ago."

We made our way through town, parked down the street from the Vellum home, and waited for nightfall. After a time, I became fidgety. I knew I would be late for dinner and Papa would want to know where I had been all day. Also, I was thinking about Billy, about that mad dog mug of his.

I was worrying the edge of my dress so bad that Jay touched my wrist and said, "Soon."

"Who did you see at the carnival?" I asked, recoiling from him.

"What do you mean?"

"Did you see Billy? I thought I saw him at the funhouse, in the hall of mirrors. Is he after us?"

"Don't worry. We're safe."

I didn't believe him.

"I'm tired of waiting," I said, crossing my arms over my chest.

"It won't be long," he said. As if cued by his voice, a light came on in the bay window. The Victorian wedding cake of a house had been slowly vanishing in the twilight, the fading blues and grays in the sky making cardboard silhouettes of the entire scene. The living room lamp must've been close to the floor, because it cast long shadows up across the ceiling—shadows of figures, moving, then stopping, then jumping to life again, like crickets caught in a porch lamp.

"Why are we here?" I said.

"Just wait."

"Not even a hint?"

"No."

"Mama and Papa will be steaming mad if they find out I was with you."

"After I show you what I need to show you, I'm going to tell you a story."

"What sort of a story?"

"True crime."

So we waited, and as we did, I became more convinced I was going to receive a beating when I got home. I tried to think up a good lie: "Sorry, Papa, I lost track of time. Sorry, Papa, I fell asleep while I was reading. Sorry, Papa, I got turned around in the woods." But he wasn't going to believe me. You know how he was—guilty men are always the most suspicious.

Instead, I began to think of ways I could defend myself. Could I catch his hand with mine? Could I duck in time? Could I sprint up the stairs and barricade myself in my room? If I stopped him initially, he'd probably back down and think better of it. But could I make him feel guilty *before* he did it?

"Look," Jay said, nodding toward the Vellums' house. A man and a woman came out of the front door. The man was Frank Vellum. Although I couldn't see his face, I recognized his shape and his mannerisms. His arms moved in angry jabs, and his voice was loud and biting, but just noise, nothing we could make out. The woman ignored him and kept walking to a dark sedan at the edge of the road. She wore a black, wide-brimmed hat, carried a makeup bag and a small suitcase, and was wrapped in a dark raincoat, which, for summer weather, was peculiar. She was young and moved quick, but her steps were uneven, like she was off-balance, even drunk. I couldn't see her face, but I didn't think she was Bernice Hersh. She seemed too young, too short. Could it be Aunt Kathy? Was she involved? She might know what happened to Lily.

The woman dropped into the passenger side of the car, and Frank hesitated at the driver's side, his hand on top of the car. Then, in a furious motion, Frank got in and slammed the door.

"What are they up to?" Jay said, genuinely surprised.

The sedan's lights shot on and the car pulled out, its wheels tearing through the gravel. Jay started the wagon, and we were in pursuit.

We followed them back over the mountain, swinging through all the curves and blind corners again, this time in the dark, insect-speckled night. Jay kept a tight grip on the wheel and sat a little forward, his eyes like glass beads catching the beams from passing cars. We cut through Royal Oak, north to south, and bright-lit windows like candid snapshots passed us by, exposing the interiors of people's lives—families having dinner or washing dishes or listening to the radio or dancing or playing cards or just sitting and staring back.

As we neared Hersh's Pharmacy, I thought maybe the woman in the car was Bernice Hersh, after all. Frank's car slowed down in front of the pharmacy, but it kept moving through town to the train depot behind Main Street. The 10:00 train to Charlottesville, Culpepper, and Washington would be passing through soon, its whistle echoing down the valley.

Frank swerved and braked at the curb, and the woman flung herself from the car, still clutching her bags, tottering a bit like she was still tipsy—or emotional. I saw her face under the streetlight, just for a second. It was beautiful, bright, and blank like a clean sheet of paper, not a face I knew. She smacked the door closed with her suitcase. Without a good-bye, Frank made a U-turn and drove back past us, his face as still as a statue in the dim light.

"Go," Jay said. "Go talk to her."

"What?"

We heard the hollow sound of the train whistle. It wouldn't stop for long, maybe five minutes, if that.

"Go," Jay said.

I jumped out of the car. "Come with me," I said. I could see the engine's light growing brighter, a dot, then a circle of light down the tracks.

"Go—before she's gone."

"*Please* come with me!"

"Go! Now."

I had lost sight of her, so I headed to the platform. By the time I reached it, the train was pulling in. Its huge metal wheels cranked to a halt, slow and deliberate, like the locomotive was dying in little gasps. Then, the engine sent a blast of steam through a small cluster of people on the platform. The men grabbed their hats, and the women adjusted their cotton dresses as the light fabric blew back against their legs.

Just inside the station door, I saw the woman holding a ticket in her hand, her luggage arranged neatly at her feet. Her face was in shadow, but her chin, a streak of silvery skin, peeked out, inviting me to come closer. I walked toward her, terrified, wanting to know what it was I needed to see, what I was supposed to say, what Jay had wanted me to understand, feeling like I was stepping across some invisible border that divided the realm of my imagination and the real world.

"All aboard!" the conductor called out, and the woman glanced up, and we were looking at each other, dead-on. She had thin purple lips, high cheekbones, and the smooth, thick makeup of an urbanite. Her hair was pulled back and tucked into her hat, a loose curl or two drifting at the sides of her face. Her eyes, however, were glassy and raw, and a little puzzled to be regarding me. The clamor of passengers boarding the train flowed around us. I was about to speak, to say something stupid, when I noticed the pearls around her neck, and it was somehow that detail—not her clothes, not her face, not even her eyes—that made me realize I was standing in front of Lily Vellum, in the flesh.

Sheila fidgeted and dropped her purse. It had been perched in her lap while she had her drink.

"Let me get that for you," Thomas said, and retrieved it. She liked his wide shoulders, the curl in his thick brown hair, and the way his cologne brightened when he moved. She was also terrified of him. She was sure he was the man in the photos. Was she crazy? Or was this some mental trick, like déjà vu? She had dreamed of a handsome stranger arriving and sweeping her off her feet so many times since Kenneth left her. He seemed a figment of her imagination. And even if she *had* seen what she thought she saw in the album, who could say it depicted the truth? Who was to say what that even was? Besides, she had some say-so in her fate, right? She had free will. It was a law of nature. She had decided a long time ago that she wouldn't be trapped on a farm in New Jersey, growing potatoes like her father and mother. Now the world was hers for the taking.

"Thank you," she said, taking the purse from him cautiously.

"Forgive me for saying this, but you don't look like the sort of hausfrau out for the evening I'd expect to see in a joint like this. What I mean is, you don't look like you're from around here. Take that as a compliment."

"I suppose I'll have to." She frowned a little.

"Where are you from?"

"New York City."

"I *was* right. Thank God."

"And you?"

"The same."

"Why are you here?"

The bartender interrupted and asked what Thomas would like to drink. "Whiskey. Straight up."

"I should be going," Sheila said, standing from her stool.

"Stay. Indulge me a little."

Sheila liked the way he was smiling at her. He did have more than a little charm.

"Get the lady another one," he said to the bartender. "What were you drinking?"

"Just a club soda and lime."

"A club soda for the lady," he said loudly, and looked her way again. "What's your name? You haven't mentioned it."

"Sheila Fury."

"You don't say. Fury. What a fiery name! I bet you're passionate."

"You're just flirting."

"Yes—but I speak the truth. Names tell you everything about a person."

"Such as?"

"Their background. Where they come from. Who they come from. I knew a man named Walter Roosevelt. A king of a man. You can hear it in his name. I knew another man. This guy, he called himself Sid Ciscero."

"He sounds like a movie star— or a goon."

"You're good at this! He was a failed actor turned petty crook. Can I offer you a smoke?"

"No, thank you."

He took out a cigarette, caught it between his lips, and lit it with a silver lighter.

"You hang out with crooks a lot?" she asked.

"Oh, Sid? He was the friend of a relative."

Sheila's club soda arrived. She toyed with the lime but didn't take a sip. "Why are you here again?"

"Haven't said. I'm visiting family."

"I'm here because of family too."

"Oh really?"

"My aunt passed away."

"Too bad. I'm sorry."

"Don't be. I didn't know her.

She was a bit of a crook herself—or that's what they say. I shouldn't speak ill of the dead. She was glamorous, and I'm thankful to her. I'm going to travel the world and have wonderful adventures because of her. I'm saying good-bye to this dull life."

"See, I knew you were fiery!" He slapped the bar.

She laughed and smiled at him. He slid his hand close to hers. The tips of his fingers brushed against her skin. The experience at her aunt's had faded, now just a faint murmur in the back of her mind, and she slipped into easy conversation with Thomas.

His surname was Finn, and he lived in Manhattan and worked for a bank. His girlfriend had recently thrown him over for a rich head doctor. He asked many questions. She liked that he took such an interest in her. She told him about growing up in Parsippany and moving to New York City; about her first job as a waitress at Larry's Restaurant, a grubby dump in the Village; about landing her first real job at Waverly; about meeting Kenneth in the elevator; about falling for him; about his being a bum; and about her divorce finalizing in a few weeks. As she spoke, she felt better, more in control of her senses, more herself again. Eventually, she decided she had to return to her aunt's house. She needed to finish getting the papers in order and head back to her little apartment in the city.

They were outside, standing beneath the wooden bear, his outreaching paws just above Thomas's head. The light from the lounge transformed the drizzle into a fine red mist. The White Mountain Lounge's mascot seemed fierce in the scarlet shadows, but Sheila felt safe, even lighthearted.

"Good night," she said, smiled, and started to turn away.

He caught her arm and moved in. "When we're both back in town, we'll go on a proper date."

He was so close to her. She could smell the musk on his damp skin. She could see the subtle flex of his jaw muscle and the perfect shape of his lips.

"Yes," she said breathlessly.

He leaned into her and kissed her.

14

BUNNY

Before I could speak to my father, I had to wait quietly, respect-fully, for him to finish reading an article in *Life*. I fidgeted like a little girl, twisting my sweet-sixteen pendant around my finger and picking the remains of the little girl's cotton candy off my blouse.

On the cover of the magazine, in faded black-and-white, Nazi pris-oners marched with their hands on their heads. About a week before, Truman had dropped the bombs on Hiroshima and Nagasaki. The war had ended, but it hadn't completely sunk in. We were still sorting out the truth from the propaganda—one story had been told, a tale with all the correct proportions and hopeful conclusions, but another, much more unpleasant one had been lived. I wondered if the same weren't true of Jay.

"Yes, what is it? You've been sitting there very patiently," my father said. He laid the magazine on the side table, smoothing out the dog-eared page he had been reading.

Father had traditional good looks. His red-brown hair had gone gray at the temples, and his sturdy face was grooved at the dimples and the corners of his eyes without seeming weathered or dry. His cheeks and chin were always a bit grizzled, like he didn't care too much about his appearance, a nonchalance I envied because I had not inherited it from him. He had a presence about him that calmed me— perhaps it was his eyes, which were the color of silvery winter clouds, or the slow, bottomless breaths he took before answering a question or responding to a request. After what I had seen at the carnival, as much as I wanted to talk, I also just wanted to sit with him, to be his daughter for a little while.

"Daddy, I need to use the car. I want to go shopping in the city."

"Are you going with someone?"

"I know where to go. I've been with Mother. I'd rather be on my own."

"You *are* very independent. But I don't like you going alone, not with the war still on."

"They're not seriously worried about Washington being bombed. Not anymore."

"I don't care what the newspapers are saying. We just bombed Japan, and yes, they surrendered, but they could still retaliate. Another Pearl Harbor. Who knows? I would feel better if you were with someone."

"I don't mean to sound like a snoot, but I can't take friends from Royal Oak. They wouldn't appreciate the price tags on the dresses, if you catch my meaning."

"All too well. Your mother has refined my appreciation for price tags."

"I'm using the money I earned at the plant."

"If it's your money, I can't stop you. But I insist you return before it gets dark. It's dangerous at night in the city. You'll have to ask your mother too. She may not have enough gas on the ration book."

Mother immediately embraced the idea. She poured me a cup of coffee and sat across from me at the kitchen table, eager to strategize and embrace a moment of mother-daughter bonding. "I always make a plan," she told me. "You need to be a smart shopper."

I told her I needed a fall coat, perhaps something in chocolate brown and nicely tailored, and a pair of black shoes, patent leather with a substantial heel. Nothing too blocky, though.

Narrowing her eyes and smiling, she said, "How much do you have to spend?"

"Thirty dollars."

"Hmm." Her glossy red nails gleamed as she tapped her thin porcelain coffee cup. "I'll give you an extra ten, and you can pay me back. I'd hate for your trip to be less than a total success."

"And gas?"

"I haven't used my ration coupons for this week. You should be fine."

Before I left, I hugged both of my parents. I made a point of this. It was a secret apology. Of course, I hadn't told them the real reason I was going to DC.

Mother gave me her map and drew X's with red pencil to indicate all the stores that met her standards: "Go to Woodies first, and then Garfinckel's. Woodies has the best coats. Both have wonderful selections of shoes. You're sure to find something that suits your fancy."

When I stopped for gas on the edge of town, I made a call to the operator and had her patch me through to the Howard, which I discovered was on 8th Street NW. I figured I would start there. I had brought the article about Lily from the *Royal Oak Times* and the photograph of Jay he had given me before he left for the war.

The weather was particularly beautiful that day, one of those afternoons with impossibly blue skies, trees fluttering with shades of green, and limestone cliffs nearly white in the sun. My mind felt refreshed, sharp, clear. A theory began to bloom. Perhaps Lily had been Jay's secret lover and had died horribly at the hands of her abusive boyfriend Billy, who killed her because, let's see . . . he thought she was pregnant with Jay's child! It could be. And Jay was using Ceola and me to bring Billy to justice—or, at the very least, to grieve for Lily.

The intricacies of my self-deception have to be admired.

On that drive, I created an alternate emotional reality for Jay, and I convinced myself it was true. If a flaw poked its ugly head through my reasoning, I dismissed it. For instance, why did Lily write, "I can do without the pushy girls at the Showboat or the boys in uniform at Carroll's (but I'm sure you don't mind a look!)"?

Don't over interpret, I said to myself. *Detectives only deal with facts and concrete observations, don't they?*

And so my brilliant hypotheses continued. Jay kissed Ceola only because she had asked him to. She was getting curious about sex, and adolescent girls have been known to do such things. He had felt obliged to kiss her, because he knew she was grieving, too, and she needed the attention. But why there, on the Ferris wheel, in plain view of Royal Oak? Another ripple in my smooth reasoning. It made me drive faster.

My mind returned to what I thought I knew—namely, the passionate kiss Jay and I had had before the war. His kiss with Ceola was only for a moment, a messy, awkward event, but our kiss was the bright crystal of evidence, the tangible fact, indicating the most authentic of connections—the spark of true love.

📷

In the 1940s, servicemen and -women and other government workers filled DC, giving color and movement to those austere, self-important façades, those Parthenonic symbols of a democracy. Boardinghouses became overrun, and the temporary Navy and Munitions Buildings along the Mall teemed with employees like massive beehives. The newly constructed Pentagon, the largest office building in the world at the time, glowed from across the Potomac; a monolith, a vision of impenetrability.

The city went beyond the purely symbolic. It functioned practically, both by housing the offices of a nation at war and by inspiring an imaginative conception of what our nation was and who we were, particularly in the face of evil from abroad. It is no wonder my romance with DC began during that time.

I drove into the city across the Key Bridge, with Georgetown's gothic steeples and spires pitched against the sky. I made my way through Georgetown and down K Street, dodging the streetcars as I went around Washington Circle. A few blocks south, between 10th and 11th Streets, I found Woodies.

I dashed through the department store, passing by a gorgeous display of asymmetric lace and taffeta gowns in buttery yellows, emerald greens, and faded pinks, sparkling with rhinestones and intricate embroideries. In another display, mannequins posed fluidly, as if modeled from designer sketches, showing off décolletage-enhancing necklines, sheer laces, and slim-waisted silhouettes. But I didn't have time to gawk.

I usually enjoyed shopping at a leisurely pace, trying on outfits and checking the fit, so this whirlwind tour through the ladies' department was harried and unpleasant. I was brusque with the store clerks, who were being friendly and chatty, bolstered by the war's nearing end. One woman in a pink blouse said, "My dear, you have the bone structure of a starlet; your cheeks catch the light at all the best angles." I stopped for a moment, gave her my full attention, and told her of course it wasn't true, but thank you. She insisted I try on a gray felt tam. I indulged her but decided against it.

I thought of Lily trying for a job here. I imagined her modeling dresses for the fall preview, drifting through the store, smiling and spinning to show her dress to customers: "This comes in dusted rose and silver pearl too."

After taking in the bouquet wafting from the mirror-topped perfume counter, I departed Woodies, having snatched up a smart, dun-colored Vera Maxwell coat with a pleated back and a pair of faux-crocodile wedges. Once I returned to my car, I tossed my bags in the back seat and spent a few minutes reacquainting myself with my true destination—the Howard.

Although I knew DC had a significant black population, I didn't know where their neighborhoods were. I had only been exposed to the "agreeable" sections of town. As I drove north, the brickwork on the row homes became less ornate and the bay windows gave way to porches. Shiny new Cadillacs, Pontiacs, DeSotos, and Oldsmobiles became dinged and scuffed older models, from the years before the war. The sweet perfumes and powdered noses of the pretty store clerks at Woodies faded away, replaced by sidewalks of grimacing black faces, mouths opening with quiet astonishment. "What's that little white girl thinking?" they seemed to say. "Dorothy ain't in Kansas no more." Come to think of it, that memory makes me think of a line of Joseph Conrad's: "There it is before you—smiling, frowning, inviting, grand, mean, insipid, or savage, and always mute with an air of whispering, 'Come and find out.'"

The Hotel Howard was a series of Victorian row homes integrated to form one large building. A scaffolding of fire escapes crisscrossed its brick façade, and a weather-beaten canopy printed with the street address hung over the entrance. The red-carpeted lobby was cramped with a low ceiling and a pervasive odor of mildew. Against the back wall was a row of brass mailboxes labeled with residents' names. The Howard seemed to be more boardinghouse than hotel.

A young, well-groomed black woman sat at the front desk. Her glossy hair was crimped and bobbed and framed a lovely face with long, elegant cheekbones. Her bright red lipstick shone like glossy enamel. She was on the phone, lost in gossip of some sort. As I stood in front of her, waiting for her to glance up and notice me, I scanned the names on the mailboxes. None were familiar to me.

"Hang on," I heard her say to the person on the other end of the line. "Excuse me," she said to me in a more pleasant tone than I had expected. She rested the receiver against her collarbone. She articulated her words clearly, assertively, which led me to believe she was more than a concierge. I was certain she either acted or sang.

"Hello," I said. "I have a friend who I'm trying to track down. I was wondering, perhaps, if she was still here." I tried very hard to keep my voice light and direct, avoiding any inflection that might give away my eagerness.

Lifting the receiver to her mouth, she said, "Can I call you back?" She hung up. "Who are you looking for?"

"Her name is Lily Vellum."

"Don't know her. She doesn't live here."

"Oh."

"Sorry, honey."

"May I ask you," I said, "if you've ever heard of this establishment—Croc's?"

"It's a bar. Crocodile Tears." An enigmatic smile quivered at the edge of her red lips. I liked her a little less. *Always mute with an air of whispering.*

"Do you have the address?"

"I can give you directions, but it won't open until eight tonight."

My heart sank. I was expected at home by then.

Croc's was only five blocks away, at the corner of U and 11th Street. In need of familiar surroundings, I retreated to my car and sat quietly for a moment, watching pedestrians on the street. I studied their clothes, the way they walked, and their faces. Everyone was purposeful. A group of men in uniform, both black and white, passed close to my car. Their army greens were crisp and snugly fitted to their frames, the insignia and badges glinting in the sun, but they seemed casual to me, perhaps because they were laughing. The sight of their clean, handsome faces made me feel more at ease. I wondered what it would be like to live in the city, to have friends like these men or even the Howard's concierge. I wondered if they were going to celebrate the attack on Japan tonight. In retrospect, it was a horrible thing to celebrate, but at the time, it was a glorious final strike for the Allies. We hadn't seen the images of the devastation.

A sudden burst of confidence surged through me. I decided I would phone my mother and tell her the Oldsmobile broke down and I would have to spend the night. I would tell her I was safe and I could pay for the repair with the money she gave me. I would describe the clothes I had purchased and how I was looking forward to a nice dinner. I would tell her I was, despite it all, enjoying myself.

And that's exactly what I did.

I returned to the Howard and asked the woman if they had any rooms for overnight stays. They did. Once I settled in my room, I called Mother from the pay phone in the hall. She supported the idea of me making the best of it. When she asked for a diagnosis of the car trouble, I said, "Something with the ignition."

She simply said, "I see." She knew I was lying, but she understood that sometimes adventures require a little deceit.

📷

After spending a few hours wandering through the National Gallery, its paintings having recently been rehung after being held for safekeeping at the Biltmore Estate, I returned to my room. I wanted to convert my conservative pink polka-dotted dress into an evening dress, but as much as I attempted to adjust it—unfastening the top buttons, pulling the thin, black belt tighter—I couldn't alter its appearance. My hair and makeup would have to create the desired effect; I twisted my hair on top of my head, allowing a curl or two to escape, and pinned it there. I also applied a thick layer of lipstick, giving my lips a deep red luster.

It was six by the time I was ready. I was tired from my day, so I opened a window and let the evening breeze in and, being careful not to muss my outfit, lay down on the bed. The smells from the street weren't pleasant—car exhaust mingling with the greasy mist from the restaurant at the corner of U and 8th—but the cool air was refreshing, and I drifted into a deeper sleep than I had intended. When I awoke, the bright rectangle of my window was now a gaping hole, emitting echoes of laughter from the street below. It was nearly midnight. Dinner was over, and nightlife had begun to flood into the streets. I had planned to get to the bar early and search for Lily before a crowd descended on the place. My stomach growled, and I felt homesick. But I rallied a bit, fluffing my hair and freshening my lips, and set out.

Many of the windows in the buildings along U Street were curtained, a preemptive measure in case of a blackout drill during the war and now most likely the result of habit. The commotion on the street was a blur of gray shadows, broken only by the lighting of a cigarette, indiscreet automobile headlights, or the opening of doors as men and women flowed in and out of restaurants and bars. After finding my way to the corner of U and 11th, I combed the block, soon becoming convinced the receptionist at the Howard had given me the wrong address. I huffed and slapped my hands on my hips.

"Excuse me, miss. You look lost," a voice said.

I turned to find a short young man in a crisp suit and fastidiously parted blond hair. His face was smooth, almost waxen, but not uncomely, and his lips thin and pursed. A vermillion kerchief plumed from his breast pocket.

I smiled, happy to see a friendly face, and stammered, "I'm looking for Croc's."

"Oh, really?"

"Do you know where it is?"

"Are you sure you have the right place, darling?"

"I think so."

Finger to his chin, he gave me a casual once-over. "You're the real thing, aren't you?"

"Certainly," I conceded, a little perplexed.

"Very well. Follow me. We'll find out if it's the place you're looking for."

We went behind the hardware store around the corner, into a dank alley, and down a flight of steps to a nondescript door. Over it hung a small sign that read CROCODILE TEARS in dark blue letters. The man knocked on the door in a distinct pattern—Morse code, I think. It happened too quickly for me to catch the rhythm.

The door flung open, and a puff of smoke escaped, trailed by laughter. A tall, horsey woman, wrapped in a horrible bright purple evening gown, emerged. She recognized my new friend and rushed forward, giving him a hug. The little man disappeared into a blob of purple organza and then reappeared again, extricating himself from her gossamer cape, taking a moment to complain she had ruffled his freshly pressed blazer.

"Oh, Timmy," she cooed. "Wrinkles make you more rugged. Too much polish on and the boys won't want to rough you up."

"This is my friend . . ."

"Bunny," I supplied.

"Bunny," Tim repeated.

"Hop! Hop!" The purple horror screamed with joy, her large mouth gaping to reveal cigarette-stained teeth.

"She's come to see the show," Tim said.

"Little Bunny better hop-hop on inside."

"Indeed," Tim said.

The purple horror stepped aside, motioning for us to enter, her diaphanous plumage rippling and fluttering with each exaggerated gesture. Mellow guitar, a Reinhardt-esque tune of some sort, drifted across the room through the haze. I followed Tim down a few stairs, dropping below the veil of smoke.

The space was a deep, buttressed basement, supported by two or three large brick pillars. The windowless walls were painted a wine red and lined with booths. Much later in my life, the Roman underground cistern of Istanbul would conjure memories of this place. The city's cavernous architecture and lush darkness, although much grander, had a similar and equally disconcerting atmosphere, like being in the belly of a whale. In the center were round tables of odd sizes, set with mismatched chairs and lit with red votives. At the far end of the room, a thick, velvety curtain was pulled back, revealing a thin, well-dressed black man, perched on a stool and playing the guitar. His eyes were closed, deep in the moment of the music. At the back of the room stood a makeshift bar, cluttered with stools and the greatest number of patrons.

"Does this look like your sort of place?" Tim said.

"I'm looking for someone."

"Anyone in particular?"

"Lily Vellum."

"That name rings a bell. I remember hearing something about a Lily a few months ago, but I never met her."

"What about Teddie B.?"

"Why are you looking for *him*?"

"I'm a friend of a friend."

"Oh, you'll get to meet Teddie B., all right. He's crooning his dreadful repertoire tonight. Just hang around. I'll bet my toes he's the next act. God save us if he's doing Dietrich."

Remembering another name from Lily's letter, I said, "Do you know a George?"

"Which one do you want? George Abernathy? George Wills? Georgie Goodbottom? Although I seriously doubt that's his real name. George Gershwin? George Washington? You'll have to be more specific." I was bewildered, which he clearly saw, because he said, "Darling, why don't you have a seat at an empty table and let Timmy find a drink for you? What do you want?"

"I'm fine. No need to—"

"Darling, name the drink."

"An old-fashioned."

"Whatever your heart desires." He clucked and left me.

I found a small table near a pillar and sat down. My eyes were beginning to adjust to the submarine blues and ruby reds of the room, and I discovered there were several groups of patrons that I could observe without seeming conspicuous. Around the table nearest me, three young men sat together, craned over their drinks, whispering and laughing and smoking. Occasionally, one of the men would extend a slender arm over the center of the table and tap ashes into an empty glass. The gesture had a certain irreverent grace about it, a feminine haughtiness I had never observed in men, except perhaps at my birthday by the lake. Jay had seemed so different that night.

At another table, a man and a woman sat across from each other. The woman wore a dark velvet dress, the color of which was difficult to discern, and she seemed angry, or at least unwilling to look the man in the face. The man was impassioned, pleading with her. I wondered if he was in love and she wasn't—or at least not with him. At one point, she slouched and put her hands to her face. She melted into tears, and the man rose and walked around the table and put his hand cautiously on her shoulder. She shook him off. He was utterly bewildered. I decided I didn't like the woman.

The table on my right, at the edge of my peripheral vision, was half-submerged in darkness, and in that restless shadow I saw two shapes conjoined, moving against each other, in soft, uneven undulations. I stared for a moment, uncertain what I was looking at. Then the two shapes separated and assumed the more recognizable forms of two sturdy, square-shouldered men. One of the men was still leaning forward slightly, his hand gripping the other man's thigh. My heart rate increased, and I turned away. Before I could process what I had seen, Tim was standing over me, dangling my drink precariously between his thumb and forefinger.

"Here, darling. Take your drink. I hate the condensation on my palms."

As he sat, he nodded toward the two men. "It looks like Ben has a new boy tonight. They simply worship him. That's only because his favorite activity doesn't require conversation." He took a swig of his drink. "Don't mind me. That's just jealousy talking."

"I don't understand," I sputtered.

"Of course you don't." He smiled.

"Is he . . . ?"

"A fairy. Yes, darling. As am I." He tipped his glass to me. "Cheers!" He took a deep swig, swallowed, and paused to absorb the alcohol. "You really don't know where you are, do you?"

"I do. It's just . . . I've never been to a place like this."

"Are you a lessie?"

"A what?"

"A dyke. There are better places I can recommend if you are."

"I don't—*No!*"

"You look pale, darling. Have your drink. You'll feel much better."

I picked up the tumbler, removed the thin orange slice—which Tim snatched from my fingers and ate—and took a gulp of the tangy liquid. After the alcohol settled, I took another, more ladylike sip and spoke: "I'm here because someone I care about has a connection to this place and to the people I mentioned to you."

"Teddie B. and this Lily person."

"That's right."

"What sort of connection?"

"I'm not sure. The more I discover, the less I understand."

"You're beginning to intrigue me."

"Is that a good thing?"

"Indeed."

In a clumsy flutter, the purple monster was suddenly with us. I could see now that she was in fact a he. The liberally applied makeup, the waxy red lips, and the cockeyed wig served only as an immediate distraction from the burly man hiding underneath. I felt embarrassed for him, not to mention a little afraid *of* him. I moved my chair back a few inches to give him room.

"Don't be scared, little Easter Bunny," he cooed.

I sipped my drink.

"This is her first foray into the fairyland," Tim explained. "Be gentle with her."

"She a dyke?" the purple monster asked.

"She says no. She says she's looking for friends. She says Teddie may know something about these friends. It's all very mysterious."

The monster brought his arm across his face, his sheer purple dress veiling his nose and mouth in parody of the Shadow: "Who knows what evil lurks in the hearts of men?" and he mimicked the Shadow's signature laugh. To say the least, it was odd. But it made me laugh.

"She thinks you're funny, Henry," Tim said dryly.

So the monster had a name.

"Henrita," he corrected Tim.

"Why not Henrietta?" I asked.

"Henrietta is a heifer's name. Henrita has Latino mystique. South-of-the-border spice. The clatter of castanets."

Tim rolled his eyes, and I laughed again. I was tipsy. It felt good, though. I could feel my anxiety slipping away.

"You're the one to comment on names, Easter Bunny," the monster said.

"It's a nickname. My real name is Bonita."

"Oooo, I like that. Henrita and Bonita. We're going to be best girl-friends!" At that, he reached over, snatched up my drink, and took a gulp. I was taken aback. "Don't worry, Miss Hippity-Hop. I'll get you another one."

The lighting on the stage had darkened. The guitarist had disap-peared, although the lilt of his music lingered in the room. There was a shift in the mood around us, a shuffling, and the stage was suddenly flooded with light.

"Here we go," Tim said. From stage right, a tall woman surfaced, swathed in a tight black gown. Her hair was a blond bob with large sculpted curls, and she held a fur stole around her. She moved gracefully to center stage and raised a faux-diamond cuffed glove to the audience in exaggerated appreciation of the decidedly unenthusiastic applause. Her face was as white and smooth as a Japanese porcelain mask, with eyebrows like twin circumflexes and lips as dark and glossy as ink. Teddie B. was Marlene Dietrich.

An accordionist appeared out of the darkness of stage right, a still shadow in the background. The accompanying piano was in the corner of the room, lit only by the inconstant flicker of candlelight. "Lili Marlene," her signature war song, was the first of the night.

His rendition was all camp, replacing Dietrich's world-weary-woman-who's-seen-it-all with pure melodrama. I glanced around at the grinning faces and rolling eyes, particularly among the men. I couldn't tell if Teddie was making fun of Dietrich or himself or, worst of all, if he thought he was doing a passable impersonation.

As the songs rolled out of him—"The Boys in the Backroom" and "You Go to My Head" and, of course, "Falling in Love Again"—his façade began melting, literally. His sweat made the pancake makeup lose its soft, powdered surface. There were moments, though, particularly in "Falling in Love Again," where his voice—the man's voice, not the faux Dietrich—broke the surface with a touch of authentic emotion, part humiliation and part desperation to master the song and embrace his muse. However brief these slips were (and they were most definitely unintentional), I found myself cheering him on, hoping that at least for a chord or two he could make the transformation complete.

It never happened. As Teddie took his bows, the applause was respectful but far from enthusiastic. A couple of sailors even booed him.

Tim said, "So you've seen him. What do you think?"

"I'm beyond words."

"He's atrocious."

I nodded, and he shook his head.

"Hen will escort you backstage if you want to talk to him. Won't you, Hen?"

"Teddie loves to receive admirers," Henrita said. "But you had better think of something nice to say about his Dietrich, or he'll scratch your eyes out."

"Good luck, darling." Tim held up his glass in a mock salutation as I rose from my seat. "I'm staying here. I'm only three or four drinks from that lovely little vacation spot on the shore of Lake Oblivion."

📷

I followed Henrita down a dim hallway, lined with lewd graffiti scratched into the plaster walls: men coupling with men, disembodied genitalia, raunchy words and phrases childishly scrawled at angles. I wanted to pass judgment on this strange, underground world. These people assaulted my refined, good-girl sensibilities. They mocked the very values my parents, my school, my church, and the culture of my town had ingrained in me. But what was worse, they had made me laugh. I shouldn't like them, and I certainly shouldn't laugh with them.

It didn't fit. I blamed the giddiness of a few moments ago on that tried-and-true scapegoat—alcohol.

The damp, sweaty smell in the hall gave way to a rich, metallic perfume as Hen and I approached Teddie's dressing room and knocked.

"What is it?" a rough male voice barked from inside.

"It's Henrita. I have an admirer who wants to meet you."

"Go away."

"She wants to talk to you."

"'Go away,' I said."

"My name is Bunny Prescott," I said to the closed door. "Do you know someone by the name of Lily Vellum or . . . Jay Greenwood? If you do, I need to talk to you. It's very important."

There was a long silence; then the dressing room door swung wide. Perfume and pink light spilled into the hall. Teddie had removed the Dietrich wig and the dress but had yet to wipe off the makeup. He was shirtless. His skin was pasty, mole-speckled, and marked with red indentations from a bra and girdle, which now lay behind him on the dressing table. He still wore elastic, form-shaping panties and hose.

"What do you want?" he said, returning to his dressing table. I followed him in, and Hen left the room. I heard the click of the door behind me. Teddie began removing his makeup. The dressing room was no more than a twelve-by-twelve-foot cell, painted bright pink and cluttered with a sloppy costume rack and a table full of head forms, some bearing wigs, others bald. On the opposite wall was the sliver of a ground-level window.

I felt trapped, claustrophobic. Teddie was an androgynous witch whose cave I had to brave to receive the answer to my riddle. His cold cream jar was his cauldron, and his hairbrush was his broom.

"Did you know Lily Vellum?" I said.

"Perhaps . . . What do you want with her?"

"I just want to find someone who knew her, who could tell me about her."

"You mentioned another name."

"Jay Greenwood."

"I know him. He and Lily are pals."

"Can you tell me about them?"

"They were here a lot in the spring. I haven't seen them much since—" He caught my eyes in his mirror and spun around. "Has anyone told you that you look exactly like, um . . ."

"Gene Tierney."

"That's it."

"Has anyone told you that you look exactly like Marlene Dietrich?"

"No," he said and laughed out loud. "We're just a couple glamorous movie stars, aren't we?"

"About Lily and Jay."

"They were here off and on—the life of the party, very popular sorts, both of them—oh, and this other woman, Georgiana or Georgina, or something. She was definitely on the prowl. She really vamped it up at first, but when I saw her with Lily, she had toned it down a bit. She seemed to have eyes for Lily. I saw them holding hands across a table and giving each other *the* look. That's not typical for this place, if you know what I mean."

"Did Lily ever refer to her as George?"

"I never heard that. But I really didn't know her too well. She was friendly with Jay, though. They were always chatting it up. If I remember right, he had a bum leg, a war hero and all of that. He was a handsome fellow too. He didn't like me. I don't think he thought much of fairies in dresses. But he certainly liked the pretty soldier boys. Don't get me wrong—I understand why he wanted those boys on his dance card, but he could've given me a chance. I don't wear this getup around town . . . and I clean up nice."

When he said this, I realized I had mentioned Lily's name repeatedly since I had come to DC, but I hadn't uttered Jay's name once until a few minutes ago, outside of the dressing room. The alcohol had loosened my tongue, it seemed, and I was starting to ask questions I didn't want to know the answers to.

"You look pale," he said. "Do you need a drink?"

"I've had enough."

He shrugged, searched his dressing table, uncovered a silver flask, and took a swig. He fished out a pack of cigarettes from a makeup bag, placed one in a holder, and lit it. He cocked his head back and exhaled a long, feathery stream of smoke.

"I should go," I said, turning to the door.

"You're in love with him, and you didn't know he was queer."

I stopped, my hand on the doorknob.

"I'm sorry," he said.

"I feel ridiculous." I let go of the doorknob and faced him.

"You can't help who you love." His voice was gentle. "If there's one thing I've learned in this life, it's that."

"I don't understand it."

"None of us do."

He offered me the flask again, and I took a drink. The alcohol burned in my chest and warmed my head, melting the tears as they gathered in my eyes.

When I returned the flask to him, he said, "I remember another thing about Lily. It was just a rumor, but I heard she was pregnant, and she was looking for a way out, if you know what I mean."

"It's in a letter she wrote to Jay. That's how I found out about it. Jay led me to believe he'd only met her once, but he knew her well. They were friends. That's why I'm here."

"Why haven't you talked to Lily?"

"That's what started this. She was murdered."

"That's horrible."

"Jay told us he met her on the train to Royal Oak and she asked him to take photos of her for a modeling application. Jay was a war photographer, you see. He told us when he went to rendezvous with her for the shoot, he found her dead. Ceola and I—"

"Wait, who's Ceola?"

"The kid sister of Jay's best friend, Robbie. He died in the Pacific."

"A pretty soldier boy, I assume."

"I suppose. Anyway, we followed Jay to the scene of the crime in the woods, but Lily's body was gone. Ceola hunted for clues and discovered her bloodstained shoes. Then we went to Jitters Gap to watch the Vellum family's home and spy on her father and her boyfriend, Billy, who we learned about from a newspaper article about her disappearance. A day or two later, Jay produced the second half of a letter, which he claimed he'd found in the Vellums' garbage. The letter implied a motive—the baby—but didn't reveal the addressee. I found the first page of the letter on my own and that led me here, to you."

"May I see it?"

I pulled the letter out of my purse and unfolded it. The photo of Jay and the newspaper clipping about Lily I'd placed there earlier fell to the floor.

Teddie bent down and picked them up. "That's him," he said, holding the photo out for me to take and exhaling a cone of smoke. He took a moment to read the article on Lily and then said, "Poor girl. A shame." Once he had Lily's letter in his hands, he held it away from his face, so he wouldn't damage it with his cigarette. He growled with displeasure and tossed it at me. "That bitch called me 'a mess'!"

"Do you see why I'm confused?"

"Nothing that you've told me has made an iota of sense. Why would he pretend he hardly knew her? And do you think he was *really* meeting her in the woods to take photos? You better stay away from him. How do you know he wasn't the one who killed her?"

We heard muffled shouting out in the hall. Teddie stood up, wide-eyed and alert. The voices became clearer, louder: "Raid! Get out! It's a fucking raid!"

"Damn," Teddie said, and snubbed out his cigarette. He grabbed a floral patterned robe and wrapped himself in it. "Damn," he said again, and looked at me. "We have to get out of here. I know a back way."

As soon as we opened the dressing room door, several men ran past us. "Follow them!" Teddie said, clutching his robe tightly around him. The door at the far end of the hall—the door to the bar room—flung open, slamming into the damp cracked plaster. Behind it was a large, beefy, flat-faced man in sloppy army fatigues. His powerful forearms bulged at his rolled sleeves. He held a baseball bat in his right hand. His left hand was curled into a fist, and a flush of fervid malice pulsed in his eyes and his cheeks.

Teddie gasped and grabbed my arm, and we hurried down the hall, up a flight of steps, and out into the evening air. We were in an unfamiliar alley, dark at either end, cluttered with trash, lit only by a rusty fixture over the door. Teddie's fake fingernails bit into my forearm as he pulled me to the left. I resisted, stunned by all the commotion. Then the door banged open and three or four men ran past us. One man's mouth and chin were streaked with blood; another held his ear with a badly damaged hand.

"It's not the police," Teddie said. "It's much worse. Drunk soldiers, fag haters. They bust the place up from time to time. It's our lucky night. Come on!"

We rounded the side of the building, and two men, hurling out of the darkness, slammed Teddie against the brick wall. Another man knocked me back against the same wall. The tall gangly one pinned Teddie to the side of the building, forearm to his neck, choking him. The fat one, in a rumpled Navy uniform, pulled a military-issue knife on me and nervously waved its point in my face.

The shortest one, whose crumpled engineer's cap was low over his forehead, wore a thin white T-shirt, showing off his muscular bulk. He approached Teddie and hissed, "You fucking hermaphrodite," and ripped Teddie's robe off him.

I couldn't make out any of the men's features, not even hair color. The only light in the alley came from the building behind the thugs, falling on Teddie's distorted face, the twin arches of his Dietrich eyebrows smudged across his forehead as if by the hand of a frustrated artist fed up with his work. His chest was heaving, and his legs were positioned at an oddly sensual angle, spread apart, lithe and smooth against the dark brick.

"This one's almost fucking real!" the short one said. "Is there a dick down there? You have a pecker, Nancy-boy? Tell me. I bet it's all shriveled up. That's what happens to faggots."

Teddie struggled to free himself, but he couldn't. The tall man had his right arm and the short man his left.

"Let's see if you still have one, eh?" The short man cocked his arm back and punched Teddie in his crotch. He howled, and the men let him fall to the ground in a heap.

"He *does* have one! What do ya know, Jerry?" the short man said to the tall man, and then he turned to me and said, "What do we have here?" He took the knife from the fat one's hand and brought it to my neck. He pressed the cool tip of the blade against my collarbone. I held my breath. The fat one backed away. "My God, this one is as real as I've seen 'em. Jesus Christ, Jerry, I could fuck this one. Ha!"

As he came closer, I could make out the features of his face below the shadow of his cap. Something about the shape of his mouth and the edge of his jaw were familiar, but I couldn't place him. He reeked of hard liquor, sweat, and cigarette ash, and his breathing was labored.

"He looks like Gene Autry," Jerry said.

"Tierney. Autry's the fuckin' singing cowboy."

"Yeah."

He pressed the point of the blade deeper into my skin, nicking the surface. I cried out.

"Fuck, he even sounds like a woman," he said, grabbing my left breast and pulling on it as if he expected it to come off in his grip. I screamed, and I heard my dress rip. He pushed me against the wall and, with his free hand, tore my dress open, buttons popping and clattering on the pavement. He cupped my breast roughly and exhaled into my face.

I began begging: "Please, leave me alone. Please, oh, please."

His face was only inches from mine; so close, all I could see were his dark, bloodshot eyes and all I could smell was his stale body odor. Then he let go of me and stood back a few steps. He seemed discouraged. "She *is* fucking real," he said. "A goddamn dyke. Another fuckin' dyke. Just what I need." He took off his hat and wiped his forehead with his arm. The light caught his features, and I knew who he was.

I said his name as it entered my mind: "Billy Witherspoon."

He blanched with surprise.

We both heard a thud and a moan. Jerry stumbled forward with an empty expression on his face, falling into me, clutching at me, at my dress, my arms, and sank to the ground, tearing the fabric more. I glanced at the top of his head and saw blood flowing out the back of his skull. I pushed him away from me. Then another thud, wood against bone, and Billy stumbled sideways, buckling like a puppet whose strings had been snipped, landing on hands and knees in the middle of the alley. That's when I saw him.

The purple monster brought down the baseball bat, making contact with Billy's back. Billy tried to brace himself as he fell forward, but the gesture was futile; he hit the pavement with his face. Henrita, whose own face was smeared with makeup and blood, heaved the baseball bat over his head again and slammed it into Billy's back. I found myself screaming, begging him to stop. But he hit Billy again and again before his rage was spent.

Henrita now looked more like a Henry. His wig lay in a puddle, and his eyeliner stained his face like soot. His dress was torn and drooped from his left shoulder like a shabby imperial toga. He held the baseball bat limply, and his chest was rising and falling with deep breaths. A cut above his left eye was streaming blood. I backed away from him. He took a sharp step toward me, holding the bat in front of him, and I let out a high-pitched yelp. He stopped and lowered it. For a moment, I realized he must've taken the bat from the brute who had chased us down the hall. That frightened me even more. I heard a muffled moan come from Jerry, and Henry tensed, gripping the bat with both hands. I continued backing away, noticing that both Teddie and the third thug had fled. Jerry uttered something unintelligible, and Henry advanced and kicked him in the side. The wounded man groaned and curled into a ball.

"Stop!" I said. "Stop hitting him."

Henry looked at me and in a clear, deep voice, very sober, said, "They broke Tim's nose. They broke his arm."

I was going to say something to him—a condolence or an admonishment, I'm not sure which—but before I could speak, we heard sirens.

"We need to go," he said, and we both ran down the alley, choosing to go opposite directions once we came to the street. I wrapped my ripped dress around me the best I could and headed through the darkness toward the hotel.

📷

The journey back to the Howard was a blur. Once I was in my room, with the door safely locked and chained, I fell on the bed. My body quaked with anxiety—and anger burned deep inside of me, but it wasn't righteous anger. I wasn't suddenly transformed by what I'd witnessed. That would take years of reflection. No, I was angry at the

entire experience: Tim's nonchalance, Teddie's ridiculous impersonation of Dietrich, the thugs for their stupidity, Henry's pathetic rage,
Ceola for her worship of Jay, and Jay—most of all, Jay—for being the
boy Siren, beckoning to me and bashing my illusions on the rocks.

I lay there for about thirty minutes, fuming, before I decided to take
a shower. The warm water soothed my anger, and as my muscles loosened, I let myself cry. Afterward, wrapped in my towel and with hair
still damp, I fell asleep, curled on top of the coverlet. I dreamed it was
Jay who was in the alley, whose face appeared underneath the engineer's cap. When he grabbed my breast and ripped my dress, I wanted
him to keep doing it. I wanted him to push me against that wall and
bite me on the neck and do what I knew Billy was about to do. But he
stopped and stood back and smiled. I became furious, picked up the
baseball bat, and hit him with it. It bounced off him as if he were made
of hard rubber. He was still smiling. I hit him again, and he began
laughing out loud. I hit him again and again until, surfacing from the
dream, I realized my belligerence was in sequence with a knocking at
my door.

I got up, groggy and disoriented. Since my dress was in tatters, I put
on the coat I bought at Woodies and cinched the waist with the belt to
keep it closed. I smoothed my hair and called out, "Who is it?"

A woman's voice responded, "Miss Prescott?"

"Yes."

"This is the concierge from downstairs."

"Yes." I recognized her voice.

"I have someone here who wants to speak with you."

"Who is it?"

"Maybe you should open the door."

"No. Tell me who it is."

There was a brief silence, and then a lighter and vaguely Appalachian voice said, "Please let me in. I need to talk to you."

I cracked the door without removing the chain. The concierge stood a few feet away, still poised and bright-eyed for this late hour. She had on a dark green velveteen dress, black silk gloves, rhinestone earrings, and lipstick. She *was* a performer. Beside her, looking a bit anemic, was a pretty, slender woman, wearing pearls, a hat, and a dark dress. After fiddling with the chain, I let them in. The concierge held out her hand and said, "I'm Georgiana Gardner. Most people call me George. And this is Lily. We need to talk."

15
CEOLA

here she was. *Alive.* And I was babbling like a fool, and she was smiling, or trying to smile, distracted by the train behind me and her need to get on it. And then she was shaking my hand . . . So glad to meet me, any friend of Jay's, but she had to go . . . I quickly asked her about Jay's photo of her, but she looked at me like she didn't understand a thing I was saying. Then I went on about your story, and how maybe photos do tell the future, and she should be careful, but she wasn't listening . . . and like that, she was on the train, gone in a cloud of steam.

By the time I made it to the station wagon, questions were bouncing between my ears, questions I should've asked Lily if I'd had my wits about me. Was that her in the photo? If it wasn't, who in God's name was it? If it was her, then what happened? How did she go from being a bloody mess to that nice lady on the train platform? Was the photo staged? Was she trying to fake her own death? Why? And what did she mean she'd heard so much about me?

I opened the door and gave Jay a look.

"You saw her?" he said. I nodded, but before I could say a word, he held up his hand and said, "Not now. We've got to go."

He started the car, and we were on our way. I almost asked where we were headed, but I knew I wasn't going to get an answer. Instead, I filled the quiet space between us with daydreams. Seeing Lily alive confirmed for me that life was much more like fiction than adults would admit. Jay had always understood that. Robbie, you'd understood it too.

I began to fantasize that Jay and I were driving out of town, and we would keep driving until we were far, far away, leaving Royal Oak and its petty characters behind. We were going to settle in a city and open a detective agency and solve crime; we were going to be partners. We'd call ourselves the Blue Hearts Detective Agency, and we'd interview clients in a dark, musty room, smoke cheap cigarettes, drink booze, and wisecrack—and we'd always get our man.

Then, like that, Jay's kiss at the top of the Ferris wheel came to me, and it didn't fit. I could still feel the pressure of his hand over my heart and his lips against mine. I saw the photos he'd shown me of him, his naked body stretched out like a cat in the sun. And the picture of you in the boat, your hands behind your head and your swimming trunks undone. I saw Jay's countless photos of corpses that had spilled from his album—soldiers, women, children, all bent and broken like rag dolls. They seemed to spread forever across the floor, to fill up the entire room. I tried to shake them from my mind, but they had hitched in their claws and wouldn't let go.

When we turned onto Route 4, I knew where we were headed. Soon we were driving up the Greenwoods' tree-covered road, the dew bending the branches low overhead, and I was afraid. But of what, I couldn't say. Jay? The truth? My own foolishness? Mama and Papa? Definitely Mama and Papa, in that moment. It was very late—so late, in fact, that I knew no excuse, no matter how creative, would satisfy Mama's questions or temper Papa's anger. But it was well beyond the point of no return, and I was hungry to know how this story was going to end.

We parked and found our way across the weedy yard to Jay's make-shift room. Inside, he raised the wick on his oil lamp. Where he hadn't covered the glass walls with sheets or quilts, the surfaces worked like mirrors, reflecting, twisting, and intensifying the light like the inside of a camera. Jay pointed to the cot, and I sat, my arms at my sides, my back straight, aware of all the objects in the room—the picnic table, the piles of dusty books, the photos of soldiers pinned to the quilt above the cot, the Purple Heart, the trunk, the liquor bottles, Jay's body moving around, stirring the thick air.

He dropped down on the far side of the cot from me and poured himself a half-glass of whiskey. "Do you want something to drink," he said, "like water?"

I shook my head no.

He tossed back his drink, leaned against the wall behind the cot, casual-like, and stared at a dark corner of the room. He was thinking. *Ruminating* is the fifty-cent word for it. I could almost see the shadows stirring, pulsating, taking the form of his memories. But what sort of memories were they? Good? Bad? Tragic? Memories of the battlefield? Memories of you?

After a long while, he began to speak.

I'm going to do my best to relate what he told me. Not because

I have to be accurate for you—hell, you know more of the truth in Heaven than I do here on earth! No, I have to do this, because I've lived too long with his story on the inside of my head. I've replayed it so many times, I no longer understand it. It's all garbled, like the way an echo becomes nothing but noise after traveling a far distance. Maybe if I put it down here—really get it out of me—I can see it for what it is. I know it won't be Truth with a capital T, but it's what I've lived with, so it means something.

His voice came out clear and low, but I could hear a tremble of pain underneath, a rumble like a train still a distance down the track: "Not long after your brother received his orders, I went to the recruiting station on Main Street and signed up for the Navy. Grandma threw a fit, begging and pleading, screaming and cursing to high heaven. She cooked up some crazy plan for me to hide out in the mountains. She was scared to death of losing someone else, you see. It took me several weeks to persuade her to let me go. But fate was already gunning for me, so to speak."

He explained how, only days after he signed up, he'd received a letter. It was from a local draft board, ordering him to report to the recruiting station. It was unusual to receive orders so fast. He went downtown, stripped, and went through all the tests and question-naires. When the ordeal was over, he was told to go to the Army desk, where a gruff sergeant said, "Here, sign these."

"I was here last month," he said, "and I joined the Navy."

"No, you didn't, kid. You were drafted today, and our quota says everybody goes into the Army."

He was beside himself. He hadn't enlisted just to be drafted! He had words with the sergeant, but the jowly, red-faced old fool told him to shut up and sign the papers, or he'd arrest him for being a goddamned draft dodger. Jay pushed back, not intimidated by the threats, and wrote a series of letters, but before long, he was in the Army and on a train to Camp Croft in Spartanburg, South Carolina.

"Basic training was difficult," he said. "The heat was unbearable at Croft, already in the nineties by the morning run and over one hundred degrees for calisthenics. But all the physical activity distracted me and kept me from missing Robbie too much. During my downtime, to keep the blues at bay, I volunteered to take photos for the camp rag called *The 40th Column*."

His photos made an impression. The *Column*'s advisor, a Lieutenant Jessup, liked them, especially a shot of a bunch of trainees dragging a large truck out of a gully with ropes, and another of grunts crawling through the mud of the barbed-wire infiltration course. The lieutenant said they looked like stills from combat films, like authentic newsreel propaganda from the front. He showed them to members of the Signal Corps, who were designing a public relations brochure about life at Camp Croft. They included his photos in the project; that was Jay's start as a photographer.

One day, Sergeant Davis, who was a commanding officer, approached him. "You have a good eye, Private," he said. "Combat photographers are in serious need of replacements. Son, they're going to send you in shooting film, not bullets." He slapped Jay on the back and gave him the sort of cockeyed smile you give the damned.

After Thanksgiving, Jay was transferred to Camp Crowder, Missouri, where he joined the 166th Signal Photographic Company. Eastman Kodak sent technicians to train the men, since most of them had next to no experience with photography. They learned the basics about different types of cameras, lenses, papers, speeds of film, what have you. Jay knew his way around a Speed Graphic, which was the Army's camera of choice, but he had a lot to learn about setting up a shot and about how to maneuver on the battlefield. They ran drills with infantry and tanks, and in every sort of weather—rain, sleet, snow, you name it. They learned how to move with squads and platoons while juggling their heavy backpacks and bulky equipment. They had to reload film as quick as rabbits and often blindfolded. They had to learn to change it under a coat or a blanket and feel their way through it. They also had to practice changing lenses while dodging artillery fire.

"And all the time," he said, "we had to keep in mind the photos we took had to tell a story, and if we didn't tell the story right, we weren't doing our job. It was more exhausting and more frustrating than basic, but I began to understand my purpose in the war."

He poured a little more whiskey and said, "It was during this time I met this fellow from New York City named Darren West. We were having our prints critiqued, when he leaned over and said, 'Rudy Unger is a Neanderthal.' I was holding a picture of Rudy flexing his big biceps for the camera just before lights-out. Rudy was a handsome guy with a cruel disposition. I worked hard to stay on his good side. I gave Darren a sideways glance and said, 'He's swell to look at, though.' It just slipped out. I was about to backpedal when he whispered, 'You've made him look better than he is. Not my type.' It was good to know I wasn't alone, really good, but I was rattled I'd taken such a risk. It was dangerous."

Jay leveled his eyes at me, scrunching his eyebrows together. He nodded his head like he was asking, *Is it all right I'm talking about myself in this way?* I didn't know how to respond.

He went on.

Darren and Jay began confiding in each other. Darren came from a well-to-do family in New York City. His father had disowned him, and his mother had left his father because of it. "Mother is a lovely, passionate person," he told Jay. "You would really like her. She wants me to be who I am and do what I like." Jay thought Darren's mother must be like Carla Prescott, bighearted in that way.

Later on, Darren confessed that his mother had been clinging to him too much. He had joined the Army to escape her as much as his father. He ended up at Crowder because he'd made spending money by developing photos for a portrait agency while he was studying painting at NYU.

One evening near the end of their time at Crowder, Jay and Darren got drunk. They were at the back of a local dive, three sheets to the wind, when Darren reached across the table, put his hand on Jay's, and said, "I want one night before we get shipped to England. Just one night. Then I'll vanish. I don't want to get in the way of your feelings for Robbie."

Jay had told him about you!

"Robbie never left my mind, Cee," he said, his voice cracking, "not for a minute. Please believe me. I loved him and wished a thousand times for the day when the war would be over, and we could be together again."

I didn't like where the story was going, the way his eyes were shifting, the way he was talking about you. I wondered if I trusted him at all.

"When I was a little younger than you," he said, "Grandma took me on vacation to Miami. The ocean was different there, like a pane of bottle-blue glass spreading to the horizon, and the sun seemed more beautiful reflecting in it than it did in the sky. I often thought about that blue water and dreamed about Robbie and me escaping to a tropical island somewhere in the Caribbean, living out our lives with the ocean at our front door and the sand beneath our feet. We would stand side by side and look out and see nothing but waves sparkling in the sun. There we would be, the two of us together."

"Could I have come too?" I said.

He smiled, just a flicker. "Your brother wanted that life. He wanted to get away—away from everything he was here, in this goddamned place. But he would've wanted you along, I'm sure. You would've lived with us. You would've been tan every day of the year and gone to school in a hut and drank water from coconuts and built sandcastles on the beach."

"That sounds swell," I said. "Really swell."

The warm glow faded in his eyes, leaving his face dull and empty. The shadows in the room around him seemed to swirl and darken like ink spreading in water. I was frightened again.

"Do you want to hear the rest of my story?" he said.

I didn't reply.

"Cee?"

"Yes. I guess."

"Okay"—he cleared his throat—"on with it."

In early 1944, Darren and Jay boarded the USS *Susan B. Anthony* and crossed the Atlantic, landing in Belfast. Shortly after that, the 166th was assigned to General Patton's Third Army, and they were relocated to just outside Manchester, England. They settled into flimsy, tarpapered barracks, much shabbier than their barracks at Fort

Crowder, and ate stale bread, powdered eggs, and weak chicory coffee. On clear nights, they watched Nazi bombers fly over on their way to bomb Manchester, Bristol, Birmingham, and Coventry. Preparations for D-Day were under way, and everybody knew it, but nobody knew when it was going to happen.

Several detachments of the 166th would take part in the invasion, but the cold, rainy spring weather wore on Jay, and in late April, he came down with pneumonia. He was sick as a dog. He watched the majority of the 166th leave for Portsmouth to be deployed with Patton's army to France. Before Darren left, he gave Jay a letter to mail to his mother. On the envelope, he had sketched a shadowy valley in the Lake District, which he had visited while on R&R one weekend, and painted them green with splotches of watercolor. He shook Jay's hand and wished him the best.

"It was frustrating to see him go," Jay said. "I wanted to be a part of the action. I had come too far to be stuck in a damned hospital. I thought a lot about your brother during those days. I tried to imagine what he might be seeing and doing in the Pacific."

"Didn't he write you?"

"He did. I wrote him too. But we had to be careful. The military scrutinizes the mail for leaks in classified information. If they caught wind of our true feelings for each other, we could be handed our blue papers—that's a dishonorable discharge. It's happened to other soldiers and ruined their lives. So we wrote letters with messages concealed in them—cryptographic messages—but in this case, even the cryptograms had to be disguised. We didn't want the officers who were sorting our mail to think we were spies. I would send him crossword puzzles or word games or photos of camp or of me, and he would write stories for me. I received Robbie's last letter only days before I was given the doctor's clean bill of health."

By mid-December, Jay was off to Paris. While there, he met up with a few soldiers in the 166th who had taken a pass for Christmas. Before they knew it, they were summoned back to the front. The Germans had started a major offensive in the Ardennes forest and were forcing the Allied lines back.

After many miles in a jeep, navigating through barren, ice-crusted countryside and forests that seemed as empty and cold as outer space, they arrived at the Belgian town of Saint-Hubert, where they joined up with an infantry company. The weariness and frustration behind the infantrymen's eyes was plain as day. It spooked Jay but gave him purpose. He could read a silent wish on their faces—they needed him to record what they were going through.

So after a day or two, he found his bearings, joined up with a Cavalry group made up of only GIs and jeeps—no tanks—and headed into the snowy woods to do his job. They drove through forests with the trees as black and thin as bars. They came across bombed-out villages, still burning like visions of the apocalypse, and blasted tanks and jeeps, no more than shells of squashed beetles. When they found the other men, they were frostbitten and starving, some with blistered feet, others with infected wounds, all of them wanting to go home. Jay's own feet were beginning to hurt him, the cold was so intense. But all the same, he was set on recording it, making sure other people saw what he saw.

"That Christmas, a small group of us gathered around an army chaplain for a service in the snow," he said, his milky-blue eyes widening a bit. "Although I'm not religious, I wanted to be there, with those men. I looked around at them, their heads tied up with dirty scarves and their feet wrapped with rags. Many had to live in those same clothes day after day, night after night, the fabric sticking to their skin, becoming part of them. As the chaplain went on about the meaning of Christmas, about love and hope, the men stood still, some with stony faces, others crying quietly. I looked away and tried to pretend the snow was sand and over the next hill was an ocean with Robbie standing in the warm surf—"

He flinched, a memory passing over him like a swooping bird. I sensed he was about to tell me something important, something hard to tell. You see, I didn't really understand war. I'd lost you, and I knew how that felt, but to me, war was just a mixture of photos from *Life* and shots from Hollywood propaganda. It was soldiers hoisting American flags into the sky or sailors standing at attention on the bow of a ship. It was fighter planes zipping across the sky. It was Bob Hope cracking jokes on *The Pepsodent Show*. It was Uncle Sam clad head-to-toe in red, white, and blue. But it wasn't something I could reach out and touch. For Jay, it was right there, growing out of the corners of the room, a smoky reflection in its mirrored walls that swelled to three dimensions, more real than the cot under him, or the roof over him, or me beside him.

He stopped talking, reached under the cot, and pulled out a manila folder. He wiped a thin layer of dust off it and opened it away from me so I couldn't see what was inside. He flipped through its contents and said, "You're going to see my tour of duty, but through my eyes."

The first photo he showed me was of a group of fifteen or so soldiers during downtime. Most of them were sitting close together on the side of a truck, legs dangling like boys. Some of the GIs were puffing on cigarettes, others were chatting. Several were standing,

absentmindedly holding their rifles, helmets tipped back, seeming not
to notice they were ankle-deep in black mud and cold slush. One soldier grinned as wide as the Cheshire Cat, looking like he had just
heard a dirty joke. Another waved at someone beyond the edge of the
picture. One boy was studying the sky, questioning the weather with
an open face, wondering what tomorrow would bring. A little left of
center, a young man was staring at the camera. He was good-looking
with dark features, thick eyebrows, and a wide, blank forehead. A
Montgomery Clift look-alike. He smiled with his big eyes—a warm,
knowing expression, as if the joke was that no one but Jay and this
boy knew they were all having their picture taken.

"That's Darren," Jay said, pointing out the man staring at the
camera. "We crossed paths eventually. It was good to see him—and
lucky too. This photo was taken after the first few days in the Bulge."

Jay continued to show me his photos, placing them in front of me
one at a time, checking for a reaction but saying little. He was anxious
about letting me see them, but I didn't understand why. I had already
seen similar images in magazines and film reels.

But one shot made him smile. Bright streaks of white blazed across
the sky over GIs' heads. They were huddled in a ditch beside a river,
and in the background, a geyser of water, like a fountain in one of
those Las Vegas water shows, exploded midstream.

"I got a Bronze Star for that one," he said. "To get it, I had to keep
standing during an onslaught of machine gun fire. I was lucky that
day. Not a scratch."

As we went on, he began to talk more about his experience, sharing
mostly lighter anecdotes. Eventually we came to a photo—the last he
would show me—and he hesitated.

"This one," he said in a dry whisper, "is a lie in service to the truth." The ice in his voice had returned.

The photo itself, considering many of its counterparts, wasn't out of the ordinary. In the foreground, a soldier sat in a jeep. He was in silhouette, and his head was cocked to the right. Behind him, a village was on fire, and the thick sooty smoke billowed up to the sky, mingling in with the storm clouds. After a moment, Jay cleared his throat and explained what he meant.

On a quiet day, after the siege of Bastogne was over and before the first of the year, Jay struck up a conversation with Sam Bossi and Reed Daniels, two "buddies" from the same regiment.

After a bit of small talk—mostly bitching about the lack of decent rations and the bitter cold—Jay said, "I don't have a single shot of the town that's worth a damn." Weather conditions, smoke, and enemy fire had made it nearly impossible to take well-composed photos.

"Why don't you set up a shot?" Sam said.

Sam Bossi was a short, feisty Italian guy from Chicago with a body like a steamroller. Thick veins in his neck pulsed when he spoke, and his jaw muscles flexed and rippled when he listened. He frightened Jay a little. But Jay was skittish of the men who didn't know who—or what—he really was. He knew other boys, the ones who didn't pass as well as he did, were hazed and beaten. At Camp Croft he had heard stories of a swish named Linus Reynolds. Dandy Linus, they called him. The poor kid, after being whipped with a belt and kicked in the head, was stripped to the buck and tied to a barracks' window frame with "Faggot" scrawled across his chest in red paint. After all the fuss died down, the boy received his blue papers and went home in disgrace.

"If you set up a shot," Bossi went on, "then you can take your time."

"I don't think it's a good idea," Jay said.

"I've seen other members of your CPU do it. It's not like you're tellin' lies, just making the truth more visible. I even know a soldier who's willing to pose for you."

"Yep, he likes the spotlight. He sure does," Daniels said with a smirk, playing the sidekick. He was a lean, top-heavy man with tobacco-stained teeth and a head of matted red curls. He followed Bossi every-where like a puppy dog.

"Our guy," Bossi said. "He's kind of a cad."

"I just want a shot of the town, something dramatic."

"Let's make an introduction."

Bossi led the two across camp to a line of jeeps. After winding through the mud-splattered vehicles, they approached Daniels's jeep. In the back, draped with a tarp, was a large form. Daniels stepped forward, snickering a little, and yanked the cover off. Propped against the machine gun mount like a broken puppet was a dead German sol-dier no older than eighteen, who, Bossi explained, had been shot in his chest during a skirmish a few days ago. He had been well preserved by the sub-zero temperatures. His frostbitten face was clean of blood and dirt. His skin was the blue white of cold marble, and his red-tinted lips were slightly parted, like he had been killed mid-whisper. His eyes were open, glazed and empty, but not pained.

Bossi smacked him on his back and said, "Hans, meet Jay. Jay, Hans."

Daniels tried to lift the dead soldier's arm for a handshake, but rigor had set in. He said, "Krauts are so damn rude."

Jay was surprised but not shocked. Dead bodies were a part of their everyday life. Bossi and Daniels were good-natured about it, and he didn't want to challenge them on it. Hans was the enemy, after all. But another voice was also in his head. Darren, you see, refused to take photographs of the dead. He told Jay he thought it was disrespectful; a photo of a corpse diminishes the dead soldier. Jay saw his point, but he also wanted the world to know what they were going through. That meant shooting everything, even the dead.

"Everyone thinks war is constant action," Jay said, leaning toward me, "that there's no time to think about things, but that's not true. So much of what we went through was waiting for the next burst of activity. Waiting and waiting. When I saw a body, I thought, *Is that how it's going to end for me?* I had to take photos. It was a defense."

Jay gathered his equipment, and the three men piled into the jeep, throwing the tarp back over Hans. It was not something they wanted their commanding officers to see. But before they pulled out, Darren saw them and asked Jay where they were going.

"To get some better shots of Bastogne," Jay said.

Darren gave him a doubtful look and said, "New friends?"

"Yes. What of it?"

"Those guys aren't your friends."

"They're helping."

"Let me help."

"Fuck off, West," Bossi said, lurching forward aggressively.

"Look, I've got to go," Jay said, putting the jeep in gear.

"Suit yourself," Darren said. The three men drove off.

They parked the jeep near the woods at the edge of Bastogne. After pacing back and forth, and looking and looking, Jay chose an angle

that captured the jeep in the foreground and the town as a backdrop. As polite as he could be, he asked Bossi and Daniels if they
wouldn't mind carrying Hans to the driver's seat. They groaned, but
they yanked the tarp off the body and, after a litany of curse words,
lifted him. Bossi gripped Hans's armpits and Daniels took his ankles,
and they hoisted the stiff out of the back and walked him around to
the side. As they were approaching the driver's seat, Bossi lost his grip,
and Hans slammed against the side of the jeep and fell into the snow.
Daniels still had the legs.

"Shit," Bossi said. "Hans looks pissed!"

Daniels leaned in for a look. "The hell! You're right." They both
began laughing. "He's giving us a look."

"Come on! Let's get this over with," Jay said. Bossi picked Hans up
again, and the two men forced him behind the wheel.

Jay set up his Speed Graphic under a tall pine tree, fastened it to
a tripod, focused and cleaned the lens, set the exposure, and found
his angle. He took a couple of shots of Hans. The cloudy sunlight
was behind him, and his helmet was tipped forward, just a fraction,
covering his face with a shadow. And just like that, the dead German
became a living, breathing American hero, surveying the destruction
from his jeep, snow and ash drifting all around him, a scene majestic
enough for the cover of *Life*.

After changing the film and shoving several exposures in his fatigues,
Jay decided Hans needed to be adjusted. He thought about asking
Bossi and Daniels to do it—they were under a tree smoking—but he
figured it would be faster if he did it. Anyway, he didn't have to move
the body, just lean it forward a little. As he started across the snow
toward the jeep, he heard his name loud and clear. He looked back,

and Darren was there, at the edge of the woods. He had followed them from base camp. He came toward him, furious.

"What the hell are you doing?" he said.

"I set up a shot."

"This isn't right."

"C'mon. Who's it hurting?"

"You don't know what you're doing."

"Oh, leave him alone," Daniels crowed. He and Bossi were approaching from behind.

"He's not harmin' a thing," Bossi said. "He might just be helpin'."

They were exposed in the center of a field, Jay's camera yards away, sheltered by the tree.

"How's that?" Darren said. "Who's it helping?"

"If it's the right sort of photo," Daniels said, "it can tell people the—"

A spray of bullets tore through the group.

Bossi went down, and Daniels disappeared into the woods. Darren stumbled forward, braced himself against the jeep, blinked, and fell to his knees. He wasn't wearing his helmet, and the side of his head was split open, a flap of skin loose from his scalp. He swatted at the air in front of him, stirring a few stray snowflakes. His lips drooped and his eyes quieted, and he was gone before he hit the snow.

Another shower of bullets pelted the ground and the jeep, brighter and louder than the last, hitting Hans in the chest, in the head, in the face. He tipped over and fell from the driver's seat like a doll from a kid's toy shelf.

Jay hit the ground. His right leg was wounded and bleeding. He rolled under the jeep for cover, biting his lip and pressing his leg into the snow, hoping the cold would numb the pain. He just lay there, listening to the German machine guns as they went *bbrrppp, bbrrppp* for several minutes. From under the jeep, he couldn't see the Germans or, for that matter, anyone except Darren, whose face was turned toward him, eyes open and blank, blood melting the snow around his head.

Across the clearing, the camera was still perched on its tripod, observing everything.

Once the machine guns died down, Jay pushed himself out from under the jeep with his good leg. He pulled himself up using Darren's rifle and began hobbling toward the woods. He heard several pops of rifle fire, and a bullet grazed his arm. He kept moving. He passed by his camera and viciously swiped the tripod with Darren's rifle. It crashed against an overturned tree.

More pops, followed by the *bbrrppp* of machine guns.

Jay was in terrible pain, but his adrenaline was up. He kept moving west, toward the general direction of camp, blazing through undergrowth and over uneven ground. As the noise of gunfire faded, his fear eased into exhaustion, and he collapsed against a tree. He slid down the trunk, wedged his body in a crook in the roots, and looked up. Fat snowflakes floated toward him, dissolving on his cheeks and on the warm blood soaking through his fatigues.

"They were like little white hands reaching through the branches, beckoning to me," Jay said. "I thought I should say something to God—to prepare myself somehow, you know, but then I saw Robbie—the way he looked when his attention was somewhere else, peering out at something or caught in a daydream—and I got angry. I was going to see him again. This wasn't going to be the end."

Using the rough knobs in the bark, Jay forced himself to roll over and pulled himself up. Pain seized his leg, and he let out a sharp cry. But he found his feet and studied what seemed to be an endless scatter of trees. He decided which direction to go based on the angle of the shadows on the snow. He walked a few feet and fell against another tree, but this time he didn't stall out. He howled and gritted his teeth like an angry dog, found his legs again, and stumbled on for nearly a quarter mile, until he saw another American soldier a few yards ahead. Daniels, thank God Almighty. Daniels helped him back to camp and from there, he was transported to Verviers, where he learned his lower femur had been shattered by a bullet.

Jay stopped talking and shushed me. Then I heard it, too—footsteps several rooms away, coming closer. He hopped up.

"Quick," he said in a high whisper. "Hide under the cot." He shoved the photos into the folder and stashed them under his pillow.

I didn't move at first, but Jay started gesturing violently toward the bed. I snapped out of it and leapt into action, throwing myself under his cot and burying myself behind shoes and books and discarded scraps of paper.

Like the Wicked Witch of the West in a puff of smoke, Letitia Greenwood appeared in the room. All I could see were her feet, a pair of liver-spotted ankles planted in purple slippers.

"What's going on in here?" Her speech was slurred. "I heard your, uh, voices."

"I'm reading. Out loud."

"Was someone with you? That Prescott girl?"

"No. Just me."

"She was here this morning, you know. She was looking for you."

"You need to go to bed."

"She wants to know about the shoes. Are you going to tell her about the shoes?"

"Not now."

"Are you?"

"No. Go to bed, Grandma. Please."

"No more disgrace, Jay. No more," she said wearily. "This family can't take it. *I* can't take it."

"Good night."

"Give me a hug, Jay. Hug your ol' grandma."

He went to her, and I heard her mumble, "I love you, dear."

He led her out of the room and I was left alone, curled up in the dust and trash under his bed. His experience in the Ardennes flashed through my head in bright bloody snapshots, but it still seemed unreal. I thought that if I could understand what he'd gone through, then maybe, just maybe, I could understand what had happened to you, Robbie. But it was beyond me, will always be beyond me, I suppose—those men, you, him, all just actors in front of a flimsy backdrop, just cardboard cutouts of the Truth. That's all we ever get of other people's lives, it seems. But I was young and expected more.

Sheila was at home again in her apartment in New York. Morning sunlight poured through the kitchen windows, pink eyelet curtains billowed in a soft breeze, and the smell of coffee and freshly cooked bacon hung in the air. In the distance, she could hear the familiar bleat of car horns. Everything in her apartment was just so: her small velveteen sofa, her lampshade with a forest scene painted on it, her coffee table, which she'd covered with a doily to hide the scratches. None of it was fancy, certainly not glamorous, but aspiring to something. She wasn't ashamed of it.

There was a knock at the door. She moved swiftly to it, unchained the latch, and swung it wide.

"Ken!" she shouted, and threw her arms around him. He kissed her and pulled her close to him. She loved the strength of his arms. "I love you, dear!" she said. "I love you! I'm so glad you came back to me!"

He released her, and she stepped back from him. He was *not* Kenneth! How could she have called him that? It was Thomas Finn, her handsome stranger.

"Hello there, Fiery Fury," he said. "You ready for our date?" His face was tan and lean, but his eyes were dark, shifty, even. He crossed the threshold, seeming to tower over her, and held out flowers. Dried roses.

She said, "It's early in the morning."

"We have to go. It's time."

"Not until I'm ready."

She was in her dressing gown and slippers, and her scalp was tight with curlers.

"I'm not waiting any longer."

"I need time to put on makeup and dress and do my hair—"

"*You* called *me*," he said. She

didn't like his tone. He sounded like Kenneth.

"What?"

"You called me at work."

He was looming over her, his jaw set cruelly, a smirk on his face.

"You called me!" he said again. That's when she noticed his front teeth were missing. Then he gave her an ear-to-ear smile. He had no teeth at all! His bare gums were black and rotten and bloody. "Your number's up, She!" he said, slurring his words. Before she could scream, he grabbed her by her neck and forced her into a suffocating kiss, thick blood oozing from her chin.

She was awake and on her feet, her chest heaving, Aunt Majestica's parlor spinning around her as she gasped for air. She steadied herself against the wall.

When she'd come home from the bar, she'd dropped into a wingback chair, still daydreaming about her kiss from Thomas, hoping they could meet up once they were back in the city. He'd been such a gentleman. She had intended to pack as soon as she returned and head home, but the plush of the chair and the dark wallpaper and dim light of the room lulled her to sleep.

She couldn't believe she had delayed this long. She had to leave now!

16

BUNNY

I shook Georgiana's hand, registering that this must have been the George mentioned in Lily's letter, and let them in. She found the chair at the writing desk, turned it around, and sat purposefully. Lily positioned herself on the edge of one of the twin beds, folding her hands in her lap. I stood over Lily for a moment, still drunk with exhaustion, trying to figure out how this could be. The woman who had lain dead in front of me, so meticulously photographed, now sat upright before me.

But I didn't find it shocking. Perhaps it was because I was tired, or because I was already desensitized by the events of the evening, or—and this is what I think now—because I had always known it wasn't Lily in Jay's photographs. I might have believed Jay at first, but once I held her shoes—those scuffed, bloodied pumps—my instinct had told me something wasn't right, even if I couldn't articulate what that was.

I sat on the other twin bed and faced both women. Lily smiled gently, her eyes alert, blinking, but heavy with emotion. She broke the tension with a laugh; a sort of nervous habit, I imagined. She was attractive and much younger than she seemed to be in her newspaper photo, but it was a serious sort of beauty, a beauty with a few marks, a few scars. I wanted to like her, but under the circumstances, such charity was difficult to muster.

"I know it's late," she said, her voice soft and level, "but I was worried I'd miss you if I waited until morning. After the night you've had, I figured you'd head back to Royal Oak as soon as possible." She fidgeted with her dress, brushing off lint that wasn't there.

"How did you find me?" I asked.

"The minute I got back in town, George told me you'd been asking about me and you'd gone to Croc's searching for me. So I went looking for you. Billy must've followed me from Royal Oak and rounded up his sailor buddies to cause trouble. He was hoping to hurt me, not you. Henry told me what you went through. I'm so very sorry. Really. You were caught up in someone else's ugly story. I beg your patience while I explain."

"She needs you to understand," George said, leaning forward, in an attitude of motherly protectiveness. "She can't return to Jitters Gap. Ever."

"I'm listening."

Lily began. She explained how Billy Witherspoon had received a 4F from the Selective Service because of his diabetes and wasn't called for the draft. He was lonely and idle, and his job at his father's garage was boring him stiff. Lily was bored too, and as a result, easily flattered by his attempts to court her. If for no other reason than to fend off the gloom of Jitters Gap, she began seeing him. But when she attempted to pull away, he leeched onto her, resisting even a gentle parting of ways, and, in a gesture of desperation, he proposed to her. She rebuffed him immediately, sharply. He became furious and accused her of shaming him.

On the heels of Billy's proposal, she received another proposal. Her aunt Kathy, who had lived in DC for years, invited her to come live with her in her boardinghouse and work for the government. Her father reluctantly granted her permission, and within a week, she was in DC; within a month, she found a job as a secretary at the Treasury Department. Billy continued to plague her with phone calls, letters, and even gifts.

"Occasionally, a letter would move me with its sincerity," she said, "but I ignored the majority of them. I was changing, you see."

"What she's trying to say," George broke in, "is she discovered she liked girls more than boys."

Lily touched her gold earrings absentmindedly, as if she were afraid she might have lost one. I didn't want to hear about her journey of self-discovery. I didn't want her trying to draw sympathy out of me. I'd fled the underground world of Croc's, and I didn't want to look back.

"It was more than that," Lily said. "But yes, I guess you're right. For a few months, I was happy."

Then Billy had appeared on her aunt's doorstep, arms full of white roses and a box of Whitman's, wearing his Sunday best. He fell to one knee and held out his grandma's engagement ring and begged, "Lily, please marry me. I love you with all my heart. I'd do anything for you. I've left my home for you."

She told him it was impossible. He became irate, cursed her, threw the roses and chocolate at her, and stormed off. Soon enough, though, he paid her another visit. And another. He continued to beg and plead with her, but he didn't become violent again. With each of his attempts, she began to warm to him, wooed by the lowest form of flattery—desperation.

One January morning, he approached her when she was leaving for work. He was shaking from the cold, and his cheeks were flushed and raw. He walked with her to the streetcar stop.

"Lily," he said. "I've run out of money. I can't even afford a decent coat." He was wearing a thin flannel jacket.

"Why don't you get a job?"

"I didn't think I'd be here this long."

"I can't help you."

"I need a place to stay until I can find my footing. I was booted from my boardinghouse for not paying rent. I've been walking the streets all night."

"You've taken this too far."

But she was moved by his condition. Her aunt had just lost a boarder, so she persuaded her to let him stay with them for two weeks, or until he could secure a job. She made him promise there would be no more proposals.

After he had been with them for a week, Lily found him alone by the fire in the parlor one evening. Everyone else was out of the house. Billy's head was in his hands, massaging his temples with his thumbs.

"Are you okay?" she asked.

But he didn't respond.

"Billy, are you okay?"

He lifted his face from his palms, his cheeks moist with tears. "I really thought you would come to love me."

She sighed and placed her hand on his shoulder.

He gently took it in his and said, "Can I have just one kiss, for good luck?"

There was a neediness, a sweetness about him that she found compelling. So she kissed him lightly, as if he were a little boy with a crush. He kissed her back, but his kiss wasn't tender; no sign of the puppy-dog tears from moments earlier. He pressed his mouth and his body into hers and forced her onto a settee, pinning her arms against it.

In my room at the hotel, Lily faltered a little. This part of the story was hers and hers only, not for the sharing. She glanced at George, and her stoic, moon-pale face broke its countenance, and although she was determined not to cry, little tremors of pain ran from her forehead to her lips.

Why did she let such a man in her home? I thought. *Why did she believe his histrionics, his saccharine charm?*

Of course, at the time, I didn't realize I was seeing myself in her, that I was questioning myself. My own foolish belief in a boy had nearly ended in similar brutality by the same man earlier that evening. I wasn't thinking right. Lily wasn't to blame and neither was I, but I was still so raw and angry that it was all jumbled in my mind.

"I'm sorry," I said coolly.

"It wasn't the only time," George said.

Lily nodded. "The next night he forced his way into my bedroom and did it again. When it was over, I vowed if it happened another time, I was going to fight him."

And so Billy came again a week later. He shoved the door open, popping the eye-hook out of the wall. Lily, not asleep yet, snatched a pencil from her bedside table. She had been writing in her journal before bed and had several freshly sharpened pencils. He must not have seen her move in the dark room, because as he approached her, his guard was down. When he leaned across her, pressing his knee into her side, she sat up and jammed the pencil into his arm. He screamed and toppled over. He kicked frantically at the darkness around him, managing to overturn the bedside table and scatter its contents across the floor in a bright clatter of glass and metal. Then, recovering a little, he backed himself into a corner, breathing in great gasps, steadied himself against her dresser, and lunged for the door.

When Kathy and several other boarders appeared in the doorway, Lily still had her back to the wall, pencils held out in front of her like soldiers in a phalanx. She told them she had attacked Billy, because she thought he was a burglar, and at first they believed her. However, after getting patched up, Billy came back, and Kathy, having put two and two together, told him to get out and forbade him to return. She was holding her late husband's rifle on him at the time, the safety switched off. He left, taking a job as a deckhand on a cargo ship, and for a long time, Lily didn't hear from him.

"That's when I enter the picture," George said. "Lily was pushing paper over at the Treasury Department, and Vivian, a friend of mine who worked with her, invited her to drinks at Croc's. I think Viv was trying to make a move on her, but Lily—being the innocent little lamb she is—didn't know she was crossing into uncharted territory. When I first saw her, I knew she was something special. That face of hers, wouldn't you agree, is as smooth and dreamy as a silent movie star's, and that hillbilly accent—pure charm. She didn't condescend to me, either. I'm sorry, Bunny, but most white girls are that way. They can't imagine a negro woman who is as sophisticated as they are."

"I thought you were beautiful," Lily said.

"You handled all the shit that came your way with great poise. If you ask me, honey, that's the definition of sophistication."

"I was smitten, that's all."

"Being a concierge is just my day job, Bunny. My passion is the blues. Lena Horne, with that magnificent voice of hers, is my idol. I invited Lily to hear me sing at Club Caverns one night."

"And she sang 'Stormy Weather.' It was so beautiful and sad. I fell for her then and there—but we're getting off track."

George leaned toward Lily and covered Lily's hands with her wide palm. The gesture made me queasy. Hours before, Billy had called me a "goddamn dyke," and his voice still hung in my ears like stale air. Billy's violence, his ugliness, had been terrifying, but even more terrifying was, as I sat there, I could identify with his sentiment. I wanted Lily and George to tell their story and leave. I never wanted to see them again.

"It was only a week later I met Jay at Croc's," Lily continued. "I overheard him talking to a soldier about Royal Oak, and I butted in and told him I came from the same area. We compared notes on our childhoods, and we both decided the mountains were stifling, especially being, well . . . who we are. He told me I looked like a friend of his. I wonder if he meant you? You're much prettier than I am—and a brunette. It really seemed to intrigue him, though. For a moment, I thought he might be flirting with me, but of course, he wasn't there for the girls. Anyway, the three of us really hit it off, and we became good friends."

But Billy haunted her from hundreds of miles out to sea. She hadn't been feeling well for a while, and one day in late March, after a lengthy bout in the bathroom, George looked at her and said: "You're pregnant, honey."

The news was crushing. She was four weeks along and was completely at a loss. After much discussion, she decided she needed to be with her father. He could provide financial security. She phoned him and told him she wanted to come home. She told George she didn't know if she would return to DC.

Frank Vellum had been lonely in Lily's absence and had started seeing Bernice Hersh, but Bernice was needy, hotheaded, and brash, not qualities Frank particularly admired, so their affair had been waning. Frank was pleased to have his daughter home. He doted on her and bought her dresses and even a strand of pearls at Brickles.

Eventually, Lily told him about her condition. His face flushed with shock and confusion, and then softened with the gloom of disappointment. In a terrible silence, he drove her to the doctor. After the family physician confirmed it, her father said, "Whose baby is it?" She begged him not to make her tell, but he insisted. So she told him.

"Jesus Christ, Lily," he said. "You left town because of him!"

"He followed me."

"And your aunt let this happen?"

"It wasn't her fault. I was the one who asked her if he could stay with us. He was starving. I never thought . . . I thought he understood. Please don't tell Kathy. I'm so sorry."

"I'll give you that—you are sorry. You desert me and then you come crawling back when you've gone and gotten yourself pregnant. I would take a layer of skin off your backside if you were younger. I don't know what the hell to do with you now."

Lily fell quiet for a moment, her hand still in George's. Her eyes were full and tense, tears nearly at the cusp, but she seemed determined to control herself.

"I couldn't bring myself to tell Daddy how it really happened," she said, and smiled vaguely. "I know that seems odd, but I just couldn't say it. The words were like jelly in my mouth. I was afraid if I told him, he wouldn't believe me. That would've been so much worse. So he locked me in the house and refused to let me go out. He didn't want anyone to know I was pregnant. He wanted me to have the baby and give it up. I caved in. I was at his mercy. Then George's letter arrived. Daddy was screening my correspondence, but I got lucky, and he wasn't home when the mail arrived one day.

"George wrote such a lovely note. The last line said, 'Remember I love you, and remember who you are.' Her words cut through the fog I was in. You see, I hadn't asked for the baby. I had done everything I could to prevent it. It was me against the baby, each in a corner, and I was going to fight it out. I wrote a letter to George and a letter to Jay, begging them to help me."

"That's the letter I have," I said. "The letter to Jay."

"As soon as I received her letter," George said, "I started hunting for a doctor to do the procedure. I know several girls who have had it done."

George frowned at me. The disapproval was apparently evident on my face. I wasn't raised in a particularly religious household, but abortion, not unlike homosexuality, seemed to deserve my scorn. Like many other people, I simply took my cues from my community.

George said, "I was against it, on principle, but I wanted Lily's suffering to stop. In her letter to me, she told me she couldn't love her baby knowing it had Billy's blood running through its veins. I understood. I found an MD who did the procedures underground. It was going to cost a small fortune, but if it brought her back to me, then I was willing to give up my savings."

"Jay had left DC by that time," Lily said. "He didn't get my letter immediately. In fact, George contacted him first. They decided they needed a more secretive way of communicating with me, so Jay became the messenger. He would drive over to Jitters Gap, sneak up to my window late at night, and rap on the glass to get my attention. On his first visit, Daddy almost caught him. I didn't know he was coming, you see. He saw Jay running away, and I told him it was Billy. He believed me."

"Jay had been to your house many times before he took us," I said. "He lied about that too."

"That's strange. I don't understand why he would take you there."

I did, but I didn't offer an explanation.

"During his visits, we planned my escape. Inspired by my lie to my father about Billy's appearance at my window, we decided to stage an abduction, hoping Daddy would go looking for Billy, who was still out to sea. On Friday the thirteenth of July—I remember being nervous we had picked that date—Jay forced open my window to make the abduction believable. I spent the night at his house, and the next day, we drove to DC in his grandmother's car."

"I saw the article and your photograph in the paper," I said. "I thought it was odd Jay said he'd planned to meet you to take your photo for a modeling application four days after you'd disappeared. He slipped up on that one."

"A modeling application?"

"You never rendezvoused with Jay to have your photo taken?"

"No. I wonder why he'd tell you that."

"You never met on a train either, did you?"

"I took the train, but never with Jay. Come to think of it, he did shoot photos of Viv, when she thought she might try out modeling, if I'm remembering right. Nothing came of it, though."

For a moment, I stared at her, taking in her nervous eyes, the pale pink of her blush. "He needed to find a way to connect himself to you without giving away how well he knew you. It was to make them believable."

"I don't follow you—"

"The photos. He wanted us to believe they were what he said they were."

"I'm so sorry. I'm confused."

"Just finish your story," I said sharply.

A little flustered, Lily continued: "When I arrived in DC, I stayed here at the Howard. George rented me an inexpensive room. I was too afraid and ashamed to contact Kathy. George took good care of me, and we talked about what we might do together. We fantasized about traveling abroad, visiting exotic locations, inventing new names and identities for ourselves. My anger gradually subsided, and the bitterness eased. I'm not sure what it was. Maybe it was George's kindness, or maybe it was being away from Daddy. Either way, I began to believe I could keep the baby. I told myself the baby was part Billy, but she was also part me, and that counted for something—for a lot. When the day of the appointment came, I didn't go. George was surprised by my decision."

"Yes, I was," George added. "I was pleased too."

"We decided then and there we would raise the child on our own, even if we had to live on the fringe. A black woman and a white woman together—who's going to want to have anything to do with us?"

A pang of resentfulness shot through me, but I tried not to show the displeasure on my face. I still wanted to know everything they knew about Jay, so I steadied myself and listened patiently.

"Unknown to us," George said softly, "Billy had returned to DC and heard about Lily's disappearance. He wasn't happy to discover he was the prime suspect. He decided the best way to clear his name was to find Lily and bring her back, so he started asking around. He went to the Treasury Department and bullied Viv, who knew nothing about Lily's disappearance, but stupidly, she mentioned my name. Then a few weeks ago, he showed up in the lobby of the Howard spitting fire.

"I was on duty then. When he asked me where Lily was, I played dumb, but he wasn't having any of it. He said, 'Tell me where she is, or I'll beat you to a pulp.' He meant it too. I told him to hold on a second while I got the manager, and I slipped into the back office, sliding the bolt behind me. He hopped the desk and came after me and began pounding on the door, calling me all sorts of things. Nigger this, nigger that. Sticks and stones, I always say. He quieted down, and I came out after a few minutes. He was gone."

She paused. "I should've been smarter," she said. "I should've thought . . ."

"It's okay," Lily insisted.

"Billy saw the hotel register on the front desk. That's what made him stop huffin' and puffin'. He found Lily's name and the room number beside it. It was stupid of me to leave it out in the open. Plain stupid."

"Billy didn't knock," Lily said, holding herself a little straighter. "He kicked the door in, splintering the frame, and came bounding into the room. His stint as a deckhand had made him stronger. I jumped to my feet and started for the bathroom. He caught me by the arm and shoved me against the wall, cracking the back of my head against a painting. He clapped his hand over my mouth and said something like, 'You ran away and blamed it on me. I loved you, and you treated me like that. Why would you do that?' He reeked of alcohol, sweat, and dead fish. I've never hated someone as much as I did right then. I slammed my knee into his crotch, and as he grabbed himself, I shoved him hard. He fell against the bed and sank to the floor, arms and legs splayed like a rag doll. I told him, 'I can't love you, even if I wanted to. I love Georgiana.' I had never said it out loud, like that."

Emotion surfaced in Lily, brimming at the corners of her eyes, moistening her lips. George put her arm around her. What did they want from me? Didn't they remember what I had just been through? Sympathy and anger, selfishness and sadness collided in me, bewildered to be crossing each other's paths in the same mind.

Not knowing what to do, I touched Lily's knee and said, "Please. It's very late."

George looked at me and nodded as if she understood. "I reached the bottom of the stairs just as Lily reached the top," she continued. "I saw her smile at me—can you imagine that! And then I saw Billy. He pushed her from behind and she fell forward, tumbling, her body hitting the steps hard until she was at my feet. Billy stood and watched her. When he saw me, he tore down the stairs and barreled past me, knocking me back against the wall. I yelled at him, 'She's pregnant! Pregnant, you hear!' He paused for a second, didn't look back, and then was gone. Lily was bruised and bleeding but still conscious. I called for an ambulance. She was lucky. He could've killed her."

"We weren't that lucky," Lily said, looking at George.

"You lost the baby," I said.

She nodded and wiped the dampness from her cheeks with the palms of her hands. "Once I recovered," she said, "I decided to return to Jitters Gap and confront Daddy. I didn't want to hide anymore. I lost my baby in my fight with Billy, but I discovered I had it in me to tell people who I was. Doing that made me feel real, like I was somebody.

"So a week ago, Jay picked me up at the train station in that rickety car of his and drove me over the mountain to Jitters Gap. You know, Bunny, he seemed different then—sullen and out of sorts—and he said a peculiar thing to me. He asked, 'Have you ever tried to explain something, something difficult to explain, but the harder you tried to straighten it out, the more you bent it out of shape?' I told him no, not really. To be honest, I didn't know what he was talking about. He's always speaking in riddles. I asked him if he was okay, and he said, no, not at all, but he knew what he needed to do, and that was something. He didn't seem to want to talk about it anymore. When he dropped me off, he told me to give him a ring if I needed him."

Jay had gone a long way to bend the truth out of shape for Ceola and me, so I had a hard time imagining he was trying to explain something to us; it seemed like he was striving to do just the opposite.

"That first night home," Lily continued, "I told my father Billy had kidnapped me, which of course wasn't true, and that he'd beaten me, which *was* true. He was sympathetic at first, maybe a little relieved. But yesterday, when I finally told him about George, about falling in love with her, he aged ten years right in front of my eyes. He didn't shed a tear, or yell and carry on. He just left the house. I called Jay and asked him to pick me up around dusk, but to wait down the block and out of sight. I didn't want Jay and my father to get into it. When

Daddy returned, he just said, 'I want you to stay missing. I never want to see you again as long as I live.' He gave me an envelope full of cash and said, 'Consider this your inheritance. Now, you need to leave.' Even though Jay was waiting, I let Daddy drive me to the train station. I didn't want to risk the two meeting. Besides, I was sure it'd be the last time I'd see Daddy."

I wondered how my own father would've taken such news. I didn't understand how Lily withstood it. I also wondered if Ceola had been with Jay, waiting for Lily in the shadows. Did she know? She'd been with him at the carnival, after all.

"On the station platform, a girl came up to me," Lily said, shaking off her sadness with a halfhearted smile and answering my question as clearly as if I'd asked it aloud. "She told me her name was Cee and she was Jay's friend. I didn't know what to make of it. She kept saying, 'I can't believe you're alive.' She had a funny look on her face, like she thought I was the Second Coming or something. She asked me about photos, too—some snapshots of Jay's. He'd shown me photos of himself and his boyfriend, Robbie, but she meant photos of me. I didn't know what she was talking about. I really wish I knew what you're both talking about. Anyway, Billy was probably at the station too. She may have kept him away until I could board the train. I'm thankful for that."

"So you really don't know anything about the photos of the dead woman?" I pressed.

"Dead woman?" George echoed.

"The girl didn't mention a dead woman," Lily said.

"Jay showed Ceola and me several photographs of a murdered woman, who he led us to believe was you," I said slowly. "He pretended he'd only met you briefly on the train and had agreed to take your picture for a modeling application, for a department store in the city. But when he went to meet you, he found you murdered in the woods, and he took photos of your body—which of course was gone by the time we arrived at the crime scene. We even went to Jitters Gap twice and spied on your father under the pretense of an amateur investigation. He planted a pair of expensive shoes for Ceola to find in the woods and told us he discovered the second page of the letter you sent him in your father's garbage. I found the first page on my own; that's how I arrived at the Howard and Croc's. He didn't plan on that. I suspected he was up to something, and I wanted to find out what. That's why I'm here."

"You got more than you bargained for," Lily said, seemingly uninterested in Jay's treachery. "I'm truly sorry about Billy. He's a monster. Henry put him in the hospital, by all accounts, so he shouldn't be bothering you anymore. I wish he had killed him. It's a selfish wish. I wouldn't want that sort of trouble for Henry, though."

"How are Teddie and Tim?" I asked.

"Tim has some broken bones. Teddie is bruised and hysterical. They'll both recover, but it has taken something out of the place. I bet they'll close their doors for a while. But they're a resilient bunch down there. They have to be."

Lily smiled at me and gently placed her hand on my forearm. "I wanted to meet you and talk to you," she said, "because I need you to stop looking for me. I want to honor my father's request to stay missing. I never want to return to Jitters Gap. I want to begin a new life with George and be happy. Can you understand that?"

"I was only looking for you because I was looking for Jay."

"Maybe he's looking too?"

I knew what she meant and jerked my arm away from her.

"She needs to get some rest," George said, looking at me disapprovingly. "We've kept her up all night."

As I was showing the two women out, Lily spun in the hall and said, "Oh, I remembered another thing that girl mentioned. It was a story called 'A Date with Murder' or 'A Date with the Dead,' or something like that. I don't know why she thought I'd be interested, but she told me it has something to do with photographs and predicting the future. She asked if I had ever read it. A very strange girl."

I shut the door and curled up on the bed. I heard the chirping of birds, and the sky had brightened to dull lavender. As I drifted in and out of sleep, the title "A Date with Death" surfaced in my mind. It was the name of the story Ceola and Jay had read together several times. I'd seen the magazine in Ceola's hands. On the cover, the Grim Reaper loomed over a blonde in a tight evening gown, its skeletal hand reaching for her throat.

A few hours later, I awoke gasping for air.

17

CEOLA

When Jay came back from taking Letitia to her room, I was relieved to hear his voice calling to me. I dug out of the clutter and dusted myself off.

In that short period of time, the gloom he'd watched duck and skitter in the shadows of the room had entered him like a possessing spirit. His shoulders were drooped, his shirt collar twisted, his hair tossed forward, his eyes down. He even mumbled to himself as he searched for his whiskey.

After pouring a tumbler full, he gave me a hard stare, like he was sizing me up. Then, without a word of warning, he began unbuckling his belt. I backed away, pressing my shoulders against his dresser and pulling my arms tight around me.

"What are you doing?" I demanded.

He unbuttoned the fly of his trousers and shoved them down around his knees. Although his white undershorts weren't revealing—I'd seen much more in his photo—I was shocked and terrified. First, the photos, then the kiss, and now this!

"Look," he said, stepping forward and yanking up the hem of his shorts. Running from the top of his right knee to mid-thigh was a deep red scar, crosshatched with stitch marks. "Do you want to feel it?" he said, and gave me an odd half-smile.

I shook my head no.

"Here," he said, and shuffled over to me. "Come on. It's not going to hurt you. Really. I was going to show it to you before Grandma burst in."

I shrank from him, twisting my face away. It felt like he was a little boy threatening me with a frog or a water snake.

"Okay," he said. "That's okay." But I could hear the muddled disappointment in his voice.

"I'll touch it," I said, letting my arms fall to my sides. "I guess it won't hurt."

He reached out, caught me by the wrist, and, being gentle, guided my hand to his leg. I stuck out my index finger and ran it down the hard, puffy tissue. It was cool and dry, not what I expected.

"That's what the Germans did to me—what I did to myself, really. I just didn't want you thinking I made up that story." He released me, and I inched away from him, still leery. He pulled up his pants, buttoned them, and buckled his belt. "So it's time for me to tell you what I brought you here to tell you."

I found my place on the cot. He sat beside me, took a swig of his drink, and began again.

"I returned to England to recover at Netley Hospital on the southern coast," he said, his voice drifting, like he was a little unsure of himself. He recovered and continued.

After going under the knife, he was finally on the mend. He read a lot—the latest Christie or Carr novels—and several books on photography, even some books on writing codes. He studied the Victorian molding on the ceiling of the ward, tracing the rosettes and plaster curlicues over and over, anything to keep his mind off what had happened. But when he was sleeping, Darren's empty, snow-speckled face rose up in his mind, and he'd wake with his heart pounding, drenched in a cold sweat.

Once he was in a wheelchair, he set out to explore the hospital. With his leg propped in front of him like a knight with his javelin, he knocked open the French doors from his ward and rolled into another long hall that was subdivided by curtained cubicles like his own. Nurses scolded him for being in the way as they rushed from station to station, but despite the tsk-ing and finger waving, they seemed pleased to see a soldier up and moving around. He wound his way through the hospital's long, telescopic wings, observing the hustle and bustle of the staff. Occasionally, he would steer into a quiet corner, where he could study the gingerbread molding, or the shafts of warm sunlight, or whatever caught his fancy.

It wasn't an unhappy place for him. The way the morning sun hit the walls reminded him of the whitewashed art deco hotels on Ocean Drive in Miami. He pretended the beach he had dreamed about was just outside those windows. Eventually, as he healed, he grew bored with mystery novels and plaster ceilings and got the itch to take photos again. He wanted to replace the awful image of Darren with a new one, anything that would drive that moment from his mind.

He asked the head nurse if she could find a camera for him. It took several weeks, but finally, a handsome young sergeant paid him a visit. He handed him a Miniature Speed Graphic and said, "If you fix it, it's yours." Jay lit up.

The sergeant said, "Daekins is the name. Write to me if you get it fixed, and I'll make sure you have plenty of film." Jay spent the rest of the week tinkering with the camera. He wrote to Daekins when he was done, and within a week the film arrived.

He kept a photo journal, snapping photos of Netley's rooms and halls, its columns, towers, and brickwork, and its long stretches of arches and windows. He caught soldiers taking walks in the sunshine, leaning on one another out on the lawn, reading magazines, hitting croquet, playing cards, grinning and flipping him the bird. He wanted to capture the mood of the place, what life was like there. When he felt stronger, he snuck into the intensive care ward and snapped photos of dying soldiers, always taking time to talk to them and tell them what he was doing.

"I wasn't trying to be rude or hurtful," he told me. "I just wanted to record what was happening. Always, if they asked, I would stop."

"Did anyone want your photos?" I said. "Like *Photoplay* or something?"

Jay smiled. "The *Eagle's Eye*, this GI propaganda rag, published a couple—a shot of one-armed soldiers playing Ping-Pong and another of a local winter dance with perky British girls tugging on the arms of unsteady soldiers. They wouldn't publish any of the dead. They told me it was disrespectful and bad for morale. 'No one wants to end up like that.' But I never stopped. I wanted them to know someone was paying attention. I didn't care what the higher-ups said. Or what Darren said. The truth is the truth."

I placed my hand on Jay's forearm, trying to show sympathy the best I could, but the gesture rang false. I wasn't touching him for the same reason I had touched his scar. He looked at my hand like it was a big bug that had landed there, and then he glanced up at me. Right then, I recalled peering over the edge into my grandpa's well one night and seeing the moon's reflection in the rippling water at the bottom. Jay's eyes glittered just like that water. I felt like I did at the top of the Ferris wheel, like he wasn't looking at me but through me, at something he was remembering. I hated that feeling.

"Cee," he said, breaking away, "I haven't forgotten. You want to know why Lily Vellum is alive and who's in those photos I showed you and Bunny. I promise to get to that, but I had to tell you about the Ardennes and Netley. It has everything to do with what I'm about to tell you."

Once Jay could walk without crutches, he started taking leave and going to London. Large sections of the city were destroyed during the Blitz, but it was still buzzing with life. In a GI bar, he overheard drunk soldiers joking about Soho being London's "magical land of fairies." He was feeling lonely, so it seemed like the best place to go searching for others like himself. He began haunting bars and clubs, seedy places tucked behind dilapidated storefronts, holes-in-the-wall disguised by rubble, the remnants of air raids, but every boy he met was interested in only one thing. Their easy smiles and hungry, wandering glances made him uncomfortable, even angry. Jay just wanted someone to talk to. So he said to hell with Soho.

On February 10, a letter from Letitia came in the mail. It was a date he would never forget. After going on about the winter weather and complaining about the upkeep of the farm and pleading for him to return home, his grandmother scrawled in her loopy, uneven lettering—"A boy from town, who you may have known, is missing in action and is thought to be dead. His name is Robbie Bliss."

"Before I left Royal Oak," Jay said, stopping to catch the emotion in his throat, "I cornered Grandma in this very room. She sensed I was about to tell her something unpleasant and pulled away and shook her head no. I told her I was in love with a boy, that I loved boys, but she wouldn't hear it. She tried to push past me, but I held her by her shoulders. The expression on her face was pure agony, as if I was driving a stake through her. She began rambling about how I was aimless and wayward, that all I did was walk around with my camera taking pointless pictures, that hard work would straighten me out, that since I didn't grow up with a father as role model, I'd never learned how to be a man. When I told her that wasn't the case, she called me a fool and threatened to kick me out.

"'I love Robbie Bliss,' I said, calm as I could manage. I repeated *Robbie Bliss*, wanting his name to sink in. She spat at me, and I let her go.

"That afternoon, she was wailing in her bedroom, which I knew I was meant to hear. I tried hard not to hate her. When I saw her the next day, she was gloomy but said nothing about the argument. Gradually, her mood lightened, and she began treating me better, even joking with me. I became convinced she had come around. But when I read that letter on February 10, I knew I was wrong, very wrong. Her letter wasn't written to inform me of his death but to let me know, to her, he had never existed at all, and neither did I—at least not the boy who said he loved another boy."

I wrinkled up my forehead and frowned at Jay in a way I'd seen film actresses do. I wanted to show him love or at least understanding, but it wasn't how I felt. I was full, right up to the brim. I wanted to yell, "I've heard enough. That's all I can take!" but I just sat there, dumb and pretending.

He knocked back his whiskey. His facial muscles gradually loosened, and his eyes became watery and began searching the darkness. In a hushed, attenuated voice, he explained that, after news of his disappearance, Robbie began coming to him in dreams. He saw him by Culler's Lake, standing very still, the sun reflecting behind him. Then by the ocean, his feet sinking in the sand, the blue water shifting and deepening with the passing clouds. In these dreams, Robbie's face was calm, not smiling, and then sad and fixed. He was in ripped-up fatigues, snow on his shoulders and in his eyelashes. He had creases around his mouth, and his eyes were rings of ice, and then he was bleeding and his head was loose and open like Darren's—

"Stop!" I shouted, and launched to my feet. "Just stop!"

He looked at me, startled.

"Why would you think of him that way? It's, it's . . ."

"It's just what happened."

"He could still be alive."

"I don't think so, Cee."

"You're wrong!" I snapped loudly, not caring if I woke Letitia and the world, and like that, I was out the door, not in control of myself, throwing my body at the night like a goddamned lunatic.

I ran across the weedy lawn, the damp grass soaking my socks and shoes and the hem of my dress. Then I stopped, dead center of the yard, mosquitoes rushing to feast on my neck and forearms. Right there, I made the decision to never, ever talk to him again, just like Mama and Papa had wanted me to. I cursed him. I imagined lashing out, beating him with my tight fists. How could he be so hopeless? How could he imagine you dead, his friend, his lover? He *was* perverse or inverted, whatever that meant. I couldn't listen to him.

But as soon as I thought it, Jay called to me, urging me back. His voice punctured my anger, and for a few minutes, I just stood there, unable to move, my thoughts spreading out in front of me like a deck of playing cards.

I remembered the day Mama and Papa received notice you were missing. When I came home from school, Mama was in the kitchen, sitting at the table with the letter in front of her. She looked up at me but didn't say a thing. Papa entered the room behind me and dropped his hand on my shoulder. He usually wasn't home so early. He turned me around, bent down on one knee, and cupped his big hands over my shoulders, holding me in place. His eyes were red, and I could smell the stink of alcohol on his breath.

"Ceola," he said, his voice watery and choked. "Your brother is missing in action. Do you understand what that means?"

I nodded. But I didn't understand. "Missing" wasn't a permanent state, after all. Papa hugged me. Then he went to Mama and tried to smooth her hair back like he would a wounded animal's, but she jerked away, her face screwing up with pain. He picked up the letter and folded it real slow, making creases in it. Mama covered her mouth and turned away from me.

What was so horrible? You would be found. It was just a matter of days or weeks or months. You'd come back to us. You'd return home in the wake of the mail truck, like I'd always daydreamed about. You'd materialize out of a cloud of dust, the mist of early-summer pollen, glowing in the afternoon sun. Wisps of it would cling to you, spiraling away from you as you walked toward me. Sunlight would be all around, transforming the road and the field and the trees into a golden paradise. As you came closer, the light would flicker away like butterflies, and I'd see your face, clear as day. You'd be smiling, but it'd be a curious smile. You'd drop your duffel bag at the bottom of the porch steps and shake the bright dust off your fatigues. As you climbed the steps, I'd dash toward you, jumping at you, hugging you, just bursting with joy. You'd laugh and pull me close to you. Once you set me down, I'd take your hand and ask you, "Will you read a story to me?"

"Of course," you'd say.

"Will it have a good ending?"

"Yes," you'd say. "A very good ending."

I needed to hear Jay's story to the end, whether good or bad, so I turned around and went back to him.

Once inside his room, he handed me a glass of water and offered me a peace offering, a few Necco wafers he'd dug out of a drawer. I took them and ate a couple, making a face at their chalkiness. Although I'd cooled down on my trip across the lawn, my anger hadn't entirely gone away.

"I'm sorry," he said. "Just give me a chance—"

"It's late, and Mama and Papa are going to be *so*—"

"Please," he said.

"Fine."

He gave me a weary look and rubbed his eyes.

After reading the letter from Letitia, Jay took the next train to London. He spent his days slumped at cafés or limping through rubble and bombed-out buildings. At night, he drank. He would wake up in strange places, sometimes with men he didn't know. He listened to the V-1 bombs fly overhead, waiting for their engines to cut, a silent warning telling everyone to take cover and now, because the sky was falling. He forgot about his work at the hospital, but he still carried his camera with him everywhere.

"It was as if my heart was trapped inside that camera," he said, "and if we were separated, even for a day, I risked losing everything." He looked at me. "Then, one night, I saw Robbie."

While carousing at the Siren's Song, a usual stop on his circuit of oblivion, Jay had glanced over, and a few tables away, you—or someone who looked very much like you—sat, smoking a cigarette and sipping a highball.

He gawked for a while, stunned and confused, playing and replaying a beautiful dream: You had escaped the war and found your way to England. You had come looking for him in Soho, hoping you two would cross paths in the magical land of fairies.

It took him a long time to muster the courage to ask the nice Brit he had been chatting up if he knew who your doppelgänger was. He just laughed and said, "That's Miss Foxy Loxie, mate, the newest best-worst act in town. She's becoming famous for being belligerent on stage, ranting about the war. You wouldn't know, though, would you? He's rather appealing without that dress on."

After another drink, Jay decided to introduce himself. He went to your doppelgänger's table and stood behind him. He turned and met his eyes, and Jay said, "Sorry, I don't usually . . . You remind me of someone I once knew."

"I hope that's a good thing." He smiled.

"You're Miss Loxie."

"Only onstage. I'm Terry Trober now."

"Nice to meet you."

They shook hands, and Terry asked, "Have you seen my act?"

"No."

"Then you're really missing something."

"That's what I hear."

"Someone has to make fun of this war."

"Is that what you do?"

"I make fun of myself. It's one and the same."

They talked for a long time, drinking and smoking. For a while, Jay pretended Terry was you. After all, isn't everyone supposed to have a double out in the world? He had your thick brown hair and black eyes, even your long, careful fingers. He also smiled a bit like you, but with more sarcasm, more confidence. There was a roughness about him, a manliness despite his swishy mannerisms. He explained why he had fled the Navy. Unlike Jay, he couldn't hide easily among straight men. His captain mocked him, calling him his "little mermaid." When he retaliated, calling the captain a self-righteous ass, the brute beat him with an ax handle for insubordination. He broke four ribs and his nose.

"Foxy was a phoenix rising out of the ashes, partially a creation of necessity," Terry explained. "She's the opposite of everything the military stands for—a man dressed as a woman, making jokes about the war." He snickered. "She's nearly traitorous, I know."

Jay asked if Terry was afraid, but he just said, "If you're afraid for long enough, you grow numb to it. Besides, they're scared of me now."

Jay told him about being an aspiring photographer and his time at Netley and his tour on the front, but he didn't mention Darren. He told him he dreamed about living by the ocean one day, far from everything and everyone. When he said this, they were leaning toward each other, their knees almost touching.

"You're the best-looking man I've seen in a long time," Terry said, and leaned in for a kiss, taking hold of Jay's hand.

Jay closed his eyes and pressed his lips against Terry's, pretending he was you, hoping when he opened his eyes, it'd all be true. As he pulled away and saw a face he didn't know, his heart sank, and he felt a terrible rush of sadness, so powerful he couldn't breathe. He grabbed Terry's beer and finished it in one gulp. Terry made him promise they'd meet up the next day. Jay nodded his head but knew he wasn't going to keep his word.

Jay started shooting photos again. He scraped together some money and purchased a collapsible wooden tripod for his camera. One sunny afternoon, not three blocks from his quarters, he came across a bombed-out hotel. The rooms had been split in two like the building had been sliced down the center with a gigantic cake knife. Jay was fascinated by the way the furniture was still situated at right angles and the paintings were still straight on the walls. It looked like a little girl's dollhouse. He lugged out his heavy tripod and set up a shot of the hotel. Just as he was bringing it into focus, Terry stepped in front of the camera. He was wearing a beat-up leather jacket and white shirt. A loop of dark hair hung loose across his forehead.

"You stood me up," he said.

"Yeah. Sorry."

"I thought we were getting along."

"We were."

"I don't understand."

"I'm just . . ."

"Scared."

"Yes."

"Of what?"

Jay sighed and said, "Remember how I told you that you reminded me of someone I once knew?"

"Okay?"

"That someone, he's gone. MIA in the Pacific."

Terry was close to Jay. "I'm sorry. But he's gone. And I'm here."

He reached out and grabbed Jay's arm, holding it tight and looking at him. The buffed leather of his jacket reflected the sun, and the noise of the street faded into the background, and then it was just Terry and his dark eyes and his likeness to you. Jay wanted to pull him toward him and kiss him.

"Let's get something to eat," Terry said, letting go of Jay.

Jay packed up his camera and tripod, forgetting all about the shot, and the two went to dinner. That night, drunk on beer and cheap wine, Jay went home with him, fell into the fantasy again, and slept with him. In the morning, hungover and miserable, he slipped out before Terry woke up.

"I'd never planned on . . . ," Jay faltered. "Everything had changed, you see."

I gave him no sign I was judging him—I didn't feel I understood enough to judge him—but I could see the fear in his face.

That night, Jay found Terry backstage before his show. He was applying makeup, stopping from time to time to take a swig from a bottle of Scotch. "Why didn't you say good-bye this morning, honey?" he asked, as he rubbed rouge into his cheeks.

"I didn't want to wake you."

"Hmmm."

"I needed to get some air and think about things."

"You're frightened again."

"No."

"Hand me my wig." Terry took it and attached it to his hair with bobby pins, arranging and fluffing the blond curls. "The war has changed us all. We're all evolving into other people."

"For the worse."

"Maybe."

"My shoes," Terry said, flitting his hand at a pair of pumps. Jay gave him the shoes, and he slipped them on. "I don't feel in character until I have her shoes on. Footwear can transform you, almost as much as a highball. Did I tell you how I got the idea for Foxy?"

"Revenge, right?"

He smiled. "That's the motivation, my dear, not the inspiration. Several months ago, after a two-day bender, I was walking down Oxford Street, feeling blue, tired of turning tricks for cash. I didn't know what I was going to do, so I was just taking in the destruction and watching the early-morning light scatter across the broken glass—the night before, the Luftwaffe had paid another visit to the West End. As I passed the blown-out windows of Selfridges, I saw Christmas trees in the street, like expensive tumbleweed, and department store debris everywhere. Under an overturned Formica dinette table, I saw a woman's legs sticking out. I took action, amazed the Selfridges employees who were busy cleaning up from the attack hadn't noticed this poor woman trapped under a heavy table. I tripped across the smashed chairs and ruined remains of a party dress display and heaved the table over to discover my damsel in distress was, in fact, an attractive blond mannequin. She didn't have a scratch on her. Perfectly preserved. I started howling like a lunatic. I laughed myself dizzy and fell down in

the middle of the street. That's when I noticed her shoes. *These* shoes."
He kicked up his foot to make a point of it. "I remember looking at
them and thinking, *I bet my feet could fit in those.* I could fool people,
just as blondie had fooled me. So, from the ashes I rose!"

Terry laughed and winked. "I've got to go, but let's meet afterward." Then he stopped and said, "You're going to survive this war.
Both of us are. At this point, that's asking enough."

Jay joined the audience, and after a showy introduction by a small
bald man in a tight three-piece suit who called himself Mr. Beet,
Foxy Loxie made an entrance. The room broke into rowdy catcalls
and jeers. She started off with bad impersonations of Eva Braun and
Hitler in bed, the Führer stomping around and squawking at Miss
Braun, demanding she spank him with a copy of *Mein Kampf.* She
did another routine making Eleanor Roosevelt and Lorena Hickok
into two giddy lovers, leading the troops into battle. She made fun of
Axis and Allies alike. As she performed, her lips smudged into a messy
clown mouth, and her eyeliner streaked down her face in black tears,
and her big earrings caught her wig and pulled it to one side. Her dress
was soaked with sweat and splattered with the Scotch she tossed back
between jokes.

The audience booed her, laughed at her, and hated her.

"Tonight, my friends," Foxy said, as she was winding down, "we
have a special guest with us." She waved her gloved hand toward Jay.
"He's a sad dreamer, dreaming of a man who will never return from
the war. I said to him, 'Stop your dreaming and find a new man!' but
he's a scaredy-cat." She puckered her lips at him. "But, hey, girls, let's
give him a hand for keeping his dream alive. Maybe dreams do keep
you warm at night."

The room booed and laughed. All eyes were on Jay. One surly-looking man in a dirty T-shirt called out, "Let me suck your dick for five minutes, and you'll forget all about him!" More laughter.

Jay shrunk in his chair, trying to hide his embarrassment and anger—and his broken heart. He wanted to get the hell out of there, to tear through the crowd and run outside, but he was frozen with fear. "No," he said to me. "Horror. I was paralyzed with horror." Eventually he unglued himself and fled.

His last day of leave was clear and cold, but Jay wanted to be out in it, nowhere near a bar. He packed up his Speed Graphic and roamed the neighborhood near his quarters, weaving in and out of Londoners as they went on their way. He wandered into Hyde Park, stopping here and there to shoot craggy, leafless trees or frozen ponds or fields of dead grass. Although his leg was hurting him, his head felt clearer. The horror that had pinned him to his seat the night before was looser around his heart.

"I thought about the photos I took of Robbie on the beach, or Robbie beside Culler's Lake, or Robbie smiling back at me," he said. "I felt calm . . . and then I heard my name called out from behind me."

It was a man's voice, but when he looked, he saw a woman. Terry had found him. Jay grabbed his camera and his tripod and limped away, using the tripod as a cane. He stumbled down a dirt path and into a thicket, ripping through the dead undergrowth just as quick as he could, stomaching the pain as it shot through his leg.

Once he broke free of the woods and into a clearing, Terry was close to him and clawed at him, catching him by the shoulder and spinning him around. As he did, Jay's camera banged hard against his side, throwing him off-balance. Terry steadied him and said, "What are you doing? Why are you running from me?" His blond wig was combed and curled, and his makeup was neat, even pretty. He was out of breath and reeked of Scotch.

"I'm headed back to Netley tomorrow," Jay said.

"That wasn't my question."

"I'm not coming back."

"You're embarrassed by me?"

"Look at you."

Terry was wearing a tailored suit with a button-front, white gloves, star shaped earrings, and black-bowed shoes. He shrugged and said, "Big deal."

"You're not who I thought you were or who I hoped you'd be."

"I'm not Robbie, you mean."

"You stood up there last night and spewed shit at everyone, like your word was the final word. You embarrassed yourself and offended all the soldiers in that room. It's all a joke to you. A fucking joke!" Jay pulled away and stalked across the dead grass and uneven stones.

But Terry followed him. "That's idealistic bullshit. The men in that room who have lost the most laugh the hardest."

"They hate you," Jay said over his shoulder.

"They hate the war."

"They booed you." He turned. "They tossed their drinks at you. They spit."

Terry reached for him. "Please, Jay."

"Get away from me!"

Air raid sirens began to wail. Everything stood still. The trees. The sky.

The self-guided V-1 bombs, like huge metal blackbirds, glided over them, their engines humming, propellers whirling—and then the engines cut, the propellers stopped, and silence rushed through the air, over the treetops, and to their ears, signaling the countdown. One–one thousand. Two–one thousand. Three–one thousand. *The sky is falling. The sky is falling.*

The first bomb hit nearby, a few blocks away, shaking the ground. Then another hit, even nearer. And another. Jay heard the screech of traffic and the bleating of ambulances. And shouts. They were closer to the street than he thought. Terry caught his arm and twisted it and said something, his face a blur of panic and curly blond hair. Jay jerked away and, in counterpoint to the explosions around him, hit Terry with the platform end of his tripod. His friend, his lover, fell to his knees, and he hit him again. He wanted to knock that wig off his head. Terry's hands were up, little ghosts flapping at him. He wanted to smash Foxy Loxie out of him.

"He was begging me to stop," he said, "but, Cee, I swear I couldn't. Something horrible had me by the throat, something I had no control over. I saw only the smirk on his face from the night before. *Maybe dreams do keep you warm at night.*"

Terry began crawling away from Jay on all fours, one foot missing a shoe. He was bleeding from his scalp. More bombs exploded. Trees splintered and debris clattered and the ground shook under his feet like it was about to open under him and swallow him whole. He left Terry and scrambled over the rough terrain and back through the woods, adrenaline overriding the pain in his leg.

When he was a few yards from the trees, nearly back to the path, a stray bomb hit in the woods behind him, not far from where he'd left Terry. The impact knocked him forward, and he tumbled down an embankment, the tall grass slowing him as he rolled to the bottom. When he stopped, he waited, holding his breath, staring at the sky, his camera still strapped to him and the gory tripod gripped tight in his hand.

"I remembered the snow drifting down through the trees in the Ardennes," he said. "I couldn't call your brother to me anymore. That dream was spoiled. I didn't want to get up."

The air raid sirens eventually stopped, and then all he could hear was a ringing in his ears. He got up and went to find Terry. The last bomb had hit the street a hundred yards away and shredded the trees nearby. Whether Terry had moved himself or not, he didn't know, but he wasn't where Jay had left him. When Jay found him near a boulder, he knew he was dead. His torso was twisted and his face was covered with blood, but his wig, his fake breasts, his white suit, and even his earrings were still defiantly in place.

"I'd killed him," he said, his eyes tracing invisible shapes on the wall across from us, "so I began snapping photos of him, loading and reloading the film fast, focusing and framing over and over, thinking of Darren's dead eyes staring back at me. It was my penance. It was my burden to preserve the evidence. *I must capture everything*, I thought. *I must carry it with me*."

When he finished, he dragged Terry underneath a tree and took off his wig, his earrings, his gloves, and his suit and balled them up. He gathered the shoes and wiped the blood and makeup from his face. He told himself he was saving his friend the humiliation of being discovered dressed as a woman, but that had nothing to do with it: "I wanted to see *him* again, even bloody and broken. I wanted to see *his* body. I wanted to see *his* face. *Him*."

He fled to his quarters and then to Netley in the morning. By the end of the week, he was on his way home, honorably discharged because of "injuries incurred in the line of duty." The real reason was, of course, he had failed to do his job at the hospital. He was a drain on their resources and no longer useful.

"And useful is one thing you must always be in a war," he said. "Even Foxy was useful."

📷

I'd heard too much that night, more than the younger me could take in. I wanted to be steaming mad, but I wasn't. I wanted to show my disgust and disapproval, like I know Jay expected me to, but I didn't. Maybe I was in shock. I had dreamed of you returning so many times, you appearing out of a cloud of dust, like some angel. I understood why Jay wanted to believe Terry could be like you, a second chance, a resurrection. Both of us had wished you back to us, but like they say, be careful what you wish for.

"It's Terry in the photos," I said. "That's who you showed us. Not Lily. That was all made up, wasn't it?"

"It's Foxy, not Terry. Don't make that mistake."

"Why did you show them to us?"

"I wanted to give you a mystery like one you'd find in your detective magazines, like the stories your brother loved, like the ones he would tell us."

"What about the shoes? Lily's shoes?"

"I threw away his wig, his gloves, all of that—but I kept the shoes. I needed to keep a part of her."

I thought about this and said, "I want to see the photos."

"They're not here."

"Where are they?"

"They're safe."

"I *want* to see them."

He looked at me. His eyes seemed to say, *That's it. That's all I'm going to tell you.* Anger began tapping at the inside of my heart, gentle at first, then in sharp jabs. I crossed my arms and said, "You hid the shoes for me to find, didn't you?"

"Yes."

"So it was all a big lie."

"A lie folded around the truth," he said, a little smug.

"We would've figured it out, you know."

"I was going to introduce you to Lily when we were at Jitters Gap. I thought she wanted me to pick her up and take her to the station, but instead of walking down the street and finding us, she went with her father. I don't know why. Maybe she couldn't get away from him. But that's why I told you to go see her before she caught the train. It was time. I needed to tell you the truth, to bend things back in shape, to set things in motion. It's like 'A Date with Death.' Once she opens the photo album, she can watch her life unfold in front of her. She sees how she'll die. She sees how all her choices will lead her to that moment. She sees everything. I'm like her." He offered me a fragile smile and reached out and touched my cheek, his thumb tracing the side of my face. I tensed up, tightening my arms across my waist.

"I've done a horrible thing," Jay said. "A horrible, horrible thing."

I withdrew sharply from his hand.

"Stories are like nesting eggs," he said, clearly wounded I had recoiled from him. "One inside another, inside another, on and on. Fucking endless."

"Nesting eggs? What do you mean?"

And then his face—no, his entire body altered, it slouched, it crumbled. His mouth fell into a big, gaping O, and his blue eyes went dark, like black holes. I thought of the groaning, foamy-mouthed zombies on the cover of the March issue of *Weird Stories*. He fumbled for my hand and caught it as I tried to pull away. I cried out and struggled, but he held on, his fingers pressing hard on the bone.

"Please, Cee . . . ," he stammered, his voice like sandpaper, "tell me there's something at the center . . . I *need* to hear it . . . from you."

"There is," I said, desperate for him to let go. He just gawked at me like he'd never seen me before. "There is something there, at the center," I tried again, having no idea what that meant, tears welling up in my eyes. "I promise."

At that, he released my arm. He wiped the edges of his mouth. "Thank you," he said in a whisper. "You need to go now. It's so late. But first, I have something for you."

I just sat there, petrified.

He slipped his fingers under the mattress, retrieved your journal, and gave it to me, his hand shaking like an old man's. "Keep it safe," he said, standing up. "It's all you really have of Robbie. It's who he was. I don't need it anymore. I'm sorry I made you give it to me. That was wrong. You were right to push me down." Then he placed both hands on my shoulders, leaned toward me, and kissed my forehead.

Before she left for the city, Sheila had to find the deed to the house. She couldn't leave without it. It was the ticket to her new life.

She turned on all the lights in her aunt's study and began her task. After a few minutes of riffling through papers, she glanced over at the safe. To her surprise, even though she had spun the dial earlier that evening, it was open. Inside, the photo album was as she had left it. She shut the door, hesitated, and opened it again. She pulled out the album and took it to the desk. Maybe it contained a clue to the whereabouts of the deed.

As she unfolded the cloth, she noticed the corner of a piece of paper sticking out from the back of the album. She must have dislodged it when she'd shoved the book into the safe earlier. She gently slid it out. In the center was a detailed design for a box camera and below it a carefully diagramed drawing of a lens, complete with measurements, specifications, and directions written in a language with an archaic-looking alphabet she didn't recognize. Her aunt had jotted a note beside it:

The eye of God sees everything, but not clearly, not with permanence. This is permanence. This is proof!

She considered the note, shook her head, and tossed it on the desk. She returned to the album.

On the first page, the photos had changed. They were empty black rectangles. She turned another page, and although it was difficult to make out, it appeared to be a photo of the front of the house, but at night. *Someone is playing a trick on me*, she thought. *Someone is here. That explains why the safe was open.* She followed the photos down the page until she reached a photograph of the front door . . . with a figure standing in front of it!

She heard a knock and let out a sharp cry. Had she really heard it? She waited. The knock repeated. Her heart was pounding. She grabbed a pearl-handled letter opener from the desk.

Before making another move, she flipped the page. The next photo was a close-up of the man. That chin! Those eyes! It was Thomas. She waited for another knock. Nothing. In the next snapshot, he was gone. Why was he here, and where did he go? None of this made sense. Was the album really predicting the future? Could it be? Even if it did have this power, then who is to say how it works . . . or what it means?

She clutched the letter opener even tighter, her knuckles whiten-ing. She flipped the next page of the album. Again, it was a page of empty rectangles—and then the lights went out.

She heard the clatter of breaking glass at the other end of the house. She crossed quickly to the door. She didn't want to be trapped. She felt her way down the hall, moving away from the sound, using the molding on the wainscoting to guide her. Her eyes were adjusting to the darkness.

Once she was in the main hallway, she could see the outlines of objects—Majestica's ornate settee, the great oriental vase by the front door, and the dull shine of the mirror opposite the settee. Nothing out of place, nothing broken. The grandfather clock boomed on the staircase, and she spun with fright, but no one was there. It was 1:00 in the morning.

All the noises she had heard had been on the first floor, so she thought she would be safer on the second. There was a telephone in the master bedroom. She could call for help. She grasped the railing and moved noiselessly up the carpeted stairs. When one of the wood risers squeaked, she sucked in her breath and quickened her pace. Once at the top, she paused and stared down the long hall, lined with doors. Terror rose up through her, but she quickly batted it away. She was determined to escape this. She dashed down the hallway to the bedroom and locked the door behind her.

18

BUNNY

drove out of DC before churchgoers woke up and before the streets filled with cars. Morning sunshine streamed between the empty, neo-classical government buildings, colliding with windshields, making them flash and glow. The journey back to Royal Oak was promising, a time to roll down the window, to let a breeze in and the chaotic events of the night before out.

As the city receded in the rearview mirror and the fresh smell of cut grass wafted in, I felt better. But as I wound my way to the ridge on the horizon, the mountains huddled together with their backs to me, as if I no longer belonged to them. As I passed through the dim limestone gateway of Culler's Mountain Tunnel, I switched on the headlights and, chilled by the damp subterranean air, rolled up the window. I heard Billy Witherspoon's voice rise up from the echoing motor: *She is fucking real! A goddamn dyke. Another fuckin' dyke.* I pressed the gas pedal and sped into the daylight, leaving the inside of the mountain far behind.

When I arrived in Royal Oak, I should've gone directly home, curled up, and slept. I should've ignored the spite and ugliness doing laps around my heart. I should've been smarter, been better. But I took a right instead of a left and drove to the Bliss home. I had decided it was my moral duty to tell them about Jay. His lies had led me into his twisted, subterranean world, and soon, those same lies would lead Ceola there. I wondered if he had taken Robbie there, if he had told him lies too.

The Blisses' farmhouse was lifeless, and I wondered if they were at church. Holes and neat piles of dirt lined the driveway, which I assumed were intended for the row of saplings leaning against the clapboard siding. It looked like the busy work of a large, compulsive gopher. The house itself had obviously been cobbled together in different stages of building. Its original builder (Old Mr. Bliss, Bob's father, I imagined) hadn't had the money or aesthetic knowledge to build an attractive, balanced architectural structure. With its sagging eves and rambling layout, it was dreary and charmless, even in the lemony morning light.

I parked the car and sat quietly, considering what I was about to do. I wanted to elicit a very specific reaction. I wanted to see Bob's fists curl and his face burn. I wanted to see his tears and spittle. I wanted him to express, as I knew only he could, what I felt. So I got out of the car, pulled my coat tightly around me to conceal my ripped dress, and approached the house.

Margery Bliss was waiting, framed in the screen door, her eyes black and hard and her mouth a grim slit stretched tightly beneath her nose. I nodded, and she pushed the door wide. Her dress was intended as a statement of her stainless morality, as if she wanted to show the people of Royal Oak she was more at home in the Depression than in the surging wartime economy.

As I walked up the steps, she said, "What are you doing here?" Her hair fell back from her cheek, and I saw the wine-colored birthmark that ran up the side of her face and disappeared into her hairline.

"I've come to talk to you."

"We don't receive unannounced visitors, especially on Sundays." She said this with great formality, and it came off oddly pretentious.

"There is something you need to know about Jay Greenwood."

She narrowed her eyes at me. "Come on, then," she said, and I followed her.

The house had the atmosphere of a summer home closed for the winter. The furniture in the living room appeared unused and positioned just so, as if it were only for display. The pale light from the windows revealed a skim of dust on the hardwood and upholstery, deadening the room's dark red and forest green motif. Margery directed me to sit and left me, making no noise as she moved. I smelled coffee and craved its warmth, but I didn't dare ask for a cup. Such a request from an unannounced guest, I imagined, would've been beyond insult.

Both Margery and Bob emerged from the back of the house. Bob had been sleeping, the side of his red face marked with lines from a bedspread and his wisp of thin brown hair mussed. He glanced at me warily, as if he were a little afraid of me, and then crossed the room, opened a wooden cabinet, and poured himself a whiskey. Margery made a gesture of protest, but he scowled at her, and she turned toward me, closing her expression with a frown.

"Mr. Bliss," I said, growing impatient. "I don't mean to bother you this morning, but I need to tell you something about Jay."

Bob knocked back his whiskey. "Do you know where my daughter was last night?"

"No. I've been in DC."

"Why would a man's only daughter, only remaining child, want to cause him so much pain? Can you answer me that? Can you? You're a daughter. Would you do that to your father?"

"I don't know where Ceola was last night. I was in the city."

Margery crossed her arms. "Was Jay with you?"

"No."

Bob finished his drink and came to his wife's side, hovering close but not touching her. "What were you doing at the carnival?"

"I was following them."

"Why?"

"They were keeping something from me."

"What were they keeping from you?"

"Why were *you* there?"

He paused for a moment, swaying a little.

"I was at the stop sign on Slater's Road and they drove right past me," he said. "I couldn't believe it. To see them together. In the car. Even after I warned Cee about him." His eyes were growing wider, more pained. "Now, answer me. What were they keeping from you?"

"That's why I was in DC."

Margery huffed and shook her head. "You come here and you interrupt our morning and you—"

"Margery, let her talk," Bob interrupted.

"I went to DC, because I thought Jay was lying to me, to your daughter too. He was telling us a story that wasn't true." I didn't mention the photographs or Lily's name. I didn't want to explain everything to them, just what was essential. I focused on Bob Bliss, his watery eyes open, almost welcoming, and his bottom lip slack. "At a place called Croc's, a bar, I learned Jay has been living a double life in the underbelly of the city. He made friends with degenerates, cross-dressers, and thugs. I had to go there and talk to these people. I was attacked." I pulled the collar of my coat back, revealing the bruises along my collarbone. My self-control faltered, and I allowed tears to come.

Margery was suddenly by my side, her hand gently taking mine. "I'm sorry, dear," she said. "I didn't realize . . . I was thoughtless."

Bob was standing over me, the expression on his face unchanged and demanding. I wiped away the tears and said, "He's a homosexual."

"How do you know?"

"I talked to people who knew him. I went to one of their bars."

I heard Margery exhale. She withdrew her hand.

"And our daughter has been spending all her time with him," Bob said.

"He's trying to destroy us," Margery said in almost a whimper. "First Robbie, then Ceola."

First Robbie, then Ceola. I was beginning to understand.

"He twisted his mind out of shape," Margery said, looking at Bob now. "And we lost him because of it. We sent him away because of it. It was the only thing we could do."

Bob brought his rough hand to his forehead and turned away from me. I couldn't tell if he was crying or just hiding from us.

Again I found myself in the middle of Culler's Lake, crying out. *Wait for me! Wait for me!* But this time, as the memory echoed through me, I finally understood that I had been utterly irrelevant to Jay and

Robbie. They were never going to wait for me. In my heart, I had known it since my eighteenth birthday, but I couldn't admit it. I hadn't come to the Blisses' to protect Ceola; I'd come for revenge.

I stood up abruptly. "I should go," I said. Bob still had his back to me. Margery nodded and gave me a smile so queasy, so pained I will never forget it. It was horror and pleasure all in one. For a moment, I saw myself in her, and my heart sank.

I crossed the room toward the front door. Before I reached for the knob, something on the stairs caught my eye. Sitting on the top stair, her hands gripping the wood plank beneath her, was Ceola.

To this day, I've never recovered from the look on her face. It was dark, petulant, and accusatory, but it wasn't a childish look. It couldn't be easily dismissed. She saw through me. We both knew I had just set something horrible in motion. She rose and started down the stairs, her eyes fixed on me. I fled.

The door to Jay's lair was ajar, and I gently pushed it open. Despite the glow of sunshine through the windows, the shaded lamp in the corner was on. Jay was curled up on his cot like a boy, fast asleep. His blond hair was swept forward across his forehead, and his lidded eyes twitched when I came close. I sat near his feet and watched him for a few minutes. I wondered what he was dreaming about. The war? Robbie? Lily? Ceola and me?

Peeking out from under the bed, I saw the Ferragamos, one of which was on its side, the sole turned toward me. The initials FL L were visible. What did that mean? Was it a person? Who was FL, and why did she or—I had to consider this possibility—*he* mark the shoes left and right? Perhaps I was correct: the shoes belonged to someone in show business. Teddie? George? But none of the initials matched.

Jay stirred, and I placed my hand on his leg and shook him lightly. He jerked awake and propped himself up on his elbows. "What are you doing here?" he asked, wiping the bleariness from his eyes.

I had planned to be angry with him, to demand the truth or else, but I couldn't summon the energy. Already, my anger had begun to collapse in on itself. Despite all I knew, when I was with him, when I could see him and touch him, I was still in love with him. I could only hate the idea of him, not the man himself. I never was a coldhearted person, despite what Ceola thought.

"I've been to DC," I said.

"Yes."

"You haven't been honest with me."

"No."

"I know what you are. I know what you did there. I know Lily is alive and well. I met her, and she told me how you helped her."

Jay was sitting up now. He blinked several times, astonished but calm. "So you know," he said.

"I went to Croc's. I met Teddie and Henry and a fellow named Tim. Billy Witherspoon showed up with a bunch of sailors and tore the place apart. He threw me against a wall and threatened me with a knife." I didn't want to tell him about my ripped dress or what Billy had said to me.

"Are you all right? You look all right."

"Nothing that won't heal." I kept my tone flat.

"How did you find Croc's?"

"I snooped around your room and found the first page of the letter Lily wrote to you, the second page of which you oh-so-cleverly tried to pass off as a clue . . ." When he didn't respond, I asked, "Jay, why did you do it? Why did you lie to us?"

"For Cee."

"I don't understand."

"It was my way of trying to explain it."

"What?"

"Everything. The truth. But it was useless."

"The truth about what?"

Jay frowned and said nothing. I wanted to grab him and shake him. I wanted to slap him and pull his hair. I remembered my dream of him, my blows bouncing off him as if he were made of hard rubber. I want him to just say it—whatever it was. After all, didn't I deserve the truth?

"Who's in those photos, if it's not Lily?"

"A friend."

"Does she have a name?"

"Terry Trober—but in that outfit, he was Foxy Loxie."

I laughed. Jay remained grim.

"He died in London, during a bomb raid," he continued. "The photos are of his body."

"The shoes are his," I said. "F for Foxy and L for Loxie. He was a performer."

"Yes."

"Like Teddie."

"Much better than Teddie."

I put my hands together. Using my powers of deduction had given me a rush. "I still don't understand why you made up a fake story to fit the photographs. What was the point?"

"Boredom."

I leaned toward him and took his hand in mine. Looking in his eyes, his irises like rings of cool blue neon, I said, "I don't believe you. It's more than that."

There was a flicker, a brief acknowledgment, and then a door, imperceptible but instantly recognizable, slammed shut, like a secret hatch snapping back into place in one of Ceola's detective mysteries. He wasn't going to tell me any more. He didn't trust me.

I let his hand go and rose to my feet. "I've just come from the Blisses'. I told them about you and about the sort of people you cavorted with in DC. I told them about what happened to me. I thought they should know. They need to protect Ceola from you."

Jay lurched forward, his right arm back, his chest forward, as if he were going to hit me. "Why would you—?"

I steadied myself against the picnic table; a stack of books toppled to the floor.

"How could you do that to her?" he shouted. "Bob Bliss is a drunk and a goddamn bastard. He sent his only son off to war because he was in love with me. And he beats Cee. Who's going to protect her from him now?"

I just stood there, speechless.

"You don't have any idea what's going on, do you?" he continued. "You've been blind from the beginning. When you look at Cee or me or anyone, all you see is what *you* want. But do you even know what that is, what you *really* want?"

I tried to speak.

"You want someone to fuck you. You want someone to end the pretense. Well, I'm not that guy, Bunny. I'll *never* be that guy. So just move on and leave me the hell alone."

With that, he spun around and was out the door.

I slumped on the edge of the picnic table and stared at the books scattered across the floor. On a scrap of paper beside one of the books was the encryption—XF XJMM LFFQ B TFDSFU. "WE WILL KEEP A SECRET."

I wrapped my arms around myself and wept.

I heard a noise behind me. Letitia was there, her shotgun wedged in her armpit, aimed at me, her blue-veined claw on the trigger. I jumped to my feet and backed away from her, wiping tears from my face, tucking away my self-pity like a dirty handkerchief. Her thin jaw was set and her eyes furious black slits. She came forward, the heavy shotgun swaying unsteadily. "Where is he? Tell me. *Tell me.*"

"He went to the Bliss farm, I think. He thinks Ceola's in danger."

"Why can't he leave those people alone?"

She lowered the gun, and I said, "Do you know about him? What he is?"

She nodded her head. "I know him best."

"Do you approve?"

"What does it matter if I approve? He's all I have." At that, she turned her back to me, said, "Get out," and left the room.

I was alone again. I wanted to scream and shatter the conservatory, but I wasn't going to indulge myself. I wasn't going to lose control. Instead I just sat there, forcing my guilt back into the corners of the room, back under the bed, back in the trunk, trying to resist the terrible revelation about to surface . . .

The engine of a car started, shaking me from my stupor. I was confused. I thought Jay had taken his grandmother's car. I went to the
door and flung it open. Letitia was driving away in the station wagon.
My mother's Oldsmobile was missing. Jay had stolen it.

19

CEOLA

hange, it seems to me, happens in one of two ways, Robbie. Usually it just inches along, visible only in the proverbial rearview mirror. Most things in the world change this way. Massive glaciers, grinding away, sculpt entire regions. Rivers hollow out canyons over thousands of years. The Appalachians, once as tall and impressive as the Rockies, so I'm told, crumble into the mossy, tree-covered slopes we grew up on. Humans grow taller and sturdier—and plumper!—than their ancestors. The low doorframes in colonial homes remind us a smaller, more compact people lived here before us.

But in some cases, change happens, well—just like *that*. A tree is struck by lightning and split in two. A house buckles and slides into a sinkhole. A man is vaporized by a bomb. There, and then not there. Only violence can bring about this sort of change. Maybe that explains why Jay turned on Terry Trober and beat him. He had reached the point at which anger had to flow out, not in. It was a force of Nature, a change that would lead him to me, to Mama and Papa, to his own fate.

When I made it back to the house after leaving Jay, it was well past midnight. Papa was passed out, snoring up a storm in the guest bedroom, and Mama was in the kitchen, sipping some cold coffee, reading the Bible. When she saw me, she started in on me. Who did I think I was? How could I be so thoughtless, so cruel? She said they'd been searching high and low for me, that Papa went over to the Greenwood place two or three times, but no one would come to the door. He even went to the police and reported me as a missing person. Later I discovered that wasn't true. He had been too drunk and embarrassed to go to the authorities. Mama sent me to bed and told me they'd discuss a suitable punishment for me when Papa was awake.

The next morning, I woke up to Mrs. Prescott's Olds pulling into the driveway, its long green hood and polished chrome reflecting the sunshine. I crept to the top of the stairs and listened to Bunny betray Jay and me. I heard every coldhearted word of it, but I was too scared, too speechless to stop it. I just sat there, biting my lower lip, feeling like a coward. When she left, she saw me, and I gave her the meanest eyeball I could. I wanted to run her over with the car, or push her off a cliff, *anything* gruesome. Maybe a pit of vipers or an iron maiden or some clever deathtrap from one of your magazines. But as much as I wanted revenge, my experience with Jay had made me doubt him too. I didn't know what to believe.

After Bunny was gone, Papa found me and dragged me downstairs by my arm. He started cursing me, calling me "stupid girl" and "little slut." I braced myself, flattening my spine against the wall, turning my head away from him, hoping he would hit me so it would end. Mama just stood stock-still, her eyes hot and red like coal embers.

"What have you done?" Papa demanded. "You were with him after we told you not to be. You encouraged him. *You know* what he did to Robbie. How could you, Cee? How could you be so goddamned stupid?"

He didn't hit me. Instead he went on, threatening me and shaming me until he ran out of things to say and left the house.

I wanted to hide. I wanted to escape from the room and the house. I took a step, but Mama caught me by the arm and bent over me. All I could see was her skin drawn tight over her cheekbones, her thin, mouse-fur eyebrows, and the deep creases lining her mouth. It was an old woman's face, though she wasn't even fifty.

As she leaned in closer, the locket she'd worn since I could remember slid out of the top of her dress and dangled in front of me. When I was a little girl, she'd let me hold it and open it. Inside, there were baby photos of you and me. "That's you," she'd said. "Just a little thing. You were such a happy baby. You were both happy babies." I wanted to grab the locket right then and yank it away from her.

"Ceola Elizabeth," she said, pressing her fingers into the fleshy part of my forearm and gritting her teeth like a wild animal. "It's a terrible thing to disappoint your father. It's ugly and selfish."

I shook her grip and made a beeline for your room.

As always, everything was just so. The red cowboys on the wallpaper. The beat-up dresser. The twin beds draped with those thin, threadbare bedspreads. The keepsakes. Postcards from the beach. Academic awards. Photos of friends. It was a shrine to Mama's idea of who you were, Robbie, and I tell you, I wanted to destroy it. I wanted to set fire to it and watch her scream. *It's not him,* I would tell her. *Don't be sad. There's no reason to be. I'm burning a lie. Deep in the drawers, under his underwear, between the pages of detective magazines, that's where you'll find the real Robbie, lusting after hand-some boys and caught up in the intrigues of his own imagination. That's him, Mama.*

I approached your bed and pulled back the dusty linens. I paused and stared at the place where you had slept. I took off my shoes and got in, covering my head with the bedspread.

I dreamed of you again. You were there, sitting on the edge of your bed, writing as you used to do. I didn't know why, but I was worried about you, worried that something in the house, some unknowable something, was after you; we needed to leave. I grabbed your arm, and we began searching for a way out, but our house had grown. Every door opened to another hallway, endless. Then, just like that, we were outside, lost in the maze of a fairy-tale forest with large mushrooms and silver flowers and insects the size of dogs. As the dream went on, I grew more and more frustrated. And then you stopped dead in your tracks. You heard something, heard *it* coming for you. I looked up at you and—

I woke to the sound of wheels crunching in the gravel. I went to the window and again saw the Olds as it came to a stop around the edge of the house, just out of sight. Had Bunny come back for round two? I heard a car door open and close, then voices. Papa was shouting. I heard another voice, not Bunny's, a voice that first sounded angry, then, after a couple of words, was frightened like a whipped dog.

A cry split the air, rattling the panes of the dormer windows—or at least that's how it seemed. I forced the window open. I couldn't see a soul—they were toward the front of the house—but I heard the second voice clear as a bell.

"You sent him to die! How could you?"

It was Jay. I froze for a second, trying to think what to do.

I heard another cry and bolted from the room, flinging the door open so the knob banged the wall, jangling the hardware loose. Mama was standing at the bottom of the stairs, observing the scene out front through the screen door. She spun around and blocked my exit. "You're not going out there. Stay in your room." I gave her a furious look and dashed down the stairs and out the back door. "Don't you dare!" she screamed like a banshee. "Come back here, Ceola! Don't go out there!"

I jumped from the top step of the porch to the ground but lost my footing and fell. I rolled on the dry grass and got up again. The voices were louder and clearer now, but I wasn't paying attention to what they were saying. My anger was so deep, so tangled around the roots of my soul that I didn't understand what I was doing. I scrambled across the yard, grabbed a rusty clothesline pole, swung my body in the right direction, and rounded the edge of the house. My heart was in my throat, and my body—so slim and boyish then—felt like a bullet whizzing through the air toward the two of them.

Jay crouched near Papa's most recent sapling ditch, his back toward Papa, head tucked under his arms. Papa towered over him, the trench shovel he used for planting cocked over his right shoulder. The red blade whipped through the air like a catapult released from its catch and made contact with the center of Jay's back. *Thunk.* Jay moaned and curled tighter into himself. Again there was red against the blue sky, just a flicker, and then the flat of the blade connected with Jay's shoulder and his neck. *Thunk.*

I barreled toward Papa and threw my arms around his waist, trying to pull him away. He jabbed his elbow at me, hitting my cheekbone hard. I tumbled to the ground.

Papa kept on striking Jay from the side, Lou Gehrig with a shovel, the blows coming faster and harder. Jay kept trying to stand, like he wanted to open himself up, like he wanted to be an easier target. I failed to find my feet and, rolling to my side, became aware of another car in the driveway. The station wagon.

Standing straighter, Jay took a few steps forward. *Thunk*. The shovel caught the side of his head, and he twisted toward me, his arms swinging out like a ballerina going into a spin. His eyes were so sad and blurry. The next blow came, and it threw him off-balance. He stumbled sideways to the edge of the hole Papa had been digging.

I forced myself up and belted out, "Stop! Papa, stop!"

Over my shoulder, I was aware of movement. The glint of metal. I heard Mama scream from the front porch, "She's got a gun!"

Behind me, about twenty feet away, Letitia stood, her raggedy housecoat hanging off one shoulder and her shotgun aimed at us, the end of its barrel making little shaky circles in the air. Her face was horrible, like a bull lowering its head. "Move out of the way," she said to me. "Move!"

I recalled her words from the night before. *No more disgrace, Jay.* Everyone was attacking him; everyone wanted to tear him to bits.

I moved quick as I could—toward him, not away—thinking I could knock him out of danger. But Letitia wasn't aiming at him, so when I stepped out of her sightline, she fired. There was a loud pop. I planted my feet so I wouldn't fall over.

The shovel fell to the ground with a clunk.

I turned again. Jay was in front of Papa and then against him. Papa held him from behind, his hands under his armpits. The fabric of Jay's shirt was shredded on the left side, near his rib cage. His lips were lined with red, like he'd been eating cherry pie, and his eyes flickered with pain. Papa supported him for a second and then released him, refusing to help him.

Jay hit the ground and rolled over the hole Papa had been digging, his face away from me. His left foot twitched. I heard him moan. Letitia lowered the shotgun, her eyes as large as spotlights and her boney body shaking like a skeleton on a string. Papa moved past me and snatched the gun from her.

Later I understood that the shot had been meant for Papa. Letitia was trying to stop him from attacking Jay. Jay had hurled himself between the buckshot and its intended target on purpose.

Jay was losing a lot of blood. His shirt was soaked through, and his breathing was just a faint gurgle in his throat. He mumbled something, and I ran to him, putting my arm around him. *Get up!* I screamed inside my head. *Just stand up!* I tugged on him. He nodded like he understood what I was trying to do. But I couldn't do it alone. My twelve-year-old muscles weren't strong enough. "Papa!" I called out, but he was preoccupied with Letitia. He had ahold of one of her arms, the way you would hang onto a bad child, and she was struggling and clawing at him with her free hand. Mama was coming toward us from the porch.

"Mama!" I cried. "Help! Help me!"

Jay put his arm across my shoulder, and with all my strength and a surge of adrenaline, I had him standing. The station wagon was only a few yards away, and the driver's door was open. The key was still in the ignition. If I could get him in the car, I could drive. He had taught me how. *It's all about balance.*

We headed for it, moving slow, hobbling, Jay's fingers digging into my shoulder for support. "Help us, Mama!" I cried, over and over.

Blood was streaming through the grooves in Jay's leather boot, leaving a trail through the dusty grass. I would need those boots to drive.

He tripped and nearly fell on me. I braced myself against the force of his weight, but I couldn't hold him. We both stumbled and slammed into the side of the station wagon. Jay cried out with awful pain and slid to the ground, leaving a smear of blood across the side of the car. As quick as I could, I opened both the back doors, hopped in, grabbed his shirt collar, wedged my feet against the doorframe for leverage, and dragged him across the smooth leather upholstery until I was out the opposite door. He pushed with his good leg, screaming something horrible. His hair was a tangled mat over his eyes, and his face was a mess of tears, blood, and spittle.

Pain had altered him. First the war, then this. The boy in him was gone.

Mama was near us. "Help me!" I shrieked at her. "Help me take off his boots." She stepped back a hair instead, like she wanted to think about it a little while. "I need his boots to drive. Please, Mama."

I didn't ask her to drive because she didn't know how; she was afraid of automobiles. Regardless, she didn't move, as if she'd just been struck dumb. I didn't have time for it. Once I had Jay in place, I ran around the car and began unlacing his boots. The right boot came off easy as you please, but the left, suctioned to his ankle by the blood, was stubborn.

"Mama!" I yelled again. She didn't budge. I yanked on the boot, and Jay screamed and writhed, but it didn't come off. I couldn't do that to him again. My heart was breaking.

I heard him mumble something through the blood. As I leaned in, he took my arm and said, "I did this. Let me go."

The photograph he had first shown us that day in the sun porch was a picture of three different people in one—Lily and Foxy and Terry. So many layers. Nesting dolls. But was it a photo of all those people—or none of them? Jay had asked us to see what he wanted us to see, and we had continued to oblige him. Now, in the middle of all his blood and agony, what was he asking me to do?

I would drive with one foot, I decided. I removed Jay's sock and stuffed it into the boot, then tossed my right Mary Jane into the grass and wedged my foot into the wide engineer's boot. I stood up, lopsided and bloodstained.

Mama had moved. She stood in front of the driver's door, holding the key in her hand. For a second, I thought she was offering to drive, that maybe she had overcome her fear in a state of emergency. I took a step toward her.

"You're not going anywhere," she said, cold as ice. "This stops here. Now." She slid the key into a pocket on her dress.

"Mama, he's hurt!"

"It stops here."

"If I don't get help, if we don't get to a doctor, he'll—"

"Go into the house, and go to your room. Do you hear me?"

"Mama! Mama!"

She crossed her arms tight over her stomach.

Change comes in two ways. For me, right then and there, it was sudden. Veils lifted, curtains drew back, and I saw our mother for who she really was—a sick woman who'd been disguising her guilt in the shabby clothes of grief, who had been so frightened by who you were that she'd sent you away. In the darkest regions of her heart, she'd hoped you wouldn't return so you could be reimagined in retrospect.

You could be the son she'd wanted you to be, as long as she had control of your memory—Jay threatened that. He had to go too. I couldn't put this into words at the time, but I understood it in my heart, and I began hating her.

I lunged at her, forced forward by Jay's boot, and hit her in the stomach with my small fists. She fell against the inside of the car door and crumpled to the ground. "Give me the key!" I yelled, steadying myself against the station wagon. "The key, Mama!" She shook her head. Her eyes were like the hollows in a skull. If she could've breathed fire, she would have. She hoisted her body up by the car door and found her footing. I backed away.

Mama caught her breath, reached into her pocket, and took out the key. She held it out like she was going to sling it into the tall grass at the edge of the yard, and I stumbled toward her, tugging on her arm with all my weight. She gritted her teeth and dropped the key. I snatched it from the dirt, shoved her away from the open door, and jumped into the driver's seat. She grabbed my dress. I looked back, into the black panic of her eyes, and said, "You killed Robbie! It was your fault!" My words hit her harder than my fists. She let go of me the way you let go of someone hanging off a cliff. I whipped the door closed, pressed the clutch, and started the car.

The wagon rolled across a few of Papa's newly planted saplings, and we were on our way down the drive. It was difficult to work the pedals with the boot twisting from one side to the other, but I steered the car onto the gravel and pressed the gas. We sped toward the road. I glanced in the rearview mirror, hoping to see Jay awake and hanging on, but I only saw my home receding in the distance, windows flashing in the sunlight, and Papa running after me, yelling, waving his arms in the air.

When I looked forward again, there was someone smack-dab in front of the car, right where the gravel ends and asphalt of the main road begins. For a second—no, a fraction of a second—it was Lily, and then it was Foxy, and then Terry, and even you, Robbie, returning to me in that golden mist.

I slammed Jay's boot into the gas mistaking it for the brake, and the car exploded forward. I tried to twist the steering wheel, screaming, gasping, my sweaty hands slipping on the smooth wood. I smashed into the mailbox, and shot across the main road and into a ditch.

As I came to, dust was still settling on the hood of the car. I heard a voice off in the distance, but I couldn't make it out. The engine was hissing and popping. The passenger-side window was smeared with purple stains. Blackberries. Half the bush was in the car. Something cool and wet ran down my cheek. I touched it with my finger. Blood. I began to panic. Jay's boot was wedged between the pedals, but my foot was out of it. I tried to pull myself out from under the bent steering wheel, but I cried out and stopped. I didn't know it, but I had broken five ribs and whacked my head pretty good. The entire frame of the wagon groaned and shifted like a ship going down. I attempted to pull myself up again, but the pain was too much. I whimpered and slumped over in the seat.

That's when I heard her voice: "Ceola, sit still. I'll get help." She was at the driver's window. The morning sun softened her face. Her dark curls were messy, but her lips were still a perfect and glossy red. Bunny. I had swerved for *her*? She gripped the edge of the door and pulled on it, but it didn't budge.

I said, "Jay is—"

"We'll get help for both of you."

"He's shot. His grand—"

"Not now. Help is coming."

"You're a murderer. You did it to him . . . to me."

"Not now."

And the door burst open. There was light, and the fresh smell of ripped and split vines, and the sound of irate insects buzzing, and birds crying for the loss of their nests. And then I was up in the air, hands underneath me—Papa's? Bunny's? And there was terrible, terrible pain. I blacked out.

And then I was in a car, the Olds, and I was lying across the back seat, holding my side, trying not to think about the pain, watching the trees pass by and the blue sky flickering between them and the clouds, so thin and high—and I knew, before Bunny hinted, before Papa told me, even before we reached the clinic, Jay was dead, that he had died before he was taken from the wreck, that what I had tried to do had been for nothing. I knew this.

After locking the bedroom door, Sheila felt safer. She thought about her mother and father, about the potato farm in Parsippany, but even in the midst of her panic, she didn't yearn to be there. The future held too many possibilities, her fate was still her own. After all, magic was a sleight of hand, a trick of light, a con. She wouldn't be denied her freedom. But she held that thought for just a moment before the reality of her situation returned to her.

The curtains in her aunt's bedroom window were open, and moonlight poured in. The storm had broken. Aunt Majestica peered across the room from her place above the mantle, her eyes bright and devilish, her face whiter than ever. She seemed to be laughing at Sheila. By the window, her crystal ball glowed as if it were lit from inside. It made Sheila think of the note on the diagram: "The eye of God sees everything, but not clearly, not with permanence. This is permanence. This is proof!"

"Golly, like a photograph!" she said aloud—and an idea, a connection, occurred to her. She went to the crystal ball and picked it up. Its ornate brass stand fell away, revealing a circular two-inch section of crystal missing from the bottom, cut, she imagined, by a diamond saw. Could a lens be made from this? Had her aunt made a camera from her crystal ball? Did the album downstairs contain the photos taken by that camera?

There was a burst of light in the room, and it wasn't lightning. She dropped the ball, and it rolled heavily toward the corner of the room, stopping at a pair of shiny black oxfords.

Thomas stepped forward. In the moonlight, his handsome face was as pale as a drowned corpse, holding none of the charm it had earlier that evening. He grinned at her, his teeth white, canine. His uncanny appearance grew darker, more wolflike the nearer he came. As he loomed over her, she felt as though she were already being devoured.

She backed away, tripping a little on the edge of a rug. "I thought you liked me. I really did. We had such a good time. You were so easy to talk to, so gracious."

"What can I say, I'm a charming guy."

"We were going to go on a date. We made plans. You kissed me! It was real, that kiss. I could feel it."

"Don't make this harder than it has to be."

"I'll pay you. I have the dough. Just look at this place. It will be mine. It *is* mine!"

"It's time to say night-night."

"Please don't hurt me! We can work this out."

"I have a job to do. I can see the bigger picture."

"How could I have been so blind?"

"You saw what you wanted to see. All the sad girls do."

He lunged forward with a snarl, and she stabbed him with the letter opener. It entered his forearm near the crook of the elbow. He yelped and gnashed his teeth and backed away. Its pearl handle flashed in the moonlight. She made for the phone, but as soon as the receiver was in her hands, as soon as she heard the buzz of the line, his good arm swept around her, closing tight on her throat. His muscles tensed, the bulge of his biceps squeezing her windpipe, the rough fabric of his coat burning her flesh. She struggled, kicking her feet and beating him every which way with her small fists, but it was useless. After a few moments, she stopped.

She saw his face in a mirror above the phone—it was cruel and cold, a mask of thin skin stretched over the demon underneath—and then she saw bright flashes of light like shooting stars, like fireworks over the Hudson, like diamonds against black velvet—and then darkness closed in.

When Thomas had finished the job, he released her. From a bag he had stowed in the corner of the room, he retrieved his camera. He found a good angle and took a picture of her. She looked pretty, he thought, but she was no dish. Just the usual sort of dame. He didn't mind killing her. There were thousands of girls just like her. It was good money after all.

He picked up the phone: "Operator. New York City. 111 East 65th. Yes, I'll wait . . . Mr. Addison. It's done . . . Yes, I have the proof. Just bring the money, and I'll bring the photograph."

PART II

February 18, 2000

Washington, DC

Ceola dear,

I'm shocked and, I must admit, relieved you received a photo of Lily as well. It does seem as though someone wants us to talk.

Where do we begin? In both of your letters, you've been kind enough to share a bit of your personal history, so if you will indulge me, I would like to do the same, to bring us closer again. That Shakespearean quotation keeps occurring to me: "What fates impose, that men must needs abide; it boots not to resist both wind and tide."

A year after the incident that summer, after I last saw you, I left Royal Oak and headed to DC, against my father's wishes. I worked in the secretarial pool at the State Department for a year and then went to Georgetown. After I graduated, I met and married a young representative from Minnesota, Kirk Kimble. We settled down and had two fine boys, Rick and Kevin. Also, during this time, I began writing The Black Box and, with a great deal of luck, became the novelist you know as B. B. Prescott.

In the early '80s, Kirk and I grew apart and divorced. I never remarried. My father sold the Dixie Dew plant to Pepsi in 1983, retired, and died of cancer a year later. My beautiful mother is still alive, nearly 98, and living in a retirement community in Northern Virginia. My first son and his wife have produced two fine grandchildren, a boy and a girl. Kevin—God's sense of humor in full form—is gay and lives with his partner, a detective for the DC Metropolitan Police.

Of course, there is more, but I don't want to wear you out. Please, call me. You have my number.

Your friend,

Bunny

20

BUNNY

T he room was quiet and empty, and the afternoon sun fell in bright trapezoids across the floor. Everything around me, the familiar arrangement of furniture, the architecture of my little kitchen, nestled inside the townhouse at the corner of 5th and A Streets that had been mine (and only mine) for the past twenty years, felt undeniably remarkable. I truly hadn't expected Ceola to call me after receiving my last letter, much less want to trek all the way to DC to see me. I sat down, dropping my hands to my lap, still clutching the telephone receiver.

We had spoken for only a few minutes, at first in halting exchanges. I allowed her, with her nasal (although not charmless) Appalachian accent, to drive the conversation. After she established the parameters of her visit—she would come up at the first of March, stay downtown, only for a day or two—we warmed to each other and began to discuss the photos.

She had a theory. She surmised Jay had sent the photos to Lily, that

when, all those years ago, he told her the images were safe, he meant
they were safe with Lily. And then, to my surprise, she told me she had
heard Lily was still living in DC, that I might have walked right past
her! Indeed, Jay could've sent the photos to her for safekeeping. And
of course, she could still be in DC. Why not? She loved it here. But
why wait fifty-five years to send the photos to us, and why be so coy
about it? Why not just contact us directly?

📷

My son Kevin and his partner, Parker, took me to lunch at Café Bou-
vier on 7th Street a few days after Ceola called.

Kevin was especially handsome in a blue sport coat, pressed shirt,
and cropped haircut. He reminded me of my father, whose sober eyes
and strong forehead had concealed a quiet wisdom, a depth I admired.

After salads and drinks were ordered, he said, "We have news."

Parker offered me a tense smile. Out of uniform and in jeans and
a gray blazer, Parker looked more like the sweet man he is than a
policeman. Although he has curly black hair and weight lifter's shoulders, he reminds me of Jay, particularly in the eyes, which are deep
blue and so expressive. Whispering eyes, my mother calls them.

"Mom, we've made the decision to adopt," Kevin said. "We want
to be fathers."

I didn't respond immediately.

We've come a long way as a society, and indeed, I've come a long
way since I was a young woman, but the world is still a cruel place.
It's hard enough for children these days, much less a child with two
fathers. The possibility of Kevin and Parker adopting had occurred to

me—both of them being so good with Kevin's nephew and niece, eyes brightening at all the childish glee and nonsense at the holidays—but the idea worried me all the same. A child whose biological parents are unknown, whose background is a mystery . . . well, it's a genetic grab bag; you never know what you're going to get, do you? But if they were aware of the risk—which I'm sure they are, both being practical men at heart—I couldn't stand in their way.

So I broke the silence: "I'm so pleased you want a child. It's admirable. Truly. You have my blessing, of course."

They smiled with relief.

We chatted through lunch about the rigmarole of the adoption process. After my son excused himself to go to the bathroom before dessert, I turned to Parker, who for the moment was studying something across the room. He seemed so like Jay then. He had that far-off look—eyes outward, but studying what? The sunlight on the wall? No, his eyes were on the past. I thought, *If I could only have a photo of that.*

He caught me looking and smiled.

I said, "Was it hard for you when you were growing up? You've never said much about being a boy. What was it like?"

"What do you mean?"

"Did your parents love you even though you weren't—well, what I'm sure they'd hoped you would be?"

"Oh. Well, my mom came around. She understood. My dad . . . he never got over it. I went to visit him in the hospital when he was dying and he wouldn't see me. It was terrible, but I survived. It was his loss."

"Indeed."

"Why are you interested?"

"When I was a young woman, I was very cruel once—to a young man, a gay man. It's something I've regretted deeply for years. It ended sadly."

"I'm sorry to hear that."

"I need your help." I reached across the table and covered his strong hand with mine. "I also need you to keep a secret. I don't want Kevin to know. It's best for children not to know their parents too well. It undercuts our authority. You understand, don't you?"

"What do you need?"

I gave his hand a little pat and released it. "I need to find someone. It's been years. I thought with your resources in the police department, you could help. It's important. It has to do with that young man I just mentioned."

"What can I do?"

I reached into my purse and handed him an envelope. Inside was Lily's name and address from years ago. I had briefly communicated with her after Jay's death. It was a place to begin. "Take this. See what you can find out. Lily would be about my age. At one time, she had beautiful blond hair—and dark eyes. Do it quickly, if you don't mind."

"I'll do what I can."

"Thank you, dear."

📷

A week later, Parker dropped by the house unannounced. I invited him in, but he declined. He was on duty.

"Here's a list of names, addresses, and phone numbers," he said. "I've narrowed it down to about six based on the information you gave me. There was only one who fit your description in terms of age, so I decided to pay her a visit. Don't worry. I didn't tell her who I was or that I was connected to you. But Kevin would kill me if I sent you into the city searching for a strange woman without checking it out first. There are people out there who take advantage of the elderly."

"I don't need a watchdog, and I detest being referred to as 'the elderly.'"

He smiled. "Do you want to know what I found out?"

"Yes, of course!"

"The Lily Vellum who lived at that address died a few weeks ago. The woman who answered the door was still visibly upset."

"Oh, dear."

"I'm sorry."

"What was she like—the woman at the door?"

"She was an older black woman. Tall. Striking."

I felt a little thrill in my heart. "Did she give you her name?"

"She didn't *give* me her name."

"Don't be coy with me! Did you *discover* her name?"

"Yes. Georgiana Gardner. It was on her mailbox."

"You did it! You found her. Oh, how wonderful! Poor Lily. I must pay Georgiana a visit."

"She lives in Shaw."

"Will you take me there?"

"I don't know."

"You must."

"All right—but Kevin should know."

"No. Don't tell him. I need this to remain private."

"Bunny."

"I need you to do this for me."

"This weekend, then. He'll be out of town."

📷

When Georgiana opened the door, she said, "Well, I'll be! You found me." She looked as if she had been expecting me for lunch, as if I'd merely been running late. "Come on in, honey."

She was still tall, slender, and graceful. Her body had resisted the slow collapse inward, the osteoporotic crumble. She was wearing a simple black dress, her thin waistline defined by a patent leather belt clasped with a gold, snail-shaped buckle. Her hair was pulled back, flat against her skull, and silvery-white, the color I imagined my hair was underneath the chestnut colorant.

I followed her down the main hall of her dim, rosewater-scented townhouse into a living room with high Victorian ceilings and a jumble of oak and mahogany furniture, positioned at artistic but inefficient angles. Georgiana stopped, faced me, and asked if I would like something to drink. I asked for water, and she disappeared into the back of the house.

The walls of the living room were cluttered with art. Personal photos mingled with bright, amateurish abstract works and African tribal masks. A stereo and speaker system, circa 1980, were tucked into a recessed bookshelf, surrounded by a dusty collection of vinyl. A large mirror loomed over the fireplace, leaning outward and reflecting the deep red Turkish rug in its surface. I sat on the love seat and looked up at myself in the mirror. My powdered, rouged face stared back at me from under my hood of dark hair, and my lilac cardigan shone brightly against the dark tones of the decor. I'm not unattractive for a woman my age, still bright around the eyes and not too much plastic surgery, but I can't claim the elasticity of motion that Georgiana possessed. She seemed years younger than she actually was. I was a little jealous.

When she returned, she was holding a weathered manila folder in her free hand. She sat beside me and laid the envelope on the coffee table, as if she wanted me to ask about it. Parker would be back in thirty minutes, so I wanted to get on with it. I took the water, sipped it, and spoke: "I won't beat around the bush. Did you send Ceola and me those photos—the photos Jay told us were of Lily? I'm sure you know the ones I mean."

"Yes, I did."

"Why?"

"Jay always wanted you to have them."

"I don't understand."

The regal haughtiness in Georgiana's face melted. She brought her hand to her mouth as if to stopper the emotion rising up through her.

"When did Lily pass?" I asked gently.

"Just a month ago. She didn't wake up one morning. Everyone should be able to die so quietly."

"You must be distraught. I'll come back when you're feeling up to it." I made to stand up.

"Don't be ridiculous. I wanted you to come. I just don't know if I'm doing the right thing. God knows, Lily and I fought about it enough. We had a wonderful life together, but *this* we never agreed on. I feel like I'm betraying her, you see. When I was a little girl, my mother told me there were two important rules to live by: 'Don't make promises you can't keep, and keep all the promises you make.' Lily didn't do that, and I've never approved. I sent you and Ceola those photos as a sort of test of fate. I wanted to know if you were still interested in them. If you were, I knew you would find me. And here you are."

"You've lost me, dear."

She reached over and picked up the folder on the coffee table. "Jay sent this to us only a few days before he died, the day Japan surrendered."

"August fourteenth?"

"Jay was already dead when we opened the package. The photos I sent you and Ceola came from *this* folder."

I took it and opened it. Inside were dozens of photographs, images from the war. Snapshots of soldiers at work and at play, both the healthy and the hospitalized, were shuffled in with the bruised and torn landscapes of central Europe and occasional studies of natural settings—the woods at dusk, snow on a wet bow, and the like. For the most part, they were artistic, not journalistic, in their composition. There were also photographs of Robbie, a lover's images. Robbie was handsomer than I remembered, his grin puckish and wise, his countenance more self-assured. There were a few of those startling, extraordinary images of me from my eighteenth birthday party; there was a shot of me from our picnic by the creek. There were several photos of Ceola too. She had a funny smirk on her face in each one, as if she were a little shy to have her picture taken. And of course, there were many shots of the dead Terry Trober.

A note was with the photographs:

August 9, 1945

Dear Lily,

I need you to keep these photos and keepsakes safe. When I'm gone, I want you to give them to Ceola Bliss, Robbie's younger sister—who you will have just met, I imagine—and Bonita Prescott of Royal Oak, Virginia.

You must deliver them in person when no one else is around. These images are only for their eyes. They are the only ones who will really understand them.

You are probably wondering why I didn't give them to you in person, but of course that would mean explaining to you why I'm leaving them in your safekeeping. I no longer have use for them. As I told you, I've bent everything out of shape, I've made a true mess of things. I'm going to tell my story if I can bear it and then be done.

You and George have seen me through so much. We've been good friends. It's important you do this for me. It's the only way to end things right.

—Love, J

"Lily thought he was planning to kill himself," Georgiana said. "When we heard news of the accident, Lily couldn't believe it. In fact, she even returned to Royal Oak to speak with Jay's grandmother. Mrs. Greenwood refused to see her, so she never found out more than the newspapers told us. Eventually, she decided she would hold on to these keepsakes and not send them to you or to Ceola. She didn't want to confuse you. If it was truly an accident, she thought, then why tell the people who loved him he was planning to kill himself? I disagreed with her. We fought about it, but it was her decision in the end. The note was addressed to her. She took the contents and placed them in a safe-deposit box. She thought she would send them to you one day. That, of course, never happened.

"When she died, bless her soul, she left everything to me. When I came across them again, well, my conviction held. It became my decision, so I sent those photographs to you, although it took me a little while to track down your current addresses."

"What's this?" I said. I had discovered an envelope stuck to the back of a photograph. It had accidentally adhered to a spot where removed tape had left a tacky residue. I removed it carefully like a forensic pathologist from one of my novels would. It was a V-mail envelope addressed to Jay in southern England. The return address had been ruined by the tape's adhesive. It had a red inspection stamp on it—"Passed by Army Examiner, 24610"—and the inspector's signature. I slid two pieces of paper out of the envelope. The first was a letter:

September 5, 1944

Jay,

Your letter cheered me up when I was feeling blue the other day. You always know when to send them. It's so damn hot and muggy down here. You wouldn't believe it. It never stops raining. Water from below, water from above, they say.

I've been thinking—when I get home, I'm not going to

return to Royal Oak. Mama and Papa deserve that. I'm going to a big city. Maybe we can get an apartment together. Can you imagine the two of us in DC or NYC! Or maybe we can go somewhere south, where there's a beach. I remember what you said about the beaches in Miami. Anyway, I could write stories about the war, and you could take pictures, and maybe we could even make a little money doing it.

I met this Aussie here. He says I'm such a "dag," which he tells me means I'm a funny guy. He's the funny one. He talks a lot about leaving the Navy. He says it would be easy to switch tags with a fallen soldier and then vanish under a new name. Even if they came looking for him, he says, they'd be looking for someone else. I know he's joking—it's just the heat getting to him—but he talks about hopping a cargo ship and not stopping until he gets to the other side of the world. I told him he wouldn't belong to a country, he'd be a nobody. He said he didn't care, he was okay with that, but he was drunk, you know. I wish I had his guts! I hate this place. It's hell, perfect hell.

Anyway, I've enclosed a crossword puzzle. I made it hard. Have fun! Oh, by the way, thanks for the word search! But I never know where to begin. I'm terrible at it.

I'll be thinking of you, hoping you avoid the worst of it. I can't wait for this to be over. There's so much I want to do.

—R. B

I handed Georgiana the letter. She read it. Then she edged close to me, and we inspected the crossword together:

Across

2. Took a bite from the forbidden fruit
3. _____ and Andy
5. A hot week in October
7. Black, not grene
10. We never have enough of this.
11. _____ isn't everything.
12. All gerunds have these.
13. More or _____
15. Leave of absence
16. "No man is an _____."
17. Captain from *20,000 Leagues Under the Sea*
18. Walt's Elephant
19. Submarine
21. Charles Foster Kane

Down

1. A cat with spots
3. Absent from your post
4. Royal Oak, _____
6. Arch enemy
8. _____ you were here.
14. "Friends, Romans, countrymen, _____ me your ears."
20. Eclipse
22. Peek-a-boo Girl
23. Bird of prey
24. "First you say you do, and then you don't, and then you say you will, and then you won't..."

Jay had finished it. However, he hadn't filled in all the letters of the final word. I didn't know the answer immediately. To my surprise, Georgiana began to hum, eyes closed, swaying a little, the words slowly emerging from her throat.

"It's Ella Fitzgerald," I said. "'Undecided' is the final answer."

She continued to hum for a few minutes, lost a little in the song.

"Do you still sing?" I asked.

"Every day, honey."

"Did you make a career out of it?"

"For a time. In a small way."

"Lena Horne was your idol. I remember."

"Indeed." She looked at me and winked. "Here, you should have these." She handed me the entire folder. "You should share them with Ceola too." She glanced at her watch and stood up. "I need to run a bath. I have choir practice in an hour. Show yourself out, if you would."

"Thank you, George."

"Come and see me again, you hear."

"Yes."

21

CEOLA

Seeing someone in the flesh after so many years, someone who'd taken up so much room in my memory, someone who I had once hated, was downright intimidating, so I told the cabbie to drop me at the corner, a few houses down from Bunny's place.

As I made my way up the sidewalk, I dug my Slims out of my pocketbook and smoked one to settle my nerves. The street was empty, just a few dry leaves scraping against themselves in the trees, the city honking and screeching the next block over. Although many of the row houses were peeling paint and slouching forward in their foundations, Bunny's three-story home was a prime example of top-dollar gentrification. She had herself a garden lined with a wrought iron fence and decorated with a marble birdbath and miniature Greek gods. In the spring, it would be something of a showpiece, I imagined. The house itself was red brick with shiny black shutters and a wreath of holly berries hanging on the front door. I stopped at the bottom of the steps, my nerves buzzing again.

Then, like that, the front door opened, and there she was.

"Hello," she said. "I saw you coming!"

She was wearing an expensive beige suit with a peacock scarf tucked under her lapel and a double strand of pewter-gray pearls around her neck. She had her face on, lips painted deep red. I'd given up the layers of makeup and manicures ages ago. I wonder what she thought of me with my red-brown curls, my drooping, mannish face, my neglected fingernails, my QVC jewelry. I remembered her, all primped and puffed, on the day Jay first told us about Lily. She had looked so beautiful and haughty in that strawberry-red dress. So I said, "You look good, Bunny," although I'm not sure how I meant it.

"Do not go gentle into that good night," she replied. "It's my motto."

"Well, it seems to be working."

"It's good to see you, dear."

"It's been a long time."

"Come inside. We have a lot to talk about."

For most of the afternoon, we sat in the kitchen, sipping lukewarm coffee and snacking on ladyfingers and ginger snaps, which she had displayed all nice and neat, like she was trying to impress me. We gabbed about everything. I asked her why she decided to write. She just smiled and said, "My dear, you know the answer to that." I told her I liked *The Black Box*, her novel about the newspaper photographer who witnesses a murder, but I thought the solution to *Guilty by Midnight* was as plain as day from the get-go. She took my criticism in stride, which made me feel better about being there. I was hoping she'd be open to what I had to say to her.

She told me about her father and that lovely mother of hers, Carla.

She told me about her ex-husband and her children, especially her son, Kevin, whose application for the adoption of a little boy, she'd just learned, had been approved. She was proud of him.

She asked about Sam and the boys. I elaborated on Sam's fall from the roof, and how it was raising three boys on my own, and how it was working with doctors and patients up at Twin Oaks. I even told her I'd started to write down my thoughts about that summer, about Jay and you. I also let her know I had pulled away from Mama and Papa after Jay was killed and that Mama had stopped speaking to me once I graduated high school. Papa had made nice, but our relationship had always remained strained.

"On his deathbed, he reached out to me," I told her, "his painkillers blurring past and present, and touched my hand and said, 'Robbie, I'm sorry. Please talk to me, son. I'm sorry.' I didn't correct him. Instead, I told him I loved him, and I rubbed his head awhile."

Taking the coffee cups to the sink, Bunny asked, "Whatever happened to Letitia Greenwood? I know she lived into her eighties."

"Everything was taken from that woman—her son, her husband, her grandson, her wealth, her position in the community. Everything. She even ended up in Twin Oaks for several months following the accident. She was completely off her rocker there for a little while."

"I couldn't have survived all of that."

"But she did. And wouldn't you know it, when she was in her seventies, she started turning up at church again. Sam and I were newlyweds, and although we weren't especially religious then, we decided to go the Presbyterian Church when I was expecting my first child. It seemed like the right thing to do. During those years, from time to time, I would see Letitia sneak in after the beginning of the service.

She was always dolled up, wearing hats and dresses that were fashionable decades earlier, her hands always in gloves. Often men in the congregation would tend to her and offer her a seat, but no, she refused politely and said she preferred to stand at the back. I sang in the choir, so I could watch her from where I was sitting. She cocked her head back and closed her eyes, trying to take in the sermon. Her body language broadcast two messages across the sanctuary—'Leave me alone' and 'Look at me.' The guilt that clung to my family had left no visible traces on her. Not a bit. Every now and then, she would stop listening to the minister and look out over the congregation. 'I'm Letitia Greenwood,' I imagined her saying, 'and my family created you people. You're all *my* children.'"

"How did she die?"

"I'm surprised you don't know."

"I didn't get back to Royal Oak often, and Mother didn't talk much about the town. She never liked it there. And Daddy—he wanted me to forget about the entire incident with Jay. He wouldn't have brought it up."

"I see. Well, the day Letitia was diagnosed with cancer, only a few days after her eightieth birthday, she went home, took the same gun she shot Jay with, so they say, and shot herself in the heart. She had to use her cane to press the trigger, but she managed it—willful to the end."

"Did she leave a note?"

"No—but an article ran in all the local newspapers detailing her life. That was her note, I suppose."

"What a remarkable woman."

"When I was a girl, I was terrified of her."

"Me too!" Bunny laughed. "I'm still a little frightened." She cleared her throat and then looked at me dead-on. Her eyes seemed like they were made of the same dark, silvery substance as the pearls around her neck. "It's time to get down to business. Follow me into the living room. I've uncovered something you must read."

Bunny crossed the living room to a sturdy, cherrywood desk, topped with a new laptop and a cluster of framed photos of her sons and grandchildren. Behind the desk, built into the wall, was a bookshelf stacked high with rows of mystery novels and thrillers. I recognized some of the authors' names, and for a second, I considered asking her if I could borrow a few. She picked up a folder and gestured for us to sit on a cream-colored damask sofa that faced out the bay window. It was patterned with little gold lions.

"What are you working on now?" I asked, curious about the computer.

"Well, I was working on a novel about a famous double murder from the '80s, the Bakker-Jones case. But I stopped when I received the package. Recently, I've been writing about this." She handed me the folder. "And I guess you have too."

"Just for me, you know. Not to be published."

"I'm sure it's wonderful."

"Not by a stretch."

"Pish—don't say that!"

"I've been writing off and on for years. I started back in my early twenties. I wrote it like I was writing a letter to Robbie. Everyone needs an audience, right? When those photos arrived in the mail, I decided it was a sign I needed to write about that summer, so that's what I've been doing. Writing it all out, filling the gaps best I can."

"Look inside the folder," she directed, smiling and sitting on the sofa beside me. "Tell me what you see."

I sifted through the folder. "Where did you get these?" I said, amazed. "I thought they were long gone."

"I found Lily's partner, Georgiana Gardner. I paid her a visit after our last phone call. She's the one who sent us the images. Lily kept them all these years, because of this." She pinched a piece of card stock out from under the photos and handed it to me. Jay's handwriting was scribbled across it. "She received this folder only days after he died. This note was attached. She saw no point in telling us about it. Georgiana disagreed with Lily and, after her death, wanted to honor Jay's wishes."

I read Jay's note, folded it, set it aside.

What it implied, that Jay had planned to die, rattled me, but it also gave me greater courage to say what I had come to say. I mustered my strength and took Bunny's hand. She shrunk from me and gave me a nervy glare, but I went on. "I need to say something to you. It's something I didn't understand when it happened, only years after the fact. This note confirms it. The last time I spoke to Jay, he told me the story behind the photos."

"You mean the friend in drag. Terry Trober. I know."

"That's right. Robbie's doppelgänger."

"He died in an air raid."

"That's not how he died. Not really."

"What do you mean?"

"Jay slept with Trober and betrayed Robbie. In a guilt-ridden mental break—a fugue, they call it—he beat Trober and left him to die. The air raid just finished him off. Jay didn't tell you the whole story."

Bunny's mouth opened. She was about to tear up.

I wanted to comfort her, but I needed to tell her everything, so I went on, still holding her hand in mine. "The last time I spoke to Jay, he was talking about that tale in *Weird Stories*, 'A Date with Death.' Do you remember it?"

"I do. You read it over and over that summer."

"It's Robbie's. What I mean is, the story is *his*. He wrote it and submitted it to *Weird Stories*, but he never saw it published. He was in the Pacific. In it, a woman sees her future in a magic photo album but does nothing to stop it. That's where Jay got the idea to create a story about a photo—"

"My mother helped me pick out lingerie for my wedding night," Bunny broke in, slipping her hand out of mine. "It embarrassed me, but she gave me some good advice. I'll always remember it. She said, 'Bonita, sometimes a woman wears her clothes like a fortified wall, and sometimes, for the rare individual, she wears them like an open door.' For you and me, those photos of Lily were an open door. Jay was inviting us to pull back the layers—Lily, Foxy, Terry—and discover him."

"The more we saw who he really was, the more he loved us."

"And feared us."

"The woman in Robbie's story has her future shown to her but doesn't believe it. It's not the future she wants. So she doesn't do a thing, not a damn thing. She denies it even when it's right there with its hands around her throat. That's what Terry was, the ugly truth about things, about the future, about love especially, and Jay beat him to death for it."

"Jay was like a code with no cipher," Bunny added, "so he brought his photos to us, hoping we could tell him what they meant. But he started rearranging the facts, spinning a different tale, telling himself we needed the veneer of one story to understand the other. But that didn't happen. We all fell in love with the lie."

For a second or two, we didn't say a word. The sunlight in the room had a strange pink glow. Then, straightening my posture and gathering my nerves, I said, "I'm going to tell you something I've never told another living, breathing soul."

Bunny clasped her hands in her lap.

"On the day Jay died, when Letitia raised her shotgun to shoot Papa, Jay stood in the way on purpose," I said. "He saved Papa's life. He wanted to die. I think it's why he confronted Papa in the first place." Her hands were balled into fists now. I continued. "The night before, after he told me about what he did to Terry, he kissed me on the forehead. It was odd to me then, but now I know it was a kiss good-bye." It was difficult for me to look at her. She was so still, and her face was blank as marble. "The guilt I dropped on you, what I said—I never should've called you a murderer, Bunny. It wasn't right. I was an angry little girl. I didn't know what the hell I was saying."

We sat there in silence for a time, Bunny looking away from me, out the window. As the sun crept below the homes across the street, the light seemed to retreat and advance, changing the very nature of the objects in the room. It warmed the faint beige of the area rug in front of us and the pale fabric of the sofa, the little golden lions blazing to life, but cast the bookshelf cubbies into shadow and darkened the living room's red walls to a musty wine color. I felt gloomy but relieved. The truth was out.

Bunny pulled out a handkerchief, dabbed her eyes, and said, "It's cold in here." She stood up and walked to the fireplace. "I apologize. I'm not being a thoughtful hostess." She pressed a button, and the gas log clicked then caught. The blue flames began toiling away at the fake firewood. I thought, *If only those damn flames knew the wood would never burn.*

From beside the fireplace, she said, "We're all responsible for his death. All of us. Your father, your mother, Letitia, Lily, you, and me— and Jay himself. Not to mention the war. Hitler. Mussolini. Hirohito. The list could go on and on. But I'm not interested in doing that. We must let it go."

I nodded.

She returned to the sofa and switched on a floor lamp. "Would you like more coffee?"

I didn't answer her. One of the photos of Terry Trober's beaten body was lying there on top of the folder's contents. In the light from the lamp, it looked different somehow, like it was shot from an angle I hadn't seen before. It wasn't a print Jay had shown to us or Georgiana had mailed to us. I wasn't sure what I was seeing—and then, like that, I was. "Look, Bunny," I said. "You can see his face better."

She fidgeted with her reading glasses, picked up the photo, lingered over it, and set it down. Without a word, she went to her bookcase and started hunting for a book.

"What is it?" I said, but she held up a finger.

Once she found what she was looking for, she flipped through it, earmarked a page, and brought it to me. It was a how-to book on photography. The chapter she'd marked was called "Dodging and Burning."

"I had to research photographic techniques for *The Black Box*," she said, picking up the photo of Terry again. "I think Jay dodged this."

"I don't understand."

"He held a cardboard cutout or even his finger between the enlarger lens and the paper as he developed it. Doing that alters the exposure and brings out the details of Terry's face. He used a similar method to create the images of me at my eighteenth birthday party."

"I see," I said, still confused. She was moving fast.

"It's even possible he burned-in the originals."

"Burned them?"

"Another technique. He dropped a photographic veil over Terry's identity by doing a localized overexposure of his face."

She removed her glasses. "Well," she said with a sigh and an uneasy smile. "I have something you must read and take with you." She placed the photo upside down on the coffee table and slipped a yellowed envelope out from underneath the stack of photos. She handed it to me, and I slid the letter out and unfolded it. It was addressed from Robbie to Jay.

I read it.

To see your handwriting, Robbie, to hear your voice, to imagine you wedged in a bunk on a destroyer writing that letter before lights out, was—I don't know what. Magical, that's the only word for it, as cornball as it sounds. What you said about the weather in the Pacific, about Mama and Papa, about Royal Oak, about living in the city and getting an apartment with Jay, about the funny Australian soldier— everything you put down, each determined word of it, had flickered out years ago, but here in my hands were the remains.

When I reached the lines about the crossword puzzle, I stopped— an idea in my old brain had flapped its wings. I glanced at the puzzle and again at your comment. My heart nearly flew out of my chest. "Bunny," I said. "Do you realize what this is?"

"What do you mean?"

"This is a message, a secret message. Because the military examined the mail, Robbie and Jay hid messages to each other in cryptograms, love letters in code. Jay told me about it that night."

"All those notes in the tree trunk."

"That's right. The inspectors might've thought they were spies if they came across a cryptogram in a letter, so he and Robbie had to disguise them."

"I'm not sure if I follow you."

"Jay's cryptograms were always based on a connection between numbers and letters. A=2, B=4. That connection is just as plain as day here. Don't you see it?"

"The crossword puzzle?"

"Yes."

"But how do we figure it out? We need a cipher, don't we?"

"I just don't know. Let's see. Maybe the words, if put in a particular order, make a sentence."

Bunny went to her desk and grabbed a pen and paper. We listed Jay's answers in order and checked to make sure they were right—Eve, Amos, Indian summer, gangrene, R and R, winning, -ings, less, furlough, island, Nemo, Dumbo, U-boat, Orson Welles, leopard, Virginia, nemesis, wish, AWOL, lend, lunar, Veronica Lake, eagle, "Undecided."

It didn't make a bit of sense, so we tried something else. Many of the answers were related to the military—gangrene, AWOL, R and R, furlough, U-boat—which seemed fitting given your surroundings. Other answers were related to movies or entertainers—Amos, Nemo, Dumbo, Orson Welles, Veronica Lake, and "Undecided."

Others were animals—leopard and eagle. What were you two up to?

"Orson Welles!" Bunny blurted out. "There's a word we need that will unlock it. We need our Rosebud."

I nodded, but we were still nowhere. We just stared and stared, our eyes burning a hole in the paper. We were hungry to solve this last mystery—and that hunger made me feel like I was a twelve-year-old girl again, following Jay through the woods, staking out the Vellum house, reaching out for his hand in the funhouse, driving the station wagon down the mountain, stopping Lily on the train platform. I felt close to Bunny too. We'd finally understood something about each other. We both loved mysteries, and we loved Jay because he was a mystery.

"Why do you think Jay didn't write in 'Undecided'?" she said. "He finished all the other answers but stopped on the last one."

"Maybe once he knew it, he didn't feel like writing it in."

"That doesn't sound like him."

"Wait!" I said. "Read the part of the letter about the crossword. What did Robbie say?"

"'Anyway, I've enclosed a crossword puzzle,'" Bunny read. "'I've made it hard. Have fun! Oh, by the way, thanks for the word search! But I never know where to begin. I'm terrible at it.'"

"'Where to begin.' It's an odd thing to write to Jay. It's a message. He means the first letters of the words."

"Do they spell something?"

We listed the first letters of each answer. First, we ordered them "Across," then "Down," but it was gibberish. Then, we wrote the first letter of each word in the order of the numbers for each crossword prompt. Number one was leopard, so the first letter was L. We wrote down the following—

LEAVINGWARWILLFINDULOVEU

And then, it became clear—

LEAVING WAR WILL FIND U LOVE U

I was speechless. It seemed impossible, all of it, just impossible.

Did you die in the war or simply disappear, Robbie? If you went AWOL, how'd you do it? Did you switch tags with a dead soldier, like the Aussie had suggested? Were you hinting to Jay about your plan? Could you have really pulled it off? *Did* you pull it off?

As I was sitting there, you came to me again, materializing out of a cloud of dust, the mail truck speeding off and you walking toward me, the sun dodging and peeking around your head, transforming your messy brown hair into tufts of gold. And I saw your strange smile, a little cocky but sweet, meant just for me, and I ran to you. *Will you read a story to me?* I said. *Not this time, Cee,* you said. *I've got a life to live. I'm going to live it even if it means breaking the rules. Important rules. Let that be* your *story. Tell that story yourself.*

"He could still be alive," Bunny said with a punch of excitement. "He could be out there, an old man. He could've had an entire life. A happy life."

I remembered Jay's dream of Miami—he was there with you, standing beside you, holding your hand and staring out at the water, digging his feet in the sand. It had saved him in the Ardennes. It had pulled him out of the snow and set him back on his feet. But it hadn't saved him from himself. But maybe, just maybe, you *had* lived that postcard dream, away from Royal Oak, out from under Mama and Papa's cruel expectations. Maybe you escaped. Maybe.

"Are you all right, dear?" Bunny asked, touching my arm.

"Fine. Just fine."

"A Date with Death" came to mind again. I never liked the ending, but I always felt closer to you when I read it, hoping with each read I'd find a new way for it to end. I never understood why you didn't give the main character a way out. The best part of a story is the escape, and you knew that.

So I'm going to believe you were like a hero from a better story: you braced yourself against the side of the ship, dodged flak from antiaircraft gun, ducked enemy fire, grabbed a life vest, and jumped from the destroyer before it sucked you under the water—and I know, I just know, you found your way to shore and to a town right out of *South Pacific*, and then on a cargo ship heading who knows where. And maybe you never contacted me because you heard news of Jay's death, and it broke your heart. You figured Royal Oak—all of us, even me—stood for everything you were trying to leave behind. That may not be what happened, not exactly, but it's what I'm choosing to believe. It's an old woman's right. I know somewhere out there you're warming your old body in the sun with a stretch of ocean at your feet and thinking about me, wondering if I'm alive, if I've had a good life.

"This should be yours," Bunny said, handing me the folder, which she had carefully reorganized while I daydreamed.

"I just want Robbie's letter. I'm tired of looking at photos."

"I understand what you mean, dear."

"I'm sure you do."

22

BUNNY

He could still be alive," I said. "He could be out there, an old man. He could've had an entire life. A happy life."

Wonder crept out of the edges of Ceola's mouth and the soft wrinkles in her cheeks and the corners of her dark eyes. It spread across her face, a wave of emotion, loosening her expression, releasing the tense muscles in her forehead. She grew younger, gentler, the feisty girl-detective coming out to play, the Blue Hearts Club back in action, the impertinence, the frustration. I saw her following Jay into the woods, blithely ignoring the branches scraping her arms or catching in her hair. I saw her combing the "scene of the crime" for clues, her Mary Janes rooting around in the dust and dry weeds. I saw her looking intently at Jay, the mingling of a schoolgirl's crush and a sister's grief. I saw her, up on the Ferris wheel that beautiful August day, Jay leaning toward her, kissing her. I saw every minute of her sad vigilance. I saw her in the wrecked station wagon, distraught, angry, her face bloody, her body bruised. I again met her accusing gaze.

"You're a murderer," she'd said, and I'd believed her for fifty-five years. It was the story of my life. But that had changed—I had been released—and as I sat beside her, I watched as the story changed for her. I certainly wasn't going to do anything to stop it.

While I was watching her dream about her brother's life, one of my mother's favorite Kipling poems came to mind, one I had chosen to memorize years ago in school. It begins:

> *Once on a time, the ancient legends tell,*
> *Truth, rising from the bottom of her well,*
> *Looked on the world, but, hearing how it lied,*
> *Returned to her seclusion horrified . . .*

What I saw in those photographs, what I read in Jay's note and Robbie's letter, and what had been encrypted in the crossword made me, like Truth, want to return to the well.

It came as a slow revelation. It began with the photo of Terry Trober that Jay had dodged, a version he'd never shown either of us. The "veil" had been removed, and although the face was still difficult to see, it stirred a deep, almost subconscious curiosity in me. I felt as though I had just seen something of great significance but didn't have the faculties to understand it, like seeing a ghost, which was why I turned it over and out of Ceola's sight.

In Robbie's letter, he spoke of an Australian soldier who talked about "leaving the Navy" and "hopping a cargo ship." The discovery of the hidden message—"Leaving war. Will find u. Love u"—solidified it for me: There was no Australian soldier. Robbie was talking about himself. The man in the photo wasn't Terry Trober. There was no

Terry Trober. In my quick once-over of the undoctored image, I had seen what I wouldn't have otherwise. At times, the mind works that way. If it studies something too hard, it only follows the old patterns of thought, like a needle retracing grooves in a record. But a momentary glance can reveal uncharted territory, a flash of insight. I knew in an instant it was Robbie's face, contorted and empty of life, underneath that tangled blond wig.

He hadn't merely escaped. He had made it to England. He had come for Jay. However, he wasn't the innocent young man who read detective magazines to his kid sister anymore. What he had seen, what he had done, like Jay in the Ardennes, had made him into something altogether different. He was a man without a country, without a name, and he had to be bold and creative, perhaps even courageous, to survive. He had to reinvent himself, write a new fiction, and quickly too.

Perhaps—and only perhaps, for I'll never know the absolute truth—when Jay and Robbie found each other again, Jay had been frightened by his transformation. The Robbie he knew—the sweet, shy boy who dove into Culler's Lake with him, who accepted him and loved him—had been vanquished by the war. The story he'd told Ceola was as close to the truth as he could tell her without completely falling apart, without risking his own sanity. He couldn't tell her he had murdered the man he loved, because in his mind the man he loved had already been murdered by the war. There had been no way to explain it. The story he'd told her was for him only insomuch as it could also be for her. He had wanted to confess, but more than that, he had wanted to preserve Ceola's memory of her brother. Like Truth in Kipling's poem, Jay had returned to his subterranean world and allowed artifice to reign on the surface.

So as I witnessed Ceola bloom with hope, I wanted her to believe the story she was already writing in her head, the story of Robbie's parallel life. I wanted her to take it with her, to be a light for her. For that reason, I'll never publish a word of this as long as she is living, perhaps as long as either of us is living. It would be right for it to be Kevin's inheritance, his choice.

I must confess, after we said our good-byes and made our promises to stay in touch, I doubted myself and, for a few minutes, began to believe in her version of the story. Had I been too sober, too pessimistic? I wasn't sure anymore. Ceola had referred to Terry as Robbie's doppelgänger. Perhaps Terry did look just like Robbie. As I flipped through the photographs, the veil lifted and fell, lifted and fell, Robbie's face dodging and burning in my mind, refusing to materialize and proclaim with certainty either, "I am Robbie Bliss!" or, "I am Terry Trober!" And then, I thought about the name Trober, and I laughed. Out loud, I think. It's Robert, but with the T glued on the front, inverted.

Truth had emerged again from her well.

I gathered the photographs together and dropped them on the fire. I'd seen what I needed to see—and so had Ceola. After all, hers was the better story.

ACKNOWLEDGMENTS

As my novel begins with the gorgeous and unsettling photograph of Lily Vellum, so I begin by thanking the talented photographer Nic Persinger, who took it with a period Speed Graphic camera. I'm also grateful to Julianna Corby—Nic's supremely talented partner-in-life (and patient good sport)—for modeling for the photo. I can report: She is very much alive.

For the sacrifice of time, brainpower, and expertise, I'm deeply appreciative of everyone who read early versions of this novel, either in part or in whole, and provided me with feedback: Rebecca Borden, Matthew Ferrence, Janis Goodman, Debbi Hamrick, Jeni Hankins, Maya Lang, Tara Laskowski, Bernadette Murphy McConville, Frances McMillan, Valerie Morehouse, Jessica Hendry Nelson, and Matt Norman. In particular, I want to thank Greg Hankins, who passed away in 2016, for his enthusiastic support for me as an writer and his astute thoughts about early drafts of this book.

It's clear to me that this book—and everything else I've written—couldn't have been possible without the great teachers in my life. In particular, I'm thankful to Katherine V. Forrest, who read its first chapters and set me in the direction of making it a better book. I'm also thankful to Thomas Mallon and Luís Alberto Urrea for their guiding comments on my work and their willingness to support my career. I'm also grateful to Sara Blair, who first sparked my interest in photography and its undeniable connection to the evolution of literature through the twentieth century.

I'm grateful to Lambda Literary, especially Tony Valenzuela and William Johnson at the helm, for providing a space for LGBTQ writers to find each other and learn from one another and, of course, DC Commission on the Arts and Humanities for their financial support and their belief in this project. Bread Loaf—both the School of English and the Writers' Conference—have had an immeasurable impact of me as a writer. The number of amazing and gifted teachers who have walked the halls of its yellow clapboard buildings is staggering. I'm indebted to the residencies at VCCA, VSC, and the Ragdale Foundation for providing space and time to breathe, think, and create. Finally, I'm thankful to the incredible educators, administrators, and students at Flint Hill, who offered me encouragement and saw my writing life as benefit to, not a distraction from, my role as a teacher.

To the entire Pegasus team, thank you for believing in this book, especially my brilliant editor, Katie McGuire, for her keen editorial eye and her intern Angelina Fay for initially reading and advocating for the book. Without my marvelous agent, Annie Bomke, *Dodging and Burning* wouldn't be what it is today. Thank you, Annie, for your candor and care, your energizing feedback, and your tireless championing of the manuscript.

To my family, you have always encouraged me to use my good sense, maintain a healthy skepticism about the world, and above all persevere, which have time and again, both in life and in my literary pursuits, guided me well. For that, I'm grateful.

To Jeff—my husband, my best friend, and my chief advocate— thank you for your unyielding belief in me and my writing, for urging me to keep writing and keep fighting for this novel.

NOTES

This book is a work of fiction molded into a specific historical moment, the mid-1940s—a time of great turmoil and bloodshed abroad and nationalistic unity at home. A time during which being gay wasn't socially tolerated or legally protected. A time during which LGBTQ people—even those who served in the armed forces—found it necessary to conceal their sexual identities or fear persecution. For those reasons, the rich gay culture of the 1940s was rarely recorded for posterity. To re-create this world, I spent time with the following books: James Lord's *My Queer War*, Robert Peter's *For You, Lili Marlene: A Memoir of World War II*, and Jeb Alexander's *Jeb and Dash: A Diary of Gay Life, 1918–1945*. In the absence of historical record, I used my instincts as a fiction writer to give verisimilitude to this complex and remarkable underground community.

The logistics and politics of World War II, on the other hand, have been painstakingly (and overwhelmingly) documented. My focus, however, wasn't so much the reams of documentation but the brave documentarians—the war photographers, whose images have shaped and challenged our understanding of war. For that research, I looked to Peter Maslowski's *Armed with Cameras: The American Military Photographers of World War II*, Evan Bachner's *Men of WW II: Fighting Men at Ease,* Charles Eugene Sumners's *Darkness Visible: Memoir of a World War II Combat Photographer,* and Ray E. Boomhower's *One Shot: The World War II Photography of John A. Bushemi.*

Like my characters, all the places in this book are inventions, but still they are based on the world I know. Royal Oak, Virginia, in particular, is inspired by my hometown of Marion, Virginia, a place of great natural beauty, rich history, and extraordinary people, a place that I'll always be at once departing from and returning to, the very definition of home. Washington, DC, my other home, is a place that continues to unfold in front of me, always offering new historical and cultural layers, a place where I feel at once myself and an outsider. Also, I think, the definition of home. For the other places in this novel that I don't call home—London and the Ardennes in the 1940s—I hope, if I've not managed to get them exactly right, I've captured their spirit. The documentation of war, after all, consists of at least as much opinion as it does fact.

Finally, there are a few works that have deeply influenced my interest in the problematic ways that photos represent or misrepresent reality: Susan Sontag's *On Photography* and Errol Morris's *Believing Is Seeing: Observations on the Mysteries of Photography,* and Weegee's photography; his images will never cease to compel me and repel me.

The following are the sources I consulted while writing the novel, many of which I mentioned previously, all of which were so helpful to me:

Alexander, Jeb, ed. *Jeb and Dash: A Diary of Gay Life, 1918–1945*. Boston: Faber and Faber, 1994. Print.

Bachner, Evan. *Men of WWII: Fighting Men at Ease*. New York: Abrams, 2007. Print.

Boomhower, Ray E. *One Shot: The World War II Photography of John A. Bushemi*. Indianapolis: Indiana Historical Society, 2004. Print.

Cole, Hugh M. *The Ardennes: The Battle of the Bulge*. Old Saybrook, CT: Konecky & Konecky, 1965. Print.

Coplans, John. *Weegee's New York: Photographs 1935–1960*. Cologne, Germany: Schirmer/Mosel, 2006. Print.

Heimann, Jim. *All-American Ads of the 40s*. Cologne, Germany: Taschen, 2003. Print.

Lord, James. *My Queer War*. New York: Farrar, Straus and Giroux, 2011. Print.

Maslowski, Peter. *Armed with Cameras: The American Military Photographers of World War II*. New York: Free Press, 1993. Print.

Morris, Errol. *Believing Is Seeing: Observations on the Mysteries of Photography*. New York: Penguin Group, 2014. Print.

Peters, Robert. *For You, Lili Marlene: A Memoir of World War II*. Madison: University of Wisconsin, 1995. Print.

Sontag, Susan. *On Photography*. New York: Picador, 2010. Print.

Sumners, Charles Eugene. *Darkness Visible: Memoir of a World War II Combat Photographer*. Ann Sumners, ed. Jefferson, NC: McFarland, 2002. Print.

"They Also Serve . . ." *The US Army in the British Midlands during World War II*. Web. July 18, 2017.

"Welcome to the WW2 US Medical Research Centre." *WW2 US Medical Research Centre*. Web. July 18, 2017.

The 1940's, 1940–1949, Fashion History Movies Music. Web. July 18, 2017.

Williams, Paul Kelsey. *Washington, D.C.: The World War II Years*. Charleston, SC: Arcadia, 2004. Print.